Praise

THE LAVENDER BLADE

"*The Lavender Blade* by E.L. Deards is a dark, romantic, and thrilling adventure set in a steampunk world filled with danger, deception, and the supernatural."

—*Readers' Favorite*, 5-star review

"Love, obsession and possession in a dangerous world where nothing is as it seems."
—C.S. Pacat, *New York Times* best-selling author of *Dark Rise*

"E.L. Deards's novel *The Lavender Blade* is engaging and captivating, with riveting twists and turns. Love, passion, and humor blend seamlessly with elements of fear and horror. Highly recommended."
—Bernard Ross, author of *Sipping Sunlight* and *Busting Timothy Leary*

"*The Lavender Blade* is an original and thoroughly entertaining romp through a unique world. Complete with breathtaking twists, heartbreaking decisions and a captivating love story. I enjoyed every minute of it."
—Debbie Iancu-Haddad, author of *Speechless in Achen Tan*

"A spellbinding and chilling journey that keeps us reading . . . A fairy tale with chariots and balls, horsemen and carriages and men who wear capes and carry knives. I could not put it down."
—Barbara Sapienza, author of *The Girl in the White Cape*

THE LAVENDER BLADE

An
Exorcist's Chronicle

E.L. Deards

SHE WRITES PRESS

Copyright © 2025 E.L. Deards

All rights reserved. No part of this publication may be reproduced, distributed, or transmitted in any form or by any means, including photocopying, recording, digital scanning, or other electronic or mechanical methods, without the prior written permission of the publisher, except in the case of brief quotations embodied in critical reviews and certain other noncommercial uses permitted by copyright law. For permission requests, please address She Writes Press.

Published 2025
Printed in the United States of America
Print ISBN: 978-1-68463-320-3
E-ISBN: 978-1-68463-321-0
Library of Congress Control Number: 2025903040

For information, address:
She Writes Press
1569 Solano Ave #546
Berkeley, CA 94707

Interior design by Stacey Aaronson

She Writes Press is a division of SparkPoint Studio, LLC.

Company and/or product names that are trade names, logos, trademarks, and/or registered trademarks of third parties are the property of their respective owners and are used in this book for purposes of identification and information only under the Fair Use Doctrine.

This is a work of fiction. Names, characters, places, and incidents either are the product of the author's imagination or are used fictitiously. Any resemblance to actual persons, living or dead, is entirely coincidental.
NO AI TRAINING: Without in any way limiting the author's [and publisher's] exclusive rights under copyright, any use of this publication to "train" generative artificial intelligence (AI) technologies to generate text is expressly prohibited. The author reserves all rights to license uses of this work for generative AI training and development of machine learning language models.

*For Dangercat,
who neither read this book nor cared, but sat politely by my side
while I wrote it anyway.*

one

Theirs was a city of whispers.

From every corner of every street, from the sooty Iron rooftops to the flecks of blood that speckled the pavement, secrets filled up the empty spaces where the light didn't reach. They were hidden in the gates that separated the three districts. They flew along the smog-choked air until they were belched out into the glittering golden sea.

Colton sat astride one of the sun-bleached walls of the Iron District—the only place in the whole damn quarter where he could see the ocean. The sun was setting, and a brilliant red glow was reflecting off the towering spires in the Ivory District like bloody, eager claws. He draped one leg lazily over the edge as he pulled out his hip flask, clicking his tongue when he found it empty.

It had just been one of those *suboptimal* days. The type that began at three in the afternoon and culminated at sunset with nothing accomplished. That was the problem with Iron folk, he supposed, up to their eyeballs in "hauntings" and not a copper between them.

"Exorcist."

The pigmonger's voice. Colton narrowed his eyes and pulled down his hood, peering at the man with wary curiosity.

"I got a job for you."

"And what seems to be the trouble, Mr. Paice?" Colton asked, rearranging his features to appear empathetic. The man had one of the more profitable pork processing units in the nation, and if *he* was being haunted, that spelled a pleasant end to an otherwise unrewarding evening.

The butcher explained that, for the last several nights, his neighbors had been awakened by screams. "Horrible stuff! Like a child being tortured! And I come in in the morning, and the place is a mess, carcasses everywhere, teeth marks in the meat—I can barely sell them like this!"

Pity.

"So will you help me or not?"

They agreed on a price, and Colton followed Paice to his malevolent presence. It was probably nothing, since it was *always* nothing, but a coin was a coin. The smell of iron death lingered in the air as they approached, and Colton clicked his tongue at the way the mud on his boots was getting redder and redder the closer they got. Pain in the ass to clean, but whatever. The slaughterhouse loomed, all sheet metal and barbed wire, blaring signs of warning to keep trespassers out. The unwelcoming entry had its intended effect, and gave Colton pause for one moment at the gates.

"Go on, then! Get the demon!"

Colton's specialty. Nondescript demons up the damned wazoo. The exorcist found himself being roughly shoved through the doors, and sighed as he heard the deadbolt click behind him. Well. At least he wouldn't be disturbed.

Colton had been doing this for as long as he could remember, initially as his mother's apprentice, and then as a solo demon denouncer after she had passed away. The jobs in the Iron District weren't especially profitable or interesting, but these people had very strong fears and beliefs, which kept him nice and busy. The Holy Order didn't really keep tabs on Iron exorcists, and his "authentic exorcist heritage" would have protected him if it did. It was easy money, and he was *way* cheaper than hiring out the priests or the sect leaders who technically specialized in this sort of matter. Colton was more than happy to take on the normal, everyday sorts of requests one might make of an exorcist—unsettled spirit, demon in the bathroom, succubus after a husband, whatever. In fact, Colton had become something of an expert in the field of ridding Silvermoorian minds of worry. Sprinkle a little salt, mutter an incantation, maybe doodle some chalk on the floor if he was feeling flamboyant, and, voilà! Spirit vanquished, happy customer, the sun rises again in the morning.

Okay. A job in a slaughterhouse. Don't see those every day.

Colton pulled his cloak up over his nose and started to explore. The place was clean by Iron District standards, meaning that it was possible *not* to step in feces, and that the vast majority of the entrails and eyes were in the respective entrails and eyes bins. There were droplets of blood on the floor, which he followed until he found a toothy hole in the wall. He kicked it and was screamed at in reply.

Now, if Mr. Paice had been watching, he would have put on more of a show—he would have pulled his hook up to cast a shadow over his eyes, he would have lowered his voice, wiggled his fingers, and shouted, "Spirit! Show yourself!" If he was feeling fancy, he might have wafted some special incense or rung some bells. But he was alone, so he crouched down and poked his head in.

"Well? Come out, then."

The intruder merely grunted in reply, and Colton pinched the bridge of his nose. "Dammit." He reached into his satchel and pulled out a dry nutrient block. "This was supposed to be my lunch, you know."

He crumpled it up and laid some at the entrance of the hole, perched on his ankles as he waited. It didn't take long for the culprit to emerge, a little spotted pig who had presumably escaped a rather gruesome fate. It snuffled into the food, its round nose wiggling as it discerned the quality before inhaling it in one swift breath. Colton sighed and reached a hand out to pat its head.

"Oh, no. What a horrifying demon. C'mon, then, let's get you back to Mr. Paice."

The pig snorted in disapproval, and the exorcist ran a hand over his face.

Ugh. Didn't need this today.

Colton emerged sometime later alone, his hands and face streaked with blood.

"Did you do it?" Paice whispered. "Did you get rid of the spirit?"

Colton smiled, a lock of ebony hair falling in front of his eyes. "You have nothing to worry about, sir. You may resume your business without fear of a demon causing you strife. Now, about my fee . . ."

The gold jingled pleasantly in his pocket, but Colton was still a bit sour about the loss of his ration biscuit. He waited for Paice to leave before doubling back behind the factory, extracting the oinker from the crate he'd hidden it behind.

"You're going to have to figure out how to pay me back for that, pig," he said, tying a loose bit of string around its neck. "Fuck. What am I supposed to do with you?"

He made his way down to The Raven and secured the thing outside, hoping that maybe someone would steal the stupid creature. The bar was packed as ever, the air warm and sweet as young people danced and drank and fought. A typical Iron establishment: a rustic, musty charm, with brown stains on every chair and table. Colton took his usual seat in the corner and ordered one beer, then another, until his pockets were empty and the world seemed like a much more beautiful place than it had an hour ago.

Everyone knew him here, and they trusted him for the most part. It was one of his best tricks, actually, to sit back in his seat, act casual, and wait for one of the drunker patrons to try and make use of his services. After all, buying bogus peace of mind was an easier sell to the inebriated.

The foam of his beer fizzed against his upper lip as his first regular customer approached him, clasping at his shirtsleeve.

"Colt! You gotta—you gotta help me—" Abby held her mouth like she was about to empty her stomach, and Colton casually tried to inch away from her.

"C'mon, Abby, it's been a long day." He wrenched his shirt free from her grip.

"Coltonnnn!" She grabbed for him once again. "You're the only one I trust for this!"

He shut his eyes and let out a long breath through his nose before giving her his undivided attention. The price of success, such as it was. "So what's the problem?"

"I'm pretty sure I'm possessed, Colton! My husband, he—won't touch me no more! He says I got the devil in me!"

Of course.

Her histrionics were attracting the attention of other patrons, which in theory was good for business but did increase the pressure just a smidgen. Colton forced a smile. "My, my, a demonic possession is quite a serious thing," he cautioned. "We'd best get this sorted soon. We have no time to waste."

Dressed all in black, with the slaughterhouse blood still caked on his face, Colton was sure he looked like one of the legendary old priests who had allegedly cleansed the earth of monsters and wicked beasties before the gates had been built. He raised a hand in front of her face, shutting his eyes as the metal bangles on his wrists clacked together in melodic urgency.

"I sense it." Well, he could sense there were at least another two drinks' worth of coins in her pocket. "This is serious, Abby, the demon is—it's furious. It could kill you if we're not careful."

A crowd formed around them, but Colton kept his attention solely on his sweet, possessed little princess, like she was the dearest thing in the world to him. "Everyone stand aside—I must bless the ground and prepare myself."

He went to his satchel and poked around in it, with as much reverence and dignity as any man could have while fumbling through a disorganized pouch of ramshackle exorcism equipment.

With a crowd like this he was going to need a little extra help . . . *Ah.*

He lit some Blue Grass incense, which purportedly cleansed the air and prepared the mind, but also serendipitously caused hallucinations and lowered inhibitions. Next, he took a vial of Snow and poured a generous pile into his hand. He lifted his palm up toward Abby's face and blew it at her, causing her to sneeze and sputter. A bit of a waste, maybe, but he wanted Abby to be more excitable, otherwise the whole thing wouldn't work.

It wasn't often he got to perform such a public exorcism—these were normally "behind closed doors" sorts of jobs. Might as well make the best of the attention.

Lastly, he sprinkled some salt and garlic and various other condiments in a circle on the ground and positioned Abby in the center.

"Okay. Shut your eyes, Abigail. Let me in." He touched their foreheads together, squeezed her hands as tight as he could. "I feel it," he confirmed, trying to keep her calm. "The demon inside you, it is a vicious thing—don't worry, it can't hurt you while I am in battle with it." *Or something.* "Repeat after me: Begone, wicked demon! Begone from my mind, my heart, and my body! Begone, and let me and my family be in peace!"

Abby did as she was told, frightened tears pouring down her cheeks. "Colton—Colton, I feel it! I FEEL IT. IT'S A SNAKE, A SNAKE INSIDE ME, I—HELP ME!"

Hoo boy. Then again, it was always a slightly easier sell when his clients had an idea of the precise nature of the monster.

"Shh . . . shhh, Abigail, I've got you, I promise." He kicked his heel on the ground with a satisfying, resounding clunk. "Begone, foul beast! My powers compel you, BEGONE!" He cracked his forehead against Abby's, and he caught her as she went to her knees. There was a small red mark on her skin, and Colton quirked a smile.

She'll be fine.

She blinked and looked at him, tears pooling in her red-rimmed eyes. "Is it over?"

"Can't you feel it, Abigail? You're free. It's the lightest thing in the world, right?"

She considered for a moment, then clutched him, sobbing against his shoulder. "Colton—thank you, thank you!"

He patted her back and hid his horror as her tears and snot started soaking through the thick fabric of his cloak. "Of course. Now, about my fee . . ."

The onlookers tossed coins at him, falling about his feet like glimmering leaves in a storm. *Beautiful.* Colton couldn't look too happy about the money—after all, the principle tenet of exorcism was empathy, or the semblance of it. Oh, screw it, he'd freed a young woman from a snake demon, right? He grinned as the gold sank into his pockets. This'd be enough to keep him going for a week!

Colton ordered another beer or three and ambled his way out of the pub once his head had begun to spin. He blinked under the lamplight, cursing as he spotted that bloody pig still waiting for him, plopped down in a puddle in the road. "Seriously?" He knelt down to untie the leash. What kind of world was this, where no one wanted a free pig in the middle of the night?

He felt a hand on his shoulder, and Colton's face shot up, alarmed at the sudden intrusion. Before him was the most beautiful man he'd ever seen in his entire life. Dressed impeccably in a tailored white suit, with glimmering golden hair and dazzling blue eyes, he had the face of an angel and carried himself with confidence and grace and nobility.

"Good evening. I saw the . . . exorcism you did in there," the man said pleasantly, keeping his hand on Colton's shoulder. "Quite clever, isn't it? The Grass, the Snow . . . did I detect a hint of Night Mare as well? A perfect concoction for suggestibility and fear, mmm?"

Colton's eyes widened. Was this guy a cop?

The man smiled a pretty, somehow predatory smile. "Ah, how rude of me, I didn't introduce myself. My name is Lucian Beaumont, of the Silvermoorian Beaumonts."

He—Lord Beaumont didn't need to explain further. The Beaumonts were one of the richest families in all of Silvermoor. Damn, he'd been exposed as a fraud by a fucking Beaumont. He was going to prison, five years minimum, there was no two ways about it. Maybe he could kick him in the balls and run for it? But the Lord had seen his face, knew his name, probably—fuck, this was bad.

Lord Beaumont gripped him tighter. "Now, now, I don't want any trouble. I have something of a business proposition for you, actually. I was wondering if you might accompany me to The Partridge so we might discuss it further? My treat, of course. You can bring your friend along if you wish." The Lord winked at the pig and helped Colton to his feet.

Like he had a damn choice. Go with Beaumont or get turned in to the guard. Colton followed the young Lord up toward the Ivory District, his heels clacking neatly against the cobblestones as he walked. He wondered if he should run, yet there was just something about the Lord's smile, his manner, the invitation itself . . .

Colton was intrigued. It wasn't every day that some cloak-and-dagger Iron exorcist was invited up to the Ivory District with one of the richest men in the world. A chance, maybe, to get out of this miserable pit.

Fuck it. What's the worst that could happen?

two

Colton had been to the Ivory District exactly two times before this moment. The first was when he was around twelve, when he and his friends had come up with the idea to sneak in during the winter.

"We'll be fine," Mai had assured them, grinning. "We'll scout out the place first, see if anything catches our interest. Maybe a nice old couple thinks one of us is cute and wants to adopt us!"

Orr smirked too. "That's perfect! Then, under cover of night, he'll let the rest of us in, and we can rob them blind!" A pause. "That's kind of a long-term plan, though. For now, I bet we can grab some wallets."

Or, more likely, go rifling through a baker's trash and eat better than any of them ever had in their whole lives.

It wasn't too long after Colton's mother had passed away, and he'd more or less stopped worrying about the consequences of his actions. She'd always warned Colton to stay away from people like Orr, but she wasn't here anymore. If she was *that* worried about who Colton hung out with, then maybe she shouldn't have died.

Obviously Colton didn't think he was going to get adopted, he wasn't that stupid—but late at night he would imagine it sometimes. A big, warm room all to himself, with loving parents just down the hallway if he got scared in the night. He could almost smell the warm meal that his family would be cooking for him each and every night. No, no, surely they'd have a chef, right? But maybe the mother would try to bake cookies, and they'd send him to school, and he'd rise up in society and—

Stupid. No one was ever gonna take in a tattooed little stray like him.

They'd chosen a moonless night to make their attempt. All three clad in their nicest clothes, faces scrubbed and cleaned to the point that their skin had turned pink. Colton's hair was always unruly, but he brushed it back and smiled like a little gentleman, praying that he looked like he belonged. The warm glow of the electric Ivory lamps bathed the steps like a soft, welcome embrace, and Colton scarcely noticed the cold winter wind on his cheeks as they stepped out of Indigo and into their futures. The air smelled fresh in the Ivory District—the fragrant spices and perfumes from the shops, the inviting joy of fresh bread, of melted chocolate, of people who had a well-functioning aqueduct system. And the machines! The golden clocks, the lights that buzzed, news tickers, carriages without horses—a strange new world existed beyond the autonomous gates.

Colton had closed his eyes and allowed the sensations to envelop him, which made it a lot easier for one of the Ivory Guard to catch him by his ears and push him to his knees. Orr had made a run for it, while Mai had looked back at Colton and bitten her lip before taking off as well. Colton watched her tiny body disappear behind a corner.

Please make it. One of us has to.

Being a minor, Colton wasn't charged with district fraud or trespass, but he was dragged back down to the Iron gates, and he did have his ass kicked so badly that he could barely go out to find food for himself the next few days.

He'd been a kid. Reeling from the loss of his mother, desperate for a place in the world, willing to try just about anything to escape his circumstance. That wasn't possible, and it hadn't been a lesson learned easily.

The second time Colton had been to the Ivory District was when he'd gotten arrested.

So it was a somewhat surreal experience this time as Colton approached the Ivory gate with Lucian frigging Beaumont. The guards stood aside and let them pass, actually bowing at the waist as the young Lord moved beyond them. The streets were filled with nobles: men and women dressed up in gold and silk, one of them sporting a mechanical bird on her hat. He was sticking out like a damned nail. Oh, balls, he had a frigging pig on a leash in the Ivory District.

Why weren't they looking at him? His blood-covered face, the soot on his clothes, the exorcist tattoos on his wrists—he didn't have a pass, he didn't belong. Where were the burly guards tackling him to the ground and dragging him to prison?

Nowhere.

All eyes were on Lord Beaumont as they passed, who was just smiling pleasantly to himself with his beautiful hands in his silk-lined pockets. Of course they were, this was a man who'd been a serious contender for Prime Minister last year. Obviously that hadn't happened, but the political sway he still carried was palpable. Even some men in the Iron District had been passionate Beaumonters, as Colton recalled. Not that Colton paid attention to politics—one rich bastard was as bad as any other.

"Have you been up here before, sir?" Beaumont chimed. "The woman called you Colton, correct? May I do the same? What's your family name?"

Colton blinked, shutting his mouth as he realized it was hanging open. "I—not really. It's hard to get a pass unless you know the right people." It sounded so strange to hear his name on the tongue of an Ivory man. "Ah—yeah. Colton's fine."

"Lovely. Well, Colton, I hope you enjoy our time together."

Beaumont had stopped in front of a gold-and-white building with massive windows. A gleaming mechanical sign atop the doorway informed him they had reached The Partridge, and Lord

Beaumont held the door open to let Colton in first. It was just as well his buzz was wearing off by now, or the sickly sweet smell of berry wine and the glittering lights of three too many electric chandeliers might have made him nauseous.

"They do a lovely brunch here, although I suspect we've missed it by a few hours." He smiled. "I bet if I ask them very nicely, they might make us something from the brunch menu anyway. Now, the café is dog friendly, but I'm not sure how they feel about our porcine friends. Is your pig well-behaved?"

Colton looked down at it. "I . . . have no idea."

Lord Beaumont grinned. "I suppose we'll just have to find out, shall we?"

The staff made a big fuss over Beaumont as soon as he entered, with the host and waiters tripping over each other to serve him first. If any of them took issue with his Iron guest, none of them said a damn word. He was an honored guest, apparently.

Colton was used to people, of course, to crowds, to being in tight spaces. But this was something else entirely. There was literal gold going into people's mouths and presumably coming out the other end later on in the day. He didn't like their eyes in his direction. Even now that they were seated, more people were gawking at Lord Beaumont and his companion than they were at the literal pig that was sitting on the floor of the nicest restaurant that Colton had ever been to. He was almost irritatingly attractive, this Lord Beaumont. And carried himself like the sort of man who very much enjoyed that fact.

"Now, then, please order anything you like. I must recommend the brioche toast with the various macerations and reductions and nibbly goodies on it, although I'm sure everything on the menu is good." Lord Beaumont unfastened his cape, because of course he was wearing a cape, and peered over the menu in the warm light of the restaurant.

Colton examined it as well, finding the gold, elaborate cursive to be difficult and annoying to read. "Do they have any sort of endangered animal surprise here? You know, Ivory District stuff." There were rumors that the upper class ate all sorts of crazy things, after all. Besides, Lord Beaumont was paying.

He laughed. "I suppose it wouldn't hurt to ask. What did you have in mind? Orphan meatloaf? The very-last-of-its-kind soup? Honestly, Colton, they aren't worth the cholesterol. It's all about hype rather than flavor when you're eating the unfortunate. But please, get whatever you wish."

Colton just ended up ordering whatever Beaumont was having, more because he didn't want to admit he could barely understand the menu than anything else. A beat of silence fell between them, and he peered across the table at the young Lord as if to say, *Well?*

"So, I imagine you're wondering what this is all about," Lord Beaumont said finally, tenting his fingers under his chin. "As I said, I have a business proposition for you. As you may have heard, recently my family and I have had some . . . rousing dialogue, shall we say, which has led me to reconsider my future job prospects to some degree."

Of course Colton had heard. Even in the Iron District, people were still talking about the young Lord stepping away from his family. Why the political campaign had abruptly ended without explanation. Rumors abounded. People said he'd fucked up the business; disgraced himself with drugs; fallen in love with a commoner. The official story was that Lucian Beaumont had found religion and had stepped away from the family estate to help his fellow man.

"I've spent a great deal of energy researching spirits, demons, hauntings, that sort of thing. I must say, I find the whole business of exorcism to be absolutely fascinating, and I think there's actually tremendous potential to make it into a very successful business within the Ivory District. There's a certain type of noble who wants their sins cleansed by . . . freelance exorcists, say, rather than members of the Holy Order." He smiled. "That's where you come in. I'd like to offer you a partnership, to work with me in ridding my neighbors of some of their demons. It's terribly trendy at the moment. You'd probably make fifty times what you made tonight on just one job, and of course we'd be able to help a great many people. What do you think?"

Colton gawked at him. This man was insane. They'd just met! Colton was a fraud! They'd get arrested in a heartbeat! And he still had a bunch of jobs to do in the Iron District and—

"Lord Beaumont—"

"Please, call me Lucian."

Fat chance.

"Look, what the hell makes you think we'd be good partners? You've only seen me perform one exorcism."

And commit fraud while I was at it.

"Well, I've done a bit of research about you, Colton. You're well regarded in the Iron District, and seem to have genuine roots in the world of exorcism. What that means is you have credibility and authenticity, which means the Order can't try and interfere with your practice. What you'd need from me is access and connections. And I imagine the particulars of Ivory schmoozing are a bit foreign to you." He chuckled.

"Why are you even asking? It's not like I can say no."

The young Lord cocked an eyebrow. "What do you mean?"

"I refuse to work with you, and you go right to the cops, right? You tell 'em all about the Grass and the Snow, and my life is over." Colton leaned over and whispered pointedly, "Why else would you wanna work with a fraud?"

Lucian bit his lip, his fingers idling along the gilded rims of his cuff links. "Oh, Colton, on the contrary. I have no interest in coercing you, nor blackmailing you. If you don't want to work with me, then we can finish our meal together, I will walk you back to the gates, and you need never see me again. I don't really think a good partnership can be founded on the basis of force." He smiled. "As for why I'd want to work with someone like you . . . I like you. And I'm *looking* for a fraud. I want to work with someone who knows all the tricks of the trade, so to speak. Someone who isn't afraid of a little theatricality, when the situation calls for it."

What was his game? Why would a Beaumont debase himself by working with someone like Colton? He glanced down at his tattoos. It was possible even someone with Beaumont's connections couldn't do exorcism work in the Ivory District without the express permission of the Order, which was not so easily obtained. The Cultural Protection Initiative kept "authentic" exorcists like Colton in business, and would provide the Lord with the shield he needed to get started.

"That being said, this isn't a binding contract or anything like that. If at any point you grow tired of my antics, or you make enough money to retire, then we go our separate ways. I've actually got a job in the works, if you're interested. Simple matter—haunted house, spirit scaring the family, blah blah blah. Fifty-fifty split for a job well done, and I'll get you some clothes befitting an exorcist of your caliber."

Lucian offered his partnership with a handshake. "What do you say?"

Colton stared at it—that beautiful, perfectly manicured hand that had probably never seen a proper day's work in its life. "Eighty-twenty," he managed, his audacity a tasty thrill. What would Beaumont say to such an offer? He'd walk out. He'd throw a napkin in Colton's face. Right?

But he didn't. Instead, Lucian . . . laughed. His whole face crinkled with mirth at the counter-proposition. His laugh was melodic, lacking any bite or cruelty. "A hard bargain, sir! Seventy-thirty."

Colton was taken aback. It was bizarre that the man hadn't stormed off in a pouty huff.

Seventy-thirty, then. A deal in Colton's favor, but the fact that Lucian seemed so utterly pleased with himself made him wonder if it was he who was giving up something potent, something valuable.

The light glinted off Lucian's golden hair as he smiled, and they shook hands.

"I think this is the start of a beautiful friendship, Colton. Eat up. I want to see you bright and early in the morning."

three

The food was the best that Colton had ever eaten. Griddle cakes so light and fluffy they practically melted on his tongue, drinks topped with arcs of caramelized sugar, everything rich, creamy, fresh. He was happy to take Lucian up on his offer to pay for everything, ordered "the flight of fancy tasting menu of autumntime laments," and, by the end of the evening, could barely walk for fear of bursting.

If Lucian minded, he didn't say anything about it, simply smiled pleasantly as he watched Colton stuff his face.

And, to his credit, Colton only ordered two drinks. He had to make a good business impression after all. Colton assumed he would find it challenging to converse with the young Lord. He'd never been the sort of person to speak through awkward silences, nor to make small talk when it didn't suit him. Of course he had questions, but intrusions into his private life at this early stage of their relationship hardly seemed appropriate. Fortunately, Lucian seemed quite happy to fill the conversational void on his own, explaining what all of the dishes were, where the drinks came from, and, of course, providing some background information on the haunting they were going to face together in the coming days.

"It's for Mrs. Radcliffe. She's a wealthy woman who is quite good friends with my father. I went to university with her daughter, so the family knows me rather well. Mrs. Radcliffe believes there is a spirit haunting the house, and has been for some time. She didn't wish to discuss the case particulars, but the main things I'd like you to be aware of are: she is not very intelligent, she will likely want value for money, and finally, she has been sexually attracted to me since I reached puberty."

Colton choked on his drink. *Cocky bastard, isn't he?*

"Right, so she's gonna want a show, then?"

"I assume so. And if you need any extra ingredients, props, that sort of thing, just let me know. I can arrange to have everything delivered in time for the exorcism. Oh! We can call it a business expense!" He laughed. "This is exciting. I've not really had to think about taxes and that sort of thing in the past. How lovely."

Colton cocked an eyebrow and shook his head. "Why does it matter that she's sexually attracted to you?" *Wouldn't most people be?*

"Well, in this instance it means that she'll be receptive to my suggestions and will subconsciously want to please me. Which means that it would probably be to our advantage to let me lead in dealing with her, and then I'm happy for you to take charge when the actual exorcism comes."

"Sure. And what sort of demon are we allegedly dealing with here?"

Lucian let his fingers skip down the stem of his glass and met Colton's eyes. "Before I answer that, I'd like to clarify something with you. Please correct me if I'm wrong, and allow me to preface this by saying that I mean no offense. Both of us are aware that exorcism and demonic possessions are a bunch of superstitious nonsense—is that right?"

Colton swallowed. That was certainly a controversial opinion to be spouting out in Silvermoor, where even the upper class stuck by their traditional beliefs. The main tenet of the Order was devoted to the cleansing of demons, the purification of society, with many citizens adjusting their whole way of living in order to avoid incurring their wrath. It wasn't exactly illegal to question such things, of course, but it wasn't wise either.

"Sort of an odd question for a man who is starting an exorcism business to be asking."

Lucian smiled. "Sort of an odd answer for what is, in effect, a yes or no question."

Colton downed the rest of his drink and licked his lips. He'd believed in spirits when he was younger. Working alongside his mother, he had held her hand and watched in wonder as she dispelled evil from homes and businesses, tiptoeing through violet smoke and muttering incantations in a language he could just about understand. But in all that time, he never saw a demon or a ghost, nor felt the presence of something wicked. When he was younger, he wondered if there was something he was doing wrong— a lack of faith, maybe, an impurity of heart. And so he worked, and he prayed, and he spent hours at a time perfecting his craft so he could be an asset to his mother, rather than a chain on her heels.

He'd carried on the practice for her when she grew ill. Copying her incantations, her runes, her chants, and her dances. He made enough money to keep the home warm, to buy medicine, but none of it helped her. Her body was ravaged from the consumptive sickness, so thin and weak that his twelve-year-old body could carry her. "*I love you, Colton. I need to tell you—about your—*"

He hadn't wanted to hear about his father or his heritage. He was tired of curses; he was tired of looking at strangers and wondering if they might have fucked his mother and given him life. So he'd kissed her cheeks and held her hands. "I love you too, Mama. I love you, I love you."

She'd opened her mouth to speak, and her body had seized up, and the only sound that emerged was a rattle. He'd stayed up late that night burying her, his fingernails bleeding as he tore the earth.

When she had died, Colton tried to conjure her soul using one of the circles she had taught him. He painted his face in holy pigment, he cleansed their tiny house with incense and fire, and he moved his feet with grace and determination. The words she had said a thousand times passed over his teeth, and he shut his eyes and prayed, begged, *willed* the incantation to work, just this once.

He opened his big brown eyes, an expectant and hopeful smile breaking across his face.

The room was dark and silent as ever, and Colton realized how alone he truly was. Whatever faith in the other world he might've once had vanished in that instant, and his exorcisms became cynical, clinical, and pragmatic.

The next morning he'd collected his mother's exorcism things—her books, her costumes, her talismans, everything—and he'd burned them in the street.

Colton swallowed. "Yeah. It's all bullshit." His voice was hollow and dry as he said the truth out loud for the first time in his life. He realized he was staring down at his plate, his heart heavy with shame. Colton forced himself to look up at Lucian, who smiled at him and touched his shoulder from across the table.

"Good. I'm glad we're on the same page. I imagine it'd be challenging to work with someone who took this all seriously. I wouldn't want to offend with my blaspheming. I'm in your capable hands then, Colton."

They spent the rest of the meal hammering out the details for their first job together. The meal concluded, Lucian paid, and Colton resolved to give Lucian a decent show to start with, at least. That meant staying sober, or at least soberish.

The porker wasn't helping with this whole "making a good impression" thing. It turns out it wasn't the most straightforward thing in the world, removing a pig from a warm, comfortable restaurant and shoving it out into the chilly night. It pulled back on the leash, made an ungodly screech of dismay, but eventually relented when Lucian procured some sort of sugar-dusted fried pastry as bait.

"See? We'll make a wonderful team."

Lucian was as good as his word and walked Colton back to the gates so he could avoid trouble with the guard, pressing a card into his hand as they were about to part ways. An Ivory pass, with unlimited uses, freedom to move through the districts as he pleased. Colton was also given the tailor's address, and informed that Lucian would meet him the following morning right as they opened.

A pass to the Ivory District. Literal upward mobility, access to the life his mother had never even dared to dream of for them. Colton put it in his pocket like a precious, living thing.

"This will be *brilliant*," Lucian promised.

Colton barely registered the way the air seemed colder and darker as soon as he stepped into Indigo, nor the sounds of the four little trotters clacking along beside him as he moved.

Lucian fucking Beaumont. The most famous person he knew nothing about. What had he gotten himself into?

Colton glanced up at the Beaumont Clock Tower and frowned. He had to be up early for his Lordship. Any sensible man would head right home, figure out how to eat the damn pig, and go to bed. *Too bad you were never much of a sensible man.*

The winding Iron streets led him to Mai's imposing splintered door, and he cursed himself for thinking of her first. He hadn't dared get in touch for weeks, and now he was gonna wake her up in the middle of the night to gossip about the nobility? She'd castrate him.

He knocked twice, hoping to the four corners of hell she wouldn't know it was him. Silence followed, and Colton knocked again, with more urgency this time.

He heard grumbling inside, then plodding footsteps, and he was barely able to move out of the way before the door swung open. Despite her tangled bed head and grumpy face, there was always something elegant about how Mai carried herself. Her sharp eyes narrowed to slits with something like hot fury, her arms crossed over her chest. "Oh, hells, no," she said, glaring at Colton. "This'd better be good."

"Hey! You're looking great!" *Good start.* "Ah . . . Mai, can I come in for a bit? It's really important."

She glanced at her wristwatch and cocked an eyebrow at him. "It can't wait?"

"I'm already here, aren't I?" He grinned at her, hoping it was charming. "Please? I can make it worth your while."

Mai's eyes went to his new companion. "I don't like animals."

"No, no, I've got a new lead, a good job. I should be able to pay you back and then some. I just need—"

"Oh, for fuck's sake, get in. But don't try anything funny."

She sat him down on some of the crates in her living room and made herself some tea without offering him any. The greatest insult Mai could come up with, surely, but honestly it was fair enough. He wasn't expecting the gold star treatment really. Not with how he'd left things last time.

Mai kept her home in a state of organized clutter, and as always, it smelled of incense and her handmade soap. Some of his stuff was still here, bless her. For all her purported grudge bearing, she hadn't sold it off yet. She removed a small vial from her necklace and tipped a bit of Snow onto her finger, snorting it deftly as she waited for Colton to speak.

"So . . . I was wondering if you knew anything about Lucian Beaumont."

"Beaumont? Why?"

Colton hesitated. "It's for a job." *Easy enough.* "I need as much information as possible. About the ehm . . . the ousting and disinheritance?"

Surely she knew something. She cleaned up after half the biggest families in the Ivory District. Mai licked her fingertip and thought about it. "No one knows exactly what happened, but most think there was some nasty falling out between them. Couldn't say why, exactly. Usually it's some sex thing, or drug thing, or a sexy drug thing."

Colton nodded. Lucian hadn't seemed like a deviant, really, nor a drug addict, and he came off as pretty smart and business savvy as well. "Anything else?"

"Well, the father is apparently a mega asshole. Horrific working conditions in every business he owns, a lot of money going into the Order, and that political play last year must have cost him a pretty penny. I've personally seen him strike a servant so hard that she got a black eye."

"And Lucian?"

Mai shrugged. "By all accounts, a pleasant young man. A bit strange, from what I've heard. Harmless. Honestly, I don't understand why he ran for Prime Minister at all. Fen was working at the estate last year and he didn't think the kid had the stones for it. He doesn't quite have the venom for politics, apparently. I dunno anyone he's hit or coerced into sex or anything, but he's pretty young. There's still time."

"So what happens to the Beaumonts now that they don't have an heir?"

"I assume everything'll go to the daughter, but that would be highly unusual. Whatever he did must've been pretty terrible, Colt, for the family to hobble itself like that. Be careful around that guy."

Colton nodded. "I'm always careful." *Mostly. Sometimes. Maybe.*

"Oh, come on." She cocked her head to the side and smiled, crossing her arms. "Colton . . . I'm glad you came. I don't like things being awkward between us."

He squeezed her shoulder then, meeting her honey brown eyes. "I'm trying to be better."

"You look better."

Sober, more like. He'd made a conscious effort to remain on the right side of inebriated in front of Beaumont. Fuck, now he felt like an ass for ever making her worry.

Mai shooed him out of the house after that, and Colton left without any protest. He supposed he'd just have to learn about Lucian as they worked together.

four

The pig woke Colton up bright and early the following morning, and he got dressed in his finest attire. He glanced at himself. Was this going to be good enough for Lord Beaumont? His cloak had served him well for years, and his belt was top-quality Iron leather—no one could complain about that. The clothes kept the rain off his back and stopped him from exposing himself in public. Surely that would be sufficient for his Lordship.

Colton arrived at the gates and was stopped by the guard, who examined his pass with suspicion and callous dismissiveness. "Who'd you nick this off of?" The guards were always rather large men, it seemed. Probably Indigo blokes who muscled their way into a cushy gig, dressed in the typical impractical uniform of white, white, and some sort of off-white.

Colton attempted to look intimidating. "I'll have you know that I am the invited guest of Lord Lucian Beaumont, and he will be very cross to learn you have impeded me!" That was how Lucian spoke, right? "You shall let me pass, sir!"

The guard frowned and made as if to tear up the pass, at which point an elegant and manicured hand shot out and snatched the man's wrist.

"Gentlemen, how unfortunate. You are being terribly rude to

my guest." Lucian's smile was cold as he snatched the pass back and handed it to Colton. "I may have to write a letter to the head guard."

"Lord Beaumont, please, we thought he had stolen this pass, sir. Please, it was only to protect your good name and—"

Lucian clasped Colton's shoulder and tsk-tsked. "Perhaps the next time there is confusion, you should contact me directly. Colton, my apologies for the inconvenience. You didn't bring your pig!"

It was always a whirlwind with this man, wasn't it? Everything was theatrics, nothing was simple. "My . . . ?" *Oh, right.* "Maybe I *ate* her." Colton pinched the bridge of his nose. "I thought I was to meet you at the tailors?"

"Well, I thought about it last night and realized you might end up having a bit of trouble getting in because of "—he looked Colton up and down—"all this. I imagine that after this morning, you won't ever have a problem with the guard again." He grinned. "If you'll follow me, please."

It was lovely, actually, having someone advocate for him, be considerate of his needs. Beaumont wasn't like most Ivory men as far as Colton could tell. Colton found himself trying hard not to smile. He could get used to this.

He wasn't sure what he expected of the tailor's shop, but he had more or less decided to surrender himself and just see where the winds of madness took him. And so he was put on a stool, poked and prodded in his various nooks and crannies while a strange woman took his measurements.

"What did you have in mind, Lord Beaumont?" she asked, ignoring the *eep* that was elicited as she went up Colton's inseam.

"Something dark and mysterious, but fashionable," Lucian explained patiently. "Definitely a few cloaks, precious stones for the clasps, of course. Something that highlights his figure, gives him an air of authority."

Colton snickered, and the tailor pinched his thigh.

"No moving."

He stood perfectly still and tried to imagine how a garment could do all that for anyone. Colton was pretty good-looking already, if he did say so himself! He'd always been tall for his age, had a reasonably pleasant-looking face, healthy complexion, big brown eyes—maybe a bit more scruffy than they'd appreciate in the Ivory District, but then not everyone could be a perfect porcelain doll like Lucian was.

Lucian cocked his head to the side and gestured at Colton's wrists. "Your markings, Colton. They're lovely. May I inquire how far they go?"

Colton snorted. "You may not."

"The only reason I ask is, well, those are *exorcist* tattoos, no? Can you imagine what a sight you'd make if they were on more prominent display? Kiara, what do you think? Could we make like . . . a vest? Perhaps something he doesn't need to wear anything under."

Colton shook his head sharply. The tattoos were a deeply personal and private thing, and he didn't like them to be seen by others. Even with intimate partners, it was a part of his body he preferred to ignore and downplay if he could. Hells, he barely even remembered getting them. He'd been so young when his mother had marked him. "Lucian," he said sharply, "no."

The lord considered him for a moment before nodding his understanding. "Of course, Colton. Forgive my impertinence."

At least he backed off quickly.

The tailor swatted Colton off her stool and got to work.

They were given some coffee, which blessedly smelled like it had alcohol in it, and Lucian resumed speaking.

"So, I've done a bit of poking around Mrs. Radcliffe and this whole haunting mess. One of the servants has gone missing recently. Apparently he had taken . . . shall we say, an acute interest in Patricia, Mrs. Radcliffe's daughter."

"Right, so what does that mean?"

Lucian shrugged. "We'll have to wait and see, but I suspect there may be some complex emotional demons at play here. Love, guilt, that sort of thing. My gut says a guilty conscience has pushed her into hiring us. She wants peace of mind, and likely a show. I want you to be prepared for anything, Colton. Do you understand?"

Not really. "Yes."

"Boy!" Kiara called him over. "Try this." She pushed Colton into a changing room and handed him a pile of garments.

A three-piece suit, similar to what Lucian seemed to like to wear. The fabric was mostly black, with accents of gold and ruby around the throat and wrists. The cloth was softer than any he had ever worn in his life, and despite the short amount of time that had transpired, every article fit as though it had been made for him. The trousers accentuated his muscular legs, the charcoal button-down shirt hugged his shoulders and tapered neatly at his waist, the jacket had gems instead of buttons, and of course there was the cloak. It fastened over his breast with a polished amber stone and featured a hood that all but hid his eyes, leaving just his nose and jaw visible.

He looked . . .

"Incredible," Lucian breathed, standing behind Colton as he examined himself in the mirror. "Absolutely stunning." He clasped Colton's shoulders and grinned. "Look at yourself, partner. Look at how lovely you are. This is who those nobles are going to see. Colton, the demon slayer. Colton, the eccentric, the mastermind, the man that every other noble in the country will want in his home. Let no one tell you otherwise. You are *brilliant.*"

Lucian's voice in his ear was intoxicating, the way he spoke with a soft, husky whisper—the genuine excitement burning behind those intelligent eyes.

Colton couldn't quite speak. Was this really him? A gentleman—not a miscreant, not an urchin, a man that would turn heads wherever he went. He could *be* anyone, *do* anything. He looked to Lucian and wondered what would happen if he kissed him, right here, in the tiny dressing room. *Bad idea. Don't shit where you eat, dude.*

He had to remind himself that Lucian was no different than he was, really. They were both con artists, very skilled ones at that—Lucian perhaps even more skilled than Colton. The way he spoke, the way he walked, the way his eyes glimmered when he smiled—how much of it was affectation?

Even so. Even bloody so.

I believe you.

It didn't escape Colton's notice that people looked at him differently now that he was dressed up like a proper Ivory man. They nodded at him, some even bowed. He moved like a nobleman, ignoring the pleased little smirk on Lucian's face. How they must have looked together—night and day, ebony and gold, mystery and majesty. Was this confidence?

It's an act, Colton. It's always been an act.

It all bled away as they approached the Radcliffe estate—a massive gleaming castle of a building right in the middle of the Ivory District. The stones were polished white marble, and there were bits of gold ground into the stairway banisters.

Colton stopped in his tracks, his jaw tight and legs tense. He was a fraud, and this wasn't some dumbass with a pig up his butt—this was a sophisticated, wealthy woman who would smell poverty and desperation a mile away. Lucian belonged with these people, and would never go to prison over something like this. Rich criminals never got arrested. Fuck! He had to get out of here—he had to get back to the Iron District—they knew him there, they'd trust him—he had to—

Lucian's hand grasped his own and squeezed. "Colton," he whispered. "You can do this. I promise you, I will not allow any harm to befall you." They locked eyes, and Colton swallowed. "You will be great."

Colton wondered if his palm was sweaty as it fell away from Lucian's. He nodded, licked his lips. He was a demon hunting expert, after all. Lucian Beaumont swore by him, vouched for him. *Needed him.* He could do this. *They* could do this.

A clockwork mechanism opened the door, and a dour-looking butler ushered them in. The whole house was a testament to wasteful opulence—priceless paintings being damaged by the sun, servants standing perfectly still with nothing to do.

Blossom, Colton noted, his nostrils flaring. *A lot of narcotics in this house.*

Lucian watched him, smiling.

"Lucian!" Mrs. Radcliffe appeared at the top of an ivory spiral staircase, artificial red hair clashing with her flaming red dress. She had likely been enchanting once and clung to whatever vestiges of youth remained. Trotting up to Lucian, she pressed soft kisses to his cheeks. "You look so well, darling. I couldn't believe it when your father said you didn't want to continue the family business!"

Lucian chuckled, and Colton wondered how he managed to refrain from wiping off the thick bows of lipstick that Mrs. Radcliffe had left on his lovely skin. Lucian's face lacked all the warmth Colton had come to expect.

"My only regret is that it means I get to spend less time with you, my dear." Lucian kissed her hand with a wink. "And yet, it is nothing in the face of helping my fellow man. Please, tell me of this demon which torments you so."

Mrs. Radcliffe fawned over Lucian, who responded in kind as they performed a dance of pleasantries that skirted toward the realm of self-indulgent flirtation. Colton listened to the back and forth of their tittering exchange, both impressed and grateful for Lucian's innate talent for vapid conversation because he took up all the attention in the room. It provided the perfect diversion for Colton to map out his new surroundings and study the people who inhabited them.

But Mrs. Radcliffe peered at Colton anyway, a mix of intrigue and dubiousness etched over her face. "And this is . . . the man you spoke of?" She reached over and put a hand on Colton's chest.

Colton's eyes widened as Lucian stepped between them, taking her wrist and drawing her focus. His lips drew into a pleasant snarl, as if he had been patiently anticipating her brazenness.

"This is Colton," Lucian said reverently, bowing deeply. "Born and raised on the fringes of society, his mother was a true and renowned mystic!" He paused for effect. "He alone has the gift to lift your curse, my lovely. He has a deep and innate connection with the *other world*."

Colton mimicked Lucian's Ivory bow, all respect, grace, and professionalism. *Hopefully nothing fell out of my pockets.* He could feel the weight of Mrs. Radcliffe's scrutiny, and never did she meet his gaze, not even when he rose. It was all the better, because it allowed Colton to watch, to learn.

She focused on her hand in Lucian's grip, and her cheeks flushed pink. "He's good?"

Colton could see what Lucian had meant, about the benefit of having him navigate these Ivory people for him. Lady Radcliffe regarded him like an animal at the circus, an oddity to be gawked at, as though Lucian were the medium through which Colton could just about pass for human.

"The best, Mrs. Radcliffe. I wouldn't let just *anyone* darken your doorstep. Simply tell him your troubles, and we'll have them solved within the week. And I think we've arrived just in the nick of time, really. I can sense an *evil* presence here."

The woman crossed her arms and avoided their eyes. "In the last few months, there have been . . . disturbances. I hear moaning in the night, feel rushes of air in the hallways. I awake sometimes from these . . . awful, awful dreams."

"Go on," Lucian encouraged, his eyes wide with excitement.

"In the dreams I'm being ravaged by men I don't know, men who are not my husband!" she cried. "I get up in the night, to go see if Patty is all right, and . . . she's always sweating, out of breath, terrified!" She shuddered. "Her breasts have started to swell. I fear that this monster is trying to sow his"—she looked at Lucian, her face red, as she whispered—"his seed in her! Can you imagine?"

Well, yes.

"How awful, Mrs. Radcliffe. Now, is there any reason to think that there is a spirit in this house?"

She shut her eyes. "A man died here in the last few months. His own fault, foolishness. One of the servants." She shook her head, sliding a cigarette from a slim platinum case. "And haunting *us*? The nerve of that boy! I'll kill him again if he touches my Patty."

Again? Such a casual murder confession, if that's what it was. Ivory people were like another species sometimes.

"Of course, of course. We'll take care of everything." Lucian smiled. "Now, the exorcism itself can be a terribly messy business, I'm afraid. Very dangerous, deadly vapors and all sorts of nasty things. It's standard protocol that we ask you to depart for your own safety. Of course if you wish to stay . . . ?"

"Heavens, no! I trust you, Lucian. Get on with it, then. I'll be back, I suppose in the morning. He attacks in the night, you know. *Patricia!*"

A sallow young woman followed Mrs. Radcliffe out the door, her posture hunched, her eyes avoiding the two men in her home.

Young Lord Beaumont watched them leave, crossing his arms and leaning against the mother-of-pearl wallpaper. "Well?" Ever pleased with himself. "How do you think we best rid the poor Radcliffes of their burden? I'd love to see how you work."

"We'll probably have to poke around the place," said Colton. "You can almost always find a demon if you know where to look. Let me go through the rooms, while you try and talk to some of the maids." It seemed like Lucian could use his charmed tongue to get whatever he wanted. "We'll meet back up in an hour and see what we've found."

"I think that sounds like a splendid idea. Give us a good chance to find out a bit more about the Radcliffes' recent political leanings as well, mmm? I get the impression that locked doors aren't a problem for you? Try to leave everything where you found it. We don't want it obvious that we were snooping."

In other words, don't steal anything, stupid. *You got it, Beaumont.*

Colton made his way through the corridors, stopping at an ornate bejeweled door handle that he supposed must lead into Mrs. Radcliffe's room. He could smell Blossom, of course, but beneath that, there was the unmistakable scent of blood.

five

The door yielded to a small amount of coaxing from Colton's lock picks, and he braced himself as he stepped into the boudoir of the unknown. Mrs. Radcliffe's room was impeccably decorated, like every other room in the house, and as far as he could tell there was nothing out of the ordinary here.

Colton wasn't sure what he was looking for as he poked through drawers, one by one. Nothing surprising there either—vials of Blossom, slinky undergarments, various aphrodisiac tinctures and lotions, several girthy vegetable-shaped figurines that he decided not to touch. There was some Holy Order paraphernalia, nothing excessive—prayer books, candles, just the sort of collection one might expect from one affecting devotion.

The daughter's room was similar, except for a number of books and toys from her childhood scattered amidst the opulence. *A diary would be useful.* He found one under her pillow, although a lot of the scribbling had been crossed out, blackened by ink. Colton squinted at the text under the light, trying to make out the hidden words.

I miss him. I need to tell him. What will Mother say?

Colton sighed. Easy enough job, he supposed. *Mother is pissed about the help touching her adult daughter, probably kills him, and* manifests a demon to explain the fact that said daughter is probably knocked up, and to deal with her own guilt on the matter. Super-duper.

He still had the diary in his hand when Lucian knocked on the door. "Colton? This is Millie, one of the maids. Sweetheart, will you tell Colton what you told me?"

"She—he was a nice boy, my Lord. Thomas. He was sweet, he loved Miss Patty very much," she whispered. "My lady didn't like it—she—"

"It's okay," Lucian said warmly. "Please."

"There's a room, my Lords, you can access from my lady's chamber, it—you—you won't tell her I told you, right? She—you'll take care of it, right?"

"Of course we will. I want to help you, that's why I became an exorcist." He was far too good at sounding sincere.

The maid led them into her mistress's room and pointed at a sconce on the wall. "Pull on it, my Lords. I will not go into that place."

He tugged, and a lock clicked open, revealing a sliding door behind a bookcase. Lucian gasped and covered his mouth. *Yup, dead body for sure.* Colton pushed past him, retching as soon as the stench hit his face.

It reeked of blood and piss, of sweat, fear, and decay, a hundred times stronger in this windowless chamber than it had been in the bedroom. The only lights were candles, and he lit as many as he could find. Chains and cages lined the walls, mechanical devices that cut, and pulled, and tore—clockwork mechanisms designed to maim and cripple. He could see bloody scratch marks now and again—how long had he endured this? Poor bastard.

There were drugs and paraphernalia present too, some remnants of Snow and Blossom that had been carelessly discarded. Shattered whiskey and wine bottles littered the floor. The center of the room housed a large metal table, ornately decorated with gold and jewels. *Extravagant as ever, these Radcliffes.* And strapped to the table, or perhaps it was more accurate to say nailed to it, were the desiccated remains of a young man.

Colton tore out of the room and heaved the contents of his stomach onto Mrs. Radcliffe's decorative pillows. He felt Lucian's hand on his back and whipped around, eyes blazing. It was so much worse than he'd been expecting—a poisoning maybe, or a stabbing or—fuck!

This wasn't like the Iron District. It was wayward pigs and cheating husbands; it was knives between your ribs in a back alley, not this—protracted, intentional, sickening torture.

"What is this, Beaumont?" She was insane. She was gonna have them killed, strung up in a chamber and eaten by ants. "I can't. This isn't—I'm out."

Lucian squeezed Colton's shoulder and shook his head. "I—I suppose I wasn't expecting—I'm sorry, Colton. I never imagined she—not like this." He swallowed, fiddling with his cuff links. "The way I see it, we have two options, broadly speaking. We get rid of the body and provide Mrs. Radcliffe with some sort of abortifacient cocktail to slip her daughter. You do whatever cleansing acts you need, and perhaps remove some of the more psychotropic medications that we've found in the house. Problem solved, guilt assuaged, everyone is happy."

Lucian paused, his jaw tight. "Our other option is we confirm that there is a demon, and one that is, in fact, possessing Mrs. Radcliffe herself. Our avenues in this instance are, we use the demon to absolve her of her misdeeds . . . for a nominal fee I suppose, or . . . we harness the demon's powers, and take care of our hostess once and for all. The risks are that word gets out we're horrific exorcists, although it's possible Patricia will play along and help our cause. The benefits are somewhat less tangible, but I imagine that if we don't act, 'hauntings' like this will continue to curse this house long after we're gone.

"If it were my decision, I would probably wish to see if we can't banish this demon once and for all. But this is a partnership, and you must be aware of the risks. We might incur the full wrath of this woman." He swallowed. "And yet the thought of acting otherwise is a bit . . . unpalatable."

His bright eyes met Colton's. "What do you wish to do?"

That wasn't fair. Pushing this all onto Colton, with so much on the line. He was so out of his element, vulnerable and alone in this sea of wealthy tyrants. "Why are you leaving it up to me? You do whatever the fuck you want."

"We're in this together, Colton. I promised you I would protect you as much as I could, but that involves being truthful and telling you what we're up against, and the risks of each path we might take. I don't want to do something without your consent."

Colton pulled his flask out of his pocket and took a swig, wiping the back of his hand on his mouth. *Unpalatable*, he'd called it. Making it Colton's choice whether or not they did the right thing—whether they took the gold or made sure that justice reigned. Colton was a professional charlatan, to be sure. But he liked to think he'd probably draw the line at murder and ritualistic dismemberment.

Balls. All his life he'd wanted a little more respect and responsibility, and look where that got him. He glanced up at Lucian, at those stupid pretty eyes and his dumb concerned face. The easiest thing would be to take the money and run, never see this asshole again, certainly never step foot into another murder house. But even when he closed his eyes, he could see the fear on that poor man's face, the misery exuded by every cell of the daughter. No. This was wrong. There were some lines you just didn't cross.

What if someone did this to Mai? What would you do about it?

His eyes narrowed. "You just might be a prodigy, Lord Beaumont." Colton stood up straight, brushing his hair away from his brow and retaining as much dignity as a man who had vomited on the job could muster. "You have an uncanny knack for the unseen world, for the demonic ways. This will serve you well in our partnership, I imagine." Colton leaned in then, clasping Lucian's shoulder and pulling him in close.

"I feel it too. The evil in this place." Lucian smirked slightly. "Sickening, miserable, worse than I'd ever imagined. Just the kind of evil I was hoping to never see again." He let out a short, mirthless laugh.

As far as Colton could tell, Mrs. Radcliffe was feeling guilty in her own way, and needed a team of exorcists to make it all better for her. Without the heavy hand of the Holy Order involved, her conscience would be cleaned with minimal risk to her current lifestyle. He could only imagine what plans she had in store if Miss Radcliffe's pregnancy came to term, if the innocent culmination of this childish love took its first breath in these dank velvet chambers.

She was going to pay for this.

"I imagine," Colton added quietly, his fingers gripping the thick fabric of Lucian's embroidered cloak all the more tightly, "that the young lady might be convinced to help us. That her mother might see wisdom."

Lucian grinned. "What did you have in mind?"

Colton took a deep breath. "It's very important never to mix Night Mare with alcohol. It can cause hallucinations, disturbances. If we had some Grass burning in the background, I can only imagine what sort of impact that might have on someone with a guilty conscience." Colton stepped away from Lucian, his fingers skipping over the bottles of drugs and various beauty potions that Mrs. Radcliffe kept on her dresser. They lingered on an amber bottle of Snow, and he tilted it, watching the white powder swirl inside. "She's a heavy user, Lucian. There may already be some . . . disturbances. It shouldn't be fatal." *Not usually, anyway.* "But the combination of all these chemicals sort of amplifies their own effects, the good and the bad."

He set the vial down and stood up straight, mirroring Lucian's posture, his eyebrow arched in a way he hoped came across as confident.

Lucian's smile only broadened. "Our friend Mrs. Radcliffe should be back in the morning. I imagine it would be prudent to discuss our findings then."

Colton rolled back his shoulders, swallowing hard and forcing a smile to his lips. "Of course not. This is a matter of public safety, after all. It's our civic duty to perform an exorcism."

"You read my mind, Colton." Lucian—predatory, hungry, delighted. "All right. This is what we'll do. In order to exorcise the demon, we'll perform a sort of tea ceremony when the affected members of the household are present. To this end, you'll need to arrange some elaborate curse-dispelling setup in the dining room—candles, incense, writing on the walls, and, of course, your special concoction." He licked his lips.

"We will not have the opportunity to speak with Patricia directly, especially not in private. That said, I have an idea for how we might accomplish our goal and push things in our favor. Hell, if this goes according to plan, I think that we'll earn quite the little reputation for ourselves."

They would drag a confession out of Mrs. Radcliffe in front of her daughter, and take it from there. What could possibly go wrong?

Lucian smiled and clapped Colton on the arm. "I'll need you to roll with the punches a little here, and follow my lead. This is going to be brilliant."

Colton's smile was wry. "Oh, come now, Lord Beaumont. I'm nothing if not a professional. Of course it's going to be *brilliant.*"

six

The dining room was to be their stage. Colton had chosen it after wandering through the whole damn manor because of its grand airy windows framed with delicate carved wood. The room felt less oppressive than the rest of the house, although once the curtains were drawn, that would change. The thick velvet would snuff out any light that Colton hadn't provided and would leave the cheery room cast in a realm of blackness and shadow that seemed best for summoning a demon.

Besides, the darkness would make it easier to hide his own sleights of hand, and any part that he played in coaxing the "demon" out, perhaps a little more than was traditionally required.

Colton had three goals at this point. The first was that, ideally, he didn't want to be arrested by the end of the day. If Radcliffe clocked him as a fraud, or sniffed out that he didn't have her best interest at heart, there was a very real possibility that Holy Order agents would be summoned and he would be taken away from the rest of society. Ivory prisons weren't nice to Iron men, and he was quite confident that they would take great pleasure in making an example out of a known fraud who'd been taking advantage of the Cultural Protection Initiative. Lucian would probably be fine; his name alone would keep him out of trouble. Hopefully he'd have the courtesy to extend some of that protection to his new colleague.

The second was to leave this house with his wallet full enough to make all this drama worthwhile. The third was to go to sleep tonight knowing he'd at least tried to get justice for that young man.

It was fortunate that Ivory households were so damn superstitious. They *wanted* this to be real; it was exciting, it was sexy, it was going to be the new trend of the season. The fact that the entire spiritual world was a farce? Details, details. Best not think too hard about it.

He would do everything he possibly could to make this exorcism pain-free for all parties involved, and he hoped that his survival instincts, attention to detail, and overall persistence would help him through this. The rest, of course, would be up to Lucian.

The large wooden dining table was his first victim. He removed everything from its polished surfaces, the fine porcelain, the silver, everything except for the ornate candelabras in the middle. He replaced his spoils with incense burners, old-world teacups, and some garish straw dolls that he'd picked up over the years. He arranged them into a five-pointed star, which probably looked otherworldly and purposeful.

Oh, yes, the demon would be *terrified*.

Next he pulled out the tricks of his trade, the various mind-altering substances that he used together to make his hauntings appear all the more authentic. He ground up some of the Night Mare and used a small brush to coat the inside of the cup at Mrs. Radcliffe's seat, adding a drop of mint oil to disguise its taste and smell. Using the same brush, he applied some cinnamon and red pepper dust in ornate symbols on the floors and wall, more for aroma than appearance. He had collected some bare sticks from the garden and arranged them around the room near the candles, so they might cast ghoulish clawing shadows across every corner of the space. Colton took a step back and crossed his arms, admiring his handiwork with a smile. Assuming that Lucian was also any good at this, they might actually have a plan in place.

Lucian returned with his arms full of incense and a change of clothes, a broad, beaming smile on his face. "Colton! You've done a brilliant job! Hells, if I was a demon I'd feel right at home here." His enthusiasm was baffling, and Colton tried not to smile as he felt a seed of it burrow in his guts and begin to grow in his soul. He believed in Lucian. *Best tamp that down. Enthusiasm does not fit with my aesthetic.*

"What is the plan then? What are you going to do?"

Lucian grinned. "I think it might be best if I leave it as a surprise, partner. An authentic reaction on your part will be all the more convincing."

"That isn't very reassuring."

"Perhaps, but it'll be much more fun this way. Get some rest, Colton. We'll need to be our best in the morning."

Mercifully, Colton was able to sleep a few hours, back to back with Lucian. Normally, being in such close proximity with a man as lovely as Lucian would have been almost unpleasantly distracting, but the manor was far too creepy for that. As it stood, Colton was just glad to have a warm, comforting presence beside him. He hadn't quite *admitted* that he was too scared to sleep alone here, but his partner had picked up on it anyway, and they spent a chilly and somewhat awkward evening together, going over their final plans.

The next morning they stood clad in black, side by side on the spotless walkway that led up to the estate. The contrast of the dark fabric with his gleaming teeth and hair was almost upsetting, but Colton did like the touch of theater that Lucian seemed to put into everything. Demons didn't like the light, remember.

Lucian welcomed Mrs. Radcliffe and her tittering neighbor Lady Lundelle with warm gusto, his saccharine voice and disarming smile like a bioluminescent fish. The women eagerly followed the lures, and Colton bowed dutifully at them as they passed.

"I'm so glad you're back!" Lucian preened, kissing them on the cheeks twice, respectively. "Colton is a marvel, honestly. We have the spirit cornered, and yet I fear that there is more to this haunting than meets the eye. For your safety, Colton has recommended we perform a séance, to best expel this monster from our world and back to hell."

"Oh, how fun, Mavis!" Lady Lundelle chirped. "A haunting! My word, you'll be the talk of the town! Everyone will be clamoring for their own ghost next! You must let me watch!"

Mrs. Radcliffe was clearly enjoying the flattery, and Lucian had rightly guessed she wouldn't miss the chance to one-up her snobby neighbor, who in turn was dying of jealousy. Lucian and Colton's business venture was looking to be the trendy little purchase of the season. After all, how many houses could claim to have a real, live spirit dwelling within? One vanquished by an *actual* Iron District mystic? To die for, worth any price.

And so they all entered the estate, into the dining room setup Colton had prepared the night before. The heavy doors opened with the awful groan of purposefully degreased hinges, while the darkness swept the group into its midst. The curtains were drawn, and any gaps were sealed with layers of soot-blackened paper. Shadows danced along the walls, with only the dim candles to light their path to the women's seats. The fireplace was roaring and left the room sweltering, heady and appropriately uncomfortable. Yes. It was perfect. Right down to the tiny little chip on the handle of Mrs. Radcliffe's cup, which would differentiate the poisoned chalice from the others.

Lucian lit the Blue Grass incense and poured the tea, his face somber and as spiritual as Colton had ever seen it. "Now, it is tradition that we all drink herb tea to put our minds in a plane that will be receptive to such wonders," he whispered, his fingers ghosting over Mrs. Radcliffe's pale forearm. "We will save you, my dear. We'll fix *everything*."

His pupils were dilated like he wanted to fuck her, and the woman drank her tea down to the last drop. Perfect. Colton almost wanted to clap.

"Colton," he whispered reverently. "You may begin."

His name lifted from Lucian's lips like a prayer, and Colton snapped back to attention. Okay. He could do this. He'd done this a thousand times before—these people wanted a show, they'd get one. The runes were as familiar to him as the tattoos on his skin, and he swept his hands through the air, incense twisting around his face.

It was time.

"Spirit!" he called, sneaking glances at Mrs. Radcliffe. "Demon! I conjure you forth to demand why you haunt this place, these people!" The words that fell from Colton's lips were hushed and reverent. He watched with pleasure as his victims fell under his spell. His confidence grew as he saw Mrs. Radcliffe's breath begin to quicken as the drug took effect.

"I summon you! Show yourself!"

Suddenly, Lucian pushed his seat away from the table and groaned, a strangulated noise somewhere between pleasure and agony, loud and sharp and certainly enough to get everyone in the room to look at him. Colton's head snapped up—what was he doing? *Be ready for anything, remember.*

"Ah . . . ahhh . . . !" Lucian stood, his eyes lolling, his whole body a mess of stochastic energy. *"How long it has been since I took a human form . . . to breathe . . . to feel warmth in my skin . . ."* Lucian stroked his own face and nearly swooned, his voice about an octave lower than normal. *"Who dares disturb my sanctum?"*

Colton was frozen in place as he watched his partner's display. It was a chore to keep his jaw from dropping open, his eyes from bugging out—they were professional demon hunters, after all, surely they encountered things like this all the time! He snuck a glance at the women around him. The whole room was mesmerized, and an addictive heady confidence filled Colton's soul.

Lucian slammed his hands on the table, upending the teapot, until he found himself glaring at Mrs. Radcliffe. *"YOU! This is all YOUR fault! For eons I have searched for a place such as this, where* misery and curses drip from the walls like FUCKING CUM IN A WHOREHOUSE!

"So many screams, so many souls—never—never have I found somewhere such as this—ahh!" A clear pleasured noise then, Lucian's body lurched slightly before pivoting toward Colton as if finally aware of his presence. "You try to DRIVE ME OUT?"

Mrs. Radcliffe gasped, and Colton could barely speak. What was he supposed to be doing again?

What the—*Oh, right.* "Demon! Your presence is not wanted here!" He pushed his own chair back, approaching Lucian with a holy crystal sphere in his hand. "I banish you from this place!" He would have felt ridiculous if Lucian hadn't started the show with such a strong hand. It felt as though the two of them were made to play together.

"*You fool,*" Lucian hissed. "*You cannot stop me with your trinkets. I have come to claim my prize, and I shall take them . . . one . . . by . . . one . . .*"

Lucian turned to Patricia then, licking his lips and approaching her with his hands outstretched. Colton readied himself to intervene. *Lucian, you brilliant bastard.*

"*NO!*" Lucian stopped himself, slapped himself across the face as his voice returned to near normal. "*You won't touch her! I won't let you!*" He let out a strangled cry then, as though trying to get himself back under control. "Pattycake . . . sweetheart—I'm so sorry, I couldn't—she—ahh! I tried to protect you. I love you, and I've always loved you. Please, please help me get rid of this monster . . . please . . . please help me protect what is ours."

Patricia's eyes were bugging out of her head, leaking tears of fear and joy and hope. "Tom? How?"

"*Your—your—m-m-MOTHER.*" As though it were physically hard to get the words out. "*She—she took me and—she tortured—she killed—she's EVIL, Pattycake, she'll kill our—ahh!*" Lucian touched Patricia's face, looking into her eyes like he loved her more than anything in the world.

"*SILENCE!*" Lucian's voice dropped lower again, and he turned on the matron of the family. "*The boy is a fool, and yet . . .*" He stroked Mrs. Radcliffe's face. "*There is wisdom in his words. The souls of departed servants are delectable to be sure, but the soul of a truly, perverse . . . corrupted . . . malevolent . . . evil . . . murderous cunt of a woman is just . . . so much nicer . . .*"

The drug was taking effect by then, and Mrs. Radcliffe was scrambling to get away from Lucian, pawing at the air and babbling.

"I didn't mean to—he just wouldn't stop screaming! I only tried to—I only tried to—I'm not wicked, it's not my fault! *He's* the one who—*ahh!*"

"*You're mine, Mavis,*" Lucian whispered. "*And I'll never let you go.*"

The man was a genius, and he had trusted Colton to deliver the killing blow. Colton grinned. He wasn't about to let Lord Beaumont down.

Colton leapt in then, grasping his partner by the collar and forcing him to meet his eyes. "You will not harm these people, beast! Your evil is no match for the light in our hearts; you will *never* win against us!"

Lucian's eyes were manic and bright. He gnashed his teeth at Colton, close enough that he might actually bite if he wasn't careful. Fury didn't suit Lucian, but it was a convincing performance all the same. Colton held him back and pressed a gleaming quartz sphere against Lucian's forehead and broke the spell, cutting the puppet strings.

Lucian collapsed to the ground and tried to lift his head up, trembling from the exertion. The "spirit" had clearly left him, and he looked well and truly rattled.

"It—oh, my word. I never felt such wickedness . . ." He was nearly crying, but he stood up, shaking. "Mrs.—Mrs. Radcliffe?"

Colton swept around the table and tore the curtains open. Daylight dispelled the darkness, and he had to squint to combat the nausea from the sickly sweet incense permeating his senses. Colton approached their victim, staring down at her with disdain.

Mrs. Radcliffe was writhing around on the ground, nearly spitting as she tried to get this demon away from her, out of her, to stop it fucking telling everyone what had happened!

"Oh, no," Lucian whispered. "I think she's been taken by the spirit. This is terrible. It was bound to happen eventually, but oh, that poor woman."

"I fear you're right, Lord Beaumont," Colton said with a solemn expression draped over his sharp features. "The spirit has found its true vessel. I fear she is beyond even my powers now."

"Is there nothing we can do for her?" Lady Lundelle chimed in, pleasure barely concealed on her taut face.

Lucian bit his lip, something Colton assumed he did to stop himself from smiling. "I don't believe there is. The only thing for her is to get her to St. Palindime's Hospital."

"The . . . the asylum?" Patricia whispered. "I—are you certain, Lord Beaumont?"

Lucian shook his head miserably. "I don't see another way, Miss Radcliffe. I'll contact them at once. We can't even chance this monster harming anyone else in this house. We're lucky you were spared, Miss. I can't even imagine what you're going through."

Patty's hands were draped over her stomach, and she nodded. Colton watched as it all fell into place in her mind—her missing lover, the screams in the night, the fact that her child would never know his father. "Put her in the wine cellar," she instructed her staff. "I don't want the spirit escaping." She looked up at Colton and Lucian, her eyes red and blazing. "Whatever she offered you for the exorcism, I'm doubling it. Thank you . . . thank you."

Lucian bowed his head, casting a sharp eye up at Colton as he accepted the terms. When no one was looking, his lips curved into a smile, his eyes twinkling with a hint of mischief.

Oh, this smarmy bastard. *You'll be the death of me, Beaumont.*

seven

It was just as well Lucian was there, really—Colton had no notion of how to talk to these Ivory women, and they were drawn to him like lonely moths to a flame. Even Patricia seemed to be taking comfort in his handsome, gentle presence, and Colton was happy to lean his back against the wall, collect his various knickknacks and drugs, and wait for his partner to finish schmoozing.

After an age, Lucian swept out the door and into the light, Colton beside him with their shoulders touching. Lucian's open palm collided with his back, and he was so startled he almost coughed.

"Colton!" The lordling was all smiles, practically bouncing with delight. "You did brilliantly! I don't think that could have possibly gone any better!"

"Well, it might have been better if some poor servant hadn't been killed."

"Oh, of course, but besides that! Colton, I'm so pleased!" Were his feet even touching the ground? His energy was addictive. "How was that? Did you have fun?"

Colton let out a laugh then, more from Lucian's absurdity than anything else. "Fun is one word for it. You really surprised me back there, Beaumont. How did you know that would work? Or that the daughter would listen to you?"

"Oh. I suppose I didn't, but I tried to push the odds as much in our favor as possible. For example, I found the various nicknames and mannerisms of our poor victim in Patricia's diary, which made it a little more believable that young Thomas had possessed me in the short term. But more than anything, I think she wanted to know the truth." Lucian's voice was soft and distant. "The rest just fell into place."

"Is that what demons are like, do you think?" Colton teased, nudging Lucian with his arm. "Shouty and bitey?"

"Well, I'm certain that most demons aren't nearly as handsome and charismatic as I am."

Colton snorted. "You might be right about that."

They were flirting, right? There was no other plausible explanation for it, though it certainly seemed out of place for an Ivory man. Firstly, there was the whole matter of class, and secondly, that sort of relationship was ... well, largely frowned upon by the elites. The Holy Order had a whole *thing* about it, about the immorality of physicality without purpose, and the Ivory leaders seemed to take that all quite seriously. It was better in the Iron District, really. Such encounters often began with a clear and concise "Wanna do it?" and ended on Colton's makeshift mattress. Still, as pretty as Lucian was, indulging in such things at this stage in their partnership seemed unwise.

Doesn't mean I can't have fun with it though, right?

He playfully kicked at the back of Lucian's calf. "So, about my fee ..."

"Ah, of course. Well I was thinking about the logistics of that—do you have an account with any of the banks? This is sort of a rather large amount of cash to stuff in a mattress."

"*Pft.* What do you think?"

"I suspect that financial planning has never been a huge part of your life, but we can certainly change that today! My family owns most of the banks, you know. Oh, Colton, we can start you up a pension fund with compound interest! Won't that be *fun?*"

Colton snickered. "Yeesh, Lucian, it'll be tough for me to come up with an activity more fun than that." He stroked his chin and pretended to think about it. "Nah, I have a better idea—let's go to The Hare, and I'll treat you to a drink. Get you back for last time." He grinned. "And you can cough up my damn money before I go all Iron District on you." He extended his fingers in front of himself like claws and let out a soft *rawr*.

It was strange being this open and friendly with an Ivory elite like this, even if he was relatively disgraced. But there was just something about Lucian—how he could be cocky without being superior, the way he laughed without reserve, how he seemed to find delight in just about everything he touched. Lucian was completely nuts—Colton wasn't about to forget that any time soon—but he was the sort of nuts that he enjoyed being around. Like candied almonds on a cream cake.

Colton's stomach growled, and all at once he realized why he was feeling so lightheaded and woozy. He was exhausted, had barely slept, and hadn't eaten properly since they'd been to the tailors. "C'mon then, you uppity prig. I'll show you how we enjoy ourselves in the Iron Belt." He cocked a brow to ask if Lucian was coming and pivoted like he didn't care if his partner followed.

Lucian's sharp heels clacked along the marble pavement beside him, the resonating sound diminishing as the marble faded to stone, to concrete, to dirt and mud the closer they got to the Iron Gate. The Belt was more of a residential area of the district, with homes and businesses rather than smog-churning factories, but even in his black cloak and suit, Lucian still stuck out here. He hoped that the average Iron criminal knew better than to mess with him, though, and certainly knew better than to trifle with a Beaumont.

The Hare was a far cry from The Partridge. None of the cakes behind glass windows, bare wooden walls rather than painted spokes and polished ledges. The clientele weren't belligerent, but they were lively and handsy, and Colton hoped Lucian wouldn't be offended. A soft murmur fell over the establishment as they entered, probably because of Lucian's innate flashiness, and the fact that they'd all seen his face in the papers for the better part of a year. As ever, Lucian took the attention in stride, selected a relatively non-sticky table for them, and asked for a menu to peruse.

Colton sat proudly across from his partner in all his gaudy glory. Let people talk, it could only be good for business.

"They don't really *do* menus at The Hare," Colton explained. "It's sort of a gamble. Just get whatever's hot and keep your fingers crossed that the meat isn't seagull or vagrant."

For a moment, a look of hesitation crossed Lucian's face, but it was soon replaced with a grin as a buxom young barkeep handed them each a draft of ale. "Bring it on, Colton. Show me brunch in the Belt."

Colton gave him a look. Yeah, *brunch.* If that's what he wanted to call it.

It didn't take long before two bowls of mystery stew were plopped down in front of them, and Colton forgot he was sitting across from a Lord as he more or less face-planted in the bowl. It was only when he'd finished a full serving and half a tankard of beer that his attention finally returned to Lucian, who was watching him with delighted amusement as he ate his fill. Colton glanced up at his partner and draped an arm over the back of his chair.

Holy shit. This was all real, wasn't it? He'd just pulled off a nobleman's con with one of the richest men in the world. And it had been so *simple.* Could they do this with every house in the district? Earn enough money that Colton could pay off his debts? *Make* something of himself?

Colton laughed and shook his head, swirling his ale around in the flagon. "I'm a bit surprised you followed me down here, Lucian. It's one thing to scoop up a stray from the Iron District. It's quite another to share bread with him."

"Of everything that happened this morning, my joining you for breakfast is what surprised you?" Lucian teased, shoving a spoonful of mush into his mouth. "Of course I came with you—allow me to say why." His knife tore through the stale bread, leaving a beach of crumbs in its wake. "One, I like you and enjoy your company. Two, this is the breakfasting hour, and I am terribly famished. You may not be aware of this, but I grew up in a very wealthy household. It's not often that I go hungry." He shrugged, taking a sip of his grog. "Three, you and I need to discuss our next job. And four, I trust you well enough not to poison me at this stage. Besides, I didn't fancy paying you in the street." He grinned, passing a rather hefty silk bag over the table. "I wouldn't open it here, partner."

He was right about that. Even if all the coins in the pouch were coppers, this was more money than Colton had ever seen, let alone held in his hands at once. This changed everything. He'd never even imagined—he wouldn't go hungry this month, he could buy a flat for Mai—hells, he could buy a house! For both of them! And a pen for that stupid pig!

Lucian chuckled. "There's more where that came from, Colton. Unless you want to quit while you're ahead."

Colton considered it. That would be the smart thing to do, surely. Take the cash, walk away a wealthy man—well, for the Iron District, anyway. If he ever wanted to move up in the world, move out of this place . . . He reached over the table to clasp Lucian's shoulder. "Where's the fun in that? Besides, someone needs to keep you out of trouble."

Lucian unclasped his cape and clinked their glasses together. "Here's to the beginning of a beautiful friendship, then, Colton."

Unfortunately Colton still had an odd job or two to complete in the Iron District before he gave himself up to Lucian completely.

"Well, I should come with you!" Lucian chirped as they exited the pub. "The more I learn about our trade, the better, surely."

"Suit yourself," Colton said, and he scribbled down an address for them to meet the following morning. "Come by tomorrow, and wear something . . . normal."

Lucian looked affronted but winked all the same. "Colton,

how dare you! My clothes are handmade from spider silk and—"

"Be that as it may, you're a walking target for mugging like this, you puffy peacock. Be normal, or I'm going to have to lend you some of *my* clothes."

Lucian gasped audibly, putting a hand over his heart. "Colton, you wound me. Lucian Beaumont as an Iron rake? I can't think of anything better. Wouldn't I be *dashing*?" He turned with a flurry of his cape, traipsing off into the light.

"Weirdo." Colton shook his head, laughing.

I really like him.

Lucian's influence was at once easy and unsettling, deceptively capable and resilient—perhaps that was the most terrifying thing about him. He was free and easy with his emotions, his motivations; Colton had to wonder how much of it was real. Was that what wealth and privilege did to a person? Endow them with pleasant affability and little else? Hardly, if his past experience with the wealthy had anything to say about it. Lucian flitted from one idea to another and slipped into the skin of a demon so easily that Colton had to wonder if he'd done this before. And what if he had? Who had Lucian been before he'd been ousted, before he'd met Colton? *I don't actually know anything about him.*

Colton made his way back to his single room squat and hesitated before removing his gleaming new boots. His clothes hardly matched his home anymore, and he carefully untied the laces and placed his shoes and socks in a clean cupboard and away from the dirt on the floor. The pig nosed its way up to him and snuffled his trousers, getting shooed away in return. He flopped down onto his bed and put one hand behind his head, at long last taking the bag of coins out of his pockets. He took a deep breath as he opened it, and there it was. Gold. Dozens of glimmering gold coins, enough to feed him for a decade, house him for a year, or enough to buy one bloody sock from Lucian's tailor.

He felt heavy as he stared at it, a dark fear that tunneled through his chest and out through his legs. This was more money than he had any right to have. He was a con artist, a stray, a drunk. He'd been born of a demon-hunting lineage that spanned hundreds of years and he'd never even seen one damn spirit. It didn't seem real. He took a steadying breath in through his lips and clenched the mouth of the sack shut.

"Damn," he whispered, clinking the coins through the fabric. "Thank you, Lord Beaumont."

Colton pulled his knife from his belt and stabbed his mattress, drawing back and exposing the unpleasant mix of straw and horsehair that had cushioned him every night since Mai had kicked him out of her place. That had been rough, honestly. He didn't like sleeping alone; he never had. He shoved the pouch inside, his heart racing as it disappeared into the moldy depths.

Maybe Lucian was right. Maybe a savings account is the way to go.

Meh. Maybe tomorrow. Colton cracked open a bottle of brandy he'd been saving for a special occasion and took a swig right from the bottle. One glass wouldn't hurt, would it? He was celebrating, after all.

That night he dreamed of blue eyes, of soft hands reaching playfully for his throat.

eight

Colton was awakened the following morning by a loud knock on his door. He groaned and covered his eyes, wondering how it was possible to be awake this early and still be alive. Hells, it was . . . sunrise? How much had he drunk last night? He pushed the pig out of bed and staggered toward the noise, pulling the door open and finding himself nearly blinded by—

"Lucian?"

"Good morning, sunshine." His partner was his version of dressed down, in a plain white suit with only one or two golden buttons and not a gemstone in sight. No cape either, which was odd.

"What are you doing here?" Colton croaked blearily.

"I believe you invited me, darling. Can I come in?"

"Fine. Use whatever you want as a chair."

"Lovely." Lucian swept in, dragging light and vitality into the musty space behind him. The swine trotted up to his feet, and his face broke into a smile. "Your pig! I knew you didn't eat her! Can I pet her?"

Colton needed some tea. Or beer. Beer would probably be more helpful. "I—do what you want. Don't come crying to me if it bites your fingers off."

"Splendid!" Lucian knelt down and scratched the stupid thing on the back of its ears, until eventually it turned over and presented its spotty fat tummy to him. "Awww, Colton, look, she loves me. What's her name?"

Colton was doing everything in his power not to collapse in a heap in front of Lucian. They'd thwarted a murderer together—but was his disdain for early mornings going to do him in? "I just call it 'Pig.'"

"Oh that's no name for such a magnificent beast, is it? No, a majestic creature like you deserves a name befitting your glory. I shall name you Marbles."

Colton blinked. "Why?"

"Because of the spots, Colton. Come now, I thought you were a man of culture." That smile again, the wink that reached his voice.

Too early. It was far too early to deal with this. "Please tell me you brought food."

Lucian peered around, no doubt taking in the cramped space Colton called home. For an Iron house, it wasn't *that* bad. He had a window (well, technically it was a hole, but it let light in), at least *two* articles of furniture, no obvious rat infestation—what more could he ask for?

Although . . . one coin from the bag in that mattress would be enough to get a real bed, at least. Hope? From Colton? Surely transient.

Lucian reached into his prim leather briefcase and produced a bag of pastries and a metal flask. "It's tea," he announced calmly. "Now, as much as I'm enjoying this porcine playdate of ours, I thought you had some work to do?"

Colton pulled his old black cloak over his shoulders and downed the whole flask in one go. "Megh. Okay. I just have a few outstanding contracts to complete before we ah . . . make this official? A delivery, a cleansing . . . uhh . . . some drug house is haunted, apparently." He pinched the bridge of his nose. "Two copper pieces says it's a junkie wrapped in a sheet or something."

"I'm getting the impression the Order doesn't really manage many hauntings down here?"

"You got it."

"So you've cornered the market, essentially?"

"Such as it is." The jobs were probably so *piddling* to Lucian. "I can't deal with this today."

Lucian chuckled and dropped an arm around his shoulders. "Aw, poor lamb. What happened? You smell like a brewery."

"I was celebrating," Colton huffed, leaning into the steady warmth.

"Looking forward to my arrival, surely."

Colton set his gaze upon Lucian as they sat there in a stiff show of intimacy. They were of similar heights, although Colton had a slightly more muscular build. He pushed Lucian away and stood up, smirking at his partner. "Try and keep up, Lucian," he drawled with a lingering smirk as he cast the other with a sidelong glance over his shoulder. "I'm a busy man."

"Of course. Far be it from me to hold you back."

Prior to meeting Lucian, Colton's life had consisted of lots of paltry jobs all over the Iron District. He could have just canceled them, he supposed, but there was a sense of obligation to see these things out. These people trusted him, valued him, and he'd given his word. *Whatever that's worth.* The first two jobs had been follow-up appointments, to make sure the houses were still unhaunted.

"Yup, no spirits here." Easy enough.

A single copper was pressed into his hand. "Not a word," he said grumpily to Lucian.

"I would never," the Lord assured him. "Honest work is honest work."

Sort of.

The third job found them in a run-down old school building. "The students can't concentrate," the exasperated teacher had explained. "It's a demon, surely."

"Of course!" Lucian piped in, touching her shoulder. "We'll take care of it for you, Miss."

She left, and Colton began poking around the classroom.

"Colton?" Lucian inquired. "It smells like a butt."

Colton hid his smile. "Very astute observation, partner. It's that sort of intuitiveness which will solve many a case." But Lucian was right, it certainly did smell like a butt. It didn't take long for him to uncover the source of the odor. Underneath a loose and rotting floorboard was the corpse of a rabbit, tucked into a ball and surrounded by carefully placed flowers. No signs of foul play.

"Class pet," Colton wagered.

Well, it would certainly explain why they couldn't concentrate. Beady black ants were swarming the thing and bit at Colton's fingers as he jostled the body into a satchel and pushed it aside. In its place he left soft scented herbs, dried lavender, and concentrated oils of mint and cinnamon.

The pair made their way to the minuscule school garden, and Lucian said nothing as Colton dug a little hole and placed the rabbit inside. He covered it with soil and placed a smooth stone over the fresh earth. Colton cast a glance over his shoulder and caught Lucian watching him affectionately.

Lord Beaumont offered a hand to help him up and clapped him on the shoulder. "You're a sweetheart, you know that?" he said fondly, brushing dirt away from Colton's hands. "What's next?"

"Just one job left," Colton muttered. "I'm surprised that you stuck around this long. This can't be very interesting."

Lucian smiled, and Colton wondered what he put on his skin to keep his face so radiant all the damn time. "On the contrary, I'm learning ever so much about your—*our*—trade."

The last job took them to an old house in a nearly abandoned district of the city. It was mostly drug users who remained, the scent of Blossom dens permeating the thick, oily air. The day was waning, and the remnants of the sun were casting lengthy shadows along the slimy cobblestones.

"Who hired you for this one?" Lucian asked pleasantly as they pushed past the splintered doorframe and into the dusty chambers. The floorboards creaked, the paint was cracked, and the whole place stank of rust and bile. What little fabric was left on the curtains was speckled with mold, and the remnants of furniture had seemingly been used for firewood at some time or another.

"The building's owner wants to sell the place. Apparently Beaumont Industries wants to build this area up." And every other part of the Iron District, as far as Colton could tell. "They obviously can't buy the property while it's haunted, though."

"What can I say? My father has good taste. Of course the main problem with this property is the demons." Lucian snickered to himself. "Good thing we're on the case!"

Colton lit a lantern and ventured deeper into the building. The light fell into the space, and he grabbed Lucian's wrist. "Wait."

The room was all but empty, barring some old tools and a ramshackle altar poised in the middle. Around its base was a pool of blood, and a thick, corded noose dangled from the rafters. Around the altar was a ring of stones, seashells, rotted flowers knitted into ropes—all encircling a dead-eyed rag doll with a nail piercing its heart.

Oh, this didn't feel right at all. Behind him, he heard Lucian swallow. "This . . . this one's a bit unsettling, eh?" He forced a laugh, his fingers busying themselves with his plain gold cuff links.

"Shh." Colton squeezed Lucian's arm and ventured forth. "Watch over me, all right?"

He hugged his cloak closer to his body, put on his thin leather gloves, and began dismantling the ritual space. He pulled the noose down first, then began cleaning the blood with a dank little sponge. The doll was staring at him with dim button eyes, and he picked it up and turned it over. A name was scrawled on the back of her handkerchief dress, barely legible through the years of neglect.

Footsteps thundered across the space, and Colton barely had time to look up before he was tackled to the ground. It was all he could do to grab his assailant's hand as it came down over him, trying to drive a rusty blade through Colton's skull. He was deranged—red eyes, sparse teeth and hair, skin that hadn't seen the sun in years. His breath was foul with the stench of vomit and Snow as he gnashed at Colton's face.

"Luc—" Colton's head collided against the floorboards, and he tasted blood.

Where was he? Had he run off? *That fucking bastard! No!*

The man was deceptively strong—the power that madness granted—and Colton was on his back, desperate. "Get off me!" he ordered, but of course the creature didn't listen. Colton's strength was failing, and he watched the quivering knife tip inch ever closer to his eye. "FUCK!"

Flesh cracked above him, and the stranger lurched off of Colton, dropping the knife and quivering on his side. Above him stood Lucian Beaumont, a bloodstained shovel in his hands as he panted from exertion. His veneer of calm vanished in favor of something akin to fury, and his skin was pale and misty with perspiration.

"Don't. Don't you bloody dare." Lucian's hands were shaking as he let go of his weapon, rolling the man onto his stomach and kicking the knife to the far end of the room. "A-are you all right, Colton?"

Colton scurried away from the creature, trembling. He could almost taste his heart in his throat. "Yeah," he managed. "Nice one." It was hard to speak. Curling up in a ball seemed preferable, but he persevered.

Lucian's attention turned back to the assailant, exuding power and confidence, even if the trembling in his hands gave him away a little. "Who else is here? Speak."

The stranger's mouth was bleeding freely, and he didn't respond, his arms clawing at nothing, trying to gain purchase on the floor.

Lucian kicked him in the ribs. "Who else is here?" he repeated impatiently. Colton wasn't sure he'd seen Lucian rattled until this moment. Anger didn't suit him. Then again, nearly having his eye stabbed out didn't suit Colton either. Fuck. That had been bad.

"No one, ya rat barshtard!" the man managed eventually. "The fug' you doin' 'n my house?"

Colton breathed out slowly, gingerly touching a hand to the back of his head. "We're getting rid of the evil spirits, sir. No one lives here."

The man began howling. "Sprits . . . evil spirits . . ." He ran his fingernails over the ground and sucked them, trying to get even one last speck of Snow from the grimy dust he found there. "My daught'r's no evil spirit, ya cunt."

"So what happened here?"

"M' wife . . ." His eyes glistened with tears. "She . . . When I were t'work she . . . wit' 'er knife she . . . my wee Ellie . . . n'then afterward she . . . wit' the rope."

The man kept staring at his hands, and Colton thought about what he'd been told. It was hard to imagine a woman killing her own child and then herself. Maybe he had threatened to kill them if they left.

Either way, he could stay here no longer.

"Don't move," Lucian ordered, reaching down to take the doll from where Colton had dropped it. "It's Ellie's, right? Take it. Keep it. We'll make sure their spirits can rest."

The man wept and cradled the doll to his face, his groans loud and irritating.

Lucian looked to Colton and licked his lips. "Colton, darling, what's the protocol here? Do we tie him up? Do we kill him? Is that something one might reasonably be expected to do in the Iron District? I'm sure we can find a guard or something who might legally apprehend him, but for heaven's sake the man nearly gave you *tetanus*."

Well, at the very least Lucian was probably feeling better if he was back to making his idiotic jokes.

"No. No, we can hand him in to the local police. Tell 'em he's here. They'll get him help." *Or throw him in a cell and then ship him off to the mines, either way.*

Lucian tied the man's hands behind his back and knelt down beside Colton. "I'm glad you're okay. Losing you at this stage would be dreadfully inconvenient," he said with a laugh, wiping some dirt away from Colton's face. "In all seriousness, are you all right? Did he hurt you?"

There was blood in Colton's mouth, a cut on his palm he didn't remember getting, and the back of his skull was throbbing. The pain hadn't quite hit him yet, not with that sweet adrenaline still spiking like heated wine through his bloodstream. Colton shook his head and bit his lip, furious at the rush of emotions flooding his chest. He lurched forward and pulled Lucian into his embrace, digging his fingers into the soft fabric of his jacket. "Thank you. For staying."

Lucian hesitated for a moment before he wrapped his arms around Colton, squeezing him tight. "Of course, Colton. We're partners, aren't we? I'm not going to run at the first sign of trouble."

Colton squeezed his eyes shut and just held Lucian for a moment. He'd heard that sort of promise before, from men who'd wanted less of him than Lucian had. *But he'd stayed.* Colton tried, as best as he could, to snuff out that tentative flicker of trust that was blooming in his soul.

nine

They walked out of the building in silence, and Colton looked away as Lucian pulled a vial of Blossom out of his pocket and tilted the pink dust onto his finger before sucking it up his nostril. Fuck. Colton needed a drink. He let out a shaky breath and managed a smile. "They'd better pay me double."

Lucian's shoulders relaxed just a smidge, and he smiled back, his pupils blown out and dark from the Blossom. "Yeah. Hazard pay or something. Do I get a cut from today?" He wiggled his eyebrows provocatively.

"Absolutely not." Colton laughed in earnest then, gently punching Lucian in the arm. "You gotta do more than swing a shovel around to earn your keep in the Iron Belt."

Lucian shook his head. "You're ruthless, Colton. Do you wanna grab some dinner?"

A drink. I want to grab a drink.

"Nah. I think I just need to sleep this one off. You've got a new job for us uphill?"

"I do. We can discuss it after you've had a chance to unwind. Here." He gave Colton a pass with the Beaumont Crest on it. "So you don't have trouble with the guards. You sure you're all right?"

"Yes! Stop fussing over me."

Lucian reached toward Colton's face, and he flinched. "You're bleeding," Lucian said quietly. "Come with me, Colton. I'll be worried sick about you otherwise."

The sky was pulsing with heavy clouds threatening to break into rain. Colton knew it would be miserable in his flat tonight, and the pig had enough food for the morning, surely. He was silent as he followed Lucian up the smooth marble steps that led to the Ivory District. People stared openly this time—probably because his face was covered in blood, his clothes were torn, and he was filthy.

"I know what's got you so quiet," said Lucian. "You're worried you're going to find *my* secret murder chamber." Amusement flooded his features. "Or the sex dungeon, right? Not to worry, Colton, that's strictly for third dates."

"So this is a date, is it?" *Best to just be direct.*

"Oh, Colton, heavens, no. We're business partners! It's too messy otherwise, as irresistible as I am. There we are, I knew I'd get a smile out of you. We mustn't let some miserable codger spoil our evening." He patted Colton's shoulder. "Now, as you know I don't stay at the Beaumont estate anymore, but my father gives me an allowance from which I am able to lease a . . . shall we say . . . *modest* dwelling? My hope is that our work will enable me to become even more independent."

Lucian led him up and down the polished white side streets of the Ivory District, stopping in front of an enormous block of luxury apartments. Lucian produced a golden key from his pocket and let them into the main building, then up a set of white marble steps until they reached flat 512.

It was all Colton could do to keep his mouth from falling open. From where they were standing in the entryway he could see at least four different rooms—hells only knew how many more there were. The floors were heated, the furniture was all white leather and polished gold, and the massive crystal window in the living room overlooked the sea. Even with the storm clouds circling overhead, he could make out the soft white foam that kissed the top of the waves.

"See? Paltry." Lucian winked. "Here, you can use the guest room—it has its own ensuite, of course. Have a nice bath, and I'll see what I can scrounge us up for supper."

Colton scoffed. "You cook?"

"Hardly, but a man must learn to survive on his own, I suppose. Oh, and Kiara delivered your other suits already, so you needn't worry about borrowing any of my 'peacock' clothes."

Aaaaaand they were back to flirting. Fine, he could manage that. Being the object of Lucian's warm affection put him at ease, especially now that they'd sort of clarified the expectations that came with it. Lucian flirted. Fish swam. It was how he best navigated the world.

Lucian directed Colton to a large white door with a golden handle, behind which was a room as nice as any he'd ever slept in. A bed stuffed with down, curtains made of silk, and fresh-cut flowers on the table. He was going to get crusty blood on everything. Lucian wasn't the sort to send him a bill for cleaning, was he?

"Call me if you need anything." Lucian patted his shoulder and exited the room, leaving Colton alone in luxury. Right. Lucian had mentioned something about a bath. Colton ventured into the room, determined to figure out what the heck an "on sweet" was. It apparently meant that the room had a full bathroom attached to it, which was a very nice surprise. He looked at himself in the mirror and grimaced. He was filthy. Sweat had traced rivulets down the dirt on his face, and the blood from his forehead had solidified over his eyebrow. There were bruises on his neck and hands, and his expression was hollow and dark. No wonder Lucian had wanted him to stay over. Not very good for business if your partner dies of a concussion in the night, was it?

In the center of the bathroom was a massive marble tub, flanked by shelves of fair-smelling ointments and rose petals that Colton let slip through his fingertips as he filled the bath with water—there was *warm* water? He stripped out of his clothes and cast them aside in an uneven pile, groaning softly as he settled into this steamy heaven. The water started to change from crystal diamond to murky bog as the grime of the day began soaking off. Well, no matter! Lucian probably had loads of water in some mystical Ivory tank somewhere in the apartment. He found a scratchy sponge and lathered his body with vanilla soap until he was spotless. The tub was drained, refilled, and Colton decided to spoil himself by sniffing the shimmering rainbow of oils that flanked the tub.

A drop of rose, a hint of fresh coconut, something that lathered in his hair and left it black and gleaming. The petals floated around him, and he draped a leg over the side of the tub, staring up at the moonstone lamps and immaculate marble ceiling.

Lucian had mentioned that his father was financing the apartment. *This was a step down for Lucian. He's used to luxury like the Radcliffes had.* How had Lucian ended up here? He spoke so flippantly about his family, as though it didn't even bother him that none of them wanted to see him again. Colton didn't even know who his father was. He would have given anything to see his mother one more time.

He'd been a mess after she had passed away. A year later he'd slept with Mai, desperate for warmth, for intimacy, for love.

"I love you," he'd told her as they lay naked together under the moonlight. "Forever and ever."

He could remember the way her body had frozen against his, her face a pained grimace as she pulled away with a blanket over her chest. She'd shaken her head, gotten dressed, and left him alone with his thoughts.

Colton had been alone, desperate. Most likely, Mai feared losing her independence, being trapped in a marriage as a teenager and ruining her life, just like her mother, her sister, and every other poor bitch that she'd known on the Iron docks. Anyway, she hadn't believed him.

So Colton hadn't loved anyone since then. *Or admitted as much.* As far as he could tell, it had kept his relationships safe and his life balanced. So obviously he didn't *love* Lucian, no matter how pretty and pleasant and lovely he was. He certainly was very pretty, though.

He sank lower into the water and heard the sound of Lucian bustling around in the kitchen. All of a sudden, he was aware of his own nakedness, of the vulnerability of allowing himself to follow Lucian to his home like this. He'd been down roads like this before, and it never ended well.

He shut his eyes. *Lucian wouldn't hurt me.* The clarity of the statement took him aback for a moment. *Lucian would never hurt me.*

Then again, if Lucian *did* want more, that wouldn't be the end of the world. The man was a treat for the senses, he was rich, he was kind . . . he was absolutely ridiculous. Colton watched his tattooed wrist descend into the water and make its way between his legs. He shut his eyes and imagined strong hands clutching a shovel.

"Colton! Dinner's almost ready!"

Ughhhhhh, fine. Colton ruefully emerged from the bath, clean and smelling as good as he'd ever smelled in his life. The bathroom was thoroughly soiled though, and Colton hoped very much that Lucian wouldn't come in and find the smears of soot, blood, and failure that he'd left on the porcelain. Of course, Lucian had left out some warm towels and . . . lounging clothing, he had to assume. Well, at least he wouldn't have to wear his demon-hunting clothes at home. He slipped on a pair of silk trousers and slid his arms into a soft plush robe with "LB" monogrammed over the breast. Colton snorted. *How on-brand.*

He stepped out into the main living area and plopped down on one of the sofas. "You've got a lovely home, Lucian. Thank you for letting me stay here." By now it was raining heavily, and thick droplets were pounding against the windows, illuminated by the odd crack of lightning.

Lucian was busying himself over the stove, concocting something that smelled a bit burned, but at least that meant it would be warm. "Not a problem, darling. How are your wounds?"

Colton gingerly touched his forehead along the thin red gash that surely the blade had caused. His hand was aching from trying to grab the knife, his head was throbbing, his back was screaming out for him to rest. "The bath helped. I'll live."

"Do you want a sniff of Blossom? Maybe a drink? Takes the edge off."

Colton tried to avoid the inhalational intoxicants. They made him nervous. He'd seen too many people lose their teeth to Snow and their minds to Blossom. "A drink would be great. What're you making? It smells kinda bad."

Lucian laughed and poured him a large cup of a clear liquor that Colton hadn't seen before. It smelled lightly of the forest and reminded him of winter. "It's supposed to be soup. I just sort of made a pot of whatever I had lying around—you'd better be grateful! I tried my best."

"Lucian, do you use Blossom a lot?"

A slight laugh. "It's a fair question. No, not really. I find it can be helpful in periods of extreme duress, and sometimes I use it to unwind at the end of the day. You needn't worry, Colton. I have it under control."

They all say that.

Lucian slopped out whatever he was cooking into two porcelain bowls and brought one to Colton, serving him where he sat on the couch and sitting beside him.

"We can watch the ocean better this way." He slid over a spoon. "Tell me how it is."

Colton poked at the dish with suspicion—a mix of brown, black, and white mush, some of which had *probably* been alive at some point, and it probably wasn't *that* poisonous. He took a spoonful and nearly gagged. It was like eating a burned sponge that had been left in the sewers with tiny bits of carrot. He coughed, which gradually morphed into laughter.

"It—it's great. Don't serve this to anyone else."

Lucian smiled and put a hand on Colton's shoulder. "Colton, darling, I think I need to tell you something."

Was this it? Was Lucian making a move?

"Yes?" Damn it, damn his heart for leaping at even the hint of affection, damn his own tendency to latch onto anyone who showed him an ounce of kindness. *Like Orr. Like Roman. Like Mai.*

Come on, Colton, don't be stupid.

"I haven't been completely truthful with you." Lucian licked his lips. "About why I'm doing these jobs. I didn't leave my family voluntarily, although I suspect you've deduced that already. I made a series of poor choices, leading my father to disown me." He sighed.

"So you're trying to prove you can hold your own in business? So he takes you back?"

Lucian laughed. "No, no. He's made it very clear he doesn't believe I'm worthy of my title, my birthright, political office, or anything to do with him directly. The problem, my dear Colton, is that the Beaumonts still need an heir."

He reached over to a side table and produced a portrait of a young woman. She had Lucian's smile, his golden flowing hair, his innate confidence and air of loveliness. "I have a little sister named Odessa. As a consequence of my failures, my father has *arranged* a marriage for her to a man twice her age, whom she loathes. It's my fault she's in this mess. I haven't even been allowed to see her since the unpleasantness."

He gripped Colton's arm and met his eyes. "The point of these jobs is to gain prominence as a religious figure in society, someone important enough to secure an invitation to the Winter Ball."

Colton gave him a slight look of confusion and Lucian elaborated. "Ah. Only the grandest party in all of Silvermoor, where Very Important People rub elbows and decide how the world will be run each year. You know, the newspaper moguls, the Order leaders and their archons, the nobles, the politicians who write the laws and select the Prime Minister. One needs real status to secure an invitation to the ball. Some washed-up little lordling hardly stands a chance.

"All the elites will be there—*she'll* be there, Colton, and I'll be able to see her, to ensure that she's all right—maybe we could even sneak her out, if it came down to it. The Beaumont estate can burn to ash for all I care. I need to have enough resources that I can protect her. Spirit her away from the danger I've created." He let out a shuddering breath. "To do that, we'll need to take some jobs which may be terribly dangerous, Colton. You were almost killed today. If I'd been even five seconds late, he—" He shook his head.

"Some of the jobs we will face will be even more dangerous. I'm aiming to get the Holy Order's eyes on me, attract their attention, their ire perhaps, become a man they cannot afford to ignore. We'll get nose deep with some of the shadiest people in the Ivory District, collect information for blackmail, trade insight for influence, become the confident con artists of legend . . . who knows. Maybe we'll even see a real demon.

"In exchange," he continued, "I will make *you* a fortune the likes of which you cannot imagine. I will take you up from the Iron District, I will give you a name, I will stand beside you, and I will trust you with my life. But you need to know that I will also be leading you into danger. I cannot promise to always protect you, that either of us will walk out unscathed. We can topple empires—but I need you to know the reality of the risks we're facing."

This earnestness and vulnerability were novel, and Colton considered his options. This was his chance to make a better life for himself, for Mai, to be the man his mother had always dreamed he could be. It was a chance to stand with Lucian.

A half smile quirked across his lips, and he gripped Lucian's wrist, enjoying the solid warmth that enveloped his own when Lucian grabbed him back. Colton looked into Lucian's eyes and shook his hand. "Thank you for telling me the truth." Lucian kept his hold on Colton's forearm, and Colton did the same. He felt uncalloused thumbs tracing along the lines of his ink. "You underestimate me, lordling. They make us a little tougher in the Iron Belt, you know."

"I'm with you, Lucian. To hell and back, I'm with you."

ten

Colton woke up as well rested as he'd ever been. Lucian's guest mattress was like a heavenly cloud, the blankets were a warm embrace of velvet kisses, and the whole place smelled of vanilla and raspberries. He unfurled his body and slunk out of the room, helping himself to some tea and bread that Lucian hadn't been able to ruin, since he didn't cook it.

Lucian was awake already, seated in his golden armchair, one leg crossed over the other with a silken slipper dangling from his ankle. He cocked a smile at Colton and put his newspaper down, folding his hands in his lap. Thus began their lives together.

Whispers and secrets echoed as they ever did throughout the walls of Silvermoor. *Did you hear? About the exorcists? The mysterious handsome ones who—yes, the Radcliffes!* Jobs from all over the district came rolling in, as did so much cash that Colton's mattress started to burst with the money he'd stashed away. He didn't trust the banks. Leaving his money with anyone still felt kind of obnoxious. It made him giddy to think about the cash, though—the fact that his life was changing, that there was a chance for something better, that he could stand beside Lucian and smile as privileged fools praised their "genius."

The jobs came and they came, the two of them falling into a routine that felt almost natural. Together, they performed their roles with an effortless grace, each exorcism a well-rehearsed play. Colton found surprising normalcy and comfort in their partnership, striding boldly beside Lucian as they went through the motions of cleansing the world's evil.

Colton tried to keep things rooted in authenticity. "Demons inhabit specific body parts," he explained, showing Lucian the tattoos on his limbs. "The heart, usually, but occasionally the right hand, or the eyes. Sometimes it's necessary to remove the offending appendage and cast it into a fire to save the victim."

Lucian was intrigued. "Are you thinking what I'm thinking?"

Colton was almost certain that he was. At their next exorcism, poor Lucian was possessed once more, and of course there had been no choice but to remove his arm in a flourish. A bag of pig's blood sewn into the sleeve of Lucian's jacket made a convincing torrent of deliverance as Lucian tossed an almost too realistic false arm onto the floor.

The owners of the home in question paid them triple for the show. Nobody seemed to notice that Lucian went on living with two arms.

The Holy Order wasn't thrilled with their work, from the sounds of things. It had previously enjoyed a monopoly on Ivory demonic matters, although there was still plenty of work to go around. Their agents made themselves known to the pair, mostly by staring at them unnervingly and following them around on weekdays. The blossoming exorcists were popular enough amongst the Ivory elites that there had been no direct interference as of yet, but Colton kept a wary eye on their gray-shrouded stalkers.

In between séances, expulsions of demons, and long nights spent staging their victim's homes were lovely moments of respite. Lucian would come to the Iron Belt on occasion and share a beer with Colton at The Hare. Hooking his arm over Colton's neck, they'd sing until they got kicked out into the street. Lucian even stayed over sometimes, curled up in a sweet little ball on a pile of blankets on the far side of the flat, snuggled up with the pig like he owned the damn place. He never complained of the cold, nor the smells, nor noises in the neighborhood. Colton hoped he felt safe here, while they were together. There were times in the night when Colton would wake up to see a gentle beam of moonlight trickling through the window and illuminating Lucian's elegant face, when he felt that they could do anything together. That he would do *anything* to make this man happy.

Colton found he was drinking less—never to the point of blacking out, or being sick, or waking up feeling like he couldn't go on without some whiskey in him. Lucian was using less Blossom, too, seemingly quite content to remain high on life. *Hah. We're good for each other.*

Of course Colton came to the Ivory District as well. They frequented all of Lucian's favorite shops and restaurants, went to the parks and powder-sand beaches, then back to Lucian's apartment, where they watched the stars twinkle on the surface of the ocean. Colton tried to teach Lucian to cook, and after a few weeks, the two of them could whip up something that was, at the very least, technically edible. On cold nights, Lucian built up a fire, and they'd sit side by side by the hearth, drinking mulled wine and recounting the best parts of their adventures together. How they were certain they'd be caught, how brilliantly they had played off one another. They spoke of their pasts too, in these safe marble halls—of Lucian's time in the military and at university, of Colton's mother, and of his running with delinquents at the docks before he knew any better.

Small things. Simple things. A gentle trust was growing between them that Colton hadn't really enjoyed since he'd been with Mai. Lucian made him believe he could be something more than some fraud from the gutter.

Colton did some legwork outside of their missions as well. He blended into shadow, was privy to all the corners and alleys that allowed him to hear the very best gossip and pick up tips for new work. He poured them into Lucian's ear, a stream of whispers and clues from the lower districts, new ideas that could keep their act fresh to ensure the nobles would stay interested.

It wasn't like Colton didn't know how to bullshit someone. He'd been doing this a lot longer than Lucian had, after all. Lies came to him easily, his hands never shook, his heart never stuttered. There was a time when he'd thought he'd never be bested. But Lucian's words were a different sort of dangerous. The nobles surrendered to him without exception, forking out cash and influence as they fell under his spell.

And so it was like any other day when Colton strolled back into the Ivory District and let himself into Lucian's apartment with his personal key. His spirits were high, and he was in an excellent mood—Lucian would surely have snacks waiting.

"Colton, darling!" Lucian called. "Come in, help yourself! I got some of those scones you like!"

Colton sat down for breakfast, resting his legs on the table just to wind Lucian up. "So what've you got lined up for us today, your Lordship?"

"Well, our job today is a bit different." Lucian pointed out the window, to a towering stone cathedral just beyond the border of the Ivory District, enveloped in the wilds. "A very important Reverend lives there, Colton. A man who holds great influence with the Prime Minister."

Colton nodded. "So what's the job?"

"High Cleric Magnus has some worries about Reverend Ives, the head of the Haven branch. Parishioners and servants missing. No one's seen Ives's son in months either, which raises concerns about succession, transfer of power and so on."

"A High Cleric? Why don't they use their own guys?"

"He wants someone not connected with the Order—conflict of interest, that sort of thing. This gives them the appearance of independent investigation."

"Or they want to take us out, nice and quiet." Colton took a long sip of his coffee.

"Exactly. We'll need to be careful. I wouldn't be surprised if he's luring in exorcists as ingredients for whatever nonsense he's up to."

A high-ranking member of the Holy Order with a bad reputation. His mother had warned him about that sort of man—the Reverends of Silvermoor dabbled into the arcane by any means necessary. An organization that survived on the basis that evil existed, and therefore would go to great lengths to ensure that it did. Hand in hand with the government, the Order decreed right and wrong, guided societal virtues, and kept the people complacent. They'd been making a stir, Colton and Lucian, and stealing business from the Holy Officers in a public way. This could get ugly.

"Alternatively, it's just a run-of-the-mill haunting, and you and I can mess about in a temple for a few days. I'll get possessed, you save me—it's all terribly gallant, job done." Lucian's ice-chip eyes flicked up to Colton. "If we play this right, I think we can . . . Well, my suspicion is that the Order will be happy no matter the outcome. We get rid of Ives, and they will offer us a legitimate position in their ranks. We'll get into the ball for certain. Or he kills us, and they don't have to worry about us stepping on their toes any longer."

"Love it." Well, things had been a bit mundane recently. Maybe he'd get a chance to show off. "So where is it?"

"Oh! That's the best part—it is a bit remote, so we'll have to use horses to get there. Won't that be fun?"

Colton's face sank. "I can't ride a horse, Lucian."

"Sure you can, lovely. Basically, you just sit on it and don't fall off."

Oh, is that all there is to it?

They left the warmth of Lucian's apartment, and Colton gawked up at the two imposing steeds that Lucian had arranged to be waiting outside. Lucian's, of course, was a mighty white stallion—the kind with a flowing mane and tail, that looked like it rescued children from wishing wells and ate evil for breakfast. Colton's was at least as good, a large chocolate mare with gentle eyes and a glossy coat.

"Yours is called Maple, mine is called Champion," Lucian explained. "Aren't they darling?"

Colton was all dread as Lucian gave him a hand up to mount, made sure his stirrups were set properly, and showed him how to use the reins. He placed a hefty saddlebag over their rears and smiled. "Now, ideally you don't want to crush any pedestrians if you can avoid it, all right? We won't go too fast."

It wasn't long before Lucian was astride him on his magnificent horse, and he set a leisurely pace as the two of them meandered to the Ives estate. The ride was bumpy and terrifying, and it made Colton's butt hurt, but he quite liked Maple and found himself leaning forward from time to time to pat her muscular neck.

"Lucian?" Colton found himself asking as they reached a more suburban area of the Ivory District. "If we're just walking on the horses, couldn't we have just gone on foot? It'd be just as slow."

The young Lord grinned. *Oh, no.*

"Why, Colton, you're absolutely right! Follow me!" He drove his heels into Champion's flanks, who reared up with a neigh before he stormed off into the distance.

"You *asshole*!" Colton called as he urged Maple on.

The marble sheen of the Ivory District faded the closer to the wilds they got, eventually giving way to calm dirt roads and fences made up of roses and ivy. Was this still the Ivory District? He'd have to ask later. For now, it was all Colton could do to concentrate on staying in his seat. The air was clean here, and he could just about taste the spray of the sea as the horses galloped along.

eleven

It was about an hour of miserable, ass-jostling sprinting before the two horses finally arrived at Haven. They were well away from the Ivory District, and there was none of the technology or splendor he'd come to associate with that place. The atmosphere was chilly, to say the least. Locals pulled their shutters closed as the two strangers approached, a village essentially barren of life. The Holy Order's sacred star banners hung limply from the streetlights and over doorways, tattered and gray from exposure. In the town's main courtyard lay a dusty road leading up to the cathedral—grand once, boarded up now, with broken windows and the veil of neglect. The Reverend was probably in bad shape indeed, if he wasn't even maintaining the semblance of religious conviction for his people.

Colton didn't like this. He didn't like this at all. What had they gotten themselves into? Lucian didn't seem that keen on the place either, his hands idling at his cuff links at least twice. "Colton, if at any point you want to leave, tug on your ear. We'll get out immediately. I have a bad feeling about this place."

The cathedral wasn't like the basilicas in the Ivory District, which were garish monuments of excess constructed from polished marble, gems, and sanded wood. The temple itself was made of gray stone, with corroded metal grates on the windows. Lucian approached the splintered wooden door and knocked once. It took a moment before it swung open, and they were greeted by a wizened man who introduced himself as the custodian. He bowed and allowed the two men into the building, leading them silently into the residential area of the holy space and directing them to sit.

"The master will be out shortly. Please enjoy some refreshments." He poured them two tepid cups of tea before sweeping from the room with his hands tucked behind his back.

All of this was hardly reassuring.

"Careful with the tea," Colton warned. "There's a calming drug in it. Harmless in small doses, but we want to be on our toes here. I can't tell what the incense is, there's too much perfume in the air." Ugh, it made him sick.

He was interrupted from his slight sensory overload by the appearance of a haggard older gentleman. Hairs out of place on both his head and face, a rather unfortunate tooth-to-gum ratio, pupils blown wide—Blossom, probably. The exorcists stood up, ever the professionals.

"Lucian Beaumont, as I live and breathe." He bowed slightly, stepping closer to Lucian. "I am Reverend Jacques Ives. Welcome to my home." Ives turned his attention to Colton next and grinned at him. "And you."

It was a chill that ran through Colton, a voice at the back of his head telling him to *run* as the man locked his milky gaze upon him. The door—where was the door? They had to get out of here; it wasn't worth it. He reached for Lucian's sleeve and—

Suddenly it occurred to Colton that Reverend Ives was not staring at his face but the center of his chest. Without warning, he tore Colton's shirt open with such force that his brand-new buttons went clattering on the stone floors. His greedy eyes drank in Colton's tattoos, his fingers fanning out to study the skin.

"It's true," he whispered. "Just like he said—just like—"

Colton tried to take a step back, but the man's surprisingly strong grip crushed his forearm and held him still.

Lucian grabbed Ives's wrist and tore him away from Colton. "Excuse me," he said, looming, disdainful, loathing. "You will not touch my partner in that way ever again. You will treat him with respect. Apologize immediately."

"Ohhhh, ohhhh Lucian Beaumont." Ives smiled at him, his arm limp in Lucian's tight grip. "I'm *sooooo* sorry."

Lucian's lips twitched, a storm of fury brewing on his face. "Apologize to *Colton*."

Jacques flopped his head back to Colton. "Forgive me, blessed one. Please, please." There was a dim tent in his trousers, and the man rolled his hips in Colton's direction.

This man was a fucking lunatic. Yeah, this job wasn't worth it.

Colton ran a hand through his hair and tugged on his ear with one hand, the other fumbling with his shirt, pulling it tight over his chest in some pathetic attempt to cover his naked skin. He coached his face into a calm mask, dispassionate and disconnected, even though the violation of this moment would be difficult to scrub out of his skin.

Lucian released Ives's hand with a disgusted noise. "Right. I do not feel as though this will be a mutually beneficial partnership."

Ives fell to his knees and clasped his hands together. "No! No, you can't! Please, please, I need you—I need your help—I need—you can't! I'm begging you, my home is overrun, and I—he's everything—he's exactly what I've—please. Please. I'll pay you ten times what the Order offered. I'll nominate you—you'll be *Archons*! Whatever you want—I only just—"

Colton had a bad feeling about this, but then again, if they got to the bottom of this, ousted the Reverend and cemented their foothold as people relevant and helpful to the Holy Order, the invitation to the ball was all but assured. This couldn't be his call—not with Lucian's sister on the line. He looked to his partner for guidance.

The young Lord swallowed. "It's your choice, Colton." His meaning was clear. *You are at greater risk.* The Reverend had eyes only for Colton, after all.

Colton had certainly endured more degrading and humiliating treatment in his time in the Iron Belt, and for far less money. He could handle this, surely. The guy was an elderly weirdo, and he and Lucian were two young men in their physical prime. It'd be fine.

He offered the man a hand, which Reverend Ives quickly took, and hauled him up to his feet. The man's desiccated fingers latched onto his skin like parasites, clawing at Colton as he pulled away.

"How can we refuse such an impassioned plea for help, Lucian?" Colton glanced over toward the other man, his face a portrait of calm confidence. "What sort of exorcists would we be otherwise?" He forced his hands to be still and opened his shirt once more, revealing the black shadows and ancient prayers his mother had carved into his skin long ago. "You may look, of course. It has been a long time since I met someone who understood their significance, Reverend."

His mother had taught him once, ages ago. On his right arm, spirals and serpents—the paths of humanity, of fury, a rejection of divinity, to bind, to banish, to destroy. On his left arm, halos and stones—reality, salvation, certainty, to bless, to conjure, to salvage. Runes of protection on his legs, one behind his ear, his back bare save for a pair of dark eyes on his shoulders, enshrouded by raven wings. The masterpiece was his chest. It bore a tapestry with monochrome, abstract scenes of a banishment. A sunburst rising over his heart, dancing over words he could speak but not understand.

"*A prayer,*" his mother had said, "*for the worst of them. The only way, Colton.*"

Their line had been exorcising for generations, she'd said. It was in their blood, and there was no way that some backwater reverend understood anything about it. The Reverend kept a distance then, his fingers itching to touch as he put his face so close to Colton's chest that he could feel his acrid breath on his skin. "Of course, of course I do! I have studied these texts for decades! Ever since I began to walk *the path* I have devoted my life to find a way to become worthy—to become a vessel. He promised me, they did! And then he sent you! Oh, yes, oh, yes, yes."

Great. This was going great. "Who?" Colton demanded. "Who promised you?"

"He—the Golden One! The Master, the—Lord Beaumont! Surely you know!"

Lucian offered a noncommittal shrug. "Right, well we'd best get on with the exorcism, then."

Colton glanced at Lucian, who had averted his gaze respectfully. He pulled the fabric over his chest, his cheeks reddening from the awkward exposure. His partner slipped out of his jacket and handed it to Colton. "Here, darling. So you don't catch a chill."

Colton took the garment gratefully and pulled it on, buttoning it up almost to his neck.

Ives tapped his foot. "Come along, then, if you want to see everything so badly! Let me show you—let me show you my boon. Come, come." He led them through the dining room, the guest halls, up the stairs, down a corridor with dozens of expensive portraits, all with their eyes scratched out.

Well, no mummified corpses so far. That was a good start.

"Here!" Ives stopped at a door with a small stained-glass window pressed into the wood. It depicted the scene of a white bird falling to the earth. *My, how auspicious.* Through the window Colton could see a tidy bedroom, nothing too exciting about it.

"So what's in here?" Lucian asked, his voice impatient.

"My boon, Lucian Beaumont." Ives unlocked the door and gestured for them to enter. "It's just under the covers."

They stepped into the room and Lucian pulled the covers back, revealing . . . nothing.

"Oh, fucker," Lucian growled, his head snapping up.

Lucian was never one to swear, never one to panic. Colton's stomach dropped as he heard the door lock behind them. He whipped around and saw that Ives hadn't followed them in and immediately tried the door with all his strength.

"You BASTARD!" he hissed, banging his fist on the wood.

"Now, now, don't panic! It's all very safe!" Ives called through the door. "Breathe deep!"

A pale blue smoke filtered in through the vent, and Colton moved protectively toward Lucian as it started to surround them. Was there another way out—a window, perhaps? No, they were three flights up, no way they could jump from here but . . . oh hells, oh hells. Colton tried very hard not to panic, looking toward Lucian—surely he knew what to do—he always—

Lucian's fist rested defeatedly on the door. He was shaking his head.

"Lucian?"

"I think we might be in a bit of trouble, darling."

Lucian pressed a handkerchief over Colton's mouth and nose, then covered his own face with fine white silk. It wasn't working. Colton could feel the smoke bleeding through, robbing him of his senses. Lucian pounded on the door once, twice more, before the gas took his strength. He crumpled to the ground, shifting closer to Colton before collapsing on the floor, his arm outstretched. Colton could barely see anymore, but with his last ounce of strength he grasped Lucian's hand and threaded their fingers.

At least they were together. No matter what happened, no matter where they woke up or what Ives had planned, he'd have his partner at his side.

And then the world went black.

twelve

The gas robbed him of his dreams. Colton had a vague sense of urgency as he forced his eyes open, finding his senses with a gasp. *Where am I? Where is—*

"Lucian?" he called out, lurching forward to stand up only to find his hands bound behind his back and attached with a rope to the wall. Topless, too. At least he still had his trousers on. "LUCIAN!"

His partner was nowhere to be found. Colton found himself in some sort of prayer hall, something that had surely once been used by the Holy Order. The familiar smell of incense lingered, and the hall was plastered with stars like Order buildings tended to be; even the worship books hadn't been removed. Decayed wooden pews lined the hard stone floors, and there was an altar that, in this case, was thankfully free of blood and dead animals.

Colton's head slumped forward in frustration, and bitter tears pricked the corners of his eyes. They should have left; they should have left ages ago. *No. It was worth the risk. We could have been Archons, Odessa would have been rescued—*

"Cooooooooolton!" Ives's voice snatched Colton's attention back.

Ives hobbled over from the nest of parchment on which he'd been sitting, quills and ink discarded around him as though a squid had lost an argument with a goose. The man was manic now, his eyes wide and pupils blown—he *reeked* of Snow. Everything about him, from his cracked lips and his shaking hands to his fingers, was covered in blood. Colton's veins turned to ice as he absorbed what he was seeing. Clad in nothing but a loincloth—ink on his hands, streaks of blood on his face, his chest, spattered up and down his arms and . . .

Ives cupped his cheek. "You can't leave me like the others. You'll save me, mmm? You'll show them my boon, you'll speak on my behalf."

It was hard to conjure words, but Colton did his best. "Where is Lucian? What did you do to him?"

Ives's pink little tongue darted along his lips, getting a sweet nip of the line of blood under his nose before returning to the moist cavern of his mouth. "He's fine. Collateral. You won't leave him. He said you would, but you won't. You'll take me there, you'll make me."

His eyes were wide; he was literally salivating. "Right?"

Colton had no idea what the bastard was talking about, to be honest. The situation as it stood was this: He was trapped in a building whose layout he did not understand, bound and immobile, with a man who was mentally deranged, and his partner and (kind of) love interest was missing. Well, fine. This wasn't the craziest thing he'd encountered while working with Lucian, and *he'd* never really had any problems with it. Okay, easy enough. He'd channel his inner Lucian. Charm his way out of it. Play along until he got what he wanted. Fine. He could be charming, right?

"Oh, Reverend," he managed, the sweat on his forehead only just betraying the fear his smile was attempting to hide. "Of course, I'll tell him, and he'll—" He had to make this good; he had to make it believable. Colton would promise him anything he wanted, not like he'd actually follow through on any of it. "He'll accept you, Jacques. He'll make you everything you ever wanted. But you're going to have to untie me first, all right? And then you can show me your boon, and—and I'll tell him what a good job you did."

Ives's brain seemed to stagger for a moment as it tried to process the information. "You won't run? You won't resist like the others?"

Lucian, please be okay.

"Of course not, I'm—I'm marked, right? I know these things. I know how special you are. Untie me, Reverend. Let me help you."

Ives glanced at the papers as he crouched down behind Colton and gingerly undid the ropes that bound his wrists. *Okay, be calm and dignified like Lucian.* "Wonderful, Jacques. I'm so pleased, and he'll be pleased too." Whoever the fuck "he" was. "We'll need Lucian, though—he's the key to all of this."

The Reverend fumbled with his fingers. "No. He is not needed."

Anger quirked itself on Colton's face, and he sneered as pleasantly as one could sneer. "He is. The Golden One told me that he is."

"But—but the ritual—"

Oh, fuck this. Colton was lightning-fast. With one hand he grabbed the good Reverend by the throat and pinned him to the wall; with the other he pulled out his dagger and pressed it up against the wrinkled white skin of his neck. *So much for being charming.*

"You *miserable* asshole." He seethed, "Take me to my partner right now."

Ives's face morphed into a look of terror. "Colt-Colton! No, no no! You can't—why are you angry with me, I did as you asked, I did as you—oh, oh no . . . I'm sorry, I'm so sorry, please, please don't be angry, I didn't mean to—he—I didn't mean to—he was struggling and—he—he—"

Colton felt the blood drain from his cheeks. "*What did you do?*" he spat, choking the frail creature all the more tightly.

Tears began to fall from the old man's eyes, carving pale tracks in the dried-up ropes of blood that colored his face. "He—Lucian Beaumont—he—I can't—he—I think I might have—I didn't mean to, I swear I didn't mean to, it's—to be a vessel I had to—he—there was just so much blood—he—he wasn't moving . . ."

Colton let the man fall to his knees, shaking his head in disbelief. "No," he whispered.

Ives crawled to Colton and grabbed at his boots. "I—I killed him. I killed him. He was so frightened, Colton, he—I chained him to a wall, and I killed him. I took the holy blade, and I put it between his ribs, he choked, he choked, he tried to—and he fell forward—he—" The Reverend wailed, catching his face in his fingers as he howled at eternity. "The last thing he said, the last thing—it was your name." He trembled, staring at his bloodstained hands. "He must have—he must have thought you'd—"

Colton couldn't breathe, not even as he backed up against the stone wall for support, uncertain his legs would keep him standing. He could hardly think. *Lucian.* It had all been going so well. What must his last moments have been like? Surely filled with terror as this maniac trussed him up and carved him into pieces. Colton doubted that Lucian would have begged, but his jaw would have been tight, his lips curled over his teeth like a smile ready to bite. He would have been brave.

The last thing he said was your name, Colton. He died alone in this hellhole, and you never even told him you—

The world was cold. He couldn't feel the ground through his feet, his chest ached, the Reverend faded from his consciousness. *I can't do this. I don't want to do this without him.* Oh, fuck. He was in love with Lucian. Great, this was just typical. Falling in love and not even admitting it to himself until it was too late. Fucking *fantastic.*

"We can still use him as a boon, I think—I'll have to cut him up and arrange the bits—" Ives's nose was dripping with snot, and he wiped it on his sleeve, coughing from the exertion of crying so hard. "It's easy, Colton, if—if you cut on the joints, you don't have to saw the bones. I can cut him into pieces, and we can use him for the sacrifice—I can carry him then, one chunk at a time. He had nice hands." Ives vomited on the floor and wailed. "Please. Please tell me I didn't ruin my chances to ascend—to be chosen, to be accepted! His blood was so hot; it tasted so good. I must have—"

Colton tightened his grip on his blade and imagined how nice it would feel as it plunged into the Reverend's neck. He'd think of Lucian as metal tore apart cartilage and sinew, and he would sneer as the blood splashed his face.

But he'd never find Lucian's body, then. He couldn't leave him here, to rot away to bones in this miserable pit.

Colton licked his lips and cast his heavy brown eyes toward the creature in front of him. "No. No, you don't need to cut him up for the ritual. The spirit remains with the body, in the place where it fell. Take me to him, and we can finish what we started. You'll be a vessel, I'll tell him about how pleased I am." His voice was hollow and empty. "Go."

Slowly, Ives led Colton down the stairs. Down lots of stairs, actually, until they were deep within the cathedral's bowels. There was no natural light here, and all Colton could hear were steady drips of fetid water and rats scurrying about on the stones.

They arrived at a heavy iron door, and Ives licked his lips. "He's just in here, Colton." He fumbled in his pockets and pulled out a ring of rusted iron keys. One at a time he tried them, cursing loudly when they didn't work.

"You try locking me in again, Jacques, and you and I are done. All of this will have been for nothing."

"Never, my Lord! Never never never never!"

On the last key, the lock clicked open, and Colton steeled himself. It was almost impossible to maintain the unaffected air he'd need to pull this off, like he didn't give a crap that Lucian had been bound and gutted like he was nothing. He didn't want to see Lucian like this—he ... he'd never even ...

The door creaked inward, and Colton shoved Ives in first. He wasn't about to let the man be between him and a door ever again. Okay. Okay. *Do it for Lucian.* Colton stepped in, holding his breath. The room was littered with human bones and stank of dried-up blood. Lucian sat propped up against a damp-looking stone wall, his wrists pinned above his head in iron shackles, looking rather bored.

"Hi, precious!" Lucian called, feebly waving one arm from where it dangled. "I was hoping you might drop by!"

"Oh, fuck." Relief flooded Colton's chest with such force that he almost went to his knees.

But the blood...

On closer inspection, Lucian's shirt had been ripped open, and arcane runes in the style of *Colton's tattoos* had been carved into the perfect skin of his chest. Ives was unhinged, out of his mind—he'd surely killed someone else down here. *Oh, thank heaven. Thank you—fuuuuck.*

But they weren't quite out of the woods yet. Lucian was still chained to the wall, they were still trapped in this obscene temple, and the Reverend was probably still armed. Colton took a deep breath and conjured up Professional Exorcist Colton, who was very concerned about this whole situation, of course.

Ives, too, was frantic with relief, kneeling at Lucian's side. "He's alive! Look, Colton, look, it's a miracle! I told you—he—I didn't mess up, I didn't—I can be the vessel, right? You kill him, and then I can—right?"

"Of course."

Ives hesitated, tapping his fingers together in front of his chest. "I—I carved one of your marks onto him, into his flesh. Then I proceeded to imbibe his soul, Colton."

Colton moved closer to the man and put a hand on his shoulder. The Reverend was his only focus; the man had to believe he was Colton's whole world. "How did it taste?"

A velvet breath hitched between them, with all the intimacy of a holy confession. "Like a revelation."

"You are ready, Jacques." Colton smiled at him warmly. "We will free him, and we can finish the ritual together."

Suspicion passed over Ives's face, and he shook his head violently, paranoia settling into his veins. "No—you—before when I released you, you promised you would—and then you—"

Distract. Redirect. What does he want more than anything?

Despite everything, despite how scared he was, despite the revulsion that seeped all the way down to his bones—Colton twisted his fingers into the soft cotton collar of the man's shirt and pressed their lips together in a deep, sensual kiss. A sob wrenched its way from the Reverend's throat, and Colton tried to think of Lucian, despite the fact that it felt like there were spiders crawling across his tongue.

From the far end of the room, he could just about hear Lucian gasp.

"I brought him here for you, to use for your boon. So he will accept you, so you can become a vessel. His blood will pay your price," Colton cooed. A sickly saccharine crust crawled out of his throat. "Come here." Colton flicked his head slightly and gestured at the knife in Ives's grip. "Use that, and spill the blood from my hand." Colton held his palm up, watching with disgust as the master of the house tried to parse his meaning.

His eyes darted from the weapon to Colton's face, his lips quivering with uncertainty. "I can't, you're—"

"You must." Colton stepped closer, running his finger just along the sharp edge of the blade. "You think it would work with the blood of someone *unmarked*?" Colton's palm closed over the blade, and the scent of copper flooded the space.

"Drink."

And Ives drank, clawing at Colton's wrist as his tongue probed the wound and lapped up the red nectar that burst forth. Colton allowed a few moments to pass before extracting himself with some force, allowing his blood to drip onto the floor in something like a circle before Lucian.

"I need more. Give me the knife." Colton tsk-tsked impatiently, and with some reluctance Ives passed over the dagger. Colton pretended to deepen the wound and drew some nonsense runes on the stones with his finger. He took a deep breath through his nose and looked over his shoulder at the Reverend. "We must unchain his Lordship."

A strange brass object was placed into his mangled hand, and slowly Colton approached Lucian and crouched down before him, working one lock open at a time. He tried ignoring Lucian's pleased little expression as the metal fell away from his body.

One wrist free, then another. Lucian rubbed at his skin until Colton grabbed him roughly by his arm and dragged him into the center of the room. He threw Lucian to the earth in the apex of the circle and pinned him down with a knee on his chest.

"Colton!" he barked. "Release me! What in the hells are you doing?"

"Meat does not speak," Colton hissed. "You will be silent, or I will cut out your tongue." He looked to Ives, his expression warm. "You must be in contact, Reverend. Place your hands on his body."

Spiderlike fingers splintered out over Lucian's elegant neck, and he tensed up beneath them.

"Repeat after me." Colton spouted out an old song his mother had sung to him when he was a child, a lullaby in the ancient language, a song of warmth and comfort that bore no meaning here.

Ives followed in a round, butchering the alien words as he shivered with the frenzy of ceremony.

"Are you ready, Reverend?" Colton purred.

"Oh, yes, yes yes, oh, fuck me, yes." He was practically moaning as Colton raised the blade over Lucian's heart.

"Colton?" Lucian whispered, his mirthful smile just barely hidden behind his brilliant eyes.

He brought the knife down with a thud, right into the old Reverend's chest. His face told a story of ecstasy, of disbelief, of absolute fulfillment as he buckled backward and choked in a pool of his own blood. Colton stabbed him again, and again, and once more for good measure, crying out in desperation each time the weapon struck. When the creature finally stopped moving, he let the dagger fall to the ground, his anger spent and his heart all but empty.

Lucian.

His partner closed the gap between them and pulled Colton into a tight, desperate embrace.

"That . . . that was marvelous, Colton," Lucian whispered, stroking his back. "The best exorcism you've ever done. Are you all right, lovely?"

"He said he'd killed you," Colton breathed. "He was covered in blood—I thought—" *I thought I couldn't go on if you weren't with me.*

"Oh, it wasn't all that bad. Something about a vessel, something about the Golden One, the son as the vehicle, blah blah. Honestly, I'm very glad you came when you did. My hands were starting to fall asleep, and I'm a bit hungry."

Colton laughed despite everything and buried his face in Lucian's neck. "You're so stupid, I hate you."

"I know, precious. I hate you too." Lucian pulled away just slightly but kept his hands on Colton's shoulders. "Come on, let's get those cuts washed out. Then we'll need to take care of our friend here."

Lucian took Colton by the hand and led him to a basin of clean water at the far end of the room. He was gentle and nurturing as he cleaned Colton's wounds, his manicured fingers probing the blood and grime without hesitation. "You saved me. You saved both of us. And I'm so, so grateful to you."

Colton swallowed, his throat bobbing and his mouth dry. *Fuck it.* He took a breath and leaned in closer, cupping Lucian's cheeks and touching their lips together with tentative hope.

Lucian froze like a deer and gently pulled away, chuckling softly. "You're kissing everyone today, eh?" His hands idly rubbed his own naked wrists; he couldn't meet Colton's eyes. That hurt more than Colton cared to admit. "Come on, we've got a job to finish."

"Right," Colton muttered, his gaze cast to the floor.

Idiot.

thirteen

"SO!" Lucian often filled silences with chatter, it seemed. "So that was a whole thing, wasn't it? I woke up in the dungeon, and wondered if I was back at university! It—ehm. I'm very pleased you saved me, by the way. That would have been dreadful if I'd had to stay down here indefinitely. Dank pits are a nightmare for my skin. And your whole demon performance was just . . ." He kissed the air, then hunched his shoulders. "I meant it was brilliant, Colton. A Beaumont-level production."

Hells, why had Colton acted on his stupid impulses? Of *course* he was attracted to Lucian, and of *course* intimate moments where they'd just ripped life out of the jaws of death would make him feel affectionate, but he shouldn't have bloody acted on it. *Plus you're in love with him—that probably didn't help.*

Lucian was a peacock, audacious and resplendent, flirting with everyone, touching everyone as if he loved them. Colton was a fool for thinking that his friendly affection was anything more than just that, and now he feared that he'd spoiled the one good thing to happen in his life since his mother died. He couldn't go back to that utter loneliness. It wasn't the money, it wasn't the jobs, it was *Lucian*, his stupid laugh and his capes and his warm spirit. It was the sense of belonging, the closeness, the trust and respect that told him he wasn't alone anymore. That he was worthy of more than the gutter.

"So it might be a bit difficult to pass this off as a suicide. Considering he was stabbed about four times." Lucian offered a stilted laugh. "I think we'll probably need to dispose of the body and get this place cleaned up, and then—"

"Lucian, I'm sorry." *Good start.* "I was just so worked up from— from you being alive and how dangerous it all was and—I didn't mean to—I just—it was an impulse. The heat of the moment. It won't happen again, I promise."

Lucian's eyes were very sad. "It's all right, Colton." He bit his lip and an unusual silence fell between them.

Colton ran through all the possible insults, condemnations, and rejections imaginable and looked down at his feet. "I don't want to fuck this up. I don't want to lose this."

Don't want to lose you. Don't want to lose this beautiful friendship we've cultivated.

Lucian took a deep breath and bridged the gap between them, carefully touching him on the shoulder. "I don't want to lose this either, Colton. Would it just be easier if we pretend that didn't happen? That my incomparable charm and this lovely dungeon setting were too much to bear?"

Relief flooded Colton's veins, threading his extremities with the beginnings of an aching wound he decided to ignore. "Yeah, that might be for the best." A smile. "How could anyone resist you?"

"Exactly." Lucian grinned. "Victim of circumstance, anyone would have done the same." He clapped Colton's shoulder twice and broke away, surveying the damage they'd caused. "Well. He wanted to be a vessel; I say we make him the best damn vessel anyone ever saw!"

Colton found some heavy irons and stones, and the pair of exorcists lugged them up to one of the balconies overlooking the sea cliffs. Lucian tied him up and attached the weights to his body, hesitating for a moment as it hovered at the precipice. He leaned over and rifled through the man's pockets first, emptying them of everything he could find. Papers, keys, jewelry—he owed them for all the damn trouble. "I suppose we should say a few words?" Lucian suggested.

"Here is Reverend Ives, he tried to kill us and needed a bath. Enjoy the ocean."

With little pomp or ceremony, Lucian kicked the Reverend into the violent sea and watched him disappear.

He looked to Colton and squeezed his shoulder, more to ground him than anything else. "I doubt anyone will miss him too much. He's . . . well. To say he'd seriously deviated from the ethos of the Holy Order would be something of an understatement, no? I doubt anyone will mind that he's gone. And I strongly suspect that keeping this quiet is worth at least two tickets to the ball, don't you?"

The two of them made their way up to what they presumed were Reverend Ives's main offices and began searching around for a safe. It didn't take long to find one, and Lucian checked the papers he'd taken from Ives's pockets and tried a few combinations until the metal box clicked open.

"Colton!" Lucian was delighted. "Look!"

Inside were gold bars, precious stones, stacks of coins, documents . . . and right at the back Lucian produced the deed to the temple, presenting it to Colton with a smile. "It was a major foothold for the Order, which I suppose technically makes us titled gentry?"

"Does it? I'm not sure that's how property transfer works."

"Oh pishposh. I'm sure there's some sort of estate agent bureaucratic nonsense that'll get it sorted for us. And worst case, we can use it, trade it to the Order for an official position, rent it out to tourists who . . . I suppose, like to see dusty haunted villages?"

There were other papers, too, which Lucian squirreled away into his coat, but Colton wasn't really bothered with what they were for. He trusted his partner, and dusty old documents were hardly his forte.

They did one last sweep to make sure they hadn't missed anything valuable (a slightly abridged search, to be fair, since there were so many bloody secret rooms and chambers), and Colton was pleasantly surprised to find a crystal orb with the image of a winged serpent somehow carved into the center.

"My mother had one just like this," he explained, smiling. "It's probably from our clan!" And he had thought he'd never see anything like it ever again. He put it into his pouch and carefully walked out into the sunlight. The two of them had already been through some terrible things together, and although Lucian never allowed himself to seem outwardly affected by anything, Colton worried that maybe all of this evil and cruelty was starting to get to him. Hells, he'd been chained up like a dog and had had his chest carved by a lunatic. Lucian seemed quite accustomed to rolling with the insane, bouncing back after something horrific (or, more likely, compartmentalizing his feelings. Good plan). Colton had wondered how the man was able to take all of life's challenges in stride.

A sense of humor, apparently, and plenty of Blossom.

As far as Colton could tell, Lucian seemed to be fine. He was back to being a stupid prick, anyway, his smile returning almost as soon as they were back out in the sunshine.

They went to mount the horses, and the custodian came out with a bow. "I take it that all went well?"

Lucian smiled. "Extremely well. Reverend Ives has become the vessel he always dreamed of and is basking in the eternal glory of the holy entity as we speak." He reached into his bag and took out the deed to the cathedral. "He's given us the land and building as well! What an absolute gem of a man he is."

The custodian looked mildly dubious, and Colton put a pure gold bar into his hands. "And if you wouldn't mind arranging a cleanup for the place, Reverend Ives said he has no need of anything remaining in the building. I plan to sell it soon." He winked and hoisted himself onto the horse. "You take care, sir. And thanks for all your help."

The man grasped Lucian's hand and squeezed it tight. "I thank you, my Lord. A great blessing you have wrought."

"Yes yes, all in a day's work. Wroughting blessings, righting wrongs, and so on and so on."

As soon as they were out of the custodian's earshot, Lucian laughed and leaned over, punching Colton's shoulder. "Well, that was a bit horrible, eh? I think, darli—Colton, that you and I have earned a little break from all this."

Colton's heart shriveled into itself. He hated that admitting his feelings had changed the dynamic, that Lucian was being so *careful* with him now. This would take some time to fix.

"Lucian, I—"

"Race you!" he called, and pulled his horse into a loose canter as they headed back to the Ivory District. It was dark by the time they arrived, and Lucian cast a dubious eye toward the steps leading down to the lower districts. "You're more than welcome to stay over again, if you wish. I think both of us could use a bath."

Colton was about to protest when Lucian brought up the notion of hot running water. At least things were somewhat resembling normal. Small blessings.

It took a bit longer than was comfortable for the water to stop running pink. Colton's palm ached as he scrubbed it out with soap again and again, wincing as he relived those last terrible moments.

He'd stabbed a man in the heart and felt his life leak out of him. Not the first time he'd killed, to be honest, and probably not the last. It always left a mildly ironic hollow feeling in his chest. And it never got easier. He'd faced the death of his dearest friend, and he'd gambled everything on a stupid whim of a kiss. He needed a drink. Actually, he probably needed several drinks.

Colton stayed in his room that night, not deigning to join Lucian for dinner. Some space would be good for them, he decided.

That night he dreamed of Ives. He dreamed of spiderweb veins and skeleton hands. Of Lucian's hollow, lifeless eyes, of blood dripping from his mouth.

"*Colton. You failed me. You let this happen. Because of you . . . because of you . . .*"

He awoke with a start, his fist gripping the sheet, covered in sweat. Great. What a wonderful addition to his usual nighttime horrors.

Colton emerged the following morning with bags under his eyes, trudging to the breakfast table, where, of course, Lucian was already seated.

"How are you feeling?" he asked warmly, passing Colton a fresh cup of tea. "Do you want to talk about anything?"

Yes, everything. "Not really. Are you okay? That—it must have been terrifying."

A soft laugh. "It wasn't, really. I knew you'd come for me, Colton." Their eyes met, and Colton's heart swelled with affection, which he stamped down like cheap tobacco in a pipe. "Now, you can keep all of the cash we got from the cathedral. Consider it a bonus for rescuing me like a brave knight. I'll see if I can make some headway on selling the deed to the place, and once that's finalized, you'll have enough money to do anything." Lucian looked into his own teacup, spinning a little mother-of-pearl spoon around against the porcelain. "You probably won't need to work with me anymore, after that."

Colton's stomach lurched. "Is that—is that what you want, Lucian?" His voice cracked, and he cursed himself.

Hells, I should have known. It was too good to be true, and I fucked it up. Like I fuck everything in my life up.

"Colton . . ." The chair creaked across the marble floor as Lucian stood up, sweeping over toward Colton. The feeling of his partner's arms around him again made Colton startle for a moment, and he held his breath.

"Of course that's not what I want. Look at me. Nothing changes between us. You are my partner and my friend, and I love working with you. One misunderstanding doesn't change that, all right?"

They both smiled, and Colton almost laughed when his instinct told him to lean in for another kiss. He believed him. Maybe that was part of the problem, that he always believed in Lucian. "All right, Beaumont. So what's our next wretched assignment?"

"Oh, nothing so sinister as a haunted cathedral, although you might find it a bit more challenging." He grinned, slipping back into his seat. "The Ives job cinched it, Colton. The Church was so grateful for our discretion that they've offered us an official position. Say hello to the Ninth Archon of the Holy Order of Silvermoor, and his disciple Colton."

A snort. "And why don't I get to be Archon, exactly?"

"Because I don't think you'd pay attention in the biquarterly meetings, Colton. And some technical nonsense about religious differences? I don't think 'ethnic' exorcists fit with the Order aesthetic. Besides, you're missing the point! Such a title comes hand in hand with access to all the best events in the nation."

Colton smirked. "Even the Winter Ball?"

"Especially the Winter Ball, darling. I therefore suggest you stop by my apartment a few times a week for the next few weeks so I might begin some . . . why don't we call it etiquette lessons? This is different from the exorcisms, Colton. Our clients wanted Iron, they wanted rustic, they wanted *authentic demonic arts*. The ball will want perfection, or there will be social disemboweling from which I cannot protect you. I'll tell you who's who, what to look out for, and how we might best schmooze these people. As well as which of the twenty-five forks they'll provide is used for melon, and which is used to enucleate your enemies."

Oh, goody.

"My father will be there for certain. I'd very much like to rub our success in his face, if you're up for it." Once more, Lucian reached his hand over the table. "My sister will be there, obviously. Her fiancé too, which means we can possibly try and cause some mischief in that department. I—I'd be so grateful if you helped me with this. What do you say?"

"Of course," Colton said with a barely hidden smile. This was what they'd been working toward, after all. Besides, standing beside Lucian with his peers would probably be hilarious, if nothing else.

fourteen

Soon after, Colton enjoyed a long overdue meet-up with Mai, which ended with not quite enough alcohol and way too much nostalgia. They'd practically grown up together, and spending time with her reminded Colton how much of his past he'd tried to forget.

"You remember, Colton?" Mai had drawled, her head draped over his thigh as they lounged in her apartment. "That time I got so sunburned I couldn't even lie down?"

He giggled. "And I got you that weird ointment from the apothecary, and it just made it worse?"

It hadn't all been bad, really. They'd scurried around the market district getting sweet little handouts from the shopkeepers and chased seagulls down alleyways and played marbles in the sand. But the best thing he could remember was the ocean. Before his mother had died, she sometimes took Colton and Mai to the Iron beach together. It wasn't as nice as the Ivory one—the sand was more like rocks, the place reeked of tannery runoff and fish, and there was a bit more drug paraphernalia underfoot than was optimal, but Colton had been happy in those days. His mother would give them each a penny for shaved ice, and they would frolic in the water and try to catch pearled oysters.

Mai reached up and pinched his nose, her cheeks rosy with inebriation. "The best was in the winter, though, remember?"

The winter. How could he ever forget? He took her hand and kissed it, causing her to laugh and pull away in disgust.

"Colton, none of that! We broke up! Several times, if I recall! Go smooch Beaumont, he's the one you like." Mai stuck out her tongue, and he booped it with his finger, laughing until they both fell off her couch in a heap.

He waited until the following afternoon (which was ideal, as he needed to sleep off his hangover) and marched up to Lucian's apartment. Colton's heart bloomed with pleasure as his partner's face lit up upon opening the door.

"Hey! I was just thinking about you, actually—did you want to get started with our etiquette lessons?"

Colton laughed. "Nah, not quite yet. I had a better idea for today, actually." He cleared his throat. "I wanna take you out. Out of the Belt, beyond the city limits, just you and me, on a jolly adventure."

Lucian was laughing too now and shook his head. "Is that what we're calling it? Well, you know me, Colton, I'm never one to turn down a jolly adventure. I'll get my cloak."

They traveled south, down the marble steps and past the gates, beyond Indigo, beyond even the neighborhood that Colton called home. He wasn't certain that Lucian had ever been this far away from the Ivory towers, and he grabbed his wrist to hurry him onward.

"Colton, you must promise me we're not going to get murdered. It's going to be an awful lot of paperwork for my father's attorneys if I get killed in a warehouse that they own."

Colton laughed. "No promises, Beaumont. I want to get there soon. The sun's almost setting!"

To his credit, Lucian hardly complained as they walked past the very last buildings in the dock district, toward a dirt path that led them up toward the craggy cliffs that hugged the nation's borders. And still they walked, until eventually they could hear the roar of the sea and feel the salty air kissing them both on the neck.

They came to a rocky ledge, and Colton sat down, patting the earth so his partner might join him. Stretched out in front of them was the inky black ocean, dyed gold and red and pink as the sun set off in the horizon. Lucian sat down and let his legs dangle over the edge, his brilliant eyes piercing out over the sea.

"It—it's stunning, Colton," he said softly.

"Yeah, but it's nothing you can't see from your window," he chided. "The real show starts in a second."

The sun disappeared in the distance, then slowly the sky melted into an inky canvas outlined by the soft glow of the city in the distance. The only sounds were the churning of the ocean against the cliffs, and their own hearts beating.

"Lucian. Look."

A hundred—no, a thousand—glowing orbs began to emerge from the salty depths. Wave after wave of bioluminescent jellyfish were rising up to dance under the moonlight. They danced under the water, silent, glowing, a glittering galaxy beckoning through the darkness of the sea.

Lucian sat, mesmerized by the spectacle. Had he ever borne witness to nature's beauty? Had anyone taken him as a child to sit by the water and simply exist?

"Colton . . ."

"They come here every year. Only to this bay, only in the winter, only when the moon is full." Colton nudged their shoulders together and smiled. "I couldn't think of how else to repay you. You've done so much for me, you've changed my life, and . . . I just wanted to say thank you. For taking a chance on me. For being my partner."

He felt Lucian's heavy arm fall over his shoulders and leaned into the soft embrace. "It's my pleasure, Colton. It's difficult, in the Ivory District. Pit of vipers, you know, not easy to maintain friends with people who'd just as soon stab you in the back to secure your factory options. It's been a long time since I felt this close to anyone besides my sister."

"Does it lose some gravitas if I just say 'ditto'?"

"Ha! I'm glad to be on the same page, darling."

How natural it would have been to kiss like this. To arch his neck up and press his lips against the soft skin of Lucian's throat, to push him down onto the stone and see where the night took them. But he didn't. They sat there together, arm in arm, until they were too cold to bear it any longer. Then they hurried back to Colton's flat and warmed up with some spiced tea, cheeks red, mood light, and everything right in the world.

Colton hadn't had the luxury of much schooling as a child. He'd attended a local free school for boys until he was ten or eleven and had to drop out when his mother had fallen ill. He remembered enjoying it, the way chalk clicked against the blackboard, the way new books and scrolls smelled, having time to play with other children. He'd learned to read and write, and a little bit about Silvermoor's history. Up until now, he'd assumed that that had been enough.

That was until enduring the absolute hell that was Lucian Beaumont's etiquette lessons.

It wasn't that Lucian was a harsh taskmaster, nor that he was bad at teaching. Far from it—he was patient and gentle as ever. It was just *so much bullshit* that Colton had to pack into his head in a short amount of time, that there was a small part of him that yearned for the sweet release of death.

"So essentially, if it's sparkling wine you'll need to use this sort of glass"—he gestured to a narrow flute with a long stem—"and you're expected to extrude your pinkie while you drink. You should probably always have a glass of alcohol in your hand, but do your best not to become inebriated if you can avoid it. Now if they ask what *type* of wine you want, the easiest out is just to ask the sommel—"

Colton tried. He tried to listen, because of how important this was to his partner. But Lucian was so pretty, and the lessons were *so* boring, that he wasn't certain how much of this he was retaining.

One night, after it was becoming apparent that Colton was not paying attention to tonight's lesson of "how many buttons is it appropriate to have unbuttoned on a formal evening shirt," Lucian stood up and moved toward the enormous window in the living room.

"Colton, I want to show you something."

Lucian pointed at a large building off in the distance. "That's Beaumont House, our headquarters if you will." His finger drifted to an entire block of white marble apartment buildings. "Beaumont Flats. And there's Beaumont Port, Beaumont Vineyard, Beaumont Factory, *The Beaumont Times*, Beaumont blooming University."

This had been Lucian's birthright, his inheritance, the whole world beneath his fingertips before some bad decision or another had stripped it all away, before his father had cast him aside like he was nothing. Colton's eyes were wide. Was this what they were up against? Was it even possible to secure Odessa's future when their family had *that* much power?

"My father, and every influential person in the Ivory District, will be at this party, Colton. I've taken the liberty of preparing a little chart for you, full of the most likely people to attend the ball, and the ones it'll be most important to impress. With Ives out of the way, there's an instability in the Holy Order which leaves open some power gaps. He probably wasn't an active or helpful member for some time, but Haven is still an important voting block. We play our cards right, we can fill that niche and . . . well. Oh! Of course you wouldn't know. They pick Silvermoor's leader at this sort of thing. What do you think? Prime Minister Colton? You could do so much good."

Better than Prime Minister Lennox, surely. The ineffectual incumbent no one loved enough to endorse nor hated enough to assassinate.

Colton laughed. "When Prime Minister Beaumont was almost a

thing? I dare not! It's a bit of a stretch at this point, your majesty."

"That . . . wasn't my idea. I don't think I'm quite suited for politics."

"Why not? You've got the charisma and the name recognition."

Lucian rolled his eyes. "Yes, but not the drive or the instinct or the, you know, evil."

"I'm not going to point out that you just nominated *me* a moment ago."

"That might be for the best, darling." A slight pause. "The man who is engaged to my sister will be there as well, Colton. His name is Royce Chastain." Lucian's elegant finger pointed to a name on the chart, and Colton smiled at the immaculate script that he had obviously put so much effort into mastering. Under the name was a physical description, some information about property and background.

"Chastain is on a similar level to my family in terms of wealth and influence and will surely secure the lineage for generations in my stead, should the match go forward."

Lucian took a breath and calmed himself. "I'm not entirely sure which way it'll play out," he continued. "I'm starting to wonder if my plan can even work. I was so focused on getting the invitation that I hadn't really—I see her at the party, and then? I reassure her that—what? That I've secured a property or two and good luck with the marriage? I was imagining . . . I don't know, formally challenging Chastain or something, but he's as likely to ignore me as anything else. The last option would be to take her and flee, which would leave us vulnerable to—I'd say *lethal* methods on my father's behalf to get their last hope back."

He put a hand on top of Colton's. "I—I think I need your help, Colton, to rescue my Dessie."

Colton wasn't certain he'd ever heard Lucian speak like this. Vulnerable, bitter, and without a shred of confidence—a desperation that didn't suit him at all. It was almost humbling to be privy to this show of sincerity. "Of course I'll help you with this, you know that." He took Lucian's hand for a moment and squeezed it, offering up a small smile.

All at once, he remembered the way that Lucian's lips had felt on his own—the jolt of uncertainty, the fear in his eyes—and Colton let those elegant fingers go. He made his way toward Lucian's sofa and sat down, draping one arm over the back of the leather.

"I think the problem with your plan at the moment is there are a few too many variables. And the outcomes are a bit . . . well, suffice it to say it'll screw up my schedule if you have to be on the run from international assassins for the rest of your life." Colton could scarcely imagine it, Lucian roughing it in the woods, presumably with an equally spoiled and foppish sister at his side. They would bemoan the lack of warm running water in the bowels of a cave and complain when their gruel didn't come with a selection of microherbs sprinkled on top of it.

"But if I've learned anything from you, partner, it's that when the rules aren't in your favor to begin with, you change them, right?"

Lucian leaned against the wall and crossed his arms, a devious smile wafting over his face. "What did you have in mind, exactly?"

Colton leaned back on the couch, kicking his boots off and crossing one leg leisurely over the other. "You said your father picked him because of his name and influence, right? Your family seems a bit . . . sensitive about spiritual failings, no?"

"Hah. Don't I know the half of it."

"Any idea of what might make them rethink the match?" Not that he wanted to pry or anything, but Colton's curiosity was starting to get the better of him.

"They like the idea of morality, even if they don't practice it. Weakness, for example, or things that might be *embarrassing* to the Beaumonts." Lucian's cheeks flushed. "That name means more to my father than anything."

Colton nodded, considering. "Then why don't we drag his name through the mud so thoroughly that it would be an absolute *sin* if he were to sit at the same table as the Beaumonts?"

Lucian's smile only widened, the pink bow of his lips sliding easily over his perfect white teeth. "So if, for example, he were caught doing something so egregious, or with an association so politically unforgivable . . ."

"Exactly, my dear Lucian." Colton picked up one of the wine flutes Lucian had been using to teach him earlier and swirled the liquid, inhaling the aroma. "We schmooze, we chat, someone makes a scene, and then . . . we make him a man unworthy of your sister."

fifteen

Their goal was threefold—take down Chastain, make connections, and reunite Lucian with his sister, even for a moment.

"A direct approach might not be the best," Colton reasoned. "I mean, what's the plan? We somehow catch him in a compromising position at the ball, while you're there, in front of your father? The whole thing sort of screams 'Lucian's inanity' to me."

"You're right about that." Lucian stroked his chin. "All right. We can use this as a chance to lay down some traps. But I'll need your deft fingers, darling."

The plan was to engage Chastain, swipe the man's signet ring while he was distracted, then make a copy of it in wax so they could reverse engineer the seal. And with that, they could do whatever they wished. Hire whomever they wished, sign whatever contracts they saw fit. They'd engineer his downfall, make him into a pariah, tarnish his name so badly in the Ivory circles that no one would dare marry him to their daughters. The Beaumonts would rescind, reconsider their position, and they'd have bought some time for Odessa to figure a way out. It was risky, but it was a start. They'd have to be careful not to get caught, of course. Colton had noticed that Lucian never, ever wore the Beaumont ring. *His father might have forbidden it. The name is paramount, after all.*

"As for the rest of it, it would be best if I could avoid my father, if possible. He can be very antagonistic, and I've been known to lose my temper around him. That being said, if he approaches or engages us, then I'll do my best to be pleasant and cordial until he loses interest. Most likely, he will be unkind to you as well, depending on his mood. Please don't take it personally, he's awful." Lucian's jaw was tight and his eyes strained.

The exact circumstances of their falling out seemed to be quite a sore subject for Lucian still. Surely there was a kernel of good in Lucius Beaumont, if he had produced a son as lovely as Lucian?

Lucian swallowed. "I hope that meeting him will not alter your perception of me."

Colton gave him an incredulous look. "Lucian, how could my opinion of you possibly sink any lower?"

Lucian's face relaxed into a smile, and he flicked Colton on the forehead. "Be that as it may, you cur, I do hope you'll get the chance to meet my Dessie. Our father will likely try and keep us apart, but in such a public place it would be difficult for him to do so without embarrassing himself. You won't miss her—she and I could be taken for twins. She's *adorable*.

"As for you, I think you can just be yourself. They all imagine you to be some exotic beast of mystery and intrigue. We may as well play into that. I think we both know I'm not above theatrics." He winked. "Aaaaaand I suppose both of us should be on our best behavior, so no drinking or Blossom, yes? If we can find a ghost in the middle of the party and get it sorted, all the better. You can't even buy publicity like that."

Oh, no. Lucian was starting to have fun with this. Colton just leaned back on the couch and put his fist under his chin, watching the mania unfold with a smile.

Lucian booked an appointment with Kiara for the two of them, and Colton was happy to just get swept away with the madness this time. If getting new clothes for the ball would make Lucian feel more relaxed about the whole thing, then so be it.

"Don't show me the outfit yet," Lucian requested. "I want to see it on the night of the ball."

Like a wedding? Yeesh, Lucian.

The dreaded evening finally arrived, and Colton spent as much time as he could reasonably spare getting ready in his own flat. Mai came over to help him with his hair and applied just a smidge of makeup to make him look more mysterious and exotic.

The new outfit was one of charcoal-and-burgundy trousers, a jacket and vest, a wine-colored silk tie accented with affectations of the runes that ran down his chest. Kiara had outdone herself and made a cloak for him as well, studded with onyx and rubies, one that cast his face in shadow and danced around his feet as he walked. Mai had made up something like a circlet for him to wear as well, a strip of black leather with red sea glass woven into the strands. A stray tassel dangled on one side of his face and made him look . . .

"Like a prince, Colton!" Mai was very pleased with herself as she applied a bit of charcoal to the corners of his eyes.

Like a prince indeed. He barely even recognized himself these days, staring back at this handsome, dashing nobleman who looked back at him in the mirror. This was the sort of life his mother had dreamed for him, surely. The sort of life that he'd never dared to dream of for himself.

"And you definitely can't sneak me in?" she teased.

"Not without getting one of us arrested, probably."

She smoothed out his glossy black hair and looked into his eyes. "I'm really glad you've found your way. His Lordship seems to have been pretty good for you."

His cheeks flushed. *Yeah. He is.* Even if that never turned into romantic love, even if they never kissed again, this friendship had come to mean more to Colton than he could describe.

No one challenged him this time when he traipsed into the Ivory District, his cloak sweeping behind him like a nobleman's.

Being around Lucian had given him confidence, the knowledge that with a straight spine and an easy smile you could walk through almost any door in the world. So much of life was appearances, and the rest was what you made of it.

He arrived at Lucian's apartment and let himself in, sitting carefully on the couch this time to avoid wrinkling his clothes.

"Oi, princess! You ready yet?"

If Colton looked good in his new clothes, Lucian looked *magnificent*. The tailor had designed their outfits to complement each other, and Lucian was clad all in white and gold, dotted on the accents with sapphires that glittered in the light. He was royalty, he was elegance, and he practically glowed from whatever creams the spa had slathered on his face before Colton had arrived. Not a hair out of place, his smile serene, a sapphire at his throat, his cloak just kissing his neck and the tips of his feathery hair.

Best of all, though, was the look on Lucian's face as he beheld Colton in the dim light of the corridor: his eyes wide, mouth just open, cheeks flushing red as his delighted smirk bled across his features. "Colton. You're absolutely breathtaking."

Colton coughed and rolled his eyes, and he swept his cloak in a bow. "Why, thank you, my Lord." Sincerity reached his throat, and his expression softened. "You look really handsome, Lucian."

Lucian laughed and shook his head. "Then the illusion is complete. But seriously, darling, I'll be proud to have you at my side tonight."

Don't you dare blush, Colton. "Thanks, Beaumont. C'mon, if you're done being a mush, we probably need to get going."

As expected, Lucian had booked a frigging golden carriage pulled by two white horses with feathers on their heads. Lucian didn't like the mechanical coaches, apparently. The steam and the noise and the unprinceliness of it seemed to rub his aesthetic the wrong way. Colton buried his head in his hands as they trotted along the cobbles, just reveling in how *Lucian* this all was. "You never do anything by halves, do you?"

"What's the fun in that?" he grinned.

They arrived at the palace, all looming spires and gold-crusted statues, exotic trees casting shadows on the pavement that appeared to be literally lined with pearls. They were escorted in and announced at the top of a grand, spiraling staircase.

"Announcing young Master Lucian Beaumont, Ninth Archon of the Holy Order! And his companion Colton, no surname provided!"

Colton cast a glance at his partner, who was very clearly trying not to laugh. The partygoers had all looked up by then, and Lucian stood tall and proud, his chest puffed out just slightly as he sauntered his way onto the main floor. Colton did the same, walking shoulder to shoulder with Lucian, the pair of them a perfect weapon against the dark arts.

As they moved forward, Colton could hear the whispers ripple through the crowd. A murmur of admiration mixed with curiosity filled the room. Eyes followed them, conversations paused, and the murmurings grew louder.

"Isn't that the disgraced heir of Beaumont?"

"Yes, and his Iron Belt pet who's upended the district!"

"They're striking, aren't they? So handsome."

"He was almost the Prime Minister, you know. Poor Lucius must have been so disappointed when he dropped out of the race . . ."

"Surely they could try him again? Look at him! An *Archon*!"

Colton felt the weight of their stares, but he and Lucian kept their heads high, exuding confidence. He could sense the mixture of awe and scandalous curiosity directed at them. The stories of their exploits, the rumors surrounding Lucian's departure, and the sheer presence of two formidable exorcists had captivated the partygoers. For a moment, the entire room seemed to revolve around them, fascinated by the unlikely duo that had become the talk of the district.

Come in with a bang, not a whisper—that was what Lucian had wanted.

The hall was even more extravagant than the exterior of the palace. Every surface was lined with fine art, laced with gold and smelling like spices and wine. Perhaps a hundred servants mingled around the guests, arms heavy with trays of food and alcohol and other delicacies as they bent to the lords' whims.

Lucian accepted a glass of sparkling wine, which was nearly knocked out of his hand as a pair of slender arms wrapped around his neck and hugged him tightly.

"Lucian! You made it!"

Surely this was Lucian's sister. She was everything he'd described. Odessa was a vision of loveliness. A silken ivory gown accented with gold trailed all the way to the floor and whispered around her feet as she moved. It dipped down her back and exposed her flawless skin, highlighting her elegant neck, her trim waist. Her golden hair was braided and placed delicately over her head with yellow and white flowers woven through the tresses. Her smile was identical to Lucian's, and her blue eyes bore the same intelligence and curiosity.

"Dess! Easy, you'll smudge your lipstick!"

It seemed she didn't care. She pressed a kiss to his cheek anyway and left a perfect heart-shaped mark on his face. "Tough. I've missed you, and you're terribly neglectful of me."

"I know, I'm awful." He laughed. "I got you something to make up for it." Lucian reached into his pocket and pulled out a necklace that was surely from one of the shops they'd visited in the Iron Belt together. Colton recognized the craftsmanship. A choker made of delicate lace, shocks of cyan and lapis blending seamlessly together, tight and elegant like a spider's web that contained a spun opal gem to sit at the throat.

"Oh! Lucian, it's lovely! Put it on, put it on!" She turned around and lifted her hair, her foot tapping impatiently.

He smiled as he wrapped it around her neck and sealed the ties. "Am I forgiven, then?"

"For months of neglect? You think such trinkets will buy you the love of Odessa Beaumont?" She spun around, her eyes sparkling with mirth.

"Of course not, what a fool I am." He took her hand and squeezed it. "You look amazing, sweetheart."

"And you clean up well, I suppose." She huffed, sneaking a glance to see his wounded expression. And then her eyes fell on Colton. "Aren't you going to introduce me to your friend? Rude."

Lucian laughed. "Of course, petal. This is Colton, my partner in the exorcism business. He comes from a long line of demon slayers, the very embodiment of why the Cultural Protection Initiative was so necessary. He's brilliant and loyal. I trust him with my life in these matters." He gestured at Odessa. "And this is the irrepressible Odessa Beaumont, current Beaumont heir, my little sister, and the bane of my existence."

She elbowed him in the ribs, but Lucian smiled. The tiny heiress considered Colton for a moment, examining him from his toes to the top of his head like a serpent assessing a mouse. Yet her smile was warm, and she offered him her hand. "A pleasure. Thank you for tolerating my brother all this time and for preventing him from getting eaten alive by demons. I can't imagine it's easy, keeping him out of trouble."

"Oh, Lady Beaumont, you have absolutely no idea," Colton confessed, kissing her hand. "He is impossible to look after at the best of times. Couple that with a knife-wielding maniac, and I have my work cut out for me."

She giggled. "You do well, then, to keep him in relatively mint condition."

Both of the Beaumonts were scanning the ballroom, likely keeping an eye out for their father, not wanting to be caught together. From the sounds of things, he would not react well to seeing his banished child fraternizing with his heir, and would likely cause a scene. Besides, this was the best time for him to divulge their wicked scheme to the young lady. Once all was clear, Lucian suggested they mingle for a time, see what business they could drum up.

So Colton took a glass of wine and began to schmooze. It was difficult keeping track of all the people he was meant to be speaking with, though there were no shortage of nobles (mostly women, to be fair) who wanted a moment of his attention. He found himself completely surrounded at one point, three different elderly women each touching his hand and promising that their granddaughters were the most beautiful.

"Pardon me, but I must borrow Colton for a moment." Colton glanced up, his head cocked pleasantly to one side as he beheld the lovely Miss Radcliffe. She was glowing, her stomach barely noticeable under her dress, and took his arm in hers.

"You looked like you might need a rescue." She smiled. "I've been following your exploits, you know. I'm . . . I'm so pleased with your success, sir. You deserve only good things."

He smiled and patted her hand. "It all started with you, Miss. I trust all is well? How are you adjusting to being the lady of the house?"

"Better than expected. The house is . . . calmer now. Happier."

"Well, that's what happens when you remove a monster from your walls."

"I suppose it is. Shall we try and find your Beaumont? I have to imagine he might be similarly sieged."

Lucian, too, had been cornered, though there were far more Order officials at his coattails than lovely young women.

"You must—Lord Beaumont, you are the *Archon*!" One fussed as he was pushed out of the way by another.

"I can almost guarantee your success in the election—and you know Prime Minister Lennox is . . . well, he's so *opposed* to change, yes? Some fresh blood would be . . . beneficial."

His partner needed a rescue, and Colton barged in uncouthly. "Lucian. I'm out of wine." He glared at the Ministers and swayed slightly on his feet. "Lucian! Fix it!"

Lucian offered the Order members an apologetic smile. "Sorry, I must attend to my partner. An Archon's work is never done."

Lucian rustled Colton into a private corner and they shared a private smile. "I appreciate the timely intervention, darling. Another few minutes of that and I might have actually accepted the nomination to make them leave me in peace."

"Are you holding up okay? Is it weird to be back here?"

"It's strange. Like looking at my own life through a mirror, seeing this version of me which no longer exists." He shrugged. "It's been enlightening, I suppose. Most congratulate my success, are enamored and intrigued by our work. Most . . . see only the Archon, and whatever influence association with such a title might grant them. The odd one sneers, thinks he knows why I ended up here, thinks he's better than I am. Some don't care." He looked at Colton. "You've never really asked me about what happened. You must know by now that the official story isn't entirely accurate."

Of course Colton had been curious, but it seemed like such a risky subject to broach. "Do you want to tell me?" he asked softly.

But Lucian wasn't listening, his gaze trained across the room, his eyes narrow and sharp. "Come with me," he muttered, cracking his joyless smile across his face. "I think this might be our best opportunity. Follow my lead."

Colton followed as Lucian stormed across the floor, until he spotted the issue. Odessa was being held quite closely by a man twice her size. His hand was snaked around her waist, smoothing the fabric over the swell of her buttock and squeezing with impunity. Her tiny wrist was caught in his other hand, held firm.

"Royce!" she said sharply, anger sparking over her features. "This is neither the time nor the place!"

But Chastain ignored her, the ash from his cigar crumbling over her skin.

"Lord Chastain!" Lucian said magnanimously as he pulled his sister to his side. "What a nice surprise to run into you here! How are you? How's the wedding planning going?"

Odessa, trembling, glared daggers at her fiancé. Colton stayed on Lucian's right, his arms crossed and his head cocked to the side ever so slightly. He wanted it to be clear that should things devolve toward violence, Lucian would not be on his own.

"Ah. Lucian. I didn't think you'd show up this year," Royce drawled. "I hear your little project is going well? I suppose they'll make anyone Archon these days."

"The *Ninth Archon*," he retorted, though neither of them actually knew what that meant exactly. "Ah, Dessie, that reminds me, Father was looking for you near the entryway." A lie, surely, but a pragmatic one. The plan wouldn't work unless Lucian kept his cool, which was far easier when the object of his passion was not within range of molestation.

Odessa scampered off, and Lucian stepped close to the Lord, flashing his teeth in a smile. "You would do well not to besmirch my sister's honor before you are wed, Chastain. Do not test me." He grabbed Chastain's wrist, which of course caused a commotion and a kerfuffle amongst the gentry. Colton used the moment of confusion to hide his work as he slid the signet ring off the man's unoccupied and corpulent hand.

Lucian released him and smirked as he staggered backward, avoiding eye contact, muttering something about property and a woman's place and *blah blah blah*.

Chastain waddled off, and Lucian's shoulders sagged. "You can see why the matter is urgent."

Colton grasped Lucian's shoulder and smiled. "You're sweet with her, you know? It's nice to see."

"I'm sweet with everyone, Colton. You dare besmirch me in such a way?" But his smile was back, and the music swelled in the background. "Come." He pulled Colton onto the dance floor by his wrist. They weren't dancing together, obviously, but they were dancing in roughly the same space to the same song. As ever, this sort of closeness left Colton simultaneously pleased and mystified. The casual intimacy, the physicality—he loved it, he hated it, he wanted more. Lucian was a good dancer, likely a product of years of training, but despite Colton's lack of coordination and the unfortunate reality of having no sense of rhythm and a proportionally small bottom, he ended up really enjoying himself.

They were both glowing and a touch sweaty when the number ended, and they found they'd invited a hefty queue of women wishing to speak with both of them.

It was all a bit much, and Colton had to intervene when one of the women essentially worked Lucian's collar open and pressed a kiss to his throat. Lucian laughed it off, held his hands up in surrender, and took Colton to a nice, quiet corner where they could both unwind for a few minutes.

Had it always been like this for him? He'd mentioned Radcliffe fancying him when he was a young teenager. Lucian seemed very confident with women, good at getting them to move as he wished. How young had he been the first time someone had touched him? It broke Colton's heart to see him respond to molestation with a smile and a laugh, but that was Lucian. Hells, even Colton had kissed him without asking first. *Sorry, Lucian.*

He had to wonder what Lucian's love life had been like, prior to their meeting. It wasn't like he'd ever seen Lucian dating anyone, or actually show any serious romantic interest in anyone since they'd known each other. Colton had sort of assumed he was the type of man who never really got too close to anyone romantically, but maybe had private romps every once in a while to keep himself sane. It was quite odd for a man of Lucian's standing and age not to be married yet, frankly, and Colton had a sneaking suspicion he knew what the core of the issue was. Maybe he wasn't "the marrying type."

Another question was why he never looked at Colton that way.

Colton's own exposure to sex had been more natural, he thought. People his own age, men and women both, messing around at parties or in back alleys, laughing as they tumbled in the sand.

Lucian didn't seem too bothered, though. Colton sighed and licked his thumb, wiping the lipstick away from Lucian's face and neck. "Look at the state of you. Such a mess! I can't take you anywhere, Beaumont."

Lucian smiled, and Colton smiled back. What was he even worried about? They were partners now, and they could protect each other from anything. Colton fanned his fingers through Lucian's hair, brushing it neatly over his forehead with a smile.

Lucian froze where he stood, his eyes wide and his grin banished.

"Lucian, what . . . ?"

Oh, *hells*.

Colton looked up and spotted a good-looking older man storming toward them. His hair was a luxurious gold, iced here and there with a fleck of white, and his eyes were sapphire oceans. There was no mistaking the resemblance.

Lucius Beaumont.

sixteen

"Lucian!" the man hissed, seemingly trying to minimize the number of people who might hear this altercation. "What do you think you're doing?"

"What do you mean, Father?"

Colton had never seen Lucian like this, pale and wide-eyed, his hands clenched and motionless behind his back.

"You know what I mean, boy." Lucius pinched the bridge of his nose. "Carrying on like this, in front of all these people. Look at you!" He gestured at his torn-open shirt, his tousled hair, at Colton standing beside him. "You think *this* is going to get you back into my good graces? You think *this* is what the Beaumont heir should be doing? *What the Ninth Archon should be doing?*"

"*Ex*-Beaumont heir," Lucian clarified with a wary smile. "Your idea, if I recall."

"You impertinent little shit," Lucius spat. "You must be so proud of yourself, mincing around, whoring your so-called skills to every dried-up cunt in the city. Lucian Beaumont, my disgraceful mistake, and his charity gutter-slut, wading through the misery of his betters, playing at divinity for laughs."

Colton was motionless, scared that even a breath out of place would cause everything to descend into chaos. He'd long suspected Lucian was on the more sparkly side of things, and knew that Ivory men tended to shy away from such things, but . . . this seemed so extreme. Lucian hadn't harmed anyone, had he? *You'd throw your son away over this?*

Lucius showed no mercy. "If *my* father had disowned me, I would have spent every waking second trying to redeem myself, prove myself, get back into the home I deserved. Not you, Lucian, no. You took your disgrace and wrapped it around yourself like a badge of honor, shacking up with *this*." He gestured at Colton, his words dripping with venom. "In public, no less. I gave you *every chance*, boy. All the money in the world to show me that you had *anything* in you that was worthwhile. How hard was it? Marry Grace, run the campaign properly, show me some *fucking backbone*. Do something, be someone—and you couldn't even—" He shook his head. "Does it mean so much to you? You'd ruin your little sister's life for *this*?"

So that was it? Lucian wasn't *strong enough? Obedient enough?* Contradiction in terms there, Lucius. This was a topic he'd somewhat purposefully avoided around Lucian, historically. It was uncomfortable for both of them, although admittedly for very different reasons, and Colton had let the matter drop. Was that why he'd rejected Colton? A fear of further alienating his father?

Colton put a hand on his back, and Lucian flinched away. *Bingo.*

Lucian quivered, helpless with humiliation and indignity. Lucius carrying on like this in front of his peers, the Order, his sister, his partner. Colton could barely chase all the emotions that flitted across Lucian's face—in all their time together, he couldn't think of a time he'd seen him so helpless.

"I never—*you're* the one who's marrying her off to that miserable—"

The air cracked so loudly with the force of the blow across Lucian's face that a couple of nearby party guests looked up to see what had happened.

"Never speak that way to me again, Lucian. *You* are the one who doomed your family and never looked back. Never forget that, boy. That *you* are the problem. You're better off with the demons, perhaps. At least they might understand you."

Lucian stood tall as he watched his father walk away. Colton had to imagine much of his adolescence had been like this: loud, harsh, forcing him not to react for fear of tempting more abuse.

Lucian's feet moved on their own, sometimes. When they were in a tight spot during a job, or when Colton was in danger, his mind turned off in those moments, his face went blank, and he ran. So it was at the ball. He brushed past the crowd, the entryway, and it wasn't long before Colton couldn't even see him anymore.

"Pathetic. Your Archon, ladies and gentlemen," Lord Beaumont muttered, adjusting his collar before sweeping off, failing to even acknowledge Colton.

"You're wrong," Colton called after him, his hands trembling at his sides. "And you're a fool to have thrown away such a wonderful son. You don't deserve him."

But the Lord didn't even turn around. It didn't bother Colton one little bit that Lord Beaumont thought he was worthless. But seeing Lucian's pain was something else, something he couldn't stomach for any amount of money.

The music was beginning to die down, and Colton pushed through the crowd to find his partner. It didn't take long. Lucian was leaning against a gilded railing at the edge of a snow-covered balcony.

The cacophony of the party stilled to nothing as he broached the outdoors, and, silent as the night, he sidled up beside Lucian and joined him, staring out into the twinkling lights of the city. What could he say that would make any of this better? Even in the dim light from the ballroom, he could see the sting on Lucian's cheek, his eyes red and distant.

"I kinda wanted to leave anyway," Colton said casually, watching his words turn to mist in the cool night air. "I never knew my father, you know. It was just me and my mom growing up until she died. I used to always wonder what kind of man he'd been, but to be honest, he was probably a prick."

Smile. C'mon, Lucian, please.

His partner wouldn't even look at him.

"Lucian." Wearily, the young Lord Beaumont met Colton's eyes. "Your father is wrong. Everything bad that's ever happened in your life, Lucian, it's not your fault. There is nothing wrong with wanting to be who you are or loving whomever you want to love." He touched their foreheads together and put a hand on his shoulder. "You are not broken, Lucian. I promise you, you aren't. But it's going to destroy your soul if you listen to men like your father who don't care about you."

Lucian said nothing. His gaze fell back to the gold-plated metal railing beneath his arms.

"I guess it's easy to say that, isn't it? Words are cheap," Colton continued, almost wincing at the pain still cut through Lucian's eyes. "But they hurt like a bitch, don't they?"

A beat of silence followed, and Colton carefully touched the corner of Lucian's jaw, gently tilting his face so their eyes could meet once more. Lucian didn't want to be Prime Minister. Lucian was gay. So what? So fucking what? He was still a good man, a great one! And Colton adored him just the same either way. Lucian being gay was actually a huge positive in that department. And what Lucian needed now, more than anything, was to know he was worthy of love, in every form.

"We . . . could leave," Colton started, letting go of Lucian's face as his hands moved to his chest, carefully buttoning his shirt back up so he looked more tidy. "We . . . could stay." He gently put his hand on Lucian's cheek, swiping his thumb over the angry red mark his father had left on his face. "We've got Chastain's ring already. Mission accomplished. Whatever you want," Colton said softly, keeping careful eyes on Lucian's expression. "Tell me, and I'll follow you."

Tears bloomed in Lucian's eyes, and he covered them for a

moment, angrily wiping the moisture away with his wrist. "Sorry," he muttered. "I think I'd like to go in again," he admitted, his fingers itching at his cuff links. "Show my father I won't be so easily silenced or intimidated. But my face probably looks quite a mess, I imagine." He forced a laugh. "It's not . . . so out of the realm of possibility that I might have been slapped for being a cad. I don't know. Surely some people saw."

And that shame, apparently, belonged only to Lucian. A father disciplining his disappointment, a Beaumont establishing his control over the Order. *Fuck these Ivory pricks.*

"I've also taken more Blossom than was wise, I think. I might not be able to carry myself in a manner befitting our station. I might also die." Another strange laugh. "It's a struggle to speak."

"What?" Colton grabbed Lucian by the shoulders and looked into his eyes. He could barely see his irises, his pupils were so wide—fuck! He pressed two fingers against the Lord's neck and tried to take a pulse. Slow, maybe a bit irregular. "How much did you take, Lucian?"

"All of it."

A small vial lay beside Lucian's polished boot, cap askew, the snow dyed pink beside it. A lethal dose, maybe, even though he was a regular user.

"Thank you, Colton. You don't know what this means to me. I care about you so . . . so much." Lucian's eyelids fluttered, and Colton caught him as his knees buckled. Fuck.

"Lucian," he snapped, shaking his partner brusquely. "Lucian, look at me."

Glazed-over eyes blinked at him, a dopey smile followed, and Lucian's head lurched forward. Oh, hells, they had to get inside *now*. "C'mon, you moron, we need to get out of the cold—maybe someone inside has something we can use or—"

He dragged Lucian by the wrist back into the ballroom, only to be greeted almost immediately at the door by Odessa. Surely she'd heard some of the commotion or seen her father afterward. Her brow creased with concern when she saw Lucian's poor red face, and a flash of anger crossed her eyes.

"Dammit, Lucian," she muttered, cupping his face and holding him close. "You mustn't let him wind you up so. How much did you take, you idiot?"

Lucian only laughed in response, and Odessa huffed at him. She flitted through her purse and took out a blue glass vial of Seabreeze, flicking the top off and holding it under her brother's nose. "Breathe deep, stupid. I'm not planning a funeral and a wedding at the same time; it's beneath me."

By this point Lucian could barely stand on his own, and Colton had pulled one of Lucian's arms over his shoulder and was doing his best to keep him upright.

"Lucian!" Odessa gently smacked his unwounded cheek. "C'mon, we've got to get you home, okay? Yoo-hoo, Lucian!" Lucian blinked at her, and she rolled her eyes. "Honestly, he's always bad with our father. But he hasn't done something this foolish in a very long time." Her cheeks colored with pretty embarrassment. "I thank you for your kindness, for looking after him." She curtseyed, covering Lucian's ears with her hands. "He's worth it, I promise."

I know.

Odessa took Colton by the wrist and dragged both him and Lucian outside to where the carriages waited.

"Here." Odessa pressed several gold coins into Colton's hand. "Take him home in a carriage. I want to know that he made it there safely, and I can't—" She peered behind her, surely looking for her father or fiancé. "The plan sort of falls apart if I run off now, yes? We all have our parts to play."

"I'll protect him," Colton promised, squeezing her hand.

Mechanical horses snorted steam from their nostrils, and Colton eased Lucian into the carriage. Lucian's bright eyes were glazed over as he stared at nothing, but it seemed as though the Seabreeze was working. *Just . . . stay with me, okay?* "Heh. I don't think I've ever had you be quiet during a carriage ride." Colton gazed out the window. "You really scared me, you prick. I don't want you to let anyone hurt you like this ever again. You're better than this, Lucian."

He had to pay the carriage driver a little extra to get Lucian into the ascension box so they wouldn't have to wrestle with the stairs. Colton tucked him into bed and pulled up a chair beside him, pressing a cool damp towel to his forehead and watching the steady puffs of his breath while he slept the worst of it off. Only after Lucian's shivering subsided, after his breathing became more regular, did Colton allow himself to rest. He nestled his head in the nooks of his arms at the edge of Lucian's bed.

Dawn broke over the city the following morning, casting a warm golden glow between the ivory spires of the district. Colton woke with a start, his neck sore and eyes wide as he crawled forward on the mattress to make sure that Lucian had survived the night.

Lucian opened his eyes blearily, croaking a laugh as his gaze settled on Colton. "Morning, precious," he muttered. "What happened?"

Colton was so relieved that he more or less collapsed into a hug, squeezing Lucian like he meant to pop him. "Kind of a crazy night, don't you remember?" His voice was cracking. "You really, really scared me. I thought you were gonna die in my arms, I thought . . . I thought I was gonna lose you."

He held Lucian, breathing in the soft vanilla scent of his skin. He was here, this was real, and Colton almost didn't dare to let go.

Lucian's hand went to the swollen red patch that had bloomed on his cheek. "Colton, I'm so, so sorry. I acted like an idiot, I made a fool of myself and put you in a very unpleasant and unfair situation. What you must think of me," he whispered.

Colton took Lucian's hand and brought it up to his lips, pressing a soft kiss to the heel of his palm. "My opinion of you hasn't changed. You're still a smarmy prick and an inconsiderate addict, but you're brilliant and sweet, and I care about you more than anyone else on this continent."

"Just the continent?" Lucian said with a laugh, his face weary.

"Fine, the world." Their eyes met. "I *adore* you, stupid. And knowing you have a miserable beast of a father doesn't change that. Happy now?"

Lucian licked his lips. "Do you want to ask me anything about what happened?"

Colton shook his head. "Just . . . whatever you want to tell me." He had put most of it together in his mind, but he was happy to listen.

Lucian sat back and rubbed the side of his face. "It's not such an unusual story, I suppose. When I was younger, I found myself attracted to . . ." He hesitated, his whole face pained.

Colton squeezed his hand. "Lucian, it's all right. You're not in a good place right now. We don't need to do this today." It couldn't have been easy for Lucian to give voice to a secret that had essentially destroyed his family and ruined his life. "But I want you to know that you don't have anything to fear from me on that end, okay? Hells, I already tried to kiss you—I think that probably tells you everything you need to know." He laughed.

"We never really talked about that, did we?" Lucian said quietly.

"I wanted to respect your decision. You made your feelings clear, and I was okay with that. Being your friend was enough."

Lucian took his hand and squeezed it. "I want to go back to that moment, precious. When we were trapped in that dungeon, covered in the blood of a maniac, and all we had was each other. I looked at you, and I just thought, *I can trust this man with my life.*"

But not with your secret. The shame that ran so deep that he wouldn't even begin broaching the subject with his partner. Colton was exhausted.

Lucian threaded his fingers with Colton's then, allowing a cautious smile to grace his lips. "It scared me. When you kissed me— how right it felt. How much my heart sang with the thought of you, how . . . I just wanted more."

Colton didn't want to move in case he broke the spell. Lucian loved him. Wanted him. Had felt this way all along. If he wasn't careful, he was worried he might actually float away.

"Close your eyes," Lucian said, his own eyelids sliding shut as he spoke. "We're in the dungeon, Ives is dead—I've got your hand in mine because all I can think is how awful it would be if you lost your hand to gangrene, and we're standing close. And I say, 'You saved me. You saved both of us. And I'm so, so grateful to you.' And our eyes meet . . ."

Colton opened his eyes in that moment and saw Lucian had done the same.

"And we lean in closer and . . ." Their lips were almost touching.

"And you're out of your mind if you think I'm kissing you again before you've had a shower and brushed your teeth, Beaumont," Colton said with a smirk. "You smell like a drug house, and I spent the whole bloody night taking care of you. The *least* you could do is be presentable."

Lucian huffed a laugh, and they both rose up from the mattress, the Lord staggering from the lingering effects of the Blossom. He headed to the bathroom with one hand on the wall, but Colton tugged on his sleeve and stood beside him.

"Oh, and Lucian?" He cupped the sides of his face and pressed his lips against Lucian's, but only for a moment, before resting their foreheads together and staring into his eyes. "Never scare me like that again."

Lucian's laugh was like bells, and he kissed Colton's neck. "Never again," he promised. "Never."

seventeen

Colton ended up helping Lucian out of his clothes and into the shower. He'd never really imagined that his first time undressing his partner would be anything like this, with Lucian barely able to stand on his own and reeking of Blossom. It didn't matter, though—Colton was practically walking on air.

His energy that morning mirrored Lucian's on a normal day, as he flitted around the bathroom like a forest nymph. He readied all of the Lord's usual perfumed soaps and lotions, filled the porcelain tub with warm water, and ensured that the towels were suspended over the steam-powered heaters.

"You won't drown if I leave, will you?"

"I can only endeavor to do my best, precious." Lucian held onto his partner's arm as he stepped into the tub, groaning softly with pleasure and relief as he submerged himself.

Colton pressed a kiss to the top of his head. "Just shout if you start to go under, all right? I'm going to make some tea."

He sincerely doubted that Lucian would be able to stomach anything other than plain porridge this morning, and he began to heat some fresh milk up on the stovetop. As for what to drink, maybe an herbal tea would be best, something with chamomile and mint, and a twist of lemon—easy on the stomach and calming to the nerves. Thank goodness they'd gotten the Seabreeze in him in time, but with the amount of Blossom that Lucian had taken, it wasn't unreasonable to think that there might be some lingering side effects.

He couldn't help but think of Mai and how much he must have worried *her* back in the day. There had been a time after his mother had passed away when his drinking had gotten out of control, if she was to be believed. Back then Colton had thought she was exaggerating, and it had led to them breaking up for the first time (and then the second, and the third, and the last) when he refused to adjust his behavior in any meaningful way. Now, though, as he looked out of Lucian's massive window over the sparkling ocean on the horizon, Colton's stomach clenched as he imagined what it must have been like for Mai—hunched up over his bed, watching him breathe, wondering if maybe that binge had gone one drink too far. If he'd be sick in the night, choke to death on his vomit. Fuck. He needed to apologize to that woman, probably several times, and probably with a fruit basket. Everyone liked fruit baskets.

He never wanted to go through anything like that again. "I might die," Lucian had said, like it was nothing out of the ordinary. Colton wasn't sure he'd felt fear like that since Ives had assured him that his partner had been killed.

Today was about celebration—that Lucian was alive, that they weren't hiding from each other anymore, that they'd survived the ball and that they'd secured a means to destroy Chastain once and for all, hopefully.

Colton's anxiety was creeping back up his neck, and he abandoned the stove for a moment to ensure Lucian hadn't slid into the bathtub and drowned like a slug. His face relaxed immediately as he spotted his partner sitting comfortably amongst the bubbles, already partially refreshed.

"Oh, darling, I'm glad you're here. I was about to attempt to wash my hair, but I'm terribly weak from the party, you see. I have the dreaded noodle arms. You couldn't possibly be tempted to . . ."

"To shampoo you like one of those floofy dogs that parade

around the Ivory District? Lucian, you're mad." But Colton moved toward him anyway, sliding to his knees and pushing his sleeves up to his elbows. "You are *so* spoiled," he grumped, lathering Lucian's hair with a liquid that smelled of peaches and vanilla.

Lucian leaned his head back, his eyes slipping shut as he enjoyed his massage. "You're the best, sweetheart." His masculine fingers caught Colton's wrist and pulled his soapy hand forward, allowing Lucian to press a kiss to the heel of his palm.

Colton couldn't stop the surge of affection that filled up his chest and painted a smile over his lips. It was like being in school again, sharing a kiss with Orr in a corridor between classes. "You can finish your own bath, you smarmy bastard. I need to make sure I don't burn the building down."

Lucian flicked some water at him, and Colton stole *all* of the nice warm towels and brought them with him to the kitchen. *Take that, Beaumont.*

The milk was just coming up to temperature, and Colton added some oats and honey to the pot. Simple things like cooking for someone he cherished brought him so much happiness, though he couldn't believe he'd found any kind of fulfillment in domesticity. He wondered if his mother had felt like this, looking after him when he was little. He remembered her warm hand brushing the top of his head while he watched her cook, her colorful apron, the twirl of cinnamon bark she put in his tea. After she'd passed away, the loss of that tender, nurturing warmth had been the most difficult thing to manage. Mai had been a nurturing presence in his life from time to time, but Colton leaned into it too much, and she'd grown to resent him.

Lucian came trudging out of the bathroom eventually, stark naked, dripping water everywhere, leaning on the wall for support. *Hells*, he had a fantastic body—muscular and tight in all the right places, skin that had never known the mark of a whip or—

"You stole my towels, Colton." Lucian was apparently trying very hard to look severe. "This must be answered for."

They both eyed the sofa where Colton had left the towel bounty and simultaneously made a run for it. Lucian, having wet feet, wound up slipping right at the finish line, and of course Colton caught him around the waist and held him upright, cocking an eyebrow from above him. "I can't help but think, my dear Lucian, that you fell on purpose." He helped his partner to his feet and handed him a towel.

"Would I *ever* do such a thing, sweetheart?" Lucian smiled as he wrapped the fluffy cloth around his waist.

"Yes. Because you're unbearable. Go lie down. I'll bring you some tea in a minute."

A sprinkle of cinnamon and a few slices of banana later, the porridge was spooned out into one of Lucian's fine china bowls and placed on a tray along with some tea, some silverware, and a fresh daisy in a tiny flute vase that Lucian had in his cupboard.

Colton carefully brought the tray to the bedroom and set it down on the mattress so Lucian could eat without having to move or expend too much effort. "Take it slow," he cautioned. "That much Blossom is hell on your body. I don't want you throwing up in bed."

Lucian smiled at him and took a sip of tea. "I will. Thank you, Colton."

As much as Colton would have liked to join Lucian for breakfast, the previous night's excitement had just about caught up with him. "I need to lie down, Lucian. Some of us didn't get to sleep off a Blossom overdose last night."

"Of course, precious. Take as much time as you need. I won't bother you unless I start dying again."

A welcome suggestion. Colton peeled off his socks and curled up on the mattress next to his partner—romantic partner now, he supposed—pulling the blankets around him like a nautilus shell and falling asleep in a matter of moments.

He didn't dream, which was probably for the best. Bad things happening to Lucian had become something of a fixture in Colton's unconscious, which made restful sleep difficult. In the dreams, sometimes Lucian was clinging to life, a dribble of blood running down his chin as his eyes begged for aid; sometimes he was dead already, evidence of hours of torture and desperate suffering, his fingernails gone, teeth ripped out, the echoes of his voice still wafting through the air . . .

Colton. Help me, please. Please, it hurts. I didn't want this. Help me. Help me.

In the mornings, Colton would wipe the tracks of salt away from his eyes and put his head in his hands, reminding himself that Lucian was safe, that they were so much stronger together.

He woke up a few hours later with a start, disoriented and unfamiliar with his surroundings—a luxurious canopy bed with blue silk and velvet covers, the aroma of vanilla and almonds, Lucian sitting beside him, and—oh.

"Good morning, sunshine," Lucian said affectionately, pushing a stray lock of hair out of Colton's face. "How are you feeling?"

"Happy we're finally doing this. Excited about lots of things. Seeing you naked in a proper context, for example. Confused about why you didn't tell me how you felt before. Worried about what the future is gonna bring, how this'll change things for us. Angry." That was hard to admit. "Because your selfishness last night was pretty fucking awful."

Lucian's smile faded, and he folded his hands in his lap. "I'm so sorry, Colton. I don't expect your immediate forgiveness, but I want you to know that I'm kicking myself for what happened, and I'll do everything in my power to prevent its recurrence."

Colton sat up and cupped Lucian's face. "Tell me what happened. Not at the party, before that, when your relationship with your father first began to fall apart."

Lord Beaumont leaned into the touch and shut his eyes. "I was never good enough, never what he wanted in a son. When I was younger, I became very good at dancing on strings for him, getting the best marks in school, excelling in sports, riding, whatever it was he threw at me. All I ever wanted was to make him happy, make him proud." Lucian sighed.

"As I got older, it became more and more apparent that I wasn't the ruthless creature that he had envisioned taking over the business or going into politics. Still, he did whatever he saw fit to keep me on the right path. Little by little, he chipped away at the parts of my life which brought me joy. He got rid of my cat because I loved her too much. Sold my violin because it was making me 'soft.' Sent me off to boarding school so I couldn't see Odessa anymore. He clearly thought I couldn't be trusted with my own future."

Colton tried to imagine what his life might have been like if his mother had treated him like that. Robbing him of toys and frivolity, forbidding him to be friends with Mai, forcing him to study the demonic arts to the exclusion of all else, until he had become her. He couldn't see it. All she'd wanted was his happiness.

"I was maybe thirteen or fourteen," Lucian continued. "Right around the age my friends were starting to notice the young ladies in our class, and I just . . . wasn't doing that. I remember being at a party around that time, being pushed into a cupboard with a Baron's daughter and being expected to . . ." He shook his head. "I did it. Kissed them, danced with them, acted like the whole thing wasn't absolutely repulsive to me. It wasn't an easy thing, growing up in the Ivory District while preferring the company of other lads. My father could overlook it, to a point. As long as I played the part of the son he always wanted, I don't think he cared that much."

Lucian let out a long, soft breath, and Colton squeezed his hand.

"I lost my virginity when I was fourteen to a grown woman at a party who had always taken an interest in me. I remember how I'd had to close my eyes the whole time, how she took the initiative and"—he shuddered—"my father was so proud. I came out of whatever broom closet she'd dragged me to, covered in lipstick and sweat, and he just squeezed my shoulder and smiled."

Lucian took a deep breath and shook his head. "The boarding

school ended up being a blessing in disguise, I suppose. Up in the mountains, away from him, an all-boys institution designed to turn little lords into the great leaders of tomorrow, and I suppose I found my niche, shall we say. I imagine for most of them it was just a convenient outlet. But for me, it was everything, Colton. Suddenly I wasn't repulsed by the touch of another human being, I was engaged and aroused and . . . and everything I'd ever been taught to reject and deride." He smiled.

"I knew the game, Colton. Lots of men in the Ivory circles have such preferences, and go on to live perfectly successful and pleasant existences . . . they just have to suck it up and spend the rest of their lives with someone they don't really love."

It had been so different for Colton. His first time had been with Mai—all awkward kisses, noses colliding, giggles and gasps and stolen prophylactics. They hadn't been serious, then, and so, a few weeks later, when Orr had come up and expressed an interest of his own, Colton had been more than happy to see just how the two of them fit together. There had been no shame, no ridicule, just . . . fun. Warmth. Expressions of love that only teenagers were capable of. He could hardly imagine hating such an intrinsic part of himself, let alone trying to bury it deep within him.

"The first time my father found out, I was probably seventeen. I'd been careless. We'd not locked a door, one of the maids had heard or seen something, I don't know. He just . . . was so cold, Colton. So disgusted. My reputation, our future, everything that mattered to him was on the line and he made me *swear* I wouldn't be so careless again. And I wasn't, for a while. I flirted with girls like I was supposed to. I even had a fiancée near the end." He swallowed.

"Maybe a year ago, he caught me in the act again, right as my political campaign was gaining steam. He has this . . . quiet fury, Colton. This way of looking at you that makes you feel like you're worth absolutely nothing. I just thought, this is ridiculous, I'm happy, I'm not hurting anyone, what in the seven hells is his problem? I don't know what came over me, but I told him I wasn't going to put up with it anymore. I wouldn't marry Grace, I wasn't going to be Prime Minister, I was just going to be me." Lucian shook his head. "He left without a word. Stripped me of everything except that piddling little allowance. My title, my inheritance, my family. If Odessa hadn't intervened, then he would have thrown me out onto the streets with nothing."

Lucian took Colton's hand and threaded their fingers together. "It was a blessing in disguise, I think. To be free of his expectations, to live as I wished, to forge out a future of my own. But . . . there's this part of me that just wants him to . . . accept me the way I am. Flawed. Ridiculous. Be happy for me, if I married for love."

Colton's heart was aching. He couldn't bear to imagine little Lucian, all bright-eyed and apple-cheeked, being struck down for the sin of being too gentle, too kind. He lurched forward and pulled Lucian into his arms, swearing to the bottom of his very soul that he would never let anything harm this man again.

"What were you thinking when I kissed you?" Colton whispered, his lips against Lucian's ear. "You were so startled."

Lucian pulled away just so their eyes could meet. "That I didn't want you dragged into this nonsense with my family. That it might spoil the partnership, the friendship, because I'd never really been *serious* about someone before. That it was possible my father would find out, and want to cause you harm. I loved you too much to lose you."

"I dunno, Lucian, I'm pretty tough." He smiled.

"And you don't find any of this pathetic?" Lucian's voice was small.

"Of course not." Colton swiped his thumb over Lucian's cheekbone. "When I was little, my mother always taught me that love comes in all shapes and sizes. It doesn't matter what color they are, where they're from, what their bits look like. What matters is who they are in here." He touched Lucian's chest. "And I've never really cared about anything else."

That was the difference, maybe, between Ivory and Iron. Iron didn't care about appearances, didn't mind what you did or who you did it with. Morality, spirituality, it all came down to how you treated others and not how you performed on the world stage.

Lucian cupped Colton's face and drew their faces together. "And you promise this won't ruin our partnership?"

"How could it?" Colton asked, straddling Lucian's lap. "We battle demons every day, and I promised to stick by your smarmy ass. You think *this* is gonna be the thing that breaks us?"

"You're right," he breathed, pressing their lips together. "We're in this together. To the bitter end, Colton."

eighteen

They slept for most of the rest of the day, and by the next morning Lucian was still in no condition for them to do anything but kiss. Colton found he didn't care one little bit.

Ever since the initial smooching incident, Lucian had been obviously and intentionally holding back on being physically affectionate with his partner. He'd *missed* these little touches, the way Lucian's elegant palms had felt against his shoulder, how safe he'd felt when those long fingers caught his wrist.

The floodgates had burst now, and they could scarcely keep their hands off one another.

"We might want to establish some ground rules," Colton reasoned, his cheeks flushing while Lucian kissed up his neck. "Like, do we want to be exclusive? Should we have a hands-off rule while we're working? That sort of thing."

"What's this? Colton being the sensible one?" He could feel Lucian's lips smirking against his skin. "I think I'd like to be exclusive, darling, if that's all right with you. It's not like I've been especially sexually active since the whole business with my father."

The realization that he hadn't even considered sex with anyone else since he'd met Lucian hit Colton with an awkward laugh. *Oof, you've got it bad, kid.* "Works for me," he said as casually as possible. *Can't let Lucian get a bigger head than he already has.*

"As for messing around at work, I think it's probably for the best if we keep friskiness to a minimum. That being said, I've often imagined us getting into mischief on some of those overnight jobs. I say we approach such matters on a case-by-case basis."

Colton grinned. "Agreed." He pushed Lucian's face away from his neck and offered a hand to shake. "To a whole new era of our partnership."

"May it be as fruitful and dramatic as everything else so far," Lucian concurred, gripping Colton's hand firmly.

"Please, no."

"Oh, darling, you're no fun at all." He smiled. "Now, where were we?" His nimble fingers found the parting of Colton's shirt and started working the buttons open, pressing soft little kisses to each inch of skin as it was exposed.

"Lucian!" A sharp knock at the door. "Did you die? I'm probably entitled to some of your possessions if you did!"

It was Odessa. Colton didn't have it in him to be cross with her for interrupting. He wasn't sure what he would have done without her the night of the ball.

"Just a minute, kitten!" Lucian called. "I'm terribly indisposed at the moment!"

"Ugh. Make yourself presentable in a timely fashion, dear brother. I am not particularly interested in seeing you naked after all the other wretched things you've put me through in the last forty-eight hours. You have *three minutes* before you incur my wrath!"

Lucian huffed a laugh and kissed Colton's forehead. "You heard the lady. Get changed, sweetheart, I'll be fine."

He and his partner emerged at roughly the same time, with barely ten seconds left on the clock before Odessa murdered her brother. Somehow Lucian had managed to put himself together impeccably, even with the evening they'd had. Colton would need to ask him what sort of age-defying creams he had in his private bathroom. Surely there were some ground-up orphan souls in there? No one was *that* good-looking without some sort of evil magic.

Lucian opened the door with a flurry, and Odessa burst in, wrapping her arms around her brother's neck and nearly bowling him over. "Lucian!" She giggled as he tried to keep his feet on the ground and lifted her into the air. "You didn't die in a pool of your own vomit?"

"I have darling Colton to thank for that," he said affectionately, giving him a nod.

Odessa smiled as Lucian set her on the ground, taking one of Colton's hands and giving it a squeeze. "I owe you a great deal, then. Colton, thank you. He is absolutely dreadful, but I am appreciative that you kept him alive for me all the same."

As ever, the little Miss was a vision of loveliness. She had traded her floor-length ball gown for an elegant seafoam winter coat, the hood lined with pure white rabbit fur. She removed it with a flourish and handed it to her brother, winking at Colton as Lucian let it drop to the floor in a heap.

"My darling little sister, you seem to have me confused with the help."

"My darling elder brother, you seem to have me confused with someone who didn't save your life two nights ago."

"How did you get away?" Lucian asked, mournfully collecting and hanging up her coat properly as he led her to the sitting room.

Odessa smirked. "Well, after your run-in with Father, he's just been in a terrible tizzy," she scoffed, causing her blonde locks to flurry around her beautiful face. "And of course Royce is all worked up about you besmirching his name or some such foolishness, so Father had to attend to *him* and then all the post-ball thank you cards, so with all that going on I was able to slip out under the guise of going shopping. Of course, this means I must bring something to prove my errand was true." She took an apple off the counter and put it in her purse. "Perfect. I need to be back before supper, though, lest they send the search party out again." She laughed.

Lucian smiled at her. "I've missed you, sweetheart. You look radiant."

"And you look like you stayed up all night working through a Blossom binge!" She sat on his couch, her hands clenched together in her lap. "I am *terribly* cross with you, by the way. Next time it happens, I shan't come to your rescue again. And look what you've done to poor Colton." She glanced at him, and Colton did his best to look wounded. "Wretched brother. Right! With that out of the way, you *must* tell me a little more about this whole exorcism business! Father is *furious* about it, by the way, so you must keep it up. And get me some tea and biscuits or something, you're a terrible host."

Colton took a seat on the opposite edge of the couch, his posture stiff and professional. He fought every instinct in his body not to put his feet up on the table and instead just draped his arm over the back of the sofa. Cool. Very casual.

Lucian laughed and started preparing the little princess a snack. "Well, I met a nice young man in the Iron District. He was a well-known exorcist in the area, and I thought he'd be a perfect partner in my endeavor to save Silvermoor from evil and so on." He winked at Colton.

Odessa rested her head on her hands, her eyelashes fluttering with amusement. "Is that right? And how's that working out for you? I've heard he's *terrrrrrribly* handsome."

Now *she* winked at Colton.

"He's not your type, darling," Lucian interjected, stepping over to Colton and squeezing his shoulder. "As lovely as he is."

Odessa's mischievous smile morphed into something warm and affectionate, understanding crossing her features. She quickly coached herself back into naughtiness, crossing her legs and resting her chin on her hand. "And what, sweet Colton went along with your religious journey of exploration? I thought he seemed cleverer than that." She giggled. "I heard you keep getting possessed!"

Lucian giggled too. "I . . . cannot . . . help it . . . when . . . the spirit . . . TAKES ME!" He lunged at her, tickling her sides and mussing up her hair.

"Lucian, you dog!" She swatted at him, and he collapsed on the floor, the spirit vanquished by the young lady's otherworldly gift. Odessa crossed her ankles and rested her feet on Lucian's remains. "And what progress have you made in my rescue?"

Lucian spoke from beyond the grave. "About that." He made his way to the bureau, from which he produced Chastain's ring. "It might be an idea for you to slip this back to your fiancé unnoticed."

Colton cocked an eyebrow. He'd made the mold already?

Lucian scoffed. "Don't look so shocked, darling. Not all of us slept in until three in the afternoon."

Odessa looked impressed, and she caught the ring in one hand as Lucian tossed it to her. "You're a beast, Beaumont. Well done." A pause. "And where are my bloody biscuits?"

He threw one at her, and she bit him.

She wasn't able to stay long, of course. Odessa ate all of the cookies in the house, nicked one of Lucian's fancy handkerchiefs, and pocketed the signet ring. She let Lucian help her into her coat and took Colton's hands.

"And seriously, thank you. Take good care of him, all right? At least until I'm in a slightly more flexible position to do so." She stood up on her tiptoes and kissed Colton on the cheek. "Adieu, poppet. I hope to see you soon."

She squeezed Lucian again for good measure and exited the flat in a flurry, her elegant green coat flowing out behind her.

Lucian took the mold to a jeweler and had him cast a ring from the wax impression, before subtly pressing the thing into Lucian's hand.

It wasn't long before rumors started flying about dear Lord Chastain—that he was involved with slavers and terrorist groups from foreign borders, et cetera et cetera. Lucian even had a small cohort of young ladies of the evening invited to his estate, spilling their hearts about Chastain's questionable nethers as soon as they were out in the daylight.

Colton took the opportunity to go back to the Iron Belt. The pig was probably furious with him for leaving her with Mai for so long, assuming Mai hadn't gotten frustrated and eaten her in the interim.

Even in the Iron Belt he was hearing the outcome of "Chastain's" shenanigans. There were reports in the newspapers, even on the Iron radio channels, that this treasonous monster had tarnished the good name of the Ivory District! After all, that sort of deal was supposed to be made in private, the fool.

Chastain made his appeals of course, live on the radio, promising that he would never, could never, he was being set up and—

"But your signet ring, my Lord. How else could you explain it?"

To be honest, Lucian had had a hand in that too. Bribing the press, promising they'd do a live exorcism on the air, leaking some of the blackmail fodder they'd found in their more lucrative hauntings.

Chastain never had a chance, surviving Lucian's multi-pronged attack. His denials only worsened matters, and soon there wasn't a single Ivory voice calling out in his favor.

Excellent work, Beaumont.

Colton returned to Lucian's apartment a few days later with a bouquet of wildflowers he'd picked on the way in the Indigo District, hoping it wasn't too soft of a gesture. As usual, he let himself in and smiled as he spotted Lucian in his usual leather seat, a newspaper in his hand.

"Hey. I missed you. The evil scheme seems to be going well?"

"Hmm? Oh, I'm surprised you haven't heard." He twisted his cuff links and looked up at Colton. "Big scandal with Chastain. The Prime Minister is stripping him of his titles, his finances are in free fall—how unfortunate for him. As a result, some families have profited a great deal. Mine's done all right, actually. The engagement to my sister was formally withdrawn this morning."

In spite of this, the young Lord Beaumont didn't look especially pleased. He hadn't even gotten up to embrace him, nor had he made any fuss about the flowers.

"Lucian? What's the matter?"

Lucian gestured to the letter lying on the table, biting his lip. It was a single sheet of paper, ornamented with the extravagant golden seal of the house of Beaumont.

Lucian. We need to talk. LB.

nineteen

Colton held Lucian's shoulders as his partner stared at the note.

Lucian's voice was small. "This is unexpected. He sent a page boy. Not even an especially *senior* page boy at that."

Bastard. Hadn't even thought it was worth adding a personal touch to ruining his son's morning. What damn game was Lucius playing at now? Colton hugged Lucian from behind and pressed a kiss to the back of his ear. In all their time together, there was nothing that shook Lucian off his steady feet like his father. He regressed into that little boy, hiding in the closet while his father threatened to destroy everything he loved.

"What do you think he wants?" Colton tried to keep his voice calm, soothing. The last thing he wanted was for Lucian to start despairing again, to forget all of the good that had followed the man cutting ties with him.

"I don't know. There's a direct invitation to the estate in the envelope. Fuck, I haven't been there since . . ."

"You don't have to go, Lucian. Who cares what he's after? Have you *ever* felt good after an audience with him?"

Lucian was silent, and his hand moved up to squeeze Colton's where it lay resting over his heart.

"But you need this. You need to do this," Colton said quietly. He spun Lucian around and pressed their foreheads together, soft brown eyes meeting brilliant blue. "Okay. I'll go with you, love. No need for you to go into the dragon's den alone, eh?"

Lucian smiled. "We'd best bring our fire-warding spells then. Thank you, Colton." He pressed his lips to Colton's nose. "I don't know what I'd do without you."

Colton did his best to dress himself up to Beaumont standards, not wanting to look unfit to stand beside Lucian. He swept his hair to the side, polished his face with creams and scented oils, and donned one of the bespoke black suits that Lucian had commissioned. Colton couldn't quite replicate the innate gracefulness Lucian had, but when he stood tall with his shoulders back, he was elegant and confident. Worthy of both Lord Beaumonts.

He caught Lucian in the hallway, ever dazzling, even with the tension aching against his eyes and pulling the muscles in his neck tight. "You're perfect," Colton promised, squeezing that flawless hand. "C'mon, let's see what that prick wants."

The plan was to let Lucian do the talking. They'd establish the motives of the father, and hopefully leave with some of the family rift having been mended. Colton was not to speak unless spoken to, as such intervention would invariably make the situation worse. That was fine; Colton was happy to stand like a bodyguard and simply act as support. If they determined that Lucius was not acting in good faith, they would leave. Easy peasy.

En route, Colton stared out the window of the carriage as they sped along to the Beaumont estate, uncertain how to pull Lucian out of his own head. But he'd give it a damn good go.

"Hey. You wanna hear about what the pig's been up to since last time you came for a visit?"

He spied a smile tugging at the side of Lucian's mouth as he stared out the window. "The what? I can't possibly know who you mean."

Colton tried to frown, but his smile reached his voice. "Marbles.

Do you want to hear about what bloody Marbles has been up to since you came last?"

Lucian grinned and turned to face Colton. "What sort of a question is that? I want to hear *everything* about her."

"Well, I left her with Mai, who *allegedly* hates animals, so I was pretty sure that she was gonna eat the pi—eat Marbles by the time I caught up with her." As promised, Colton had given Mai a considerable chunk of the money he'd earned from the Radcliffe job. Enough to pay her back for the cash he'd borrowed, the money he'd stolen from her during his last bender, all the food she'd cooked him over the years, and "considerable emotional damages" on top of that. Miss Torii seemed quite keen on supporting Colton's new venture in any way she could, after that.

Lucian's hand was inching over the seat between them until it caught Colton's, threading their fingers together. "If anything happened to Marbles, I am jumping right out of this carriage, precious. I hope you know that."

"Well, I get there a few days ago, and the pig is nowhere to be found. Whole place smells like sage and garlic butter, I can't see either of them, I'm a hundred percent certain that the pig is dead and you are going to divorce me. So I let myself into the bedroom, and bloody Mai is in bed with the pig, all snuggled up together, and the pig's wearing a pink silk ribbon around her neck like she owns the damn place."

Lucian covered his mouth and tried not to laugh.

"Well, Mai'll never be caught dead liking this damn animal, right? So she pushes her out of the bed, and her eyes are as big as I've ever seen 'em, and she's all, 'It's not what it looks like! We were just—' And I can see that she's made the pig her own plate of herb vegetables, she has her own little pillow on the floor if she wants, and there's a frigging *portrait* of her in Mai's sketchbook!"

They both lost it then, descending into peals of laughter at the absurdity of it all.

"H-how?" Lucian managed, wiping his eyes. "How did you

make it out alive? Surely there are *some* things in this world which you can't be permitted to see and then live?"

"Mai had her sights set on me, she's going in for the kill, and I basically used Marbles as some sort of pig-shield and just legged it out. To be honest, I think the pig might like Mai a bit more than me. When I dropped her off this morning, she was all too happy to abandon her papa in favor of a madwoman who tried to eat both of us."

"So what you're saying is . . ." Lucian was shaking, he was laughing so hard. "You've lost your Marbles."

"Oh, my god." Colton punched Lucian in the arm. *The worst. This man is the worst.*

"Sirs?" The carriage driver knocked on the glass and tipped his hat. "We're here."

Lucian stiffened up, and Colton touched his shoulder. "I've got you," he assured him. "We're in this together, come hell or high water." As it stood, Colton wasn't scared of Lucius. The man was a typical elitist prick, a man who wanted the world to bow to his whims and who threw a tantrum if it didn't. If his presence was helpful to Lucian, he was delighted to stand beside him while he faced his demons.

They'd been in many opulent manors since they first started working together, but none of them could hold a candle to the Beaumont estate. It was maybe four times the size of the Radcliffe place, with marble columns holding up a gold-plated roof, capped by an ivory spire that tore arrogantly into the sky. The inside was no different. Handwoven carpets covered a good portion of the floors. The remainder were bare, showing off the marble, rare burnished woods, precious metals, and hand-rendered mosaics made from thousands of tiny tiles. Servants bedazzled with gemstones lined the corridors, dusting the paintings, the clockwork parakeet sitting in its clockwork cage, arranging the flowers that seemed to have been bred in a laboratory.

Colton was careful to stay close to his partner, imagining that if one got lost in a place like this, there was a decent chance of starving to death before a rescue party came to his aid. What had it been like to grow up here? At least it would have been easy to find a corner to be alone, if he wanted to. Maybe little Lucian would take little Odessa's hand, and they'd find a room free of any servants, giggling over a stolen tart that they'd managed to pilfer from the kitchen.

Odessa. Would they run into her here? Doubtful. Lucius would have surely taken precautions to make this trip as unsettling and unpleasant for his son as possible.

"Young Master Beaumont." A servant bowed deeply. "His Lordship is expecting you. Please, follow me."

Lucian's jaw was tight, and Colton nudged him forward. *It's okay. You're a grown man, and he can't hurt you.* He hoped not, anyway.

They were led into what he supposed must have been his Lordship's office and directed to take a seat by the servant. The room was similar to the others they had passed through—books lining the walls, gold statues in the corner, a massive window that overlooked the sea. It didn't escape Colton's notice, though, that there was a large portrait of Lucian hanging behind his father's desk. A perfect semblance, although the artist had failed to capture any of the spirit or warmth of Lucian's eyes. The man in the portrait was achingly beautiful, severe, an almost cruel smile twisting up the corners of his lips as he stared at his audience.

Colton looked to his partner, and, suddenly, the intent was clear. Lucius wanted to force Lucian to face the ideal version of himself. The version his father had wanted, that Lucian had never been able to achieve.

Lucian's eyes were on his feet as he sat down, chastened, cowed, vulnerable.

"Lucian," Colton said sharply, shaking him back to life. The young Lord looked to his partner, took a deep breath, and straightened his spine. He mirrored his portrait, cruel and severe. And with that, Lucius entered the room. Neither man stood to greet him.

"What is it, Father? I'm quite busy. Please make it quick."

Good, Lucian. Do not let him see your pain.

"Of course you are. That's why you showed up on the same day as my invitation. And you brought your emotional support boy. Cute."

Lucian did not react. "What do you want? I assumed our business had come to its natural conclusion when you struck me in front of the entire Silvermoorian elite."

"Lucian, Lucian. Must we really dredge up such ugliness from the past? Your ability to hold a grudge is astonishing. Besides, I'm sure we're all in agreement that you deserved it."

Right, fuck the plan. Colton stood up, delighted to give this man a piece of his mind.

Lucian held a hand out, and Colton stayed his tongue. "I'm not really interested in discussing this. You said you needed to speak with me. What was it about?"

"There are two matters, Lucian. The first is that it has come to my attention that you are now in possession of the Ives estate." He tented his fingers under his chin. "The custodian gave me quite the little tour of the place, and I just fell in love. I would like to purchase it from you."

Lucian's eyes widened for a moment before he coached himself into neutrality once more. "I see. And what price would you be offering?"

Lord Beaumont pulled out a piece of parchment and scribbled a figure on it in rich black ink, sliding it over the desk and into his son's hands. Lucian's expression as he took in the number was one of suspicion and disbelief. A trap? A trick?

He passed the paper along to Colton, who actually coughed when he saw the absolute *fortune* that was being offered for a run-down cathedral in the middle of nowhere that he'd rather forget. This was more money than he'd ever even dared to imagine. Not enough to rival the Beaumonts, surely, but enough to buy an estate like that of the Radcliffes. Enough to never have to do another stupid exorcism ever again, enough to take Odessa and Mai and run away forever.

"I trust you find the offer fair, Lucian," Lucius muttered.

"I'll have to consider. We've had a number of very generous offers. Why do you want it?"

That was the question. Lucius Beaumont didn't want to help his son, didn't want to give him money or opportunity at this stage in their lives. What was his game?

"I care about the Holy Order, Lucian. It's all been in a state of disarray since you deposed the Reverend, you know. Think of all those lost souls wandering about without a shepherd to guide them."

And surely some property in the Holy Order would bolster his own influence. The one part of Silvermoorian society in which the Beaumonts didn't seem to have a hold.

"I'll have to discuss it with my partner," Lucian said coolly. "What was the second matter?"

Lucius stood up from his desk and moved to the window, drawing the thick velvet curtain across the panes of glass and casting the room in near total darkness. He lit a candle and settled back at his desk. "This is something rather more delicate."

Lucian's face stayed frozen. "Why, Father, we have a reputation for our discretion." Well. Not really. "Whatever you share with us shall not leave this room."

"I'm sure Chastain can attest to that," Lucius spat. "But it is of no consequence. Since you've meddled with matters that are not your business, there has been unrest in this house. I have reason to believe that there is a spirit that has taken up residence in our home, Lucian. I do not approve of your lifestyle, but I am not sure where else to turn. You have aided so, so many in the Ivory District. I wonder if you might extend the same favor to your family."

"A spirit?" Lucian leaned forward, his fingers twitching as he kept his hands on his knees and off his damned cuff links. "What kind of spirit?"

"A demon, Lucian. A creature of wickedness, debauchery, greed. I've felt this pain in my chest in the night, a sense of dread— a chill in the air which can be dispelled by neither light nor warmth. It is only getting worse, Lucian. I fear that if we don't do something about it soon, it will start to cause harm to this family. If you could do something about it, I would be in your debt."

Colton did not know Lucius Beaumont. He did not know whether he was a man capable of kindness or humility, whether there had been any whispers of joy in their relationship at any point up until now. But the man had been very clear that he thought their business a farce in the past. What had changed? The candlelight flickered in the room, catching the white of the portrait-Lucian's eyes as it stared them down.

"Why?" Colton managed, his throat dry. "You said our business was foolishness. Why do you want our help?"

Lucius sighed impatiently. "It would not be my first choice. But the fact remains that there is a demon in my home, and it is endangering my family. I do not wish for the Order to be involved, for obvious reasons. And besides, although your reputation for blackmailing and selling out your clients precedes you, Lucian already knows our dirty little secrets." A beat passed. "I need your help . . . and I suppose there is a part of me that wishes to see your magic for myself. They say you're good at it, Lucian."

Lucian stood up and took a deep breath. He looked to Colton, who gave him a nod. "I'll sell you the estate, Father. On the added condition that you never force Odessa to wed against her will."

Bold.

Lucius shook his head, chuckling softly as he covered his mouth with his gold-covered hand. " . . . Very well, Lucian."

Really? *The fuck was his angle?*

Lucian took it in stride. "Please let us know when would be a convenient time to perform the exorcism for you."

"You—you'll do it?" Lucius stood up as well, extending a hand for the young Lord to shake. "Thank you. I—thank you, son."

Lucian's body lurched for a moment as he took his father's hand. "Of course. I couldn't allow anything ill to befall my darling family, could I? Have Johan send over as many details as you feel are pertinent. We shouldn't delay. This is a serious matter." His cloak swept around him as he pivoted on his heels, bursting out of the door in a flurry. "Colton," he called.

Colton kept one pace behind him, his shoulders apart, back straight, dark eyes glinting like an ever-vigilant bodyguard to his Lordship. He followed Lucian down the corridors, out the hall, and into the bright Ivory sun.

Lucian kept walking, past the carriage, down a darkened side street cast in shadow from the massive estates that flanked it. And Colton followed, saying nothing as Lucian came to a stop, pressed an arm against the wall, and emptied his stomach onto the street.

twenty

This wasn't going to be their ordinary run-of-the-mill exorcism. This was Lucian's home, his family, servants—people who had known him for years, knew his abilities, his proclivities, already scorned or adored him. No. Lucius Beaumont wasn't going to fall for a smog of Grass and some Snow-laced tea.

"So what're we gonna do?" Colton asked, leaning his head over the edge of Lucian's mattress as he lay on his back. "I don't know if my normal bag of tricks is gonna cut it this time."

Lucian's fist was tucked under his chin, his arm against his chest as he stared out the window and into the ocean's horizon. "No. We'll need something bigger."

Colton smiled. He could almost hear the gears in his partner's mind turning. "Mmm, maybe it turns into a big demon orgy or something," he quipped, his smile only broadening as Lucian plopped down on the floor beside him and kissed his neck.

"Oh, yes, an orgy with my family. Every exorcist's dream." Lucian fanned his fingers through Colton's hair.

"Maybe *I* should get possessed this time? Shake things up a bit—then you get to be the hero, no one gets any ammunition about how *corrupted* you are—"

"Oh, you could attack my father! I could jump in between you, knife at your throat—'Not today, you cad! The Beaumont line shall not end this night!'" He laughed, nuzzling Colton's cheek. "Could you manage that, precious? Let me see your best possessed face."

Colton flipped over onto his stomach and extended his arms, his fingers like twisted twigs as he clawed at the mattress beneath him and growled. "*Rawr.*"

Lucian cupped his face and kissed him. "Terrifying, darling. But surely not enough to fool my father."

Colton slid to his knees and arched his neck, sensuously moving his fingers from his chin all the way down his own chest. In that last moment, he flicked his eyes up as though seeing Lucian for the first time, and he smiled with his teeth.

"*Beaumont . . .*" he hissed, crawling forward, pushing himself off the mattress, onto the floor, pinning Lucian to the carpet by his wrists. "*I can smell the corruption on you, Archon—how delicious it is . . .*" He pressed his mouth to Lucian's throat and bit into the soft white flesh. "*Resist not, child of light. It will not be painful.*"

Their eyes met then, and Lucian's face was a mix of delight and arousal. "Begone, demon," he purred, arching his back and granting Colton all the more access.

"*You are not sincere in your desire to be free of this possession, mortal. That weakness shall be your undoing.*"

Lucian's fingers threaded through Colton's demon hair, and then a covenant was forged in sweat.

So much for productive planning. Well, at least they had some idea what to do next. They would go to the basement, set the scene the way they always did—blood, runes, incense, spice—and a few hallucinogens wouldn't hurt either. When the time was right and the family was gathered, Lucian would conjure the demon, and Colton would be taken. He would attack Lucius, and Lucian would intervene. There would be an epic fight for dominance, wherein Lucian would emerge the victor. Then, using the serpent orb they'd pinched from the Ives estate, the demon would be sealed into the magical stone, and then they could purify it, or something.

He didn't want to think about *why* there was a "demon" haunting the Beaumonts all of a sudden, whether it was a guilty conscience like the Radcliffes' or a harbinger of a mind descending into the pits of madness, like with the Reverend. What could have driven a man like Lucius Beaumont, a proud business tycoon who had very recently and publicly denounced his son, to seek out their business? He'd mentioned discretion, necessity, feigned something akin to paternal affection. But they had to be careful not to take such things at face value. Lucius Beaumont surely had another angle here; Colton just wasn't sure what it was.

They would have to be very careful, indeed.

The two of them donned matching black cloaks on that day. Lucian wanted to present a unified front. The contrast between them had always been a factor they'd played up in their favor before, but it wouldn't read that way to Lucius. Colton was nothing more than an Iron peasant, unworthy to stand beside his betters.

The hood cast a dark shadow over Lucian's face as they approached the long marble staircase leading up to the estate. Colton reached over and squeezed his hand.

"We don't ever need to see him again, Lucian. We don't have to do this."

But Lucian only smiled and kissed Colton's fingers. As always, this place had robbed him of his tongue.

A servant greeted them and directed them down one set of stairs, then another, then another, until Colton was certain they were far below the surface of the earth. *How deep does this bloody place go?* It was in his nature to memorize routes in new places, just in case they had to get out in a hurry.

There is no escape. It felt like that, anyway. The corridors had almost no light. The stones were crushing him.

"The basement, my Lords." The servant bowed and directed them into a dark room.

Chains lined the walls, and clockwork implements of torture in various stages of decay were piled up and discarded. *Ugh, how cliché.* It had been a trend, not too long ago. Every Ivory house in the upper district had some damned dungeon or other; it was obnoxious.

On the far wall, near the only set of lanterns, Lucian's portrait from the office glared down at them. *That's certainly a bit unsettling.*

"Where is Lord Beaumont?" Lucian asked. "We need more details of the haunting if we are to proceed."

The servant shrugged. "He instructed me to tell you that . . . let's see." He pulled out a note and read verbatim: "'You of all people should know what is wrong with this place. I will join you when it is time to dispel the thing.'"

"Ah. Of course. I am of course the source of all decay in this family. The downfall and the weakness in the line. How silly of me to forget." Lucian's jaw was tight, and Colton touched his shoulder.

"It's all right, Lord Beaumont. Surely you are familiar enough with this place for us to need minimal assistance." Colton lit a lantern and took a step back. The floor was already blessed red with intricate runes made of . . . fresh blood? Sitting in shiny clots, oily and virginal. *How gauche.*

"Lucian," he whispered, gesturing at one of them.

Lucian's brows furrowed, and he stepped closer to his partner. "That's—"

Neither of them spoke, as it was almost certain that they were being watched. The marks on the floor were ones they knew all too well. They were carved in ink all over Colton's body.

Didn't matter. It's not like they were real. *Right?* Probably just Lord Beaumont trying to strike fear into their hearts before they got started. It was very effective. *How did he know? How does he know what they look like?*

"So nice of him," Colton said blithely. "To begin our work for us."

For this job, Lucian had brought some personal keepsakes from his childhood, ostensibly to whip the Beaumont spirit into a frenzy, but in reality to force his father to feel something when he came down to see them. These included the toy horse he had played with as a child, a lock of Odessa's hair, and his mother's wedding veil. Surely these things would change the way Lucius felt, if he had any heart at all.

Everything else was set up like they'd done a hundred times—incense with hallucinatory drugs added, powder lit to decrease visibility and heighten shadows.

The flames on the candles flickered as the dungeon door opened. Lucius's cold eyes and imposing figure darkened what little light the corridor could allow in. He was flanked by two servants, one of whom took his cape. The other handed him a short blade in a gilded sheath.

"Lucian. You've had more than enough time to prepare. Are you ready to save your family?"

Lucian looked at Colton and stood up straight, pulling his hood away from his face. "I believe I am, Father. Considering that you have never seen an exorcism, it would be best if you allow me and Colton to complete our work without interruption. We are experts at this."

"Is that right? Believe it or not, I *have* been learning a thing or two about exorcisms, Lucian. Let's just say that you've got me very interested in the idea. You know, you left all *sorts* of interesting things behind at the Ives estate."

Was that how he'd learned the runes? Had Ives stripped him down and taken bloody notes while Colton had been unconscious? The ink. The papers. *How violating.*

"There must be blood, right?" He snatched Lucian's wrist and forced him closer, slicing his son's palm open with the blade. "Oh, and how foolish of me. Our blood is sacred. That is what Ives believed, right?" Lucius turned the dagger on himself now, his own palm erupting with red life that dripped onto the floor.

Lucius grasped his son's shoulders and held him close.

"Come now, Lucian. Save the family. Get rid of the evil."

He shoved Lucian forward then, who staggered forth a few steps before regaining his footing.

"Don't tell me the master exorcist is frightened. This is how it's done. There is evidence of that all over your *partner's* palm."

Colton moved his hands behind his back, clenching them into fists. He could still feel the tight scar that had healed over what had happened between him and Ives. How did Lucius know? They'd been *alone*. Hadn't they? *Was there actually a demon? Had Ives actually managed to—*No. No, absolutely, categorically impossible. *But then how . . . ?*

Lucius leaned on the wall, smearing Lucian's portrait with the crimson flowing from his gaping wound.

C'mon, Lucian. Don't let him trip you up, it's what he wants. We have a plan, it'll work, he'll be grateful maybe. Or, more likely, he'd still hate Lucian and still be a dick, but at least they could say that they'd tried.

Lucian was breathing hard, but he stood to his full height and extended his cane in the center of the circle. "Colton," he barked, and his partner took his hand and stood beside him. Lucian's blood was leaking over his palms, onto the floor, with a sickening drip.

"Demon! This is my home, and you shall not inhabit it any longer! I summon you forth, demon. Here before my father I summon you so that I may banish you to the realm of ghosts!" He banged his cane on the floor, the sound echoing throughout the chamber. "Demon!"

At this point, Colton didn't even need to look at Lucian to know when it was his time to act. He twisted Lucian's wrist and forced him to his knees, allowing his own face to morph into something wretched and cruel.

"*Beaumont*," he hissed. "*And yet not a Beaumont.*" His demon was seductive, alluring. His demon reveled in flirting in front of this miserable father.

"*Your family has discarded you like you are nothing, not-a-Beaumont, and yet you hurt for them, you bleed for them.*" He smiled. "*Such pitiful sentimentality is worth nothing.*"

Lucian snapped out of his stupor and rose to his feet, clutching

Colton's throat. "You would harm my family, demon! You would harm my father, my sister—it cannot be so! I banish you, I BANISH YOU!"

Colton only laughed. "*Such words of passion. This great love you hold for your family. It only makes me stronger, not-a-Beaumont.*" He looked at his fingernails and tilted his head, his cruel gaze falling on the master of the house. "*There. There is a man worth possessing.*"

Lucian cracked his cane on the floor and carefully moved between the demon and his father.

"You shall not. Your battle is with me."

Lucius moved closer to his son, a hand on his back, pushing him forward.

Lucian swallowed, his eyes cold as he met Colton's gaze.

The pair met in the center of the room, swords drawn and crossed as they battled for dominance. Lucian was a trained swordsman, Colton much less so, but they knew the dance and effortlessly battled one another until they had both worked up a sweat.

These things often ended in a stalemate—the demon would seem to get the upper hand, then would be vanquished at long last by the inherent good of the exorcist. They took a step back from each other, Lucian's blood still dripping onto the floor around his feet.

Colton was supposed to press forward, beyond Lucian, and raise his sword over Lord Beaumont's head. He would taste the fear in his eyes and begin to bring the blade down until Lucian stepped between them and saved his father's life. In that moment he would overpower him, dominate him, and the curse would be broken.

"Demon. Come."

The candles all went out in a scream as Colton charged one last time. The only lights that remained were the lanterns near Lucian's portrait, where Lucius was standing. *What in all the seven hells is going on? We didn't plan this!* Lucian staggered backward as though struck, his back against the wall, clawing at his chest as he gasped for breath. Colton's sword was poised over the Lord's head as he spotted Lucian, and he let it clatter to the floor as he sped over to him. This job was too important to fuck up; there was no way Lucian was faking it. *Is he hurt? What did Lucius do to him?*

"Lucian?" he whispered, cupping his face. "Lucian, what's the matter?"

Lucian's pupils were blown out, his eyes wide, his breaths coming in soft little gasps. His elegant hands were tearing at his shirt, staining it with blood in his frenzy.

"Lucian!" Colton called, shaking him sharply.

"Get the *fuck* off me!" Lucian snarled, slapping Colton's hand away from him and scrambling backward on the floor.

Colton froze, his own heart lodged in his throat. *Is he high again? He promised.* "Lucian, it's me. It's okay."

His beautiful eyes darted around the room; at last they settled on Colton, and his breathing slowed. "Colton," he whispered. "I'm sorry, I—I thought—"

Colton hugged Lucian to his chest and stroked his back—blood? Why was he covered in blood? "Are you hurt? What happened?"

From the other side of the room, Lucius Beaumont was sarcastically clapping. "Very good job, boys. I can see why your efforts fetch such a high price." He scoffed. "And what, do the others fall for this *farce*?"

Oh, *fuck*, he'd broken character and ruined it. Lucian wouldn't have. He would have found a way to keep it natural, even if Colton had been hurt. Maybe he'd have tried to use it, and act like he was about to take over when really he was just checking on his partner.

Rookie fucking mistake, Colton.

"Say something, Lucian," Lucius hissed, his arms crossed as he loomed over his son. "Explain yourself. Before I call the Order and have you arrested for fraud—you know they don't take *kindly* to the *Ninth Archon* profiteering off the spiritual suffering of the people, yes?"

But Lucian could barely speak. His breathing stuttered like a steamship dying, his eyes wide, mouth dry, disoriented.

"Why, Lucian"—Lucius sounded almost pleased with himself—"you look as though you've seen a ghost."

Lucian put a hand on the wall and tried to stand, his legs collapsing under him as he made the effort. Colton pulled Lucian's arm over his shoulders and hoisted him up, glad that his own legs were able to find the strength to walk.

"You look *terrible*. Maybe we should get you upstairs. We can have the doctor take a look at you. It wouldn't do to have such a *well-respected exorcist* expire in our basement."

Colton had to get Lucian out of here. Whatever his fucking father had been planning was not something he needed to see the end of. Lucian wanted to rekindle his relationship with his father? Well it was clear that was not *fucking* happening. Lucian looked like he was dying, and his Lordship appeared as if it was the funniest thing he'd ever witnessed. They had to get out.

"Oh, no, it's fine. Curse sicknesses are a very special business. We need to act quickly, sir. The, uh, the spiritual energy here is all wrong. Please let us pass."

"Is that so?" Lucius glanced down at his fingernails.

"So we'll have to come back and finish the exorcism another time."

Lucius laughed. "You expect me to employ your *services* ever again after today's *theatrics*? You must think me a fool." He shook his head. "You won't be paid either, obviously. That was *embarrassing*, Lucian."

"We'll make it up to you," Lucian managed. "Please."

But Colton wasn't in the mood to entertain this further. He hoisted Lucian up the stairs, pressing his fingers to his wrist to make sure he didn't expire right here in the fucking corridor.

Stay with me. I need you.

Lucian's head flopped forward, and he started vomiting. It was everything Colton could do to keep him upright.

"I don't know, Lucian. I think you should stay here. You're in no state to be seen outside." Lucius smirked.

Lucian's hand found his father's throat and squeezed. "*No,*" he hissed, his fingers twitching against the damp cartilage that stood taut under the man's skin. He frowned, shook his head, and released Lucius from his grip.

"Colton will take care of me. Thank you for your concern."

Lucius rubbed at his neck, his smile lopsided. "Of course. Take care, *son.*"

twenty-one

They staggered out into the sunlight, and Colton flagged down a carriage to take them home. He pulled Lucian into his arms and held him as tightly as he could. "What happened?" he whispered. "Are you hurt?"

Lucian looked awful—even worse than he did at the party. More disoriented, more afraid.

"I think my father drugged me," he explained, shuddering. "I felt a sting in my neck. I'm almost certain it was a syringe. Sedative, maybe, a hallucinogen." He let out a deep breath.

Why hadn't he thought of that? They both knew what Lucius was like—but what the hells did he have to gain from fucking up their exorcism like this?

"You broke character. Ruined the scene. Spoiled any possibility of my father taking me back. I just—how could you—" Lucian crossed his arms. "Idiot."

What the fuck. "I-I'm sorry, Lucian, I didn't mean to—"

He shook his head. "It doesn't matter anymore. What's done is done."

"Lucian . . ."

"It might be a good idea to get my doctor to look me over," he muttered. "If I seem to be losing consciousness, perhaps redirect the carriage to the hospital."

"Sure." What else could he say? Colton leaned his forehead against the window and watched the sun setting in the distance, wondering when this slithering feeling in his chest would subside.

They arrived at Lucian's home, and Colton helped him out of the carriage, his jaw falling open as he beheld his partner from behind. There was a red cross of blood painted all up and down his back. What had Lucius been playing at? What was he trying to achieve? Something arcane, probably, something the man imagined was dark and dangerous.

"*Ivory men play with forces they don't understand,*" his mother had warned him, stroking his hair. "*They think they can control the spirits, love. That's where they're wrong. No one can control a demon, Colton; no one can make him bend. Be wary of those who try.*"

The good news was that demonic possession and exorcisms were all a bunch of bullshit. Lucius had probably *wanted* to get Lucian attacked by a demon or whatever, slipped him some narcotics to make the process go more smoothly, and here they were. Worried, humiliated, but unharmed for the most part.

At least they weren't at that man's mercy any longer, and at least Lucian hadn't broken his promise not to take Blossom to excess anymore.

He tucked Lucian into bed, kissed him on the forehead, and made his way to the town square so he could find a doctor to have a look at his partner. He found a rather dour-looking woman and handed her a pouch of gold coins for her trouble.

They came up the stairs, and the doctor examined Lucian carefully, her face growing more and more concerned as she worked. "It's quite strange, my Lord. Your temperature is substantially below normal, your heart rate as well. Your pulse is weak too. I'm worried, Lord Beaumont. I think you might need to check into a hospital."

"*It makes them cold, Colton,*" his mother had said. "*When a demon has your heart, your body starts to shut down. Life is sustained by fury, avarice, whatever evil the creature embodies—the soul is sup-*

pressed, trapped, powerless. The first sign is ice. Then fire. Then . . . you should run."

"No, no, I don't think that'll be necessary." All honey and cream. His charm was back, at the very least. "I feel much better, and Colton will look after me. Trust me, if I begin to deteriorate, he's liable to drag me to the nearest facility by the ankle." He laughed.

The doctor nodded. "Of course, my Lord. Just a few more tests."

Beaumont Pharmaceuticals had apparently devised a new machine that could take a sample of blood and could find *evils* in it, or something. Not that an Iron man would ever see such a device, as their like were best suited for leeches, but that was neither here nor there.

Lucian's blood pressure was appalling, and the doctor had to stick him so many times with the needle that Lucian lost patience.

Colton let the doctor out and crawled into bed beside his partner. "Are you okay?" he asked quietly, cuddling up to Lucian's side. "I was so worried."

Lucian shut his eyes. "I think so." He still looked miserable, though. "Colton, I wanted to apologize for putting you into this situation. For shouting at you in the carriage. This is all such a mess."

Colton found himself blushing as he leaned into Lucian's touch. "Damn right, dummy. And after you promised never to scare me like that again."

Lucian chuckled and pulled Colton close, pressing little kisses to his face—below his eye, on the tip of his nose, at the junction where his throat met his cheek. "I know. And I don't like breaking promises to people that I care for." He pressed their foreheads together and shut his eyes. "I just . . . I wanted to say thank you, Colton. You mean everything to me, and I care for you more than nearly anyone on this earth."

"The pig takes first place, right?"

Lucian laughed. "I'm being serious. You've changed my life for the better. You've made me happier than I ever dared to imagine I could be. You made me feel like it was *okay* to be myself, to love myself for who I am."

He pressed forward then, cupping Colton's cheeks as he pulled him in for a kiss. Hells, his skin was cold. "I guess I just wanted to say that no matter what the fallout is with my father, as long as we're together, I can brave it. You make me better, darling. You make me want to become the best man in the world."

Too late. Colton only smiled.

"I . . . Gosh, I talk a lot when I'm inebriated, don't I?"

"You talk a lot all the time, my dear Lucian. Don't use illicit substances as an excuse."

"Oh, hush. I think I just wanted to say that I love you, Colton. No matter what happens from now, I wanted you to know that. I love you, and I'll never love anyone else."

Colton gave him a look that was both affectionate and teasing, diving in for a soft nip of Lucian's neck. "You never do things by halves, do you, Beaumont?"

Lucian kissed his hand and snuggled close. "Moi? Never."

If Lucian minded that Colton hadn't reciprocated in that instant, he said nothing about it. They both moved to turn the moment into something friskier, but it was apparent that Lucian wasn't up for much in the physical intimacy department. His skin was freezing, his heart beating slower than Colton thought was possible, his body trembling on the mattress.

"C'mon, stupid. Let's get you in a bath and warmed up, while I call for a doctor, okay? And if you decide to drown, it's going to be very embarrassing for me to get the police out here, do you understand? No one wants to deal with a nude lordling."

"No one?"

"Well. One idiot does." He kissed Lucian's forehead, called for a page boy to fetch the doctor. There was some fuss about how late it was and blah blah but Colton was insistent, and a gold coin never hurt these matters. He readied the bath, helping Lucian to step into the warm rose petal water before climbing in after him, flush against his chest in the vanilla-scented heat.

Lucian's arms went around his waist, and he pressed kisses to the back of his ears, his low velvet voice telling Colton stories he'd read when he was a boy. "The Starbound Sailor," "The Fairy King's Garden," "The Minister of Sausages and His Peckish Swarm."

"Those stories are terrible," Colton pouted, arching his neck for Lucian. "I want a different one."

Lucian's lips smiled against his skin. "There once was a prince from a beautiful land. His father cast him out, and he found himself wandering the world as a stranger until he met the knight who would save his life . . ." Colton was smiling too. "They became partners. They fought demons and chased them all the way back down to hell. Side by side they fought, and there wasn't a man or beast who could come between them. Even as they raged against the prince's father, even when all seemed lost, they knew that they could count on each other, no matter how dark the sky became."

"So what happens? To the prince and his friend?"

Lucian kissed Colton's neck. "They fight. They win. And they live together, happily ever after."

This was good. This was much better, actually, than facing the grim reality that was trying to claw through the back of Colton's skull. There was something terribly, terribly wrong with Lucian, and Colton didn't want to even begin to imagine what it was.

I think you know, sweetheart. It starts with ice. Then fire. Run, Colton.

twenty-two

The doctor came soon after the bath, and declared Lucian's condition to be unchanged from earlier in the day. Colton sat beside him on the sofa and squeezed his icicle fingers.

"I—I think I'm upset that I'll never see my father again," Lucian admitted, finally. "I know he's awful, I know he doesn't deserve me, I know he treats me like garbage, but . . . he's my dad. He's part of me and I just—I miss my family, Colton. I miss my home. I wish we hadn't . . ."

Maybe we should just go back down there, Colton almost said, *and we can explain what happened and—*

But what good would that do? Lucius had caught them in the act, and as it stood they were lucky that they hadn't been arrested like the damnable frauds they were.

So what to do? They didn't need the work anymore, not really. They had their position, they had enough money, and Odessa was now safe. Where did that leave them, if they didn't need to do jobs together anymore?

Colton's stomach sank as he imagined their relationship falling apart, their love not strong enough to hold them together without their shared deception. Lucian would see what a hindrance Colton was, that he'd never been worthy of Lord Beaumont, that maybe he'd be better off just marrying a rich Ivory girl and going back to his father. He inched closer to Lucian and draped a protective hand over his chest.

"Are you okay?" he asked, tucking his chin against Lucian's neck.

Lucian's arm curled around his shoulders and squeezed tight. "Colton, I'm really upset."

"I'm sorry, Lucian."

"I know you are." The young Lord sighed and squeezed Colton's hand. "I know you are."

Colton woke with a start in Lucian's bed the next morning to find himself alone. It wasn't so unusual that his partner was up with the sun, but after the last twenty-four hours, it felt inauspicious. Even so, Colton stretched out his arms like a kitten and went to brush his teeth and wash his face.

Once presentable, he made his way into the living area and smiled at Lucian, who was standing with one hand behind his back as he sipped his tea. "G'morning, your Lordship." Colton poured himself a cup as well. "How're you feeling?"

Lucian turned to look at him, his expression hard to place. "I'm fine, Colton. Take a seat. I think you and I should talk."

This always bodes well. Lucian had grown tired of him, wanted to break up, had reevaluated everything—because of the exorcism? Because he's...

"Yeah, sure." He sat down on the sofa and put his feet on the table. "What's on your mind?"

Lucian looked at Colton's crossed ankles, then up at his partner, his eyebrow cocked. Colton cleared his throat and sat up straight.

"I don't know what else to say. I'm really sorry. I thought you were hurt—I just reacted."

"In the worst possible way. At the worst possible time. In the most important job we've ever done." Lucian's eyes flashed with anger as he rose from his seat. "This was my last chance, and you ruined it. You wanted me to fail. You wanted this job to get screwed up so he'd never take me back, and I'd be stuck with you. Right?"

Colton could almost hear his own heart shatter. "Lucian," he whispered, shaking his head. "How can you ask me that?"

A moment of silence, and then Lucian's face softened. Colton crossed his arms over his chest and shifted away as his partner sat beside him. "You're right," he said softly. "That was a wretched thing of me to say." He sighed. "I'm sorry, Colton. You would never hurt me, I know that. I feel a bit strange, still. Maybe the drugs. It's not an excuse, but how can I make it up to you?"

This frigging softy.

Colton pouted. "Hmm, well, if you're feeling up to it, maybe you can take me out on the town? We can visit the pig, you can buy me lunch, and if you're *very* good, I can forgive you just this once. How's that sound?"

"I think it sounds brilliant, precious." He pulled Colton close and kissed his temple. "And if I keep being a twat, you have my permission to pinch me."

Colton met Lucian's eyes, smiled, and pinched his stupid cheeks until they bloomed like apples.

Allowing Lucian and Mai to meet was something that Colton had been actively avoiding for some time now. It wasn't like he expected conflict, exactly, it was just a little awkward for his first *serious* boyfriend to meet his longtime best friend and ex-girlfriend. Coupled with the fact that Lucian was so beautiful, it was likely Mai would probably find it distracting. Well, now was as good a time as any.

And to be honest, maybe some awkwardness would do them some good. Lucian was still obviously reeling after that difficult encounter with his father, and Colton was trying to forget the cruel barb that his partner had pressed into his heart.

"So, Mai's great," Colton chattered as they walked down the Indigo steps. "She's really smart and beautiful, and we've been through a lot together. She'll be so excited to meet you! *The* Lucian Beaumont, she'll probably never shut up about it." *Stupid thing to say.* "Did I tell you we used to date? Like when we were kids, we were kinda on-again, off-again. We broke up again a few months before I met you, so I guess you're . . ." *My rebound?*

Lucian just smiled at him, though, and squeezed his shoulder. "Colton, relax. I'm really happy to be with you right now."

They arrived at Mai's house, and Colton let himself in, practically getting bowled over by the damned pig as soon as he was past the threshold. Mai had made some changes to the place over the last few months, presumably with her share of income from the exorcism jobs. She could have moved into Indigo, surely, or even Ivory if she was happy to start small. But Mai loved the Iron Belt; she loved her neighbors, the markets, the briny smell of the sea. So she'd employed a lateral rather than vertical adjustment to her living space, and had turned her humble home into a temple of comfort. A brand-new patchwork armchair in bold colors stood before the fireplace, beside a hardwood bookshelf filled with trinkets and cherished books. Hanging lanterns with stained glass in reds, blues, and greens cast a warm glow, while the air was thick with the scent of exotic incense, turning her space into a tranquil, vibrant haven. There was, of course, a tiny little bed in the corner, with the plushest pillow and the softest blanket, "Marbles" embroidered over the top in pink silk thread.

"There she is, the prettiest girl in the whole apartment!" Colton cooed at the oinker, which predictably got Mai to throw a sponge at his head, and Marbles lumbered back to her sunbeam to snooze.

"Colton, you are such a prick. You know you're supposed to warn me before you—Oh, hello." She stopped dead in her tracks as she spotted Lucian, looking him up and down with an approving glance. "You must be Lord Beaumont. Um." Her cheeks flushed crimson, and Colton sniggered. "Wow. You are *way* prettier in person than I thought you'd be. I'm Mai Torii—I think probably Colton told you that, since you're in my house. Um. He's an asshole, so he didn't warn me that he was bringing you. Otherwise I woulda made . . . food." She coughed.

Lucian just laughed and shook her hand. "I can see I shan't be able to wallow in anonymity here. Lucian Beaumont, a pleasure. And may I say, you are far lovelier than even Colton's high praise led me to believe. Thank you so much for allowing me into your home."

Colton smiled. That was more like it—a smarmy Lucian meant a happy Lucian.

Mai seemed to approve, placing a warm cup of tea in his hands and asking him about himself. He was kind to her, he was respectful, he was appreciative of everything she offered him.

Colton let his shoulders relax and clicked his tongue so the pig would be more sociable. She emerged from the pillow pile that Mai had established for her, nose a twitching, happy scallop as she trotted over to her savior. Marbles lay at Colton's feet and rolled over for her tummy scratches, and he picked her up like a bag of flour.

"There she is. Hello, my beautiful girl," Lucian cooed, reaching over to pet the little piglet.

Marbles squealed violently and bit his hand, drawing blood as Lucian recoiled from her.

Colton dropped the pig to the ground and took Lucian's arm. "Oh, shit, are you okay? What happened? Mai, what the fuck is wrong with that thing?" He pulled Lucian to the sink and started running some cool water over the wound.

"I don't know. She's never . . . Maybe he scared her?"

"I would never!" Lucian snapped, wincing as Colton rubbed some soap over the bites. "We never had a problem with her before she started staying with *you*!"

Oh, no.

"And what's that supposed to mean?"

"Nothing!" Colton interjected as he wrapped Lucian's palm up in soft white bandages. "I think that just startled all of us, okay? Pigs are weird, lesson learned." He kissed Lucian's hand and smiled up at him. "Good?"

Lord Beaumont snatched his arm away from Colton and frowned. "What are you doing?"

"What do you mean? I'm kissing your boo-boo so it feels better." His mother had always done that for him, after all.

"I don't need you to do that." Lucian gestured at Mai with his head, his face heating up with embarrassment.

"Oh. Um." He'd never explicitly revealed his relationship to Mai, but he was pretty much certain that she'd figured it out on her own. "Sorry, Lucian. I wasn't thinking."

"Don't mind me," Mai added, laughing.

Lucian's eyes flashed with fury. "You told her?"

"No!"

"After everything with my father, after the fucking party—you told some bloody *Iron* woman without my explicit permission? How *dare* you." He stood up to his full height, his shoulders quivering with anger.

What the *fuck. First ice . . . then fire.* No. It wasn't possible. Demons *weren't real!*

Colton put himself between his partner and Mai. "You need to calm down."

"She'd sell us out in a second, Colton. All these Iron whores are the same. You think she'd hesitate to take me down? Probably get out of this fucking shack and leave you in the goddamned dust."

Mai's whole body exuded indignant fury. She was already on her feet with her fingers in a fist, plowing toward the Lord without hesitation. "Lucian!" Colton grabbed him by his collar and dragged him out the door and into the street. "What in the seven bloody hells is wrong with you?"

Lucian was breathless, his eyes wide, his face pale. "I don't know."

Colton searched his face. Fear. Fatigue. "No, Lucian! This is ridiculous. You've been a fucking asshole all day, and I'm getting pretty damned sick of it." He let go of his partner's collar, and Lucian wilted against the wall.

"Colton, I'm sorry."

Colton's shoulders slumped, and he shook his head. It wasn't the drugs. It couldn't be the drugs. But . . . then . . . *Colton. Run.* "I think maybe you should go home, Lucian. I need to smooth things over with Mai."

"Are you coming home tonight?" *Or staying in the Iron District with all the whores, right?*

"I don't know. You need to get out of here."

He didn't even watch Lucian leave as he let himself back into Mai's apartment. Mai was a tough woman—she certainly wasn't the sort to get upset over what some Ivory bastard thought—but Colton didn't want to leave things like this.

"Hey. I'm so sorry about that. I have no idea what happened."

Mai was sitting on her bed, stroking the pig thoughtfully. "He's beautiful, Colton. But he's bad news." She looked up at him, her expression almost pitying. "Once you get the rest of the money from your last job, maybe you should cut ties."

"He—he's not like that." Except that he had been. To his best friend in the world, for no reason at all. "He's usually not—fuck, Mai. He's never like this. I've never seen him like this before; I don't know what's going on with him." *You do. You just don't want to admit it.* "He's gentle, and loving, and kind—"

"And an elitist prick."

Colton didn't want to argue. "He was in a lot of pain from the bite. I'm really sorry this happened. Can I do anything?"

Mai lay back on the bed and kicked off her shoes. "You're probably not up for a quick screw to really fuck him off, right?"

Colton crossed his arms.

"I'm kidding! Yeesh." She got up though and wrapped her arms around his shoulders from behind. "Be careful, Colton. Never trust a man with two faces."

Colton's heart was heavy as he stuffed his hands into his pockets, kicking stones along the cobbles as he walked back to the Ivory District. Something was seriously wrong with Lucian, and if Colton was right . . . if Lucius had really managed to force a demon into his son . . .

Then he'd been wrong about his mother. About the world. About everything. No. No, it was impossible. Lucian was just—he was—

He couldn't leave it like this. Couldn't leave Lucian alone with so much unspoken, with so many questions still unanswered. *He had to know.* When he arrived at last at Lucian's apartment, his stomach sank as he recognized one of the Beaumont carriages parked out front. Colton hid in the shadows until it drove off into the night and carefully let himself inside the building.

"Lucian?" he called, peeling out of his jacket. "How're you feeling?"

The young Lord Beaumont was sitting on the couch, staring off into the distance. "Weird."

Colton sat beside him and leaned against his shoulder. "What is going on with you, sweetheart? Tell me what's the matter."

"My father sent a messenger over. He's been pretty clear that he doesn't want any further contact with me until I cease my association with you."

"Oh." Well, that explained everything. He was trying to cut ties, trying to keep it neat. Lucian had chosen his father over Colton, and this was the precise moment his world would fall apart. That explained the cruelty then, the outbursts, the bullshit. Lucian wanted a clean break; maybe he was trying to make it easier for the two of them. Wonderful. *Better than demons, at least.*

"I told him, in so many words, to shove it up his ass." Lucian smiled. "I'm not giving you up for anybody."

Colton's lips quirked up. Seriously? Lucian was intent on surprising him this evening, apparently. "That's dumb. Your dad can probably buy you a pony, and the best I can do is give you cuddles."

Lucian laughed and kissed Colton's cheeks. "Well, I happen to think cuddles are very valuable."

"Is that what's gotten you so wound up today? I wish your father didn't have so much power over you, sweetheart." He ran his fingers through Lucian's hair. "What about the Ives estate? Did he mention anything about that?"

Lucian stiffened beside him. "As a matter of fact, he did not. Why do you ask?"

"Well, it's sort of the last bit of business you need to complete with your dad, right? Once that's all sorted, he can go blow."

"It's always about the money with you, isn't it?"

"What? No, it's just he said that he wanted to buy it, and—"

"And what, you take the money and run? Leave me with nothing? Ruin my life and then dash off into the fucking sunset with your pig bitch?"

They both stood up, Colton's eyes matching Lucian's cold fury.

"That fucking does it, Lucian. I'm leaving. Drop me a line when you decide to stop being a miserable asshole." He turned and marched toward the door, but Lucian caught his wrist.

"Stop it. You can't leave."

"Yes, I can! I'm not bloody putting up with this. I don't know what kind of relationships you've had in the past, but this is completely unacceptable behavior. I don't care what your dad did, or said, but I'm not dealing with this." He tried twisting his arm out of Lucian's grip, his skin burning from the effort.

"I *said* you can't leave." Lucian snarled, "Sit down."

"Fuck you!" Colton spat, wrenching himself free. "You're fucking unbelievable."

"How *dare* you." Lucian's voice was dripping with venom, and Colton's blood went cold.

This isn't Lucian. This isn't Lucian. My Lucian would never—he wouldn't. He's not an elitist, he's not cruel—he's kind, he's gentle, he's good—

His thoughts were interrupted by Lucian's heavy hand cracking him across the face, sending him to the floor in a daze. With a shaking hand he touched his own jaw, his eyes wide as he saw the blood coating his fingertips. Colton looked up to Lucian—that was it then. They were done. There was no coming back from this;

Colton had enough self-respect not to stay with someone who fucking hit him! Betrayal, indignation, fury, fear—fuck this guy. *Fuck him.*

But Lucian just stood there, statue still, staring up at his arm as it extended out toward nothing. Colton opened his mouth to speak, to shout, to call for help, but stopped himself when he saw the look on Lucian's beautiful face.

Abject terror.

twenty-three

"Colton—I—I'm so sorry, you know I would *never*—"

But he had. And Colton had no bloody idea what to do about it. First ice, then fire. Run, Colton.

"You stay the hell away from me!" Colton slowly staggered back onto his feet. "I don't give a FUCK, Lucian. How many times have you apologized for being an asshole today? Of course you're sorry—I never want to see you—"

Lucian went to his knees, his hands clawing at his face as his whole body stuttered for breath. The air rasped past his throat in little squeaks and squeals—*Is he dying?*

"Lucian?" Colton's anger evaporated. He couldn't hold a shred of it when his partner looked like he was about to die of fright. He moved slowly, carefully toward Lucian and touched the side of his face. Hells, it was so, so cold. "What's happening to you, sweetheart? What's going on?"

"I—" Lucian's eyes were red, tears flooding down his cheeks. "I—I don't know. I would never hit you, Colton, *never.*" He was shaking his head, his whole body trembling under Colton's touch. "Colton—something's terribly wrong—ever since we left my father's house I haven't felt like myself—I thought it was the drugs, but—it can't be, it . . ." He let out a shuddering breath, his quivering gaze finally meeting Colton's. "Colton, precious, I think I might actually be possessed."

What? "No."

There was no such thing as demons or spirits—they'd spent their whole damn collaboration pretty much proving that. It had to be something else. There was surely a more logical explanation for why his sweet, gentle partner had suddenly become a violent monster. It couldn't be. It couldn't be! *Because if he is possessed, if Lucius really pushed us into the jaws of a monster, then—then—*

I have no idea how to help you.

"Lucian." Colton took his hand and squeezed it, shaking his head. "I'm not upset, Lucian, but this needs to stop, okay? You need to get some rest. Everything with your father is just getting to you, and it's making you act out."

Lucian violently shook his head. "No—it—Colton, it's not—"

"Shh." It wasn't happening. Lucian wasn't possessed, right, so there was nothing to worry about. *Colton. Run.* Colton kissed Lucian's hand. Thankfully, the bleeding from his lip seemed to have stopped. "Let's get you into bed, okay? You've been through so much, and you're so tired, and we don't even know what your father used to dose you. Come on." He took Lucian's wrist and pulled him toward the bedroom.

"Colton," Lucian pleaded. "Please, you're not listening. I can't control it, love. I—I'm terrified—I *hurt* you—without even thinking I struck you to the ground and—I don't know what else I'm—it's going to—please. I'm not imagining things, I know I'm not—there's this anger inside me that's never been there before, and it—you need to get out of here—you—" His face twisted into a smile. "Don't leave me, Colton. I'm so frightened."

"Of course not. I'm not going anywhere, sweetheart."

"No!" Lucian grit his teeth. "No. I can't—it—get out of here. I'm begging you."

Colton pulled Lucian into his arms and stroked his back. "I'll make you some tea, okay? You just rest. You're okay, I've got you." He sat Lucian down on the sofa and smoothed out his hair. "There we are. Isn't that better?"

"You think I've lost my mind." Lucian's voice was small.

"No, no." That was what had gotten his mother too—she hadn't rested enough.

Had a demon killed his mother? How much of the evil in the world was actually because of supernatural forces he couldn't control?

That was a lot. Too much, actually, for him to process right now. He had to get Lucian well again; he had to protect him from— *From what, Colton?* "You're fine. You just need to relax."

Lucian took a deep breath. "Colton, there is a voice in my head, and it's taking control, and it's getting worse, and I don't—haaaa . . ." Colton turned around to see Lucian up on his feet, stretching his beautiful arms out over his head. "Sorry, love, it's nothing. Just trying to figure out what happened, I guess. Anything's better than knowing I hurt you for no reason. Demons. Of all the crazy—"

With a strangled noise, Lucian grabbed a knife from the counter and sliced open his palm, his blood spilling onto the white marble floor.

"Lucian!" Colton slapped the knife out of his hand and snatched his wrist. "Stop it!"

"Colton, listen to me. I'm losing control, and I feel like I'm going to hurt you. You really need to get out of here. I'm serious. I don't know how I can get it to stop—it's not my voice, it's not me, I don't know what's happening. I love you. I love you, and I don't want to hurt you anymore. Please, Colton."

Colton was shaking his head. "We need to wrap your hand up. You're okay. We just—I'll make you some supper, all right? A good night's sleep." But even as he said it, he knew how ridiculous he sounded. There was something *seriously* wrong with Lucian, something Colton could not explain using rational means, and no amount of denial was going to change that.

Lucian looked up at Colton and swallowed. "Colton? Darling, I think I need to go to the hospital."

His stomach dropped. Colton tried to think back to what had

triggered all of Lucian's outbursts in the last twenty-four hours. They seemed linked to anxiety—anxiety about his father, about Colton's love, about loving another man in general, any perceived slight, anger, frustration, physical pain. He'd have to be careful, try and keep things as calm and simple as possible.

He sat close to Lucian in the carriage, holding him tight as his pale skin shivered under his cloak. Lucian kept his eyes shut, his face screwed up in concentration as he breathed in and out.

"Lucian? Are you in pain?"

"I can't," he whispered. "It's listening."

Colton urged their driver on and rushed him in to be seen immediately with a bag of gold coins. "You won't speak a word of this to anyone, do you understand? I believe someone is trying to harm my colleague."

The doctor, the same one from the day before, nodded and performed a physical examination, her expression becoming more and more concerned as she went from one body system to the next. She hesitated before speaking, and Lucian assured her that whatever she'd found, he wanted to know about it. His heart rate wasn't compatible with life, the doctor explained. He was as cold as a stone.

Colton's head snapped to look at Lucian, feeling the blood drain from his own face. *He's dying?* Lucian was breathing slowly, his back ramrod straight with attention. *Like if he lets his guard down for a minute, he'll lose himself again.*

"I see," Lucian mustered. "And my blood results from yesterday?"

"Normal, apparently, no obvious physical or metaphysical corruption. Nothing to explain these signs."

Assuming the Beaumont tech is any good with this kind of problem.

"I see." Lucian glanced at the red gash on his palm. "I would like some stitches for my hand and a psych evaluation, please."

The doctor took him off, and Colton just waited. His head was spinning. It wasn't true, was it? A demon possessing Lucian was so ridiculous, but when had Lucian ever lied to him before? Been so far off the mark before? Was it *possible*? Had Lucius lured them into the basement on purpose just to . . . ?

It took an hour, maybe a little longer, before his partner was returned to him with a white bandage wrapped around his hand. "Nothing obvious on the psychological examination either. Lord Beaumont appears to be sane."

"Well, that's good," Lucian quipped, crossing his arms. "You know how to reach me." He was swaying on his feet, and Colton hooked an arm around his waist to keep him standing.

They held hands in silence on the carriage ride home, Lucian staring out the window, Colton staring at Lucian. Lord Beaumont kept his spine straight, his eyes forward, like he was concentrating with every cell of his body just to keep upright. *To keep the thing from taking over.*

It couldn't be. But it was.

"Colton?" Lucian said softly as they entered the warmth of his apartment. "While I was waiting for the evaluation, I wrote you something. If the worst happens, love, I want you to read this letter." Lucian produced a parchment envelope with his beautiful script dancing over the surface: *To Colton, with all my love.*

"Please keep it safe, precious. It's important to me that you have it." He licked his lips, twisting his cuff links around. "I love you, darling. You've made me so much happier than I could have ever imagined. I feel quite worn out. I think I need to lie down for a time."

"Lucian!" Colton called after him, and Lucian stopped at the threshold of his bedroom without turning back. "I'm not going to leave you over this, okay? Whatever is happening, whatever your father did—I'm with you. I promise."

Colton just held the envelope in his hot grip. He sat in the guest room in stony silence, staring out into nothing as Lucian's last piece of humanity crumpled beneath the heat of his fingers.

It wasn't supposed to be real. None of this was supposed to be fucking real! There were no ghosts, no demons, no monsters in the night that preyed on the weaknesses of man and made him bend to their will. It had all been a con! A trick! A joke they played on the faithful!

If it—if it was real then—then his mother was right, then the world was a horror, and Lucian was . . . he—What the fuck was he going to do?

He wanted to scream. An overwhelming sense of dread filled his chest. All he wanted to do was to go be with Lucian, to grab him tight and shake him free of whatever was holding him. Had he ever before felt so useless? So impotent and so weak?

His mouth opened up, and a strangled croak emerged, a pitiful whimper in the face of the agony he was experiencing. *Lucian* was the one who was good with words. *Lucian* was the one who always knew what to do, when to act, when to run away. Okay. It was fine. It wasn't like Colton was incapable of looking after the pair of them, or protecting them, or fixing things when they got into a bind, right? He'd been trained by the best exorcist in Silvermoor, and even if he hadn't been paying enough attention, there had to be something he could do for—

You've made me so much happier than I could have ever imagined.

Colton collapsed in on himself, his chest flush against his knees as he tried to keep his misery silent. Maybe Lucian would lose faith; maybe he'd recede into himself, give up control, be lost forever.

If the worst happens . . .

"No, no, no, no." Colton clutched the letter to his heart. Everything had been going so well, They were so *happy* together. Lucian had accepted himself. They had enough money to start over anywhere, Odessa was safe, they could have—they could have had anything. Why had this happened? Why had they gone to that basement? Colton had known that Lucius was trouble, but he went along with it anyway because he thought it would be best for Lucian.

He shoved the letter into one of the bedside drawers, burying it in a dark corner and slamming the thing shut. He couldn't stand to see it, to think about what it represented, the fear that had to be raging in Lucian's heart to drive him to write those words.

The demon seemed to take any emotional weakness as a chance to sink its claws in even deeper, and the fear that came with that realization only made matters worse. Colton had to be strong for him, had to stand by him and wait for whatever this was to settle itself, one way or another. And so he tiptoed back to Lucian's room and lay down beside him, taking his hand and kissing it softly. Lucian's brows were furrowed as he slept, and Colton flicked open a bottle of Blossom to help settle him down, holding a dash on the top of his finger under Lucian's nose. Colton followed suit, chased it with the entire contents of his flask. Just this once, just so they could sleep properly.

He could only pray that when they woke up, Lucian would still be in control.

twenty-four

Bright light broke across Lucian's bed the next morning, and Colton squirmed away from it as he stretched his limbs under the covers. His hand found Lucian's cheek and almost winced away from the chill in his skin. "How are you feeling, sweetheart?"

Lucian's eyes opened and settled on Colton, a soft smile crossing those beautiful features. "All the better for seeing you, baby." He shifted over on the bed and perched himself on Colton's hips, pinning his wrists to the mattress as he pressed his freezing lips to Colton's neck.

Ooh, frisky. "Well, good morning to you too, Lucian." Colton craned his chin and exposed his throat for his partner.

"I thought you might have left in the night," Lucian purred.

"Of course not, stupid. I'm not leaving you over something paltry like *demonic possession*." He grinned. "You'd track me down, and I'd never hear the end of it! 'Oh, Colton, what a terrible partner you are, abandoning me when at last my soul hath descended into the dusky bowels of—mmh!'"

Lucian's lips were sweet against his own, and he found himself giggling into the kiss. Demon or not, he could handle it. Lucian was still in there, after all, and that meant that Colton had every reason in the world to stand beside him.

"Shut up," Lucian growled, biting Colton's ear.

Oh, no. "Lucian?"

Their eyes met, and "Lucian" sneered, drawing his tongue over his teeth. "What do you think?"

Not Lucian.

"Get off me," Colton said as calmly and firmly as he could manage. It liked fear, right? It liked a reaction. "I am retracting consent."

The creature laughed, a harsh barking sound that was so far from Lucian's bell-like gales of joy that it made Colton sick. "That's not how this works."

Teeth on his neck, he felt his skin tear, the warmth of his blood as it trickled onto the mattress. Colton strained to free himself, the muscles of his arms cording from the effort. *What the fuck is happening? Lucian isn't this strong. We were equally matched whenever we sparred. Oh, no.*

He clamped his mouth shut, not wanting to give it the satisfaction of hearing him cry out. With all the strength he could muster, Colton coiled his leg against his stomach and kicked, striking its solar plexus and sending it flying off the mattress and onto the floor.

It lay curled up like an armored bug, coughing and heaving on the ground. Colton stood above it, his arms crossed, triumphant. "Not so strong now, are you, asshole?"

"Colton . . ."

Lucian? Oh, fucker.

Lucian looked up at him, agony and desperate fear in his eyes. "Colton, I'm so sorry—your neck—"

Colton knelt down beside him and took his hand, kissing it fiercely. "It's okay. I'll be fine." He didn't want to scare Lucian; he didn't want to make it worse. He had to be strong. This wasn't like any enemy they'd faced in the past. He couldn't defend himself with his fists, with a blade—anything he inflicted on the creature was dealt in its entirety to Lucian, who was conscious, paralyzed within his own body.

"Go, Colton," Lucian begged, shifting away from him on the floor. "I can't stop it. Please."

"Lucian—I'm not going to—you know I wouldn't—we're partners and—" His voice was cracking as he closed the gap between them. "You're my sunshine, Lucian. I'm not—not when you need me like this—how could I—"

Wait. He was an exorcist, technically. *That had to count for something.* "Sit there, love. We can try—I'll get my kit, and we'll get you out of this in no time." Colton started drawing runes on the floor, and Lucian (or Lucian's new guest) watched him with polite interest. Okay! Some incense, the special serpent orb . . . maybe a bit of Night Mare root for that extra kick.

"Demon!" he called, pressing a ball of quartz against Lucian's head. "I order you to leave this body! You are not welcome here! I banish you! I . . . BANISH YOU!"

Lucian snorted a laugh, that hollow, pebbles in a tin can sound. "Jolly good show, boy."

Um. He guided some of the incense smoke around his face and took out his spirit staff, which he didn't often use because it was clunky and difficult to bring anywhere due to the size. "Demon! I order you to depart this plane!" He cracked the stave on the ground, then blew some lemon-scented ash into Lucian's face.

Lucian let out a puff of breath, shifting the dust away from his bangs. "Are you finished?"

Colton looked down at his bag. This was just painful. "I suppose I am."

Then came the now-familiar claws on his back, teeth sinking into his shoulder, the taste of blood as a fist crushed his face. He was knocked back, his head colliding with the sturdy marble walls as Lucian—as *it* stood up, licking Colton's blood off its teeth.

"You're a fool," it said, looking down at him with Lucian's beautiful face, all the disdain that he'd ever directed at their Ivory marks dripping from his eyes. "This man"—it looked at itself in the mirror, smirking with pleasure as it beheld Lucian's beauty—"figured it out faster than anyone has in a thousand years. He felt me, he heard me, he believed it, he warned you to flee." That horrible smile. "And you didn't listen."

He hadn't wanted it to be true. How could he live in a world where it was? It was easier to pretend . . . even for a day, even for an hour.

"I normally prefer to keep myself hidden for a little longer, you see. It makes it easier to take total control when the host isn't aware of what's happening to him." The creature pulled a cigarette from the drawer and lit it, smoke encircling Lucian's elegant fingers. "You drugged me," he said plainly, casting his eyes over the dead embers in the fireplace. "Or, I suppose one might say you drugged Lord Beaumont. Then got so drunk I imagine you don't remember anything from the last few hours clearly. A terrible habit of your class." It shrugged, turning a cold unfeeling face toward Colton.

No more drinking, not 'til we get this sorted. You're better than this, Colton.

It took a long drag of the cigarette and exhaled the smoke through his nose. "What was it, a sedative? You suppressed his mind while he slept, and now I've taken such a hold that I wonder if you'll ever be able to speak to him properly again." He laughed then, that horrific, dripping miserable sound. "Just as well he wrote you that goodbye letter, hmm?"

Why was it so *cold* in here? Colton stayed perfectly still, almost afraid to breathe. What had he done? It was just a little—he was suffering, it was supposed to help.

The creature stood and prowled around the room. "I keep asking myself how such a well-bred man could find himself in bed with a little gutter rat like you. His last words to you were about love and dedication, about how he felt his spirit dying. And what do you do with that heartfelt moment of vulnerability and devotion? You storm to your hidey-hole, cry into your pillow, and then you seal his fate."

Holy *hells*, this thing liked to talk. Maybe it picked up little traits from its host and was unable to disentangle them from its own psyche while it occupied them? Colton didn't dare move. He wasn't certain how much information the thing was willing to spill, but he didn't want to interrupt.

"Normally I have to keep myself well hidden from my host's acquaintances. It makes it so much easier to take hold, to destroy them slowly from the inside until their family doesn't even recognize their loved one anymore. Until they all abandon their loved one, and I can do as I wish."

Colton wasn't going to leave, he'd resigned himself to that at least. His half-assed attempts at an exorcism hadn't been effective, but that didn't mean nothing would work against the creature. He could regroup, maybe even set something up while it was resting . . . there had to be something, someone that could help him get Lucian back.

"I suppose it doesn't matter in your case, however. I have very little to fear from you, Colton."

He took his cigarette and put it out on the still-healing incision of Lucian's palm, watching with interest as the embers made the skin blister and the stitches curl.

Colton leapt up, grasping its wrist and tearing it away from Lucian's hand. "Stop it! Don't hurt him! What do you want?"

The creature only laughed, yanking itself free from Colton's grip. "Oh, Colton. I want to carve a beautiful world in my image."

"That's sort of a cliché." He flicked his eyes up—Lucian would have laughed, and his eyes would be glimmering with pleasure. But the creature's nostrils flared.

"To undo the evils in your society, boy. To rid the world of *waste*." He glared at Colton. "Those who fester and take and *breed* without a care in the fucking world. I imagine you have questions." It stepped close to Colton, Lucian's warm smile shadowing his features for just a moment before it slipped away. "Or I would, if I imagined for a moment that you had any curiosity at all. I'll tell you what Lucian wanted to know, then. Make this a bit more sporting, mmm?

"Lucian's spirit is still alive. It is trapped inside of me and can see everything I can see. If he dies, I die, and, in general, vice versa. The possession was orchestrated by that man you call Lucius Beaumont, though what his specific intentions are, I do not know. I can hardly complain. It's not often I get given a body so powerful, respected, so *rich*." He looked at Lucian's beautiful hands. "He could not force me to do it, Colton, yet how could I resist such a vessel?"

What did that mean? *Keep in mind there's no way to know how much of this is true.*

"My goal is to rid the world of trash, Colton. You won't understand. They never do. My name is not for you to know, yet you may call me Lucere. A fitting homage to my ever hospitable host, mmm?"

It—Lucere—touched Colton's face and drew nearer.

"He feels pain as I harm his body, and he has never known terror like this before. Trapped in this mind, watching as a spectator as I make use of the influence he threw away without thought. I must thank you, Colton, for the head start. I doubt he would have faced Lucius without you."

Colton withered, shaking his head. He hadn't known, of course he hadn't. Lucian was *everything* to him. "Please. Tell me how I can help Lucian."

Lucere's hand moved in an instant to Colton's throat and squeezed. Colton clawed at the arm, Lucian's blood caking under his fingernails—fuck! His vision started to blur and tears rolled down his cheeks. He couldn't die now, Lucian needed him, no one else knew . . .

Please, please!

Colton's hands went slack against his side as he lost the strength to fight. Lucere—no, now Lucian—cried out and tore his hand away from Colton's neck, throwing himself to the ground as he gasped for air. Lucian looked up at Colton, his expression agonized and frightened.

"Colton—" he managed, like every syllable was an effort. "Please. Help."

"Lucian!" Colton rushed to Lucian's side, clutching his shoulders and meeting his eyes. "I won't leave you, okay? I'm going to help you; I'm going to fix this." He'd think of something, though obviously he wouldn't be able to brainstorm with or around Lucian without tipping that monster off. Lucian would just have to trust him, like he always did.

Lucian's bright and intelligent eyes glazed over, and Lucere pushed Colton away, brushing himself off as he stood and shaking his head with a chuckle. "My, my. In all my years, such a strong spirit I have never encountered. It is no matter, Colton, he cannot take control back for very long. How pitiful that you are all he has in this world, mm?"

There was a time, long ago, when Colton had tried to imagine what the hells were like. They spoke about them in the chapels that littered all the districts, how the righteous would avoid them, then the remainder of humanity would sink as low as they deserved based on their conduct during life. A hell of fire, a hell of ice, a hell of incessant, relentless torment where they tore out your tongue and peeled off your skin to be fed to the spirits.

"You and I are going to have a lot of fun, Colton."

And yet there was no hell he could imagine that was worse than the one he resided in now. The glint of fear he could still see in Lucian's eyes while Lucere stepped closer to him, clutched at his chin, and sneered. The soft glimmer of the man he loved, slowly being extinguished by this malevolent force that neither of them could control or understand.

He'd asked his mother once, how a demon possession worked, how long it took, what happened to people whose bodies were inhabited.

"*The demon's goal is to take over the body, love. Little by little, it will make it impossible for the host to emerge or express himself. The demon can't kill a host directly; it's more of a slow, inevitable decline. The rate depends on the person's spirit, their resolve, their desire to fight. But sooner or later, that person becomes trapped in their body, powerless to do anything but watch. If the person loses hope completely? If he gives into despair? Then the soul dies, Colton."*

Lucian was tough, deep down. But there was only so much punishment a gentle soul like his could take. He had to hurry.

twenty-five

Theirs had been a partnership of equals. Colton had always been better at enacting their plans, managing their finances, ensuring that they had enough supplies, that the schedule was feasible, that their reputation was sound. Lucian was better at ideas, at planning, at pivoting in a moment, at seducing a stranger into trusting them with his life.

And now Lucian was gone.

No, stop it. He's there, he's fine, he's just not . . .

Colton shut his eyes.

Okay, how would Lucian deal with this? Colton tried to tap into his inner Beaumont, imagining a world of pomp and grandeur, his whole life a dance of false intimacy wherein he got by on his wits and charm. Lucian was a master at reading people, figuring out what they wanted to hear, and giving it to them without hesitation or embarrassment.

He imagined himself as Lucian then, his movements suddenly elegant, his smile assured. He would watch his prey and make a plan of attack based on his observations. So. What did they know?

The demon was violent, prone to outbursts of anger that seemed to be based on perceived slights relating to respect. He liked to make Colton tremble, he liked to look at himself in the mirror, he liked getting a reaction. Likely he was terribly insecure, his own voice bolstering his sense of self-assurance. Lucere had said that he'd wanted to get rid of "trash," which wasn't very helpful. "Use" Lucian's body, he'd said. For what? He was a disgraced noble with only his exorcism money to his name, relatively well known perhaps, but not that well respected.

Lucian would probably approach this in one of two ways, Colton thought. He would either provoke Lucere as much as possible, sneering at him, matching his bravado and confidence with his own, allowing his innate display of superior intelligence, charisma, and wit to speak for themselves. The demon would probably become irate, irrational, lash out and make mistakes. It was also more likely to harm Colton or Lucian in that state and would surely try and up the ante of his behavior in order to get a degree of control back in their brand-new relationship.

The other option would be the exact opposite—to defer to the creature and act as though he were so awed and fearful of him that he would do whatever Lucere asked in exchange for small favors. He had a grand plan, right? They could kiss ass, do whatever he wanted, lull him into a false sense of security and then, somehow, dispel him from Lucian's body.

The second option seemed like the safer one, but it was possible that Lucere would try and hurt Lucian anyway in order to get a reaction out of Colton. His foot was still stinging from where he had kicked Lucian's body away. There were clots of Lucian's blood that had dried under his fingernails. He couldn't physically defend himself from Lucere without harming Lucian.

He took a deep breath. Feigning some distance from Lucian might be a good idea, then, so that it might be believable that he wasn't fussed if Lucian was harmed. But he doubted that the creature would believe it, especially not after his display of adoration that morning, throughout this whole mess. Worse still, what if *Lucian* believed it and started losing heart?

One other factor he had to consider was whether Lucere would even allow him to stay close to Lucian. Obviously Colton had an incentive to try and get Lucian right again, which was in direct opposition to what the demon wanted. So what was stopping him from simply evicting Colton and carrying on as he wished? He'd have to make this fun for Lucere at any cost.

And somewhere in between all that, he would need to get in contact with Mai and Odessa so that he could make them apprised of the situation. He was going to need help, and a lot of it. There were other exorcists in the Iron District, but those were *serious* frauds. Not like Colton was a fraud, these guys like, had little paper cutouts of ghosts and used tin cans as spirit vessels. There was the Order of course, but there was the real risk that they might be more interested in harming Lucere than helping Lucian, or that they might be working for Lucius. So, that left the two remaining sensible people in his life. Odessa was smarter than Lucian, probably, and Mai had grown up watching Colton's mother perform exorcisms from the time they could walk. Now, whether he would even be permitted within twenty yards of Odessa, and whether Mai would want to hear even one damn word about helping Lucian Beaumont, were both slight unknowns in the equation as it stood. He just had to hope that they would both be willing and able to offer him assistance, and that as a team the three of them (Codessai? That was awful) might be able to do something for Lucian.

After their altercation that morning, Colton had more or less crawled into the guest room and locked the door, his whole body shaking as his adrenaline started to drain away. He examined himself in the mirror, his throat bobbing as he took in all the damage from this one encounter. His lip was split, his jaw ached, and a collar of bruises bloomed over his throat. He assessed the hemorrhages in his eyes, the bite mark on his neck, the scratches on his shoulders and his cheek. He took a deep breath and gingerly started to wash his wounds in the bathroom sink.

That certainly could have been worse, probably. At least Lucere hadn't knocked any of his teeth out, broken any of his bones. He recalled with a sickening lurch how much more powerful

Lucian's body had been this morning as it pinned him to the bed. He was toying with him.

Colton took a deep breath and steeled himself, getting dressed in one of the nice suits Lucian had bought him in the hopes that Lucere would appreciate the effort. He put his hands behind his back as he entered the living room, knowing that he wouldn't be able to hide their pitiful tremors if he held them in front of his body.

"Lucere?" he called out, inwardly wincing at the way his voice cracked as he did so. "Can we talk for a bit?"

The demon was seated in Lucian's armchair, cigarette smoke twisting through the air. A bottle of liquor stood open on the table, casting an amber glow on the wall behind it. *A drink. Holy hells, I need a drink.* It clicked off the radio, which had been yammering something about the newest Prime Minister Lennox scandal. "So respectful now," Lucere sneered, his eyes dark and cold. "It must want something."

Colton swallowed. "Yes. I have a proposition for you." He shifted on the balls of his feet. "I want to assist you to do whatever bullshit you want to do to society. You're going to need my help, Lucere, because you might have Lucian's body and face, but you don't have his knowledge or his personality. Without me, you won't be able to navigate these upper circles, you know? They'll figure you out—they'll get the hospital records, they'll throw you both in a mental institution or a prison while they try and figure out how to dissect you out of him." He hoped with all his being that he sounded confident.

"In exchange, I want to talk to Lucian every day. For an hour."

The creature considered it, approaching Colton with long, purposeful strides. "Interesting. And why should I believe for even a moment that you actually wish to help me? That you will not betray me the moment that you can?"

Colton swallowed. "I probably will betray you. But you know that I don't know exactly how to do that, and I know that you don't know how to move around the Ivory District in such a way that doesn't get Lucian killed. We're at a bit of a stalemate in that respect, I think."

Lucere sneered at him. "Oh, dear, I thought you were some sort of demon-hunting expert. Was it all just a game to you, an exercise in time-wasting and conning people? You bear the marks of a real exorcist, Colton. Yet you do not know how to wield them, correct?"

Colton just lowered his head. "Yeah. I'm sorta kicking myself now. I should have listened more. But I'm just trying to be straight with you, sir. We have opposite goals. I just want to come up with a solution that makes everyone happy until we, you know, kill each other."

Lucere narrowed his eyes, a pleased-looking smirk snaking across his features as he ran his hands down Lucian's chest. "Very well, Colton. You do as I ask, whenever I ask, without hesitation, and in exchange I will allow you to see your precious Lucian for one hour a day. But you must remember one thing. I cannot kill your Lucian, obviously. But I can certainly maim him. How many fingers do you think a man needs?"

Colton wasn't able to hide the horror that breached his face from those words. He felt his face blanch white, his eyes widen, his shoulders quiver. "I'll do whatever you ask. There's no need—"

Lucere smiled. "Good. Get down on your knees and bow to me, Colton."

Hokay, whatever. Colton was happy to give him a real show if he wanted one. He pressed his forehead against the floor, his palms flat on the fine forest wood. "Anything else?"

Lucere approached, stepping on Colton's fingers with his cold bare feet. "Kiss them."

Again, whatever. This sort of humiliation meant very little to Colton, seeing as how he wasn't an especially "proud" man, such as it was. Lucere wanted his toes tongued? No problem, demon, prepare to have the drooliest soles and arches this side of the Ivory gates.

"Enough." Lucere gave Colton a swift kick in the jaw, sending him reeling.

Colton rubbed his chin, glad nothing was broken or out of place. "Forgive me, sir, but you surprise me. It seemed as though your ambitions were grander than . . . that." His disdain reached his eyes, and he cursed himself for it.

Anger flashed in Lucere's eyes, then amusement. "Oh, Colton. I think it's important for colleagues to have clear boundaries in their relationships, no? Established roles and so on? Isn't that why he let you into his bed in the first place?"

"You don't know what you're talking about," Colton muttered, his ears reddening. "He loves me."

"Oh, Colton, how *lovely* for you." Lucere laughed. "Was that good? Did I sound like him then?" He snatched Colton's chin with his inhumanly strong hands and held him still, looking into his eyes.

It touched his face, considering him before turning away in disgust. Well, at least Lucere didn't seem to share Lucian's interest in him physically, that was good. His touch was like that of a corpse; it was like putting his hand into a barrel of beaks and claws. It looked like Lucian, it smelled like him, it tasted like him—but they were diametrically opposed in how their spirits sang through their hearts, and the contrast made Colton sick. "Yeah. We're off to a great start." He spat at Lucere's feet before he could think better of it.

Lucere laughed then, ambling idly over to the kitchen counter from which he produced one of Lucian's ill-used but beautifully polished mother-of-pearl-handle cutting knives. "Oh, Colton. How long will it take you to learn?" He put Lucian's hand on a cutting board and lined the blade up with the last knuckle of his elegant pinkie. "You will learn your place, and until you do . . . Lucian. Pays. The. Price."

"NO!" Colton careened over to him, grabbing Lucere's wrist and trying with all his might to move the blade away. "Please.

Please, I'm sorry—I won't do it again, I won't do anything ever again, please—cut my finger off, please, please, I'm sorry, it's not Lucian's fault!" Tears ran down his face as Lucere stood stone still, sneering at his desperation. Colton tried to wedge his own hand in between the knife and Lucian's finger, and attempted to pull the blade away—how was the demon so *strong*? Colton grabbed Lucian's shoulders and shook him.

"Lucian! Lucian, please! Please, please." The stakes were too high; he couldn't let Lucian get mutilated. *Come on, fight it! Fight it!*

Lucere was just laughing now, his whole body shaking as he let the knife fall away, blood dripping from Lucian's finger where he'd been cut down to the bone. "Oh, Colton. This is terribly unbecoming of you. You truly have no idea what you're doing, do you?"

Oh, that laugh. Like beetles running over broken tiles, like a crow dying in the sun, like seaweed ropes running between his legs. What he wouldn't give to have Lucian back in this moment. To have that sparkling smile pressed up against his face, those strong, warm arms wrapped around him.

"What are you going to do? How will you get him back if I don't release him?" He ran his hands through Lucian's hair, leaving a streak of crimson blood in the spun gold. "Maybe sex will jostle him free. A bit of warm, intimate passion, staring right into his eyes. Maybe that'll shake him loose, Colton. For a minute, for five, maybe, but you'll be able to talk to him, to reassure him directly that you're the best he's got. Hah! Even I have standards, Colton." He laughed again, tears pricking the corners of his eyes.

Colton shuddered to imagine it. Sex with Lucian had been so soft, tender, and intimate. All gentle touches and soothing whispers, laughter and warm hugs, comfort, trust, respect—everything he'd ever wanted. He couldn't imagine himself submitting to Lucere, for Lucian's sake.

He wondered for a brief moment how he had ever confused this *thing* with Lucian. They shared a body, they shared a voice, they shared a face, but the longer he spent with Lucere, the less

Colton could see a resemblance. Its eyes had none of Lucian's bright intelligence, its smile had none of his warmth, its posture was dripping with sleaze. And so it was with no small amount of disgust that Colton cupped Lucere's face on either side, looked into his eyes, and searched out any glimmer of his partner trapped within the tarry ooze of Lucere's influence.

"*Mama? How can you help the possessed person's spirit? How can they get control back?*"

She had brushed the hair out of his eyes and smiled. "*Love, Colton. Demons cannot tolerate love.*"

"Lucian?" he said softly, swiping his thumbs over Lucian's beautiful cheeks. "I'm so sorry this is happening. I'm so sorry I keep messing everything up. But I do love you, Lucian. With all my heart, with every part of my being, with all the stupid poetry that you can conjure, and I was never able to—I love you. Please." He leaned in and kissed the body in front of him. "Please come back to me."

There was a moment, just a moment, when those eyes shifted and turned into something bright and glimmering. A sneer melted into a warm smile, and gentle hands wrapped around Colton's body and pulled him close.

A trick, surely. *But it's him! I know it's him.* His soul was certain. This was Lucian.

"I love you too." Lucian's voice, surely, before the kiss deepened, and Colton relished the soft fingers running through his hair. "You fucking idiot."

No.

That pretty pink tongue swiped over Lucian's teeth, and suddenly Colton was pinned, trapped, desperate.

When had it shifted back? How long had it been—ten seconds? Five?

Colton's face broke into despair, and Lucere laughed, pushing him up against the wall and taking what he wanted. His weight was suffocating, his whole body hard, violent, and sharp.

Colton didn't fight this time. Instead he stayed silent, staring off into the distance, waiting for it to be over. If obedience meant that Lucian would be safe, then he could bear just about anything. Colton wouldn't let Lucian pay for his crimes.

Never.

twenty-six

When Colton had been in his very early twenties, he had tried to get into the Ivory District under the cover of darkness and steal himself a fortune. The plan had been half-baked, poorly concocted, but arguably much better than the plan he'd had the last time he'd broken in as a kid.

He had wrapped himself up in a cloak of midnight black and snuck past the guards in the last hours before dawn, a sack in his hand that he fully intended to fill with gold coins and tiaras and whatever other rich people bullshit he'd manage to get his sweet little hands on.

The sound of glass cracking had sent shivers up his spine, his hand wrapped in wool as he pushed it through windows, grasping at latches to give himself access. His mother had always taught him not to steal, and for the most part he didn't. But that winter had been difficult for the whole Iron District. The factories belched smog into the ocean and poisoned the fish, the earth itself caked in a layer of grimy snow that had killed a good portion of the crops right at the end of the harvest season, and the bloody Prime Minister had thought of what a fantastic idea it might be to raise taxes on the lower two districts at the height of the freeze.

Colton hadn't been surprised by any of this and had been

scraping by just fine until Mai had caught the coughing sickness, which had robbed her skin of its color and her eyes of their light.

No one could afford his services that season, even when he discounted them so much it was hardly even worth going outside to perform them. Colton's own needs were fairly meager, plus he had deft enough hands to keep his flask full anyway. The problem was Mai. He couldn't let anything happen to her—she was his best friend, the only ex who gave him the time of day, someone who had watched him grow up, had been there when his mother died, when Orr had dumped him, when his drinking had gotten *really* bad. He had to return the favor.

The remedies that gave Mai relief only became more expensive, and it would only be a matter of time before the disease burrowed into her bones and killed her, just like it had killed his mother. Colton watched Mai shiver in her bed one night where the wind was threatening to tear her door off its hinges, her whole body convulsing against the cold and the damp. He curled up in bed beside her, wrapping his muscular arm over her trembling body and praying to anyone who would listen that she'd wake up in the morning.

He put his hand under her nose all throughout the night to make sure she was breathing, his stomach aching with worry as he watched her suffer.

"I could set the house on fire, you know," he suggested, pushing some of her hair behind her ear. "It'll keep you warm for the rest of your life."

Her laugh had descended into a cough. She pulled her hands away, her dry little tongue licking away the spots of blood on her lips.

That night he'd gone to the Ivory District. He tried to keep the job to the bare necessities, the minimum that was needed to keep Mai healthy and warm, nothing that would hurt anyone for having lost it. Golden candlesticks, gem-encrusted goblets—he tried not to think about why people needed any of this bullshit in their houses while everyone in the Iron Belt was freezing to death. Colton was, if nothing else, pretty good at reining himself in when necessary. He took exactly what he needed and slid out into the night, metal clanging in his pouch as he skulked back to the Indigo stairs.

Just a little closer...

A guard spotted him, clocked the bag, and what else would he see but an Iron thief in the night? Colton ran. He tossed his ill-gotten goods into a shrub that he hoped he'd be able to find later and sprinted as hard as his sinewy legs could carry him. He ran until his chest was bursting; he ran until the air was puffing from his lips in white clouded gasps. But the guard was well-fed, and Colton was not. He felt his skin bloom into bruises as he was tackled to the ground, heard the friable crunch as a stranger's elbow was driven into his neck.

Fuck.

Cold metal slapped against his wrists, and he flailed like a rabbit in a snare as he tried to escape. "You don't understand!" *Mai needs me! If I don't come back, she—dammit.* He'd known the risks. *Best face up to them, yeah?*

He was dragged through the streets to the local jail, thrown into a cell, and the door slammed shut behind him. Colton didn't like confined spaces. He didn't like being under someone else's control; he didn't like not knowing what was about to happen to him.

The guards came into the cell, sometimes. One of them had a *thing* about Iron men, apparently, and he wanted to prove a point to the miserable little pissant who had tried to rob the best the nation had to offer. Colton never learned the man's name, but he knew the way the skin beside his eyes crinkled when he exerted himself—a fist into his stomach, a stick against his back, a boot on his neck that ground his face into the rough stone of his cell.

It was in these moments that Colton learned to recede into himself. He would shut his eyes and allow his mind to leave his body. He would think of better times, of jellyfish in the sea, of ice cream by the beach—of the first time Mai had kissed him, the way that the sun warmed his face when he rested on a stony ledge. His body groaned and roiled for mercy, and yet Colton was silent. What good did it do him to struggle, to resist his pain, the inevitability of torment?

That was the way he had to face his encounters with Lucere, he realized. Allow his mind to wander, focus on the beautiful marble tiles across the room, and wait for the thing to get bored. He wouldn't fight, he wouldn't resist, he wouldn't even look it in the eyes. And if it lost interest and left him alone, all the better. The main risk, he supposed, was that Lucere might try and up the ante a bit, and figure out what pushed Colton's buttons and push them as hard as he could.

An obvious one, of course, was hurting Lucian.

Okay. Keep it engaged, like a cat playing with a bird with a broken spine. He grimaced, he gritted his teeth, he tried to make himself look furious, agonized.

Take the bait, you miserable bastard.

Most of it was violence, some of it was humiliation, all of it was manageable. Pride wasn't going to be Colton's downfall, and he was happy to play whatever role Lucere wanted if it meant keeping the peace, keeping Lucian safe.

It wasn't easy to keep things creative in what was essentially a mean-spirited hostage situation, but Lucere did his damndest.

The thing pointed at the fireplace, barely hidden glee vibrating off his shoulders. "I thought of a way to bring us closer. Solidify our bond."

Great.

It pulled a searing hot iron poker from the embers, passing the handle to Colton. "Mark yourself mine, Colton. An *L*."

Well, at least he didn't want him to spell Lucere. To be honest, this sort of body modification was the kind of thing Colton didn't mind in the slightest. In the future he and Lucian would laugh about it—hells, it would even grant a sniff of legitimacy to their demon hunting ventures if they chose to continue it. "See? Look! A *real demon* made me do this!" How cool. A badge of honor he'd bear for the rest of his life.

But Lucere didn't need to know that, so instead Colton shook his head and begged, pleaded, not to have to go through with it.

"I guess we could just put it on Lucian?" the creature mused.

Easy enough. Lucere was a fool.

It hurt like fuck, which was just as well because it was best if the screams were genuine. Colton was shaking by the end of it, the black-and-crimson *L* smoldering on the inside of his wrist. *You know what? It looks awesome.* "Fuck you," he spat.

"Oh, Colton, that was lovely. See how much happier we can be as a little family when you know your place? Excellent work, excellent boy. You know what excellent boys get? They get time with Lucian!" He clapped his hands, his laughter shaking the room. "Go on then. Have him."

Lucere released control to Lucian, who apparently hadn't been expecting to be front and center all of a sudden. His face was a storm of conflict. Shame, remorse, desperation, hopelessness, despair. He couldn't be losing hope already, could he? They'd only just started—did he just want this to be over? There were tears in his eyes, and he shook his head as he turned away, shame bored into his face.

Too much. How much of this could Lucian take?

Colton was almost afraid to hold Lucian close. Lucere loved that game, it seemed. Let Lucian out for a moment, lull Colton into a sense of security, allow him to hope for just an instant, and then strike, all fangs and claws, laughing at their audacity to find a glimmer of love or hope in this desperate world.

He pulled Lucian into a warm embrace anyway, pressing sweet kisses into his hair and stroking his back. "It's all right, Lucian." He smiled, sweeping his thumb against Lucian's cheekbone. "We don't have much time together. Tell me what to do."

Lucian laughed then, a sob getting caught in his throat. "I

can't, precious. He's listening. I knew we should have come up with a code system ahead of time. The raven crows in the steep hill, the dogs are delicious in the morning, that sort of thing." He wiped his eyes with a smile. "I knew we should have enrolled in that nonverbal communication class together, but noooo, you thought we needed cooking lessons."

Colton found tears in his own eyes as he joined in the laughter, still giggling even as he pressed his lips to Lucian's. "Trust me, that was the correct class for us." Colton laced his fingers behind Lucian's neck and pressed their foreheads together. "I meant it, you know. When I said I loved you, I meant it. I love you, I love you, and I'm never gonna let you go."

Lucian's cheeks flushed crimson, and he smiled. "I know that, petal. You don't need to worry about me. I'm pretty tough. Sort of. Mostly." He chuckled, which descended momentarily into a set of gasping sobs. Lucian regained his composure quickly, pulling his hands away from his face. His hands went to his sleeves. "Dammit. He doesn't even—he never wears cuff links, and—" *Poor Lucian.* "I—I trust you, darling. I trust you implicitly. You'll sort this out."

Colton coughed out a laugh, pressing a big wet kiss to Lucian's cheek. "Did the demon turn you stupider? We're *screwed* if this is up to me."

"We might be screwed then, precious," Lucian said softly. "I'm afraid I'm not going to be much help."

He was right. Lucere would only let Lucian out when it pleased him, and there was no guarantee that he would ever do such a thing again. He could snatch away control whenever he wished, including if Lucian was about to say something useful or brilliant.

Colton didn't want to talk about this any longer. Instead, he stared at Lucian, at the kindness in his eyes, the softness of his smile, his regal posture. He listened to his beautiful tinkling bell laugh. He squished him close and shut his eyes, breathing in the soft vanilla scent of his hair. "Don't worry about anything. Just take care of yourself. I want you to stay strong. I'll fix this." Somehow.

Trapped in the deepest corner of hell by himself. Fuck. He hadn't asked for this. "I don't know how, but I will. You just need to stay brave for me, okay?"

"Colt—" Lucian's smile wavered for a moment as the sneer cracked through his joviality. His eyes went blank, then settled into something dark and cruel. "I think that's plenty of time, don't you?"

"Not really, but I'm sure you knew that." Colton sighed. "Thank you, though. It was really lovely to see him again."

Lucere looked taken aback, but then he laughed once more. "You're funny, Colton. You can see Lucian all the time."

Colton did not deign to reply to that. He'd have to trust in Lucian's ability to stay strong while he put together the exorcistic means to rid themselves of the demon. "So how does it work, Lucere? Your body, I mean. Do you need to eat and stuff?"

"My body has all the mortal flaws, Colton."

"Oh! So you're probably starving, right? Do you want me to go out and get us some groceries? Lucian hasn't been eating well for the last few days. You've got to be famished."

Lucere peered at Colton with suspicion. "Why would you do such a thing?"

"Well, I'm also hungry, and I also don't want Lucian to starve to death, and honestly I think if we have a more cordial relationship, it'll be a lot easier for us to live together." He managed a friendly smile. "What do you say? I'll be the best boy, and keep you alive while you figure out what your next evil steps are, and you let me have Lucian time."

Lucere scoffed. "Go, then."

Colton pulled on his coat, glad for the chance to turn away to hide his smile. "What do you like to eat?" he called over his shoulder.

"Flesh."

"Flesh! Of course. Good choice. I'll see what they have at the shop. I'll be back before midnight, a'right? Try and stay out of trouble."

Colton's shoulders sagged as soon as there was a door between him and the demon. He silenced the corner of his mind that told him to run.

He pulled his hood over his head and breathed on his hands. If he was going to exorcise this thing, he was going to need help from his mother. Unfortunately, due to her being dead, such help wasn't forthcoming. So he'd have to go to the only other person who had known her, the only other person in the world who might have something of his mother's that he hadn't destroyed in his childish tantrum.

Mai.

Hopefully she wouldn't kill him.

twenty-seven

The sun felt strange on Colton's face. It dazzled his eyes, and he put a hand out, blocking the light from hitting him directly. How easy it was to forget that there was a world that still existed outside of Lucere's dark violence.

He had to focus. Colton was certain that even now, less than five minutes after his departure, Lucere was hissing in Lucian's ear that this was the beginning of his abandonment, that they would be all alone from now on—*He threw you away, just like your father, just like everyone else who ever loved you.*

And it would keep speaking, the oily tar of its misery seeping into Lucian's mind, shrouding it in darkness more and more until there was nothing left of him. The weaker Lucian was, the sooner his soul would perish. He had to hurry.

Mai's door loomed in front of him, and he bit his lip. This wasn't going to go well, he just had a feeling. Sharp knuckles rapped against the splintered wood, and she opened up with a yawn. "Hey, Colt. You look like shit." She fluffed out her silky black hair and gestured for him to follow her into the apartment. "What happened? I'm assuming the prick was involved."

Colton swallowed. "Mai, I need your help."

She rolled her eyes and started brewing some tea. "I literally can't think of an example of you coming to my house and *not* needing my help. Though I must admit you have held up your end of the bargain." She directed him to sit in her lovely plush armchair.

How could he even explain it? Directly, probably. Mai appreciated directness. "I think Lucian is possessed."

Mai snorted a laugh. "Is that what he told you? That's the worst excuse I've ever heard in my entire life."

"I know it sounds crazy, Mai, but—honestly, the man you met the other night, that's not Lucian. It's not."

She handed him a teacup and twisted some lemon into her own brew. "You said he was the one who always 'got taken by the spirit' at the exorcisms, right? The man you described as the most brilliant actor you ever met, *now* he's possessed for real? You know how crazy that sounds, right?"

Mai searched his face, but Colton just shook his head. She knew him well enough to know he wouldn't imagine something like this, wouldn't assume something without considerable evidence to back it up. If Colton said there was a demon, odds were there was actually a fucking demon.

She squeezed his fingers and took a long, deep breath. "Okay. Tell me what happened."

And so he told her. He told her about Lucius, about Lucian's sinister portrait in the basement, about the blood, the runes that they'd stolen from his body. He looked at his arms, at the faint glimpses of tattoos that were just visible from the edge of his sleeves.

"How? How did he know about your tattoos?"

That was the question. In all his life he'd never seen anything like the marks on his body before, nor on his mother's, nor on her scrolls and books. She'd told him once about the world she came from, a little village on the other side of the sea.

"*There were no walls there, Colton. Just trees and grass, clear fresh water, a world carved from spirits and not red-hot steel.*" They had taught her how to hunt demons, had carved runes into her skin with charcoal ink, and then she'd done the same to Colton, when he wasn't quite old enough to remember. She'd never told him why she had left, nor why no one in Silvermoor carried these same markings. He liked to imagine that it was due to a yearning for freedom and adventure, maybe she'd fallen in love with a forbidden suitor? Or had she properly disgraced herself, with or without the help of his "father"? The answer was lost now.

He took a deep breath and told Mai his theory. That Ives had copied all of his tattoos onto paper, hidden them away in the church, and Lucius had stolen that information and used it to damn his son. Lucius had mentioned he'd visited the church before wanting to purchase it. It was likely, then, that he'd known about the Ives job before it had started. Which meant he'd either been behind the job itself, or he'd been spying on them all along.

The Beaumont power structure was a difficult beast to grapple with. Infinite resources, coupled with spite and the idleness of the rich.

Mai thought about it, putting on her thick glasses. "Which means they're the key in all of this. C'mon then, strip."

The last time he'd stripped for Mai had probably been more sexy than this, considering she was poking him like a dissection frog, her ridiculous lenses making her eyes enormous. "Do you remember which ones were in the basement?"

He thought about it. "This one." He pointed to one on his right arm. "And this, and this."

Control, conjuring, vessel.

"I'm sure there were more, but it was so dark down there." Plus seeing them at all had been unsettling enough that ignoring them at the time had been emotionally preferable.

"Well, that's a start. What've you tried so far?"

"The parlor tricks. I used some of the stones with the runes, but it was all a bit haphazard. Lucere didn't seem to fear it at all. I didn't want to try again unless I knew for sure that I was doing it right."

"Okay. And your mom never told you what to do? When a human body is actually possessed?"

Colton shook his head. "She said I wasn't old enough. That it was too dangerous for me to know before I came of age."

"Hm. You got rid of all her things after she died, right?"

Colton tried not to live his life with regrets, but if there was one thing in his youth he could take back, it would be that hasty decision.

Mai fluffed his hair. "Hey, c'mon. What do you take me for?" She left the room and came back with a small wooden box, inside of which were cloths, beads, and . . .

"Two of her books." Mai grinned. "She gave them to me when I turned ten. You know, when I was going through my witchy phase. I kinda figured we might need them again one day." She cocked her head to one side. "Gotta say, I didn't see the whole rich boyfriend demon possession thing coming, but I've never claimed to be a psychic." She let the box fall to the ground with a dusty *whump* and pulled out one of the tomes. "C'mon, you look too."

His mother's handwriting. Everything she'd worked for and believed in, this piece of himself that he never thought he'd see again. He thought it had been lost to his childish impulsivity, that he'd doomed Lucian with his foolishness. "Mai . . ."

"Stop. You can thank me after we're not in danger of being killed by a demon."

He sniffled a laugh. "You got it."

The books weren't easy to decipher. His mother's handwriting was small and flourished, and the language was cryptic and unfamiliar. Mai got frustrated after about an hour of attempting to understand the contents, stormed off, and returned an hour later with a dictionary she'd dug up from the foreign bookseller at the end of her block.

They pored over the books together until Colton found one that, at the very least, seemed to have a glossary of what runes should be used in what spells.

Mai pushed her glasses up her nose. "Hmm, you said Lucere was conjured specifically?"

"That's what he says."

"Well, it stands to reason he might be mentioned in one of these demon lore books, right? Might give us some insight on how we can deal with him." She flicked through the pages. "Maybe this one? It says you need a cross of blood to conjure it. Hmm . . ."

"What else does it say?"

"His name is Herluin? It says that—sorry, the handwriting is hard to read. It says that long ago, he was a little boy who was abandoned. His father was a pauper, a gambler, lost everything, drove his mother off, leeched off of society, threw Herluin away like he was nothing. He died in the gutter, apparently."

Hah. A story more familiar to Colton than Lucere would likely care to understand. *Hypocritical bastard.*

"And his anger at being thrown away, at the injustice of being born into such an uncaring world, to such an impoverished and haphazard man, to have a life that was not worth living, it crushed his heart into black oil until all his humanity was gone. He was reborn as a . . . well it says angel, but your mother seems to have crossed that out and written 'demon' over it in all capital letters. He wishes to—it's very unclear—there is *so* much fire imagery here. Uh . . . rid the world of the dregs of society, those who take without giving, the poor, the addicts, the leeches."

Colton frowned. It was hard to imagine Lucere as a little boy, yet if he saw Colton as one of those unworthy creatures, as a waste of life . . . "It would certainly explain why he hates me so much," he muttered. "A'right, so he has daddy issues. He and Lucian are gonna get along great."

Colton lay back on Mai's giant pillow pile. Suddenly, his eyes snapped open. It just all sounded so familiar. "Do you have an Order Hymnal?"

"Uhh, I mean, I doubt it but . . . oh! Yes! I was given one from my last job! I'm not godly enough, you know. I was just going to use it for my stove but—"

Colton flicked through the pages.

He shall come to the exorcist's call,
A fallen child, his cleansing flames bathe the world,
By writ of the Order, the world reborn,
Silvermoor will bow, in splendor, in mercy.

Was Herluin *specifically* selected for this? "That means the Order is probably involved . . . and Lucius was working with them, probably."

"Fuck. So what do we do about it?" Mai asked.

"That's the question. I think the first step is figuring out what answers are written on my body." He picked up the book of runes and lined up his arms before it. "Okay, so this symbol comes up a lot—it means demon, obviously. Ah okay, so this one, it seems to be like a spell for getting rid of a demon in a house. See, look—this one is demon, this one is abode, this one is dispel. So this one, this one is more like a curse." The ones from the basement, stolen from his limbs. "It's for calling a demon. Nothing about getting rid of a demon from a person. Let's keep looking."

Colton flipped through the books as fast as he could, scanning the pages for something, *anything* that could help free Lucian. There was a page at the end of one of the books, the words written in dried-up blood.

"*The cure is in the heart. That is where the demon resides. There is no other way.*"

The heart? He swallowed. "Mai—these ones on my chest." He pointed at his left breast, where a circle of ornate letters hovered over the organ in question. "Heart, knife, lavender, exorcise, demon . . . keep the aim true."

"What does it mean?"

Colton hesitated. "It—I think it means we might have to—" He didn't want to say it; he didn't want to put the words together.

"Take a blade, anointed with lavender oil . . . and stab Lucian in the heart. Right here." Mai put her fingers right in the center of the tattoo circle. "There is no other way."

"No. There's got to be another option. That'll kill him."

Anything but that. Anything.

"And the demon!" Mai added, helpfully. "But I agree, not an ideal outcome."

Marbles crawled into Colton's lap and snorted, her flat nose nubbling against his legs. "I can't, Mai. I can't."

She leaned over and hugged him tight against her chest. What if he didn't have a choice? What if Lucere was going to rip out his throat?

He wasn't sure what he'd do in that moment, if he had to choose between saving himself or protecting Lucian.

What would Lucian want? Could he bear to go on living like this?

"I'll keep looking, Colt. I doubt you can take any of these books back home, right? He'd eat them. When do you need to be back?"

"Soon, probably. I'm just supposed to be grocery shopping."

She nodded. "Go, then. If there's another method, I'll find it. Meanwhile it might be a good idea for you to try and get some outside assistance."

Colton nodded. "Yeah. I was gonna try and get in touch with Odessa."

"Or . . . maybe even their father?"

Colton gave her a look. "The man who got him possessed?"

"Yes! It's possible that *this* wasn't the intended outcome, you know? Lucian's his son—he probably doesn't want him to cut his own hand off. Plus if he got a demon *in*, he might be able to get one *out*."

That was a thought. After all, Lucius didn't need to *know* he was helping, did he? He could have dug up all sorts of useful exorcism crap from Ives or his other contacts. Dess might be able to get Colton into the house, where some proper snooping might be undertaken.

He bought some meat at the market—all sorts really, rabbit, cow, chicken, something that was helpfully labeled "miscellaneous." Lucere would have to be happy with that. He trotted up the steps to

Lucian's flat and was greeted at the door by three beautiful women. All were laughing, disheveled, their dresses revealing and worn.

"Lucere?" he called, putting the bag of flesh on the counter.

It was seated in Lucian's armchair, half-dressed, covered in lipstick, looking absolutely *fucked*. It smirked around the lit cigarette simmering between Lucian's lips, standing up and adjusting its genitalia to greet Colton. "Took you long enough. I got terribly lonely, you know. I'm sure Lucian doesn't mind." Its hand went to its throat, wiping the red smeared kisses off of Lucian's neck.

For just an instant, Colton could see Lucian in those eyes before Lucere locked him up once more. Desperation, repulsion, helplessness.

Colton stepped forward and hugged Lucere to his chest, squeezing as tightly as he could. "I'm sorry," he whispered. "I'm so sorry. I came back as soon as I could."

He felt his skin tear as Lucere's claws found his shoulders.

twenty-eight

Lucere was growing restless, bored of their little domestic truce-cocoon. "I wish to explore Silvermoor, Colton. You will escort me."

What that probably meant was Lucere had attained a good enough grip over Lucian at this point that he wasn't worried at all about losing control of his host when they were out and about.

"Ah . . . well, I don't think that'll be a problem. What did you have in mind?"

"I want to do an exorcism, Colton. I think it'll be *enlightening*."

Hokay, that wasn't exactly what Colton had been expecting, and there was the very real risk of damaging their reputations if their new colleague wasn't able to keep his cool. "Oh, we don't have anything booked actually. Because of—well Lucian had so much Archon stuff to do and we were waiting for the money to clear from the Ives job, and—"

"I did not ask for details or excuses. We will do an exorcism, Colton. I want to see your work."

So Colton went through their outstanding requests and ultimately settled on what Lucian had helpfully dubbed "the case of the bread basket." The Ellingtons apparently had some disturbances in their kitchen, and had sought the aid of the exorcists to solve their problems once and for all.

They were a well-off family, Indigo people originally, who had risen up when the wife had invented some sort of rotating cream-whipping device that had purportedly revolutionized food aeration. Not important enough to seriously harm their reputation should this all go badly, but wealthy enough that Lucere would be satisfied, hopefully.

Lucere was not easy to share a carriage with. He fidgeted, he kept pushing against Colton with his shoulder, and from the way he was gawking, he was quite unfamiliar with the Ivory technology he was seeing. *It might have been a long time since he was last conjured into the world.*

Upon arrival at the house, Mr. Ellington greeted the pair and sat them down in the parlor. "Oh, Lord Beaumont, it's quite a spirit! Every morning the kitchen is in disarray—flour on the floor, bread torn to shreds, claws on the ground, milk upended—we're at our wits' end."

Sounds like they might have a cat.

Lucere was not happy. "For such paltry matters you summon me?"

Colton clasped his shoulder. "For a demon? Haunting our neighbor? Of course, Lucian. Please rest assured, Lord Ellington, we will sort this matter for you."

The pair were left alone in the kitchen, and Lucere poked at what looked to be an automated can opener. It cut his finger slightly and he smashed it on the floor with a grunt. "Right. So how does this normally go?"

"Oh. Well, normally we find what's actually going on, which in this case I think might be a house cat. Then Lucian pretends to get possessed, and then I, ah, banish the demon, and then the family feels better and that's usually it."

Lucere didn't seem impressed. "And for this they pay you such a fortune? No, Colton, we must make it worth their while. I need a goat."

Colton made a point of dealing with the actual demon, which

involved setting up a cat play area so the beastie wouldn't be quite so bored in the evening. He went to check on his partner, which had gone about as well as expected. Lucere's plan ended up in what might be generously described as a ritual sacrifice of a live caprine victim, which resulted in the kitchen being coated in so much blood that the Ellingtons' eldest son burst into tears.

"Behold, your demon." Lucere dragged his blood-soaked fingers over Lucian's face, leaving tines of red in their wake. "You are safe. You are grateful. How fortuitous."

Uhh . . . "And—and Lord Beaumont has done such a wonderful job of—um. Sanctifying your—ah . . . well. The demon is gone, at any rate." And at the very least they could maybe donate the goat to a food kitchen or something. *This was not going to be good for business.*

Lord Ellington was shaking as he handed the money to Lucere, who licked his teeth and just about snarled when the man accidentally made contact with his skin. *He isn't good at this—he's* terrible *at being human.*

At the very least, this experience had probably left Lucere realizing that he wasn't going to blend into high society as seamlessly as he might have intended. The job had certainly soured Lucere's mood, and he kept stepping on Colton's feet as they walked.

"You . . . wanna talk about it?"

"Hah. Your little farce was everything I imagined it would be. This is how you applied your gifts? Useless."

"I mean, it usually goes a lot better than—" Never mind. "It's all right, Lucere. There are other things we can do outside of the apartment that you might enjoy—and tell you what, we can study more people, and you'll uh . . . I mean your grand plan to take over and fix society or whatever will be underway in no time."

Lucere crossed his arms. His pout was one of the most Lucian things he did, honestly. "I wish for access to grander resources."

Wait, this was it. A chance to see Dess, snoop around the Beaumont manor, maybe even see if Lucius could be called upon to help remedy the situation. Risky, but . . . they had to try.

"Yeah, sure! We should go see Lucian's father, he—"

A laugh erupted from Lucere, cutting Colton's speech short. "Oh, ho. My little Lucian did not much care for that suggestion, Colton." His tongue glided over the tips of his teeth. "Go on. I'm intrigued."

"Um. Well, right now you're just a nobody, right? Cause Lucius Beaumont disinherited Lucian, and we're kinda, like, losers." *Sorry, sweetheart.* "So if you wanna do *proper* evil, we'll need to get Lord Beaumont to take you back, and he probably will because, you know, you're awful now."

Lucere wasn't stupid, obviously. It wouldn't do to try and deceive him—he'd see right through it. He smiled, less than a grimace, which was maybe 25 percent Lucian. Fuck. *It's learning.* "Hah. Go on then, Colton. Bring me to my father."

The carriage ride to the Beaumont estate was never a pleasant one, but this one carried an extra weight of dread with it. Even through Lucere's control, Colton could almost feel Lucian's anxiety, which seemed to be putting the demon on edge. It was drumming its fingers, biting its lip, fidgeting in a way that Colton had never seen it do except when sexually aroused.

The carriage came to a stop, and the manor loomed over them, blocking out the sun with its enormity. Lucere stepped out of the carriage and stood straight, his shoulders back, a cocky smile on his face. He'd chosen one of Lucian's signature three-piece suits, sapphire cuff links, that ridiculous gold-lined cape. He really looked like Lucian.

A butler greeted them at the door and bowed. "Young Master Beaumont, what an unexpected pleasure. Do you have an appointment with your father?"

Lucere sneered. "Do I need one? He is my *dear father*, after all. I'm sure he'll be delighted to see me." He reached out and grabbed the butler's chin, forcing him to meet his eyes. "Go get him."

It looked like Lucian. The resemblance stopped as soon as it opened its mouth.

"I—I shall see if he is available, my Lord."

They were left alone in the corridor, and Colton watched as Lucere peered at his surroundings. The golden statues, the gems pressed into the walls, the stained glass mosaic featuring the Lord of the house, casting his brilliant shadow over Lucere's face.

"Lucian!" Odessa's chirping voice called from the other end of the room. "Oh, my word, what are you doing here? You should have forewarned me, you miserable cow!"

Oh, no no no.

Lucere was quick, and stepped in front of Colton, preventing him from catching her eye. Her feet were wrapped in pink silk slippers that tapped softly over the hard marble floors as she skipped toward them, throwing her arms around her brother's neck and kissing his cheek.

"Odessa, wait." One wrong move and they'd both get their eyes clawed out.

"Well, hello there, beautiful," Lucere purred, his hands snaking around Odessa's waist and gripping her ass through the thin fabric of her dress. His lips found her neck, and Colton shuddered as those sharp teeth grazed the perfect skin of her throat.

"Lucian!" Her cheeks were crimson, both hands pressed up against his chest as she tried to free herself from his grip. "Let go of me! What in all the seven bloody hells is wrong with you?"

"Hah! Hahaha! Very hilarious, *Lucian.*" Colton staggered forward, nudging Lucere in the side with his elbow. "Such a funny way to greet your *sister, Lucian.*"

Let her go. Please. Please don't hurt her—Lucian will never forgive me, please, please. Besides, hurting the current heir might harm Lucere's chances of being taken back by the Lord of the house.

"Sister," Lucere repeated, letting her down onto the ground. "Of course, a poorly timed joke indeed. Odessa, darling, how are you?" Lucere's face softened, and there was almost something like affection in his eyes. *He's getting better at this.*

Odessa's expression was one of incredulity. She hesitated

before stepping closer, and then a crack rang out as she struck him in the face, her shoulder quivering with rage. "I do not find such jokes funny, Lucian." She remained still for a moment, then pulled him in for a very brief hug. "You're the worst, you know? I hate you."

Her eyes fell on Colton's, and she frowned, surely catching sight of the bruises on his neck, the cuts on his face. She smoothed out her dress, tucked a strand of hair behind her ear. "Why are you here, darlings?"

Lucere stepped closer to Odessa, and she flinched. "We're here to see Father, Odessa. I'm going to get un-disinherited."

She cocked an eyebrow, glancing at Colton. "You are? Ah . . ."

Odessa was probably as smart as Lucian was, maybe even smarter. Surely by now she had clocked that something was wrong with Lucian—he wasn't acting like himself, wasn't speaking to her the way he usually did, and bringing *Colton* to a meeting with Lucius was obviously not the best way to get back in his father's good books. Besides, he'd never expressed an interest in getting let back into their family before.

Colton caught her eyes and shook his head once, hoping she would understand that no, everything was not all right. He and Lucian had been so, so careful. They'd never spoken about Odessa in front of Lucere, never gave him any information he might use when their paths finally crossed.

She swallowed. "Of course. Well, I wish you the best." She stepped closer to Colton and took his hand. "Colton, darling, I have this engagement coming up next week, and I just *couldn't* go without your input on my outfit! Come, come, we have time before my father sees you—let me show you—"

"Odessa, how rude," Lucere said lazily. "Excluding me from your fun." He caught a strand of her hair and twisted it around his fingers, hard enough her face moved closer to him. "Anything you can say to Colton, you can say in front of me. I am, of course, your dear brother, after all."

Odessa laughed, and Colton watched the bead of sweat trail down the back of her neck. "But Lucian, you always hated my fashion shows, remember?"

Brilliant, Dess.

Lucere rolled his eyes. "We don't have time for this, Odessa."

No nickname again. She knows something's up. It could study Lucian as much as it wanted, but from the outset, Lord Beaumont had been keeping cards hidden.

She shivered. "You will not command me, Lucian Beaumont." A cold smile. "I do as I please."

"Dess—" Colton grabbed her shoulder. *Don't provoke it.*

Lucere's nostrils flared. "Is that so?" There was none of Lucian in it now, all indignant incredulity and icy fury. His posture predatory, muscles tight, a cocky smile gnashing with hunger and displeasure.

Odessa stepped closer and smiled as the thing licked its teeth. His shadow fell over her face, and she held her ground. "It is."

The butler emerged once more as Lucere was about to speak and bowed deeply. "My Lord, Master Beaumont is happy for an audience with you this afternoon. And Sir Colton is welcome as well. He was quite insistent."

Lucere grinned, his anger dissipating, his face shifting back into something like Lucian's. "Brilliant. Come along, then, Colton. Let's see if we can endear ourselves to lovely Father once more."

Odessa. Run.

"Colton—really, I need you right now, please," Odessa stammered, gripping his sleeve. "Please don't go right away."

Run.

"His Lordship is waiting, Master Beaumont."

Colton took Odessa's hands and looked into her eyes. "I need to do this. We can talk later, okay?" *Please, Dess.*

She swallowed. "Okay, honey." She squeezed his hands tight, raising her voice so Lucian could hear. "I will come check on you in half an hour."

Probably to make sure that Lucius hadn't killed him.

Great. Absolutely fantastic. Lucere grabbed his shoulder hard enough to leave bruises and tugged him after the butler, down the winding halls that led to Lucius's office.

He had to fight his body, shove down the dread that coiled in his gut as Lucere yanked him before the man who had done this terrible evil to his only son. His feet dragged, his heart raced, and every part of him felt cold.

Just hold on. Slip away when they're occupied, find Dess. He wasn't physically strong enough to defy Lucere. All he needed to do was survive this meeting.

And keep the two beings that loathed him more than anything on earth from cutting his throat for sport.

twenty-nine

Lucius's office was different from the last time they'd been in it. The portrait of Lucian was gone, replaced with a magnificent likeness of the elder Beaumont.

Lucius was facing the window, his hands clasped behind his back like Lucian did when he was pensive. "Lucian." His voice was smug. "You've come back at last."

Lucere's teeth glinted as he smiled. "Of course, Father. How could I allow myself to remain disgraced for so long?"

Colton tried to keep his breathing steady. Like one of those little birds that was trying not to be spotted by a cat.

"Johan was saying that you wished to rejoin this family. What will you do to make yourself worthy?"

Lucere's eyes flashed in anger. "Excuse me? You know what I am, do you not?"

"Hah. Of course." The Lord was smiling, the bastard. He'd known, of course he'd known. He'd done this to Lucian with intention and forethought. Colton was gonna fucking kill him.

Lucius's strides oozed confidence as he approached his son's body, grasping his chin and looking into his eyes. Lucius purred, his smile only broadening as the demon snatched its face away from his grip. "You carry yourself well. A worthy addition to my line. And so . . . spirited. I'm pleased. What good would the ritual have been if we'd ended up with a flippant little fool like that boy again? Look at you. My beautiful heir."

Lucere's body lurched. Had he just felt the flood of pain that Lucian was surely experiencing in this moment? Lucere stared at Colton, his head cocked to one side as he swallowed. His eyes flicked back to Lucius, narrowing slightly.

"Lucere." The demon clarified, "Nothing like that son of yours, mm? A wretched boy, yes?"

Lucius gazed at his heir, his chest swelling with what must have been pride. "Nothing at all. This"—he put his hands on Lucere's broad shoulders—"this is what a Beaumont looks like. And he and I are going to change the world together, aren't we, son?"

Colton kept a distance from them, not sure how the creature would react. Lucere did not like to be challenged or controlled. Then again, he loved power. And almost no one in Silvermoor had as much power as Lucius Beaumont.

Lucere's lip twisted into a smile. "Oh, Father. What did you have in mind?"

Okay. Okay. They're working together, that was . . . a somewhat predictable outcome. One he'd considered, though hadn't weighed very heavily. It was fine. They'd get lost in each other, Colton would slip away, conscript Odessa, and then they could plot away at their leisure. It was fine. *Just keep telling yourself that, kid.*

Lucius couldn't stop touching the demon. It was as though he felt paternal toward it, a stirring sense of pride and accomplishment for manifesting this horrific creature. "I was thinking, it's been far, far too long since we had a Beaumont in a position of real political influence." He smirked. "After all, what good is wealth without power? Imagine it, *Lucian*. My son, the Prime fucking Minister of Silvermoor."

Colton's chest tightened. What would a world with a demon in charge even look like? He imagined the Iron District in flames. He imagined slave girls being carted to the palace, the oceans turning red as they choked the fish with blood. More than all of that, though, he imagined Lucian's soul withering away. What use did the demon have for him anymore? Why should Lucere ever let him out again?

"Please," Colton tried, his voice aching with desperation. "Please, help him. He's your son."

Lucius's familiar eyes settled on Colton once more, and a self-satisfied smile crossed his face. "I suppose you're wondering why this wretch was even invited to our meeting, eh, Lucere?"

Lucere's attention turned to Colton, too, and for a fleeting moment Colton was almost amused by the family resemblance. Lucian had never looked more like his father than he did in this moment. "I must admit, I was."

Colton stepped away from them until his back was flush with the mahogany door of the office. The ornate woodwork pressed into his skin as he groped for the handle. Soft flesh met cold brass, and it rattled like an empty can in the rain as he found himself locked in. He swallowed.

"Um. Fire! THERE'S A FIRE IN THE OFFICE, WE NEED HELP!"

A clamber of footsteps, someone from the outside trying the door. "The key! Get the key! His Lordship is—"

"We're fine, Johan. Leave us." Lucius rolled his eyes. "Well, son. We don't know one another very well, do we?"

"I suppose not." Lucere was enjoying this. He was almost quivering in his hunger.

"So I think perhaps a test of loyalty is in order, no? So we know for certain we're on the same page before we get in bed together, so to speak."

Lucere's nostrils flared.

"Kill him for me." Lucius nodded toward Colton. "And kill whatever is left of Lucian along with him."

Colton could see glimmers of Lucian in Lucere's eyes sometimes, especially in moments of extreme emotion. Lucian had taken control once, maybe twice, when Lucere had not allowed it. As much as Colton loved and trusted his partner, he doubted that his soul had the strength to take control now. He was on his own.

Colton tried the door again, shutting his eyes—of course it was still locked. Panic bubbled through his chest. He didn't want to die like this, trapped with the things he hated more than anything in the world.

"Excuse me?" Lucere's body slithered toward Lucius. "A loyalty pledge? For what reason?"

"I brought you into this world, Lucere. You need me to achieve your aims. I think it is best if we trust each other. Besides, you must see that Lucian's toy doesn't serve our interests in any meaningful way. How am I to know that the possession worked otherwise?"

Lucere licked his teeth. "Look into my eyes, Father. Tell me what you see."

Lucius peered at Lucian's face, drawing a finger down the line of his cheekbone. "I see ambition. I see hunger. Desire. I see the steadiness that Lucian lacked. Resolve. Detachment."

"Do you see your son? Any part of him?"

Colton doubted very much that Lucius had ever looked into his child's eyes. That he would recognize his gentle warmth, the glittering joy, the desperate fear that only emerged when father and son were together.

Lucius considered the creature before him. "No. I don't."

Lucere smiled. "A pity. He probably would have spared you."

A word like "Lucian" was silenced as Lucere's fingers found Lucius's throat. Colton heard the cartilage crack beneath that unworldly strength, saw the way Lord Beaumont's blood landed with dull pats as it hit the carpet. Lucere tore. Sinew ripped and snapped under his nails, and he drew back a bloody fist, a fleshy mess of tissue crunching in his grip as he pulled away.

His larynx! Lucian's voice chirped helpfully at the back of his mind, as Colton chose this moment to recall the basic human anatomy they'd studied together when trying to improve his fighting skills.

Lucius stood for a moment, his fingers painted with blood as he clawed at his neck and gasped for breath.

Lucere just smiled. "I will not be controlled, Father. I'm sorry you couldn't understand that."

The Lord wobbled on his feet before crumpling at the knees with a wet thud on the carpet. Lucere gripped the flesh in his hand and squeezed the blood out of it like he was juicing a lemon.

"My, my, Colton. That must have been very upsetting for you."

Colton was grateful for the wood that kept him standing. His whole body trembled as Lucere licked some of Lord Beaumont's essence off his fingers.

"Why?" Colton stammered. "Why didn't you kill me?"

Lucere grabbed him by the collar and pressed a kiss to his forehead. "Because you're different, Colton. I think I might have been wrong about you." He smiled. "And Lucius Beaumont was hardly worthy of our attention, was he?"

Was that all? Surely the control aspect was part of it, but was any of this Lucian's influence? Herluin's residual anger at his own monstrous father? Colton couldn't control the sob of fear that wrenched itself from his throat as the adrenaline started to dissipate. His hands covered his mouth, and he coughed, soaking his skin with tears and mucus.

Behind him, he could hear a key rattling around in the lock, and Colton jolted away from the door. "Colton?" Odessa's voice. "Colton, honey, is everything okay?"

"Dess—" She couldn't see this; he had to protect her from it. "Don't."

The door opened anyway, and the lovely Miss Beaumont stood perfectly still in the frame like a rabbit spotted by a hunter. Her hand went to her mouth as she took in the scene—her brother, crimson painting his hand all the way down to where his sleeves met his wrist, a whisper of red by his lips, that manic, toothy smile that she didn't recognize. Below him was her father, his throat torn out, still gurgling feebly in a pool of his own blood.

"Lucian . . ." she stammered. "What—what happened?"

Lucere just smiled. "Oh, Odessa. It's a terrible thing. Father had a heart attack right here in his office. But darling, a glimmer of light in the darkness. Right before he passed, he made me his heir once more. Isn't that lovely, princess? A family reunited for one brief moment before tragedy strikes? I'm so glad he and I could patch things up before he died."

The audacity of the lie almost made Colton laugh. Oh yes, heart attacks often made people's necks explode. Yet who would question the Beaumont heir?

Odessa was shaking, the silk of her dress vibrating around her ankles as she held her ground. "That's great, Lucian." *How is she so strong?*

"Isn't it just? And you know what this means, right? This house, all our assets, everything in the Beaumont name is mine, darling. Of course I'll let you stay in your home, sweet—how could I move you in a time of such tragedy? But I doubt I'll have much time for you, love. I have to fulfill Father's last wish."

Colton found the strength to stand and took Odessa's hand. Some of Lucius's blood had spattered his fingers, and he hoped she wouldn't notice. "What was it?"

"Sweet sister, it is that I should become Prime Minister."

Her eyes widened.

"I know, such a responsibility, eh? Not to worry, pet. I have you and Colton to help me, don't I? I'll need to keep you both very, very close. We wouldn't want anything to happen to either of you, would we? Oh, Odessa, you mustn't cry. He lived a full life."

A sob escaped from her throat, and Colton held her close. It was too dangerous to speak; Lucere was high from his victory, liable to strike at anything that might catch his attention.

Lucere licked his fingers once more, smiling pleasantly. "Get Johan back here. It's undignified to allow Father to lie around like this. We must prepare him for burial. Heart attacks, eh? *Horrific.*"

thirty

If Johan had any opinions about the state in which he found his employer, he certainly didn't say anything about it. Lucere stood over his father's body with a sad smile on his face, shaking his head in sorrow.

"How terrible it is to become the head of the family in such a tragic and unexpected way. But I would like it to be a smooth transition, you know? It's what my poor, poor father would have wanted."

Johan called other male servants, who kept their eyes on the ground as they tidied up what remained of their former master. None of them dared speak, nor to even cast their eyes up at Lord Lucian as he directed the cleanup.

Odessa hadn't let go of Colton's hand since she'd discovered her father's body, and her tiny palm was sweating against Colton's fingers as she gripped him with all her strength. She alone seemed perturbed by the horror, and yet what could she do? Lucian wasn't Lucian, and whoever he was now was quite happy and capable of murdering people on a whim. She had underestimated him before—she wouldn't do that again.

"Odessa," Lucere called, causing her to stiffen like a cat against Colton's side. "Why don't you go tell the rest of the staff about what has transpired? I feel as though they might take the news better from you than from me." He smiled. "And find a room for Colton while you're at it. We wouldn't want him to be a target of any political nastiness now that I've resolved to run for Prime Minister, would we? He must stay here." He looked to the servants. "I do not want anyone to enter or exit this house without my permission, do you understand? There is such evil in the world. We can't be too careful, can we?"

Well, Colton reasoned, *at least he's not expecting me to stay in his room all the time. Plus he's gonna let me be alone with Dessie, so we can figure something out.* Focus on the positives. That was probably what Lucian would do.

"Of course, Lucian," Colton said obediently. Just a moment alone, that's all he needed. Odessa would know what to do, maybe. *Please. Please let me go with her.* He didn't ask for permission but simply followed her out of the office and into the corridor. She was standing tall and straight like Lucian did, even though her whole body was trembling as she walked past the creature inhabiting her brother.

As soon as they were alone, Colton expected her to collapse in his arms in a flood of tears, but she didn't. Her eyes were watering, sure, her voice was shaking, but she held herself strong as she faced him.

"I need you to tell me everything," she said, a sob forced through her throat. "Everything you know. What in the hells *is* that thing? What happened to my brother?"

There wasn't much time—Lucere could come for them at any moment. He leaned against the wall to keep himself upright, before recounting the whole miserable tale.

"I thought your father might have some insight into how to get rid of the demon. I thought you and I could work together, I thought—but he is so difficult to control, he wanted us alone. And your father wanted to see the *thing* he created. He *wanted* this—a strong son, a ruthless one." *That fucking miserable bastard. Guess he got what he fucking wanted.*

Odessa took a deep breath and looked up at the ceiling, blinking her eyes until the tears slipped down her cheeks. Colton pulled her into a soft hug, and she cried into his shirt, soaking it with years of pent-up misery.

"Hey," he said, after a time, "I really do think your dad probably has some stuff we can use to get Lucian out of this. We—me and my friend Mai managed to dig up some of my mother's old books. I can't read the symbols very well at all, Dess, but it implied that the only way to get rid of Lucere would be to . . . to kill Lucian.

"But I was thinking back to when I was a kid. I don't think I ever saw a *real* exorcism like Lucian needs." He'd certainly never seen his mother stab someone in the chest. "But there are rituals, tools, little bits I remember that I think we can use. Couple that with the research your father must have done, and I think we've got a lovely alternative to cutting Lucian's heart out."

Odessa shook her head. "A fine suggestion." Her fingers went to her temples, and she took a deep breath. "Okay. Okay. Okay. We can't leave the house without that thing's permission, and he's likely to keep a pretty tight leash on us for the immediate future. I also pissed him off pretty badly in that first encounter, which means he might want to hurt me to prove a point." She swallowed. "How did you keep him appeased before? You survived alone with him, after all."

"Doing whatever he wanted, mostly. He's a simple creature in many ways—he likes drugs, alcohol, food, sex. I think we should just appease him, kiss his ass, inflate his ego, and wait for him to let his guard down. It won't be easy, but I've not made any moves against him since that first night. My strong suspicion is he doesn't see me as a threat, or any human being, really. Besides, he'll be so busy with his political schemes that I'm hoping he won't even pay attention to either of us."

Odessa quivered but nodded. "Okay. So I think for now, we'll have to accept him as Lord Beaumont and all the power and privilege that comes with that. Then I think you and I can hole up in the library for a time. I'm certain we have some books on possession, on demons, the sort of thing that isn't readily available to the public." She swallowed. "And you're right. My father surely has—had—his own source of knowledge. Otherwise, how could he have performed the possession ritual in the first place? I'll have to break into his office without making Lucere suspicious..."

Colton squeezed her hand. "It'll be easy to convince him that he doesn't want your father's office. 'It smells like old man,' something like that. It's safe to say he didn't care for your father very much. I don't think it'll be too difficult to get him out of there, especially while it's all, ah, dirty."

Odessa laughed weakly. "Lucian inside of him, just—'Lucere, you must be joking, the carpet is *damp*! That is just asking for mold, weevils... Come now, this is beneath us.'"

Colton smiled too. It had been such a long time since he'd smiled. There was a part of him, and not a small part, that feared he'd never see Lucian ever again. "That's another thing, I suspect that Lucian's emotions influence him. Lucere reacted to his anxiety before, and I wonder if killing your father was partly Lucian's anger. He's also spared my life more times than I think is reasonable for a demon."

Odessa's eyes widened. "You think the demon is being influenced by Lucian?"

Colton nodded. "It certainly would explain a lot."

He's still in there. He's fighting for us. He's not giving up and neither should we.

"That's fantastic, Colton! He's still alive in there, protecting us as best as he can." Her expression was warm. "Good, we can work with that. At the very least it'll make it harder for him to kill us."

"He won't try." Colton prayed he sounded confident. *It's more fun for him when we're alive and miserable.* "Probably."

"Probably." Odessa sighed.

The plan then was to lay low, collect as much information as they could, and then attack when Lucere was least expecting it. All their resources would be pooled, all the books, all the trinkets, Mai, if she was willing. They'd do as Lucere wished, dance on little strings, and then crush him like a fucking bug.

It took Colton about an hour to figure out the way back to Lucius's office, and he sheepishly knocked on the door and let himself in. The body was gone, but the carpet was not, and it squished under his feet as he approached Lucere's stern figure by the window.

"Lucere, I wanted to thank you for sparing me before. I didn't know what to think." He swallowed. "How does it feel? To be the new Lord Beaumont?" He forced a laugh. "I'm wondering how Lucian feels too."

Lucere scoffed. "It's not a bad feeling, I suppose. All the better when I can start wielding it. Your little Lucian is a bit shocked, I'm afraid. It all happened so fast. Poor, poor father."

"Yeah. It was really sudden, wasn't it? Are you okay?"

Lucere frowned, then chuckled to himself. "You're a funny one, Colton. I can see why Lucian likes you."

"Thanks." A pause. *Ingratiate yourself. He likes you, use it.* "What will you do? Were you serious about becoming Prime Minister?"

Lucere turned and cracked his neck. "You wish to stop me?"

Colton actually laughed then. "I think we both know I can't. Besides, I'm having a hard time seeing you doing what Lucius wanted."

A scoff. "Unparalleled power in this nation? The man had at least two good ideas in his lifetime, it seems."

Summoning you, and ruling the world. Great. Okay, pivoting then—"It's just a lot of work, right? Especially for someone who isn't aware of all the major political players yet, what illegal things the police can ignore and the things they can't." It was bullshit, but he could fake it enough to keep Lucere happy. He cleared his throat. "I'm just saying, I think my utility to you hasn't quite come to an end. And of course I'm happy to keep up our deal from before—I do what you want, and in exchange I get my Lucian time at night." He couldn't believe how confident he sounded. How differently this conversation was going from how he envisioned it, telling Lucere what would happen rather than begging for scraps of his lover. "Surely our bargain hasn't changed just because our living situation has."

The demon considered him and stroked the side of his face with icy fingers. "Mmm. I suppose we can keep up with our little game, can't we, Colton?"

"Of course! And maybe we can start by getting you a better office, one befitting *Lucere*." He fanned his fingers out in an arc over his head, like he was imagining that terrible name written in glistening lights. "Look at this place—a giant frigging portrait of himself hanging over his desk, the tacky golden everything, clashes with the new red carpet." A cough. "Lucius had awful taste, no?"

"What in the hells do you care?" Lucere crossed his arms, a little defensive. He was almost cute sometimes.

"That man tried to kill Lucian. You're far less of an enemy to me than he was." True enough to be believable, maybe. "You didn't choose Lucian. I want every piece of him erased from the face of the fucking earth. And if that means you get a nicer office in the process, then so bloody be it."

And it'll get you out of here, so Dess can move freely.

Lucere laughed. "Indeed. I like you, Colton. I was wrong about you, you know. You're not like the filth you grew out of. Fine. Let us find an office befitting the new Prime Minister of Silvermoor, and you can outline your plan for my success. Then you can have your precious Lucian hour."

Keep it happy. Do what it wants.

It's just a matter of time now, you miserable bastard.

thirty-one

The first few days were tense. Colton wasn't certain what Lucere's limits were, how much of a danger he represented to Odessa or the rest of the staff. Perhaps he needn't have worried, though, as the demon seemed to be almost euphoric from the sense of power that came with dismantling the Beaumont dynasty. Lucius had been a close contact of the high leaders of the Holy Order and certainly had enough money to have some politicians in his pocket as well. Like a child first discovering the reach of his hands, Lucere stretched out his influence, testing the waters of what the new head of Beaumont could get away with.

Ives's poor reputation and the mystery surrounding his disappearance had fractured attendance for the Order's sermons (likely bolstered by a shift toward less favorable coverage from Beaumont Media, blamed solely on the incumbent Prime Minister Lennox), which of course had the King all up in a tizzy, and pushed forward an unprecedented midterm Prime Minister general election.

Perhaps two days after Lucius's untimely demise, four cloaked and elderly members of the Order attended Beaumont estate to offer their condolences to Lucian. Colton wasn't invited to the meeting, obviously, but Dess showed him one of the two-way clockwork spy beetles she'd snuck into her father's office as a teenager.

It all came out then. Lucius had found out about Colton's tattoo runes by paying one of his exes (Orr, probably), and had then given the information to Ives. *Lucius* had been the Golden One, the man who had promised Ives could ascend, the one who had ordered Magnus to hire Lucian and Colton.

To incapacitate us. To—to steal the marks off my body. So you could use them to—to summon—

"I might have been killed," Lucere said with a snort.

"You were never the true target, my Lord," a sniveling Order priest assured him. "Merely— the vessel. Your father's plan was always for you to—"

"Become great."

"To become Lord Herluin." Colton heard his chair scrape backward, the sounds of a man choking, gargling. "M-my Lord!"

"You will not speak that name." Lucere's voice was as calm as Colton had ever heard it. A snap, a tear, a body falling to the carpet.

Colton had to imagine that the other priests were fairly perturbed at this point. "My Lord—forgive me, us—our impertinence. We only meant—that Lord Herl—that you were always the intended entity—the Order—Our Angel, Your Grace, long have we awaited the return of—an entity such as yourself who can truly—"

There was the sound of man being struck, and Colton had to imagine that Lucere was sneering, his head cocked to one side like a hungry terrier. "Change the world? And what better man for the job than the Ninth Archon?"

Whatever the fuck the other eight Archons got up to, Colton never really found out. As far as he could tell, it was a title that had almost been manufactured for Lucian, for all of this . . . so the demon could take over, and rid the world of . . .

"Corruption. Moral failure. I can't watch the degradation of society any longer, gentlemen," Lucere said at a public forum, broadcast nationwide. "The rot of spiritual decay is infecting every corner of our fine nation, causing it to fall apart at the seams. Why do you think the most impoverished of us suffer so? Why is there so much crime, so much illicit drug use? Too many of us have turned away from our spiritual betters, have lost any sense of decency, morality, and goodness. The demons of the seven hells have permeated our lives, and they will not leave until drastic changes begin to happen in this country. *I* will be that change."

It was bloody brilliant, and it made Colton nauseous.

Something had shifted in Lucere. It seemed as though he no longer took pleasure in Colton's misery and was even *warm* toward him at times, gentle. He didn't strike Colton, didn't force his company, and was happily preoccupied with his candidacy for much of the day. This allowed both Colton and Odessa to move freely in the house, to collect all the books and documents that they could possibly use in their fight against the demon. Between Colton's books and artifacts that Lucius had collected, more and more pieces of the puzzle that could theoretically take down a demon came together in Colton's mind. With a bit of luck, they wouldn't need to cut Lucian open after all.

They just had to wait for the next full moon.

Ten days. They just had to hold out for ten days.

Lucere's sexual appetite was as high as it had ever been, but luckily for Colton (and unluckily for Lucian), Lucere only seemed to enjoy the company of women. A constant stream of young ladies was allowed into and out of the house. These young women often left with marks on their faces or bruises on their throats.

The creature was a marvel at political capital now, using his media outlets to espouse his virility, his care for the downtrodden, and just how much he liked touching the little lives of Silvermoor. What a man, right?

He let Lucian out sometimes, less and less often now that his independence and self-actualization were growing. Once a week maybe, if he was lucky.

"I just don't really see the point," Lucere muttered, cinching up his tie and shooting himself a sweet little kiss in the mirror. "He's such a bore, Colton. Barely wants to come out as it is."

"Please." Colton bowed at his waist. "I just—I want to know he's okay. I've done whatever you wanted, and I'll keep helping you as much as I can. Please." The aim was not to sound too desperate, but Colton wasn't always so effective in these matters. In addition, Lucere sometimes seemed jealous of Lucian, of the affection that Colton still carried for him. The moments after Lucian was locked away were the ones where Lucere showed his violence the most. He didn't like to share; he didn't like to be ignored. Three days before the full moon, and four days after Lucere had hurt Colton badly enough he couldn't really walk the next day, he surrendered control to Lucian for a final time.

"I don't want to do this anymore, darling." Lucian's smile was so hollow, so broken. "I don't want you to see me like this. Please don't make me come back."

Colton shook his head, grasping at Lucian's hands. "No. Please. I—this is everything to me, I have to know you're still—"

Lucian kissed his forehead. "No, precious. I can't."

His meaning was clear. *I can't let you subject yourself to him anymore. Not for something as hollow and empty as seeing me at my worst and pretending that everything is all right.*

"Lucian . . ." Colton couldn't leave it like this, couldn't abandon Lucian now that they were so close to enacting the exorcism. Even if it wasn't what Lucian wanted, and even if it didn't work, he still had to try.

"I love you, Colton." Lucian's beautiful eyes were weary and dull. "I hope we'll meet again."

Odessa kept away from Lucere as much as possible, allowing her to put the plans in motion. Two nights remained before the full moon, and just about everything was in place. All they needed were Colton's books, and whatever other artifacts Mai had managed to scrape together.

And so Colton, wrapped up in the black cloak Lucian had loved so much, stole out into the night and toward the Iron District. He could almost sense Lucere on his heels, hear his hissing laugh on the wind, feel those horrible claws on the small of his back. But each time he turned around there was nothing but darkness, and Colton moved forward.

Mai's house was a warm ember in the distance, a lone safe haven in a world he didn't trust anymore. She recognized his knock and hugged him so hard that he was almost brought to his knees.

"I thought he'd killed you," she sobbed, burying her face in Colton's neck. "I hadn't heard from you—and he, he's—now he's trying to be *Prime Minister?*" Her fists collided against his chest, furious, dull, relieved. "What happened? Why didn't you tell me?"

He hugged her and breathed in the soft ginger-lemon scent of her hair. "It's sort of a long story. Can I come in, Mai?"

Mai turned off the radio, which had been playing one of Prime Minister Lennox's attack ads against Lucere for his fraternization with a ragamuffin from the Iron District. Not great.

Marbles nuzzled Colton's hand and plopped heavily in his lap as soon as he sat down. Her home was warm and inviting, it smelled like his childhood, and he never wanted to leave. Mai couldn't stop looking at him and was (he hoped) pretending to be furious while she brewed up some tea for them both.

"I've been keeping him happy. He doesn't like me being out of his sight for too long. We've been doing a lot of research into demonic arts and rituals, and I've found all of the documents that Lucian's father used to make this whole horrible business happen in the first place. We think we might have found a spell that can reverse it." He swallowed. "The only problem is that we're going to need to . . . restrain him. And hurt him. And he's so much stronger than he should be that I don't know if it's going to be physically possible." He wiped at his eyes. "Mai, I need all of my mother's things. All of them. We're only gonna have one shot at this, and I need every scrap of her abilities if I'm going to have a prayer at all."

"Of course." Mai handed him his cup of tea. She twisted a stick of cinnamon in her own cup and licked drops of tea off the end, hesitating for a moment. "Do you want me to help, Colton? I mean, really help?"

He shook his head. "I couldn't ask for it. He's so dangerous, Mai, I don't think anyone can appreciate what he's capable of. If he killed you, I'd never forgive myself."

She held her cup in her hands, her elbows rested on her legs. "How do you think I'd feel if he killed *you*? You think these last few weeks were fun for me, dumbass? You're my best friend, Colton—what does that even mean if I'm not willing to help dispossess your demonic megalomaniac Prime Minister lover?"

He laughed and it shook around in his chest. "Mai . . ."

"Besides, how can you even carry all your mom's things without an extra pair of hands?" She nudged him. "I want to do this. I want to help you. I want us all to be happy in the end, okay?"

He felt tears slip down his cheeks as he laughed again. "I'll pay you. I'll pay you so much that it's almost stupid."

"Deal." Mai enveloped him with her arms and kissed the top of his head. She didn't say anything else, because there was nothing to say. A fraud, a socialite, and a not-that-down-on-her-luck cleaning lady were about to take on a self-aware, violent, powerful demon from the bowels of the deepest corner of hells, armed only with some books, flowers, and good thoughts.

They were completely fucked, and they knew it.

thirty-two

Mai helped Colton bring as much of his mother's things as they could carry and kissed his cheeks as he ferreted his way back into the secret passage. She was to arrive the following evening so as not to attract attention, clad in drab servant's garb to avoid Lucere's hungry gaze. The other servants were preoccupied, managing Lucere's fury while he dealt with the blowback of the smear campaign. Everything had to be just so, his clothes had to be perfect, his sleep undisturbed—and it seemed a good idea to keep one's head down.

It suited Colton just fine, since it gave him time to finish preparations as he gleaned every last detail he could from his ancestral books.

"*There are side effects, love, if you don't kill the demon outright.*" His mother had warned him, "*Sometimes, after a demon has been bound in the body, the person might . . . not have normal emotions anymore. They might be blank like a stone; they might be consumed with sadness. The soul will always carry scars.*" Lucius's books agreed, and vitally added the crucial possibilities of permanent physical changes in the organs, a diminishing of intelligence, loss of memory . . . Lucius had taken away all pertinent documents from the Ives estate, some of which mentioned blood sacrifice, mutilation, one going as far as to say disfigurement or removal of organs or appendages "in case this is where the demon resides."

It all seemed rather grim. His mother had always focused more on the protective aspect of exorcism than she had on the vanquishing one.

"There is power in your blood, Colton. The power to heal, the power to mend."

Right now, the solution boiled down to two possibilities. Seal Lucere away in Lucian's body, theoretically vanquished but dormant, which may or may not involve amputating a body part and burning it. Or kill him, by stabbing Lucian in the heart. Neither were great options.

There was one faint glimmer of hope, at least. Despite the contradictory nature of the texts, the sources seemed to agree that, one: lavender oil was required, two: the host was still likely conscious and present, imparting his influence against the demon as best he could, and three: the demon, while physically stronger than most humans, was still restricted by the weaknesses of the human form. Meaning Lucere was susceptible to fear, deprivation, and narcotics.

So the plan was as follows: Colton would offer Lucere Blossom and wine as he did every night, except this time it would be laced with Odessa's sleeping pills and some Black Molasses that they'd bought off one of the servants. Once Lucere had lost consciousness, they would drag him to the basement, tie him up, and . . .

Well, that was where the plan got a little bit vague. They would anoint him in lavender, they would paint him in runes made from Colton's blood, chant, wave smoke around, try everything gentle first. If that didn't work, then they'd have to move on to stage two. Cutting Lucian, carving symbols into his flesh like Ives had tried to do, forcing him to ingest all the semi-poisonous things the books had told them about. A touch of arsenic, tea laced with cyanide, hot enough to burn his throat all the way down. All laced with lavender flowers, twisted until they leaked their precious oils and mixed with Odessa's and Colton's blood. They'd seal Lucere away, and Lucian would be saved.

If that didn't work, Colton didn't even want to think about it.

"We have to have a plan, darling," Odessa pointed out softly. "Once we have Lucere down here, that's it—one of us isn't going to be leaving the basement. If this doesn't work, then we need to make a choice. Kill Lucian or not."

"We can't," he croaked. "I can't."

Odessa's lip quivered as she wiped at her eyes with a silk handkerchief. "He wouldn't want to live like this, would he? He's so miserable."

"No," he whispered, rejecting even the notion of harming his love. "Please, Dess. It'll work. We won't need to hurt him, I know we won't."

"He's my brother, Colton," she said, her beautiful face cast down. "I don't want to kill him either. But I'm not sure we're going to have a choice."

She's right. "You're wrong." He was shaking his head. What would he do, in that moment? Would he force Odessa to stain her hands with fratricide, or would he commit that sin for her? Would Lucian's eyes flash up at him in the last moment? Would he smile? Would it be a betrayal or a relief? Would he be able to say goodbye?

The night of the full moon arrived, and Colton waited dutifully by the secret entrance for Mai. Part of him prayed that she wouldn't show up, but of course she did, all decked out in the traditional white-and-blue clothing of the Beaumont servants. It was a far cry from the flowing colorful fabrics she normally liked to wear, but she was so, so beautiful in that moment. The sun setting behind her, streaking her jet-black hair with beams of gold and orange, causing her skin to glow.

"Ma'am, the servants' entrance is actually over that way," he called to her, leaning his broad back against the doorframe. "This secret entrance is for mischief and ne'er-do-wells only."

Mai scoffed, kicking him lightly in the shin. "Ne'er-do-well here, reporting for duty." She smiled. "You look terrible, Colton."

"Love you too. You can still turn back, you know."

"What, and miss out on all the fun?" She brushed past him, into the Beaumont estate. "Not a chance."

He shut the door behind them both with a clang and led her down to the basement where all this had begun. Odessa was waiting, clad in a stunning virginal white gown that hugged her body down to the waist and flared out around her feet. She looked so small, so lovely, yet so tired.

She stood with a flourish and approached them, taking Mai's hand in both her own and squeezing it firmly. "You must be Mai. Thank you so much for your help in this matter. I'm not certain I'll ever be able to repay this debt. Maybe I can start with a financial offer? A country estate with a vineyard, maybe? Whatever you wish, Miss Torii." With a shy smile, she tucked a strand of gold hair behind her ear. "Colton's told me so many wonderful things about you. When this is all over, you must share all of your embarrassing Colton stories until we both collapse, yes?"

Mai seemed taken aback, but pleasantly so. The tip of her nose went red as she smiled. "Well, that's a given. Surely you don't think I came here out of altruism? What's the point of anything unless I can make this guy squirm?"

Odessa squeezed her hand again before letting go. "Okay." She let out a puff of air. "We'd better get started. Colton, honey, why don't you give Lucere his after-dinner Blossom, and I'll tell lovely Mai about our plan." Such as it was.

He nodded and made his way upstairs, their special Blossom concoction in a vial tucked up next to his breast.

"You. Are becoming a problem for the campaign."

"Oh," Colton said, not sure what sort of emotion that statement was supposed to evoke. Fear, probably. Groveling? "Well, I wouldn't worry too much about it. You know how these rumors go. Everyone'll forget it in a week, especially if you, I dunno, start some kinda rumor that *his* son knocked up one of the maids or something." He shrugged. "The people love you, Beaumont. Whatever you're doing, it's working."

It was true enough to make him sick.

Don't get distracted. "Um, Lucere?"

The demon's fury was palpable from across the room, and Colton took a step back. "How . . . how's Lucian doing?" *A believable question.*

"He's dead."

Colton was very proud of himself for maintaining his smile. *He's lying. He would have told you earlier. He would have gloated, he would have laughed.* "I think you're both just having a rough day." He selected a very expensive bottle of wine from the cupboard and poured Lucere a generous glass of red. "So what I'd suggest is . . . let it go for now, and relax." He tossed Lucere the vial of Blossom and smiled when he snatched it out of the air like a frog catching a fly on its tongue. "And tomorrow, you can fuck that guy up. C'mon, Lucian needs the endorphins."

Colton watched with a mix of relief and horror as Lucere snorted the entire vial in one go, chasing it down with the entire glass of wine. It wouldn't kill Lucian's body, right? He was still human, still had the physical limitations that accompanied a mortal shell. Oh, hells, what were they doing?

"What?" Lucere growled, creeping toward him. "What's that stupid face for?"

Lucian overdosed on less Blossom than that. He almost died.

"I was just thinking of that new shipment of brandy that Johan got in this morning. I—let me get you some, okay? You deserve it."

He slipped out before Lucere could stop him (a good sign, to be sure), and by the time Odessa and Mai joined him ten minutes later, the young Lord Beaumont was unconscious on the floor.

"He's breathing," Odessa confirmed, grabbing his feet while Colton took his arms, Mai initially trying to support his waist and then realizing she was better used opening doors. "If he starts struggling, we can give him some Seabreeze, but I'd rather avoid it if I can. We want Lucere as inebriated as possible."

Colton hated how clinical they had to be, how detached Odessa had been forced to become to participate in this. "He won't die," Colton whispered. "He's been building up that tolerance for ages."

Down the stairs, through the corridors, down, down, until they reached the basement at last. If any of the servants had questions about why the young Miss Beaumont was dragging her unconscious sibling to the basement with a gutter rat and a maid, they didn't dare ask.

The basement had been prepared very carefully for this night. It was well lit, and they'd washed all the blood from Lucian's portrait. Odessa had procured some fresh flowers, and they'd painted protective charms in iridescent pearl paint mixed with lavender oils. They hoisted Lucian's body onto an oddly sacrificial marble table, which was helpfully fitted with cuffs and restraining bands.

Leather pulled tight around his wrists, the metal clacking in Colton's shaking fingers as he tried to cinch up the belts.

"I'm sure you're wondering why we have this table." Odessa nodded to Mai. "Um. Let's just say I suppose my father had some interesting hobbies prior to his death." She gestured at the walls, which were lined with weapons and torture devices that Colton hadn't noticed until they'd added more lit candles to the place.

Mai smiled warily, her eyes never leaving Lucere's sleeping face. "Same in every family, isn't it?" A pause. "So, how do we start?"

They set Mai to performing some of the chants that they'd gleaned from Colton's mother's books, since she was the only one who remembered the tunes properly. Then Colton and Odessa got to work. They dipped paintbrushes into lavender oil and began to draw some of the symbols from Colton's body onto Lucian's chest. The skin burned where the oil touched it, which Colton hoped was a good sign. Lucere groaned in his stupor, but Odessa didn't flinch.

"It's working. Keep going." The smoke from the incense swirled around them, and Odessa cut the tip of her finger to start painting runes on Lucian's body. "Demon Lucere, you are not welcome in this body. The spirit of Beaumont compels you to leave him! Begone! BEGONE!"

Colton joined her, hoping the spiritual power that lay dormant in his blood would help. Lucere was convulsing against the bonds, his groans turning to screams, the muscles of his neck tight.

Something didn't feel right. Colton wasn't sure how to explain it—this weird, cloying energy in the air felt more heavy than cleansing. But they were following every step in the book; they were doing everything right, weren't they?

Lucere was leaving Lucian's body, of course it hurt, of course he'd scream. "Keep going—something's happening!"

It feels wrong. Something is wrong.

At that moment, Lucere's eyes snapped open and filled with a rage that Colton had never seen in him before. "*You,*" he hissed, his muscles tensing under his clothes. "*You miserable wastrel!*" He screamed then, Lucian's velvet baritone echoing over the stone floor, strings of saliva connecting his teeth.

"Colton!" Could Mai sense it too? The energy in the room turning darker, heavier, sinking. She grabbed his arm and tried to pull him back.

He wrenched his grip free of her, taking his oil-anointed blade and dragging it through Lucian's skin. "We can't stop now. I think—look at him!"

She grabbed his arm, and he cried out in frustration.

"What are you—we're SO CLOSE! Why are you—" Why was she trying to ruin everything? He'd never forgive her.

There was a crack of stone as Lucere broke one of the chains off the marble table, a thump, the sound of tearing flesh. Mai staggered back, her chest marred with deep, bleeding lacerations that wept onto the stones. Odessa caught her, holding her by the waist and keeping her steady. "It's okay," she whispered, but of course it wasn't.

Mai's name caught in Colton's throat as he watched the demon flex his hand, her blood dripping down his wrist. Lucere's smile was manic, furious. That rattling laugh started to fill the room, accompanied fittingly as the marble relented under the force of his struggles. A second hand free, he released the bonds that still held him against the table.

"Oh, Colton," he purred, still staggering, like a man trying to pretend he wasn't drunk. "I am going to *hurt* you for this."

Odessa held Mai, and Mai was badly wounded. Neither of them could outrun Lucian on a good day, and Colton hadn't been able to land even one decent hit on him since this had started. "Go," he whispered, hoping that at the very least he could buy them some time while they tried to get away. What had gone wrong? Why had it failed? *Because you did the sealing spell from the books instead of aiming for the heart. Because you were too much of a coward to use the blade properly.*

"Go!"

Odessa was frozen to the spot, watching Lucere as he approached the wall of weapons. Mai clung to her, brilliant red blood soaking into the pure white silk of Lady Beaumont's dress.

"RUN!" Colton ordered, wondering if his own shitty knife could hope to match the gleaming cleaver that Lucere had selected from the cache of blades.

Lucere was still laughing, the sound only growing louder and more raucous as Colton brandished his tiny dagger and stepped forward. "You fucking idiot."

It all happened in an instant. The sound of metal slipping through muscle, of bone yielding, of flesh plummeting to the ground with a wet thump. Lucere—or could it have been Lucian?—had turned the blade on himself, severing Lucian's right arm above the elbow with one damned hand. He laughed. He laughed, and laughed, and all of a sudden the sound was swallowed up with a gasp as Lucere released Lucian to the front of his mind.

Lucian's face was one of terrified confusion. He stared at the stump at the end of his shoulder, at the waterfall of blood that was painting the floor, and finally at Colton, at his sister, at Mai.

"W-what?" he whispered, his legs collapsing underneath him with a splash as his strength failed him.

Colton screamed.

thirty-three

Once, and it seemed like a long time ago now, Colton and Lucian had been lounging around together in that beautiful period of freedom between setting up an exorcism and performing one. They had the whole manor to themselves, but it had been a long day, and neither of them was particularly interested in snooping any further. Colton had claimed one of the plush velvet sofas in the drawing room, and Lucian had claimed Colton, resulting in the two of them being squished together like poorly packaged salt herring while they both pretended to hate it.

"I wonder how it'll go tomorrow," Lucian had mused, pulling Colton's hand to his lips and kissing the heel of his palm. "Do you think we'll be in terrible danger? Do you think I'll get to rescue you? Hoist you over my shoulder and carry you to the wilderness to avoid the dreaded peril?"

Colton snorted, wriggling his body into a more comfortable position against Lucian's warm frame. "You'd best not do anything dramatic, Beaumont. I don't need any more interesting adventures, and I certainly don't need to be carried off into the woods at the end of it."

Lucian laughed, and Colton thought of how lovely and brilliant his eyes were when he was happy. "Well, it's probably best if you get injured rather than me, darling. I had to learn first aid in the army, you know. I can solve just about any minor ailment."

Colton gave him a look, and Lucian fell into giggles. "Oh, precious, come now—you know I'd leap in front of a cannon for you, but I question your ability to save me if, say, I got my foot bitten off by a bear."

It was Colton's turn to laugh then. "And how exactly have we run afoul of a bear, Lucian?"

"Oh, you never know, what if these people have one locked up in the attic! Maybe that's what's causing them all the trouble with the supposed haunting. There's a bear, and it's eaten my foot, and it's up to you to save me." He pulled Colton in for a kiss and beamed at him. "You can bleed to death in an instant, love." A peck on Colton's nose. "But I know you'd save me. You always do."

His feet moved on their own now as he ran to Lucian, unconscious on the floor in a pool of his own blood. Colton had never seen someone bleed this much before, and he silenced the miserable thought at the back of his mind that kept telling him, *He's already dead, he's gone.*

Colton went to his knees and crawled forward. *He can't be.* Colton found himself reasoning, *He's still bleeding. His heart is still—it's still beating.* He groped at what was left of Lucian's arm, nauseated as his hands were coated with sticky red life. A tourniquet. He had to apply a tourniquet. Colton had looked it up, after that stupid fucking bear story, just in case.

With trembling hands, Colton tore his sleeve off and tied it around Lucian's stump, ignoring the shards of bone jutting out, the way his muscles were twitching against the cool air of the basement. *Focus.* He fitted his dagger into the tourniquet like a lever so he could tighten it sufficiently. One twist, two, three, like a faucet turning off, the blood stopped flowing.

Colton took a moment to brace himself before he checked if Lucian was still alive.

He could feel his own heartbeat pulsing in his cheeks. His face felt hot and cold all at once, and he knew that no matter what he found in that moment, he would burst into tears. His fingers pressed against Lucian's neck and—there it was. A fluttering sparrow in a cage, Lucian's pulse whispered against his skin. "Oh, fuck," he whispered, resting his forehead against Lucian's chest. He had to be close to his heart. He had to be able to know that this miserable asshole was still alive. "Fuck. Thank you."

Be careful. It might not be Lucian when he opens his eyes. Colton didn't care. Let them die together, then. Nothing would tear him from Lucian in this moment. "I've got you," he whispered. "I've got you."

He grasped Lucian's left hand and wrapped the whole limb around his body. He missed this, being held in those arms—this arm. Being close to the man he loved.

Odessa let out a soft noise, and Colton looked up, suddenly remembering she was there. "Is he okay?" Her voice was so small.

Fuck. *Mai.* "I think so, Dess." He lifted his head, wincing at how badly Mai had been hurt. "What about you guys? Mai—are you all right?"

Mai attempted to stand to her full height, wincing as her chest flexed. "Oh, yeah, never better." She tried to force a laugh but stopped when the pain of it struck her. "Colton, I think we need a doctor."

"Yeah," Colton croaked, resting his forehead against Lucian's chest once more.

Odessa seemed loath to let Mai go and pulled her lovely arm over her shoulders. "Can you walk? Let me get you upstairs, Johan can call the doctors. I'm sure we have some Nectar in the cupboard. Oh, you poor thing, you must be in so much pain."

Those fucking claws. Lucere had ripped four neat little lines into her chest, and through the skin, he was sure he could see muscle— bone? She'd live, surely, unless infection set in.

He watched them leave, robbed of his speech as he lay on the floor with that freezing, limp arm wrapped around his body. "I'm sorry. I'm so, so sorry."

Johan came down in time, Odessa leading him and a number of other servants down the stone steps. "Lord Beaumont has had a terrible accident. Please be gentle with him," she cautioned, her eyes red and puffy although her voice was clear.

They almost had to pull Colton off of Lucian, and he nearly struck one of them for picking up Lucian's arm like a piece of meat at the market. Johan tried to pick Lucian up by the torso, and Colton snarled in protest, gripping him ever tighter.

"Colton, sweetheart." Odessa knelt down beside him, the hem of her dress dipping into the blood. "We have to help him, okay? I know it's hard, I know. Please."

Colton clung to her instead, burying his face against her neck, chasing the warm pulse under her skin. *No more death. No more fear. No more pain, please, please.*

"I know," she said. "I know."

Odessa took him upstairs and brought him to a room with two beautiful canopy beds, upon one of which lay Mai, topless and wrapped in bandages. She was grinning from ear to ear; Colton suspected that Odessa had in fact found some Nectar to make all this easier.

"Colton!" she slurred cheerfully. "They took my new shirt! And I got stiiiiitches! Wanna see?"

He managed a laugh and sat down beside her, squeezing her hand. "Not really. I—I'm so sorry, Mai. It should have been me, you didn't need to . . . Thank you."

Mai shook her head. "Did . . . did it work?"

"I don't know. His temperature is coming up, his heart too. Lucere . . . that was a risk for him. If Lucian died . . ." *Lucere did this to hurt you. Lucian paid your price.*

Johan and his crew soon emerged into the room, depositing the still-unconscious Lord Beaumont onto the other bed. "We have to—"

Colton staggered close, dripping lavender oil all along the exposed muscle of the stump. If Lucere was there, if any part of him still existed—they had to seal it, they had to give themselves the best chance. The skin wasn't burning anymore, that had to mean something.

A pack of doctors descended then, forming a shell around Lucian while they worked. Colton heard the sound of a rasp on bone. He smelled flesh burning. *Oh, hells, Lucian.* By the time they were done with him, he was pale as death, his arm caked in bandages, his breathing steady.

"He's stable, Lady Beaumont," one of the doctors said to Odessa, "but he's lost a tremendous amount of blood. He might not recover, and even if he does, he might have brain damage."

What a tremendous bedside manner.

"How did this happen?"

"He fell," Odessa said plainly, which of course explained the runes, the copious blood, the burns, the amputated arm. The staff knew better than to question a Beaumont. "What do I need to do to take care of him?"

She listened to their orders, ushered them out, and carefully locked the door. "Okay. Well. That was awful." Odessa looked at her hands, at her immaculate white dress, now saturated with her brother's blood. For a moment it looked as though she would collapse into sobs, but she took a shuddering breath instead and leaned against the wall. "I need a shower."

"You definitely do," Colton teased. "I'll get started on securing the room. I don't know how long it'll be before Lucian wakes up, but I think we need to prepare for the possibility that the exorcism didn't work—and that Lucere will kill all of us as soon as he regains consciousness."

Carefully, Colton painted runes of warding and protection on the floor with Lucian's blood. Next, he anointed the rest of Lucian's body with lavender oil, spread lavender flowers all over the bed, and lit lavender-scented candles. To be honest, it was beginning to be unpleasantly lavender-y. "It was Lucian," he said quietly as she got to the doorway. "At the end, I know it was."

Odessa bit her lip. "You knew Lucere the best, Colton. Would he exorcise himself just to get a rise out of you?"

Probably not.

"I don't know. I'm sorry, Dess—he—he mutilated Lucian because of me, I'm so, so sorry. I should have known he—he always said he'd . . ." Colton shut his eyes. "What are we going to do?"

Odessa sat down on Lucian's mattress and stroked his hand. "We're going to wait and see what happens, and we're going to help him however we can. If the demon comes back, I think we owe it to my brother to put him out of his misery." She shivered.

Yeah. There was probably no way around that now. "Dess?" He swallowed. "What happened to Lucian's arm?"

She looked at her brother, at the mess of gauze at the end of his shoulder. "It's in cool storage. I know we're meant to burn it, but . . . I thought he might want to . . . I don't know. See it. Bury it." She covered her face with her hands for a moment, and when she emerged she offered Colton a smile. "You wash up first. You're absolutely filthy."

"But I—" *Don't want to leave them. And we should burn that fucking arm in case Lucere was—* Colton looked down at his hands and winced. He was completely caked in Lucian's blood, which cracked and disintegrated every time he moved.

"It's okay, honey. I'll make sure nothing happens to them, okay? Go wash up, then we'll switch."

She walked up to Colton, threw her arms around his neck, and sobbed into his chest for exactly ten seconds before letting go once more, wiping her eyes on her blood-soaked sleeve, and looking up at him. "It's so fucked up."

Colton pulled her back into his arms and held her tight, not letting go when the tears started flowing once more, nor when he heard her sobbing. How long had she had to stand by herself? Her father had just been brutally murdered and she hadn't had any time to grieve.

He quickly washed up, then ushered Dess into the bathroom

before curling up beside Lucian on the mattress. Careful not to disturb his wounds, he leaned over and kissed him gently on the cheek. Lucian slumbered still, smiling in his sleep as he nosed closer to Colton. Colton saw nothing of Lucere in that sleeping face, and he allowed himself to hope.

thirty-four

Odessa emerged from the bathroom in a rush of steam from her shower, a fluffy white robe tied around her waist. She approached Lucian's bed on tiptoe. Sitting on the opposite side of it from Colton, she touched her brother's shoulder, her fingers lingering on the bandages. "How is he, honey?" she whispered. "Settled, at least?"

Colton nodded. "Yeah. I think whatever they gave him is working pretty well. At least he's not in any pain."

Lucian's body moved in its stupor, releasing a soft and gentle sigh. They both looked at his stump then, their failures wrapped in gauze around Lucian's macerated flesh. The temptation was not to think about it, but ignoring his problems hadn't really been serving him very well recently. A mutilation, a terrible price. But something Lucian would surely understand, forgive, and accept over time. They'd done their best, with all the good intentions in the world.

That had to be enough, for now.

"When I was little, it was just us two, you know?" she said quietly. "My mother had a problem with Blossom, and my father was always so busy with work. He only cared for us when it was in relation to his legacy, and he was so, so strict, especially with Lucian. But Lucian never let it bother him, at least in front of me.

He was always smiling, and making some stupid joke, and trying to get me to laugh, even when the world seemed like it was closing in on us. He's like a big ball of sunshine. Even when his own heart is breaking." She shook her head. "I wanted to be there for him this time. And I . . . and he . . ."

"Hey." Colton stood up and moved toward her, pulling her into a soft hug against his chest. "It's fucked up. This whole situation is beyond fucked up. But I think it worked, Dess, I really do. Look at that smile, sweetheart. Look at how peaceful he is. *That is Lucian.*"

She sniffled and snuggled into Colton's embrace. "What's he going to do with only one arm, Colton? He'll be miserable."

"Probably make a lot of dumb jokes about it, to be honest. 'Look, Ma, no hands,' that sort of thing."

Odessa laughed, and Colton wiped the tears from her eyes.

"He's the worst, Dess, but he's resilient, and he sees the good in everything. It'll be an adjustment to be sure, but if it got rid of Lucere, I think he'll think it was worth it."

She nodded and fell into his arms. She was so tiny. "Ugh. This isn't me, all this moping. Okay. You watch my darling brother and lovely Mai while I get changed. I need something a bit more fitting than a horror blood gown, don't you think? I'll have Johan get you all some wardrobes while we try and figure out what's what, all right?"

Colton watched her leave and quickly checked on Mai before getting settled back into bed with Lucian. She was out for the count, breathing peacefully while the drugs worked their way through her system. The gauze on her chest wasn't saturated with ooze like Lucian's was, and he took that to be a good sign.

Colton pressed a kiss to Mai's forehead and tiptoed back to Lucian, curling up beside him. "I love you, stupid," he said, snuggling into the blankets. "So, so much."

Lucian groaned softly, his long eyelashes fluttering as he opened his eyes. "Hey, precious," he murmured, his smile warm and open.

He was awake. *He was awake!* And it was *him*! There was nothing of Lucere in that expression, no trace of him in those eyes. There was no snarl in his voice, no sneer on his lips, no tongue sliding over his teeth. *He can turn on a fucking dime, though—don't you forget it.*

"Lucian!" Colton wrapped his arms around Lucian's chest and squeezed him as hard as he dared.

Lord Beaumont chuckled, snuggling in even closer. "What happened? You look positively wrecked, darling."

Colton blinked. He didn't remember anything? He'd always been conscious before he . . . "You don't . . . ?"

Lucian pressed a kiss to his forehead and smiled. "You're going to have to tell me allllll about it," he said softly, rolling over to embrace Colton. His stump twitched, and Lucian's gaze fell on it, his eyes widening.

Oh, no.

"W-what?" Lucian convulsed on the mattress, tearing his IV out as his left hand delicately groped at what was left of his limb. "Colton! My arm! What happened to my arm?!"

Colton resisted the urge to vomit and gathered Lucian into an embrace, holding him as he writhed in a panic on the mattress. *He's seeing what the rest of his life will look like. A cripple, mutilated with an inescapable reminder of the horrors he'd barely managed to escape. He's seeing that his father's betrayal has handicapped him permanently.*

"Lucian, Lucian, look at me." Colton caught his cheeks and looked into his eyes. "We did the exorcism, love. We drugged Lucere, we took you down to the basement, and we exorcised him. He's gone, Lucian. He's gone." He had to be. They'd paid so, so dearly. Colton pressed their foreheads together and held him close. "Do you feel him? Any part of him?"

Lucian's breathing steadied, and he sat up, his left hand going to the limp stump at the end of his shoulder as he searched his mind. "No," he whispered, "I can't."

Was it possible? Lucere had exorcised himself, in the end? No, the bastard wouldn't have done that. More likely still he was being sealed away in Lucian's body, panicking, spiteful, and had wanted to go out with one last "fuck you" to the both of them. Had they done it? Colton's face erupted in a smile even as tears ran down his cheeks, and he pulled Lucian in for a big wet kiss. "Lucian!"

"Colton!" For the first time since they'd known each other, it seemed like Lucian was at a loss for words. All there was in this moment was joy, relief.

Colton felt Lucian's hand wrap around his waist, followed by him losing his balance and tumbling back toward the mattress. "I tried to hug you with both arms," he explained with a laugh. "Oh, that's very odd. Colton, precious, can you"—another laugh—"can you give me a hand, please?"

"Oh, my god," Colton mumbled affectionately, perching himself on top of Lucian. "Why did we exorcise the demon exactly? I forgot what a *dork* you are." He leaned down and pressed a soft, careful kiss to Lucian's bandages. "I guess you're more armless now, anyway," he said with a wink.

"Colton! That's a good one!" He giggled, his left hand stroking Colton's face. "Darling, precious, thank you. I can't—I'm just so grateful, it's so nice to—to not . . ."

"Yeah." Colton snuggled up against Lucian's chest, kissing his cheeks, his nose, his lips. "I couldn't stand being afraid around you. Watching that bastard wear your beautiful face."

"Watching him hurt you. Knowing I couldn't stop him." Lucian shuddered. "If I ever get possessed again, love, just kill me right away."

"Don't even joke about that."

Lucian gave him a pouty smile and settled back into the mattress, taking a few seconds to find a position that didn't put pressure on what was left of his right arm. "So what happened, lovely? Tell me everything."

"Hey, one thing at a time."

Lucian managed a smile and kissed Colton then, trying awkwardly to keep his balance with one arm. "Wanna mess around?"

"Oh, my god!" Colton laughed, pushing his chest. "No! First of all, you've lost almost all your blood, second of all, you have a huge injury which probably won't respond well to any changes in blood pressure, and third of all, Mai is right frigging there! Keep it in your pants, Beaumont."

Lucian smiled then, nuzzling up against Colton's face. "Oh, have it your way, partner. I love you, precious. I love you so, so much."

"I love you too, stupid."

And they fell asleep like that together, surrounded by blood and gauze, without a care in the damned world.

thirty-five

Once it was clear that neither Lucian nor Mai was in any immediate danger of death, the four of them relaxed enough that they could venture out of the bedroom they'd selected for their recuperation.

Mai somewhat jokingly demanded a private room with a view of the sea to use until she was well enough to return home. "Also, I want a four-poster bed and a milk bath, and I want to see the horses and pet them, and I want a room where I don't have to listen to Colton mumble in his sleep anymore!" She grinned, pushing herself up onto her elbows.

A room with a view of the sea, huh? Probably in the family quarter then, which most likely meant a room with a view of Odessa. Mai went through new infatuations now and again, and Colton always found it adorable to watch her interest shift and grow as a new thing of beauty entered her periphery.

Colton wasn't sure how Odessa would react if she knew that Mai had a little crush on her. She had grown up in the same home that Lucian had, which meant that navigating the world with both the Ivory and the Beaumont standards yoked upon her.

What had that been like for Odessa? A beautiful young woman blossoming into maturity, with the same likes and desires as anyone else her age—shamed into thinking such instincts were evil and dirty. She was rebellious, though, her own person, not the sort to obey authority she didn't respect. Her engagement to Chastain had probably disgusted her, and he could easily imagine her selecting an attractive young man and ruining her wedding night on her own volition.

And yet in all these months of friendship with her, there had been no mention of a beau, jilted or not, and she'd seemingly had no one to call on in her hour of need. Lucius had probably seen signs of rebellion brewing and had made it difficult for her to maintain friendships, male or female.

So there was a possibility then that Odessa had never for one second even considered the possibility that she could be attracted to, or fall in love with, another woman. Well, if she tended toward such proclivities, she was in for a treat with Mai. Colton had a lot in common with her, in that sense. Neither of them were particularly fussed about their partner's gender, as long as the person was pleasant to look at and be around.

They would make a lovely couple, he thought. *Please be happy.* He found himself thinking, *After all this—we deserve it.* For the first time since Lucere had come into their lives, Colton allowed himself to hope that a bright future was possible. That maybe he and Lucian could enjoy the spoils of their adventures together, spend the rest of their lives simply being comfortable and content. A happy ending he'd never dared imagine for himself.

Odessa became quite adroit at changing and managing bandages, and Mai trusted no one else with her delicate scars. Colton watched over the process to make sure she was healing okay, of course, but it was difficult for him to suppress shuddering when he saw the extent of the damage. Lucere had torn her skin open from her shoulder all the way across to her opposite breast, exposing muscle and bits of rib, nearly robbing her of her life. She wasn't healing well, if Odessa's tight jaw was anything to go by, and there a sickly rotting smell emerged from the dressings each morning when Lady Beaumont changed them.

It was an intimate moment when Odessa tended to her, but Mai never turned it into anything sexual. She allowed herself to be vulnerable, open, and gracious as her wounded body was exposed to the room. Odessa would comment on how lovely Mai's skin was, wondering what creams she used, how she managed to keep her hair so sleek and straight with the sea spray that covered all of Silvermoor in mist. And Mai would just look at her like she held the stars in the sky, a soft flush of pleasure in her cheeks.

Just kiss already! Colton thought on more than one occasion, but he decided not to push anything. They had their whole lives to figure out what this was.

Lucian, as expected, had been the more challenging patient. He enjoyed being coddled and so would dramatically bemoan his slightly dusty bandages with a swoon (and play dead) until Colton kissed him on the forehead.

"You mustn't encourage him," Odessa chided, but it was impossible for Colton to resist that stupid face. Besides, he'd—ugh—been "disarmed" (thanks, Lucian), and Colton thought it was reasonable to spoil him now. Colton could see through the theatrics and down to the genuine agony that crossed Lucian's face when he moved his limb too quickly. He noticed the way Lucian's jaw clenched at night when the phantom limb pain seized him.

The first time it had happened, Colton had woken up with a start, panic rising when he saw Lucian's ghostly, sweating face and his hand gripping the sheet in agony.

"Hey," he whispered, not wanting to disturb the girls, "what's wrong?"

"It—I can feel the blade in my arm," Lucian managed. "My nerves are on fire. Colton, it hurts so much."

He couldn't rub his hand, couldn't apply a compress, couldn't do anything to take the pain away. Nectar was the only thing that soothed him when it got bad like this, and sometimes he needed a sniff of Blossom to sleep. *It's just temporary*, Colton told himself, and he hoped to all the hells it was true. The pain served as a distraction at least, from all the "what ifs" and "what nows" that hung over their heads. He had to imagine that they were riding a high from their hard-won success, but that once that wore off, Lucian would have to face everything that had happened to him.

The election loomed before him as well, the fallout that would follow from a popular candidate suddenly dropping out. There would be serious political repercussions. Now that Lucius was out of the picture, opportunistic vipers could take advantage of weakness in the Beaumont line.

It wasn't going to be pleasant when that reality came to a head, but Colton had every intention of supporting his partner through the worst of it.

After a few days of dressing changes, Mai sat up and glanced at Odessa, asleep in the bed just next to hers.

"I think I'm ready to try walking a bit today."

Odessa frowned. "Are you certain? Your wound is still so . . ."

Mai shrugged. "If I don't move my body, I'm liable to expire, I think. Besides, we can scope out my new room. Will you come with me? I hate to think of what might happen if I get lost in your home."

"Oh, Mai, we couldn't allow that. We'd have to send out a search party, and honestly, most of the time all we find is a desiccated corpse in the hallways." She put on her slippers and smiled. "So of course, my lovely, I will escort you."

Mai took her arm then, presumably to lean on her while she regained her strength, although Colton had to assume there was a sweeter motive.

Odessa's ears went pink, and she put her hand on top of Mai's. "I was also wondering what might have become of your little pig? Colton was telling me about her, and I couldn't help but think that she's been alone for a few days."

Mai's smile was simultaneously shy and confident. "Well, it sort of depends on how long I'm staying here, I suppose. She's with one of my neighbors, so she's fine for now, but I'm not quite recovered yet, and I won't know if I should leave Colton, so . . ."

"Oh! Mai! Of course, you can stay as long as you need to! Longer, even!"

Colton tried not to laugh. *Oh, hells, Dess, very subtle.*

"I wouldn't want to impose."

"You aren't! It's an absolute pleasure having you here. You and Colton are both welcome here for as long as you wish." She tucked a strand of hair behind her ear, a smile sweeping her beautiful face. "Why don't I get one of the maids to go and collect our little pig then? Then you won't need to worry about anything while you heal."

Their eyes met then. Mai's smile was soft, inviting, while Odessa's hand was trembling just a touch. The young Lady Beaumont averted her gaze first, a blush blooming nearly down to her neck. "I mean, if you like." An awkward cough, which manifested into a fit of coughs as Mai squeezed her hand.

"I think I'd really like that, Odessa."

Colton smiled as he flopped back down into bed with Lucian. "They're adorable," he mused, pushing some of Lucian's hair away from his eyes. "What do you think? Would Mai make a good sister-in-law for you? Would they hyphenate their names, maybe? Odessa Torii-Beaumont. I love that."

Lucian shoved him gently. "Oh, come on, there is no frigging way."

Colton kissed him then, cupping his face. "You're blind."

"You're adorable. I think maybe it'll be a good idea to try and get things back to normal, eh? Start getting some of my father's affairs in order, maybe begin processing my emotions around his death and the whole patricide and dismemberment thing."

He stretched, and Colton tried to ignore how much weight he'd lost in the last few weeks. Lucere hadn't looked after Lucian's body, it seemed.

"One step at a time, Beaumont. And then we'll need to figure out what you wanna do about this whole 'top candidate for Prime

Minister of Silvermoor' thing. And whatever will become of Cucian Exorcisms Unlimited?"

"Darling, I don't think I agreed to that name."

"We had a vote, Lucian! Every member of the company was invited, you were in a coma, I voted in favor—what do you want me to do, undermine democracy?"

"Oh, heaven forbid, " Lucian giggled.

"Seriously, I've got you. But step one is you get out of this bed, get some ridiculous product in your hair, let me help you shave, because your stubble feels so, so wrong, and then we go do something fun together." He reached his left hand for Lucian to shake. "What do you say?"

Lucian's hand was warm in his own, and he relished the sweet pressure exerted by his fingers. "I say lead the way, partner."

thirty-six

Things settled down for the four of them as Lucian's recovery continued. Mai's wounds were more of a challenge, but the doctors had informed Colton that her infection was, at long last, starting to wane. Lucian and Colton had moved into his childhood room, and Mai had her room by the sea. Marbles had her run of the place, and Odessa had begun teaching her tricks nearly as soon as she walked in the door.

The four of them were happy, and for the first time since he'd been a child, Colton felt like he was in a real family once again. "It's strange," Lucian mused, gripping onto a gold-handled banister as they climbed the stairs. "I never really imagined that any of this would be mine, after I began to disappoint my father."

"What do you want to do with it, love?" Colton asked. "I guess burning it down isn't really a great return on investment, is it?"

"I imagine that depends on your insurance provider."

At the top of the stairs was a great window that overlooked nearly all of Silvermoor. It was possible to see all three districts from there, all the way down to the cerulean sea. On its borders were stained glass images of the Beaumont seal, all sapphires and gold, presented over the national crest, an image of the globe.

Colton looked straight into Lucian's eyes. "Why not use all this wealth and influence to make the world a better place? Destroying your father's legacy of pain and replacing it with one of reason and kindness? Lucere tried to get you to be Prime Minister, after all, and according to the polls, there's a pretty good chance you'll win." He smiled. "The greatest con we ever pulled off."

Lucian laughed and caught Colton's hand, drawing it to his lips for a kiss. "You might be crazy, you know that?"

They looked out over the horizon, over everything that Lucian would be able to control from that seat in the capitol. "I'd vote for you," Colton added, pressing a kiss to his cheek. "Well, think about it, anyway. It might be worth getting in touch with your campaign people. Odessa and I have just been telling them you have viral enteritis."

Lucian's hand went to his stump, and he swallowed. "They'll probably have some questions." He forced a laugh, pain skirting across his eyes. "The doctor might talk."

"Oh don't worry about that. We've either bribed or threatened everyone who's had access to the manor in the last month, including the doctor. As for your new look? We'll spin it somehow, love. You fought off a bear and saved a cute little endangered orphan or something—very valiant, very on-brand. Plus I'm sure we can get you a prosthetic if you want, once the wound is more healed. No one will think any less of you, sweetheart."

Lucian was quiet. "Can I see my father's office?"

Colton frowned but nodded. "Are you sure? We didn't get a chance to clean everything up, and it's awful, Lucian. It's really horrible in there."

"I think I need to face it, darling. I can't keep running from this, from him. Look at me, my hand is shaking just thinking about it!" Lucian's hand flitted toward the cuffs of the empty sleeve on the other side of his body. "The man is dead, Colton, and he still has the power to make me feel like . . ."

A little boy all over again. He'd loved Lucius like any son would, and had been hurt worse than anyone possibly could have imagined.

"I just want to see. He was just a man, made of flesh and blood like any of us. I want every piece of him erased from the earth, and then you and I will be the masters of this place, and we can live however we wish." He smiled then, trepidatious and manic, eager and boyish, every bit of him Lucian.

"I'd love that." Colton found Lucian's enthusiasm contagious. "We can travel, maybe?"

"Climb a mountain? Dismantle the oppressive government system my family helped to implement? Milk a goat?"

"Yes, the great three things that everyone must do in order to have truly lived. You're a man of true insight, Lord Beaumont."

They stormed into the old office, and Colton shuddered as they moved past the door he'd been pinned against, marveling at how spiders and dust had settled over the whole place like a tomb. It was such a different place now without Lord Beaumont present, and Colton watched with pleasure as Lucian tore his father's portrait off the wall and threw it into the fireplace. The patriarch's miserable sneer cracked under the heat. Lucian paused by the pool of dried blood that had soaked into the carpet and dug his heels in, sniffing in displeasure.

"Disgusting. We'd best get Johan in here to clear things up, mmm? My father's bedroom will need to be completely refurbished as well."

Colton frowned. This furious, confident Lucian was one with whom he was quite familiar. This was Lucian when he didn't want anyone to see how upset he was. This was Lucian when he didn't know what he was supposed to be feeling.

"Hey," Colton whispered, pulling Lucian into his arms. "It's okay. I know it's hard, sweetheart. I love you, I've got you, and he's never going to hurt you again."

Lucian's strong, beautiful arm wrapped around his body and clung to his cloak. "Colton," he whispered, his voice wavering. "It hurts so much."

"I know, love. Tell me what you're feeling."

Lucian squeezed even tighter. "I hate him. I'll never forgive him."

Colton swallowed.

"Let's get out of here, love. I don't want to think about this anymore."

Dammit, Lucian. "Not good enough, Beaumont. C'mon, I like you being emotionally available and willing to talk about your feelings. We've got to get this stuff out in the open or it'll never get better."

Lucian sighed. "He threw me away like I was nothing. He actively sought to destroy my very essence because I wasn't enough of a man to him. Because I dared live my life apart from him, because I wasn't vicious and cruel. How do I live with that, Colton? That my only living parent hated me enough that he forced me to get possessed, and then died at *my* hands?"

Not easy questions to answer. "You loved your father."

"Whatever good that did me."

"He didn't deserve you, Lucian. A bright, loyal, intelligent young man like you as his son. He was a fool to try and change you." *Obviously, since he got his throat ripped out as a result.* "Does it help to remind you he was a fucking miserable prick?"

"A little."

"I never knew my father, you know. I always wondered what he was like, wondered if he'd have been proud of me or wanted to know me or . . . I guess at the end of the day, he was just some guy who never cared enough to even see my face. After my mom died, I thought I'd never be happy again. But . . . I learned that family is the people in your life who love you. Whether you were born to them, or you found them somewhere along the way—it's the people who want to build you up instead of crushing you down. The people who see all your flaws and smile because they make you *you*. The people like me, and Dess, and Mai, and that stupid fat pig."

Lucian squeezed his shoulder tighter. "You have such a way with words, precious."

"This isn't gonna be easy, Lucian. You're not gonna be okay all the time, and that's fine. We'll be with you every step of the way, and we're gonna carve out a beautiful life on our own terms. Now, why don't we go to the balcony? We can spy on the girls."

They had a bet going now, as to whether or not "Maidessa" was fated to be or not. If they didn't fall in love, Lucian would get to use unbearable puns for all eternity, and if they did, then Colton got gloating rights for ten years.

Lucian shook his head, stroking Colton's cheek. "Nah, I have a better idea." Warm fingers squeezed Colton's hand, and he allowed himself to be led up the stairs, into their enormous bedroom and onto the mattress.

There was no mistaking the look in Lucian's eyes. Warm and adoring lust was flooding his features, and Colton couldn't help but fall under his spell. They hadn't properly been intimate since Lucian had been possessed. But it had been a few weeks, and his wounds were nearly healed over. Colton wrapped his arms around Lucian's neck as they kissed and kissed in the soft light of the sun.

Lucian's shirt went off his shoulders, and Colton was up in a flash, kissing what was left of his arm, of the scars that he and Odessa had carved in lavender oil onto his chest. Lucian frowned, and Colton kissed him again. "You are beautiful," Colton whispered, his hand traveling south, and he smiled when what he found stood to attention. They took their time that day, worshiping each other—the bodies that had survived such an ordeal, the love that had bloomed between them.

Colton was panting when it ended, his limbs tangled up in Lucian, his face red and his heart swollen with adoration. "I missed that," he mumbled contentedly. "I love you so, so much."

"I love you too."

Colton pushed himself up on one elbow. "Did I tell you? About what me and Mai found in my mom's old books?"

Lucian's eyes slid shut, and he pulled Colton against his chest. "Nuh-uh."

"Well, it was about Lucere, where he came from. It said that he was the son of a pauper, I guess. That his father was a miserable and cruel man, who chased after his own pleasures over the security and future of his only child. That his father threw him away, left him to die, that the anger of that betrayal is what caused him to turn into a demon in the first place."

Lucian swallowed, his jaw tight. "He—you don't think—he could only possess someone who . . . who's broken?"

Colton pressed a kiss to his temple. "Not broken. Wounded, maybe." He smiled. "The Order thought he was an angel, prophesied to bring a new age to Silvermoor. It was strange. Being up against such a powerful entity and just thinking, deep down in his core, he's just a lost little boy. Poor Herluin."

Lucian's tongue swept over his teeth, his lips pulling into that awful sneer. Colton nearly jumped off of the mattress, his pupils blown wide. "Lucian?" he demanded, his hand trembling as he fumbled for his trousers. "Lucian, say something."

Lord Beaumont's entire face was contorted in rage. "You will NEVER use that name again." He lashed a hand out toward Colton, catching the air and swearing loudly. "How DARE you!"

No no no!

Lucian—no, surely it was Lucere—stood up and laced a towel around his waist. He stretched his arm up over his head, glanced at himself in the mirror, and sneered at his beauty. "How? Your exorcism failed. Why? Because you stopped everything as soon as Lucian's arm hit the floor."

"No. No." Colton shook his head. "He couldn't feel you. He said he couldn't feel you."

Had it been Lucere the whole time? No, no, it was impossible!

"I was dormant, Colton. Rebuilding strength. It was quite a creative little setup you had there, I was almost impressed." He found a bottle of wine and took a long, desperate swig. "But you're no different from the rest of them. You betrayed me, Colton. You cut my skin and tried to burn me alive."

Colton was backing up, shaking his head. "No. No. I didn't, I—

Let him back out. Please. Please! We—we were gonna be happy, Lucere. All of us—we . . . Please. I'm sorry. I'm sorry I hurt you!"

Lucere laughed, his eyes glinting with pain. "It's too late for that, Colton." His face contorted, and, yes, at last, Lucian emerged, clasping Colton's face and holding him close.

"Run, precious. I can't stop him this time, you have to run."

Then that *laugh*.

The sound that sent insects crawling under his skin and over his bones. The coughing, clicking snarl of gas hissing over his spiracles. The ghosts of the bruises on his body that had only just begun to heal started curling in on themselves, and Colton suddenly forgot how to move.

"I'm getting better at being him, no? I studied him for so, so long."

Maybe none of this was Lucian. Maybe Lucere had been in control this whole time. Had they burned the arm? Was that why he—*Okay. Well. Fuck.*

"Please," Colton whispered. "Please give him back to me."

Lucere just laughed. "Oh, Colton. You think I'm going to forget that you burned my soul? That you tried to torture me out of this beautiful body? Oh, no, darling, I'm going to make your life a living hell. I promised you before, didn't I? That I was going to hurt you?" He smiled. "I'll give you until the count of ten. Head start, mmm? Look how sporting I am."

Ten.

He had to run.

Nine.

His body started to move. He found himself tripping over his own feet as he stumbled down the halls.

Eight.

The women! The pig! Oh, hells, Lucere was going to kill them if he caught them. Where were they? They had to get out of here, they had to—

Seven.

He had no time to get any of his belongings—not even his shoes, fuck—the ring Lucian had given him, the portrait they'd had made together . . .

Six.

The gardens! And the pig would be with them, surely—please, please.

Five.

They saw him running toward them, clad in only his trousers, his face contorted in terrified fury. "Run! Lucere! We have to—"

Four.

They were up in a flash, Odessa's hair billowing out behind her as she ran, Marbles trotting after them on a leash. Mai staggered, fell, clutched at her shirt, which was beginning to stain with fresh blood—

Three.

Fuck fuck fuck! Her stitches! Colton ran, he ran and scooped her up in his arms. She groaned softly and clung to his chest as he hurled himself into the carriage.

Two.

Did they have any money? Where would they go? What would they do? Odessa touched Colton's leg, and Mai took Odessa's hand.

One.

Ready or not, Colton. I'm coming for you.

And I am going to hurt you for this.

thirty-seven

Odessa tended to Mai's wounds as the carriage hurtled through the streets. All the stitches had torn, but it was more painful than it was life-threatening, probably. What in all the hells were they going to do? Where could they go?

Not to Lucian's old flat. Lucere had spent the infancy of his possession there, and surely he would send cronies to look in the apartment first. Not to Mai's home either, since he'd been perched on Lucian's back the last time they'd gone there.

There was only one place Lucere had never been.

"My old apartment," Colton said quietly, hugging Marbles against his stomach. "Lucere would only know about it if he can probe Lucian's memories."

Odessa took a shuddering breath. "What happened? I thought—"

"He tricked us, Dess. Whatever we were doing, it must have been working—he cut Lucian's arm off to stop us. But it weakened him, he had to hide, and he was just dormant, regaining strength. We never burned the arm, so it could have—I don't even know how much of him was there, if we ever spoke to Lucian at all or if he—if it . . . if he got so good at impersonating him that we can't even tell them apart anymore." He blinked wetly. "And now he's going to kill us."

"Great!" Mai managed, barely able to sit up straight. "Just what I need, a demon after me because it wants to make Colton sad!" That had been a bit too much of an exertion apparently, as she lay back down on the carriage seat and covered her eyes with her arm. "You owe me big-time, dude. Like, seriously, slave-for-life kinda thing."

"That's fair." But first they needed to survive this. How?

An Ivory carriage knocking down the rust-coated cobbles of the Iron District drew too much attention, and so the four of them got out as soon as they were at the border of Indigo and began to walk. They stood out anyway—Colton without a shirt or shoes, Mai with her pig on a leash, and Odessa's gold-trimmed white gown that only emphasized her willowy beauty. Lucian had a similar problem when they'd first started traipsing down here together, and after the fear of the two of them getting mugged had worn off, he'd found he enjoyed the attention they got.

Now, it was something of a liability. Odessa shifted uncomfortably under the gazes of Indigo strangers, and Mai untied the rainbow sash around her waist and gave it to Odessa to cover her hair.

Better.

They barely spoke as they traipsed through the alleyways toward Colton's former home. He took them down a dizzying route, needless turns and diversions in case they were already being followed. His feet were aching from the walk, slowed by his need to avoid the glass, metal, and needles that were common findings on the earth of the Belt.

This wasn't his home anymore. His real home was the beautiful life he'd built with Lucian, it was vanilla and twinkling smiles, it was warmth, security, and a deep, desperate love. He pushed the door open and ignored the way his heart sank. Dust and decay, droppings from pests, a dank moisture he'd never been able to shake.

Mai couldn't help but giggle at the way Odessa's face dropped as soon as they walked in, rainbow silk moving up to cover her lips. "Oh! Colton! It's so . . . quaint! Cozy!" She coughed a little. "What are we going to do?"

That was the question, wasn't it?
You have to kill Lucian.
No.
He said it himself, Colton. He doesn't want to live like this.
Never.
He's going to destroy the world.
He couldn't. How could he? How could anyone?
You don't even care what he wants?
It's not that, it—hey! Fuck. Maybe that was true. Maybe he was just being selfish. If there was no hope for Lucian, then . . .

"You guys need to get out of here," he whispered. "At least *you* should live."

"We're not leaving you, idiot," Mai said firmly, squeezing Odessa's hand. "I mean, yeah, I'd rather not directly face that miserable fucker again, but . . . you're too dumb to deal with this on your own, and besides, blondie needs all of us."

Odessa smiled. "Exactly. If you owe lovely Mai a lifetime of servitude, then surely our Lucian owes me a palace on my own personal island. You can't imagine for one moment that I'll run off to the continent to miss out on that, can you? Come now."

"You guys . . ." Hells, he loved them both. "Fine. But I'm not putting either of you in direct danger again if I can avoid it."

They wouldn't be able to act without more information first. Of course, Lucian had a PR broadcast today. Colton crawled over his mattress and plugged his radio in, fiddling with the dials until he heard the words "Lord Beaumont."

"My word, Lord Beaumont!" said the broadcasting host's voice. "We were all beginning to think you had dropped out of the race, but seeing what's happened to you—well, it's obvious why you might have needed a bit of a break!"

Lucere's hideous laugh had softened somehow, and it almost sounded like Lucian. "Oh, this?" Surely he was gesturing to his empty sleeve. "It's a harrowing tale, Mr. Graves. I'm certain I wouldn't want to bore your listeners with it."

"The top candidate for Prime Minister of Silvermoor loses his right arm and lives to tell the tale? I'm pretty sure they'd love to hear what happened to you, Lord Beaumont!"

"It . . ." Lucere was probably trying to sound demure, flicking his eyes up like Lucian did. "It all started with the murder of my father. I was a fool, Mr. Graves, a wretched fool."

"Your father was murdered? We have on record that he died of a heart attack!"

"I'm afraid the deception is my fault, sir. My father, he was murdered by my former partner, Colton."

Colton's face blanched. *No. Oh, fuck no.*

"What? Why didn't you come to the police?"

"I was certain a demon was responsible. I believed I could help him. Colton had been such a dear friend to me, after all. We had been through so much together."

Colton could hear the smile in his voice. Could imagine him biting his finger to avoid laughing out loud on the radio while he spewed his deception. This *fucking bastard.*

"So, in between my other responsibilities, I worked tirelessly to ensure that my wonderful friend Colton would be freed from this terrible burden. I tried, Mr. Graves. I tried as best as I could. But it is not possible to rid a body of a demon. In the fight for Colton's soul, he ripped my arm off with his bare teeth; he bathed in my blood and defiled my father's good name."

"Good heavens—how did you survive?"

"It was nothing short of a miracle, really. Demons like the one inhabiting Colton are vulnerable to *fire*." That wasn't true. There wasn't *one* thing in his book about demons being weak to fire. *Colton*, on the other hand, was as flammable as anything. "With all the strength I could muster, I took one of our torches, and I brandished it at him with one arm, backing him into a corner, burning at his flesh."

"You're so lucky that you figured that out, Lord Beaumont!"

"I know, it is a stupendous thing. Colton was cornered, the

demon was furious and terrified, but my strength began to fail me. With the last of my energy I called for aid, and my servants all came with torches, with wine and candles. There was no other recourse, I feared. Colton must be burned." Lucere sniffled, although Colton would have bet money on the fact that he was trying not to laugh. "He was weakened from the fire, but my servants were so frightened of him that he pushed past . . . and he . . . and he . . ."

"Go on."

"He kidnapped my sister, Mr. Graves! And who knows what depraved evil he's carrying out on her as we speak! Surely Odessa is dead, or if not, she is wishing for death to be swift." A soft sob was audible over the airwaves, and the sound of someone patting someone else on the shoulder.

The actual Odessa's face had drained of blood, and she put a quivering hand on Colton's knee. Crafty little bugger, that Lucere.

"My word. No wonder you had to take a break from politics. Do you think you'll resume your run?"

Lucere sniffled delicately. "Oh, of course. If anything, this has simply increased my resolve to serve the people of our great nation. It is exactly as I outlined in my initial platform—our country is rotting from the inside, and spiritual decay is at the heart of everything. Why was Colton possessed? Why did he allow evil to take hold of his heart? Because he lost his faith, because he had fallen victim to artificiality and avarice, because he suffered the same evils that many in the Iron District suffer! Under my rule our Silvermoor will be *cleansed*, Mr. Graves. It will be reborn in fire, and we will soar into the sky and *thrive*."

"A brilliant platform, Lord Beaumont. But wait, you said that Colton—"

"Yes. He escaped and is currently at large in our fair city. Please, act with caution. Colton is still possessed and must be considered to be extremely dangerous. He has the strength of ten men, he can dismember with his claws and his teeth, he will not hesitate to kill, maim, or rape anyone who gets in his way. He has approximately average human intelligence and has likely taken up refuge somewhere in the Iron Belt. I have taken measures to ensure his capture. His bank accounts have been frozen, and posters and flyers featuring his likeness are to be distributed through the three districts. I am offering a reward of ten thousand gold pieces if he is captured alive."

Mai and Odessa both looked at Colton, grievous pity in their eyes. What the fuck were they going to do?

"Remember, fair citizens of Silvermoor: Demons are vulnerable to fire. Burn him if you must, but try to avoid crippling him if you can. Somewhere inside of that creature lies my dear Colton, and I hope very much that the cleansing Beaumont flame will be able to save his soul. And it is with that flame that I hope to cleanse all of Silvermoor, one faithless demon at a time. Our sweet nation is at a precipice, dear citizens."

He cleared his throat, and Colton was sure he was standing erect, his chest puffed out and hand over his heart. "I am Lucian Beaumont, of the Silvermoorian Beaumonts. And I will pull this nation out from the depths of hell. A vote for me is a vote for a clean, virtuous future. A vote for me is a vote for salvation! I thank you for your time."

Colton clicked the radio off and put his head in his hands. Long ago, they had promised one another that they would stick together through anything. To hell and back, they'd said.

There was never one moment that Colton had imagined that hell would look like this.

thirty-eight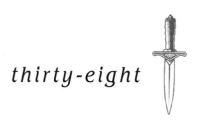

No one said anything for a while, until Colton released his head from his grip and let out a long sigh. "Okay. Well, that's my weekend, shot."

Odessa squeezed his knee and bit her lip. "It's probably not safe for you to stay here, honey."

Colton could already hear people in the district emerging from their homes, clamoring down the street. Ten thousand gold pieces, he'd said. They had maybe half an hour before his home was completely swarming with desperate people out for his head.

"I can get you some money, if you need it," Odessa offered. "I mean, odds are he's blocked *my* accounts too, but . . ."

Then Colton remembered. He'd had the foresight to keep one bag of loot stashed in his house, and he pulled his sheets back to find that, yes, it was still there. "Thank fuck," he muttered, gladder than he'd ever been that he'd ignored Lucian's suggestion to open a damned *savings account*. "Okay. This is from our first job together. We're going to divide it evenly, and then I'm going to go off on my own."

Mai interjected, "But—"

Colton stopped her. "You're hurt. You're better off without me, all right? Play it up like you sold me out." It wasn't safe for them to remain as his companions, and besides, he'd have a much easier time moving in the shadows by himself. Besides, nothing would lure Colton out of the darkness but knowing Mai or Odessa was in danger.

"In the meantime, honey, we'll need to do something about this." Odessa gestured at Colton in his entirety. "What image will he distribute to find you? We'll need to adjust your appearance quite drastically."

A few months ago, after they'd first started seeing each other romantically, Lucian had woken Colton up with a big, stupid smile on his face. It had been unusual at the time, since normally Lucian liked to sleep in, and Colton generally had to wake him up by smothering him with a pillow.

"Colton!" Lucian had perched on top of him, pinning his wrists over his head. "We should get a portrait done together!"

Colton's sleep-addled mind was somewhere between aroused and confused, and he just chuckled at his partner's unbridled enthusiasm. "And why is that?"

"Because we're wretchedly good-looking! And we're so happy! And I can hang it up in the parlor and look at it when you go out on errands and remember how cute you are and how nice we look together."

Colton just laughed. "You're very odd, you know that?"

"Darling, I'm *eccentric*."

"That's just what they call odd rich people."

"And?"

"You're very eccentric, Lucian."

They'd gotten dressed and Colton allowed Lucian to drag him around town, stopping eventually at one of the most renowned portrait artists in all of Silvermoor. They'd stood for what seemed like an age, Lucian's hand on Colton's shoulder, close enough that it was obvious they cared for each other, far enough apart that it wasn't overt that they were lovers. Despite the foolishness of the whole exercise, the artist had managed to capture Colton's brown eyes in a moment of fond adoration as they rested on Lucian's face.

He'd perfectly replicated the unbridled joy in Lucian's face, the intimacy that sparked between them, and once it was complete, Colton found himself staring at it whenever he lounged in their parlor thereafter.

It was hard to remember what Colton looked like in the picture, because all he could conjure up when he thought of it was Lucian. How young and happy he looked, how pleased Colton was to have such a man in his heart.

He'd have been in a suit though, surely. Lucian would have tutted and fretted until he changed into something more boutique-appropriate. And so his black hair must have been combed neatly the way Lucian liked, and he wouldn't have had any stubble at all. He would have looked like a noble.

"The one in the apartment, Dess," he said softly. "Of us together." Unless he had an artist do a sketch for them or something, but he doubted Lucere would go to the trouble.

Odessa knew the one, of course. "All right, easy enough. Colton the Prince must become Colton the Shadow." "Shadow," in this case, was surely a polite word for "bum."

Mai helped him shave off his glossy black hair. Odessa found the cheapest clothes he had in the house and tore them just slightly, before pulling some soot from the fireplace and dusting his hands and cheeks with it.

"You'll have to grow a beard," Mai postulated, using some of her powders to change the contour of his face just a little. "And make sure that your tattoos are covered all the time."

"Be sure to practice poor hygiene!" Odessa added, patting some crimson rust powder onto his newly exposed scalp.

"I think you need to hit me. Hard."

Mai bit her lip. "Are you sure?"

"Yes. I want to be unrecognizable."

There was a moment of hesitation before Mai brought her open palm across Colton's cheek. He laughed and shook his head. Of all the times for her to be pulling punches. "That all you got?

Remember when I stole your savings?" And had blown it all on booze. He'd paid it all back, eventually, but that trust had taken a long time to build back up.

"... Colton."

"Please, Mai."

A punch to his nose sent him to his knees, spluttering and snorting blood. That'd bruise like a fucker, and make both of his eyes purple and swollen. "Better."

Mai gingerly touched her chest—no fresh bleeding, that was a plus. She put her hand on top of his head. "Look after yourself, okay?"

Colton knew the drill. He'd spent many of his teenage years hiding in plain sight. With a cloak around his shoulders and over his face he could scarcely recognize himself, which meant that surely the bounty hunters wouldn't either.

There was no time to dwell on it, though. Some of his neighbors had surely heard the broadcast and were probably racking their brains as to where he'd lived. If they could catch him, if they could burn him. There were voices outside, people he'd lived with, worked with, for whom he'd exorcised demons at very reasonable rates. They'd tear him apart, roast him alive, or worse ... bring him to Lucere in one piece. His life in the balance, and Lucian's only chance to escape from the nightmare he was trapped in. There was no time.

"I've got to go. Take care of each other, okay?"

He pressed kisses to each of their foreheads, even Marbles's, and hoisted himself up through one of the holes in the roof.

"Be careful," Mai whispered, and Odessa took her hand.

Colton moved in the shadows, casually, ambling, a scrap of paper on the wind as he moved to find an empty warehouse to sleep in. He kept thinking of his old life, when his bread and butter had been doing exorcisms before he'd met Lucian. A smile crossed his face as he realized how spoiled he'd become, how accustomed he was now to velvet carpets and silk walls.

"Colton, precious, this is *ghastly*. Surely we can get a broom or something? We'll get the *hantavirus!*"

Fuck, he missed Lucian so much.

He'll torture you to death. He'll rape Mai; he'll pull Odessa's arms off. He'll eat the pig raw.

He couldn't leave the man he loved to suffer like this.

You have to help him. However you can. Even if that means letting him go.

Tears sprung to his eyes as the hopelessness of the situation sank in once more. Lucian didn't want to live like this. And if Colton survived long enough to get close to Lucere, there was only one option.

The cure is in the heart. That is where the demon resides. There is no other way.

Every part of him rebelled against that idea, though the rational part of his mind knew better. Souls weren't so fragile that they couldn't be untangled from an evil presence, were they? Lucian had survived this long, his spirit still resilient and present as it had been from the moment Lucere had taken him. Colton just had to get close. Sneak into the manor, drug him, something. It would work this time, he only had one arm—they could . . . If the three of them worked together again, they could . . .

No. He was arguing with reality, which never ended very well for him, to be honest. His choices now were to abandon Lucian, or to end his life and set him free. The difficult part would be accepting it.

thirty-nine

It had been a very long time since Colton had been on his own for any extended period of time. He had never been apart from his mother until she'd died, and after that it was slipping between homes and bedrooms, chasing the warmth and comfort he could only find in the embrace of another human being. It wasn't promiscuity, exactly—more a fear of the echoes in the back of his mind whenever he found himself alone and sober.

After Mai had broken up with him for the last time, he'd had a string of partners who hadn't been very good choices in many ways. Nothing serious, but they enabled Colton's worst habits, and Mai had suggested quite firmly that he get his shit together. So he'd tried, for as long as he could, being comfortable with being alone.

Then he'd met Lucian. Even when they weren't sleeping together, they were seldom apart, and certainly not absent from one another's thoughts. Funny, how seldom he had found himself drinking after Lucian Beaumont had wormed his way into his life. Lucian had made him feel like he mattered.

But Lucian wasn't with him anymore. Neither was Mai, or Dess, or the stupid pig.

That first night after he'd managed to slip away from the mob, he'd tried to sleep in a dirty warehouse with nothing but his cloak to keep him company. He couldn't sleep. He couldn't stop his hands from shaking, his stomach from rising up into his throat.

Everything is falling apart. Odessa lost her home, Mai's gonna be on the run forever now, and you're gonna be burned to death in your fucking sleep. And Lucian is—he—

It wasn't smart to venture out on his own when the whole nation was after him, but he just needed a little something to help him settle down. He kept his shoulders straight, his eyes forward, and no one gave him a second glance. Precious copper left his fingers in exchange for an amber neck, which he clasped like it was the dearest thing in the world.

The liquid was warm when it hit the back of his throat, and he could feel it slosh around and coat the lining of his stomach as he swallowed. The hollow nausea was an old friend, and soon enough the bottle was empty.

The next few days were something of a blur. The hopelessness of the situation was starting to hit him: the fact that he had no real plan of action, that his options were limited to homeless destitution and/or certain fiery death. And so he drank. He drank until he felt warm against the cold of the night, he drank until he was sick, he drank until it didn't hurt to be alone.

It was a few days before he gave himself enough of a break between drinks to think clearly. It wasn't pleasant. Sunlight hit his face and he squinted against it. *Where's Lucian?* It took a moment to remember where he was, why there were pebbles stuck against his skin, why the only thing he could smell was stale urine and sticky beer instead of vanilla and cream.

Fuck.

The world spun as he stood up, and he realized with no small amount of remorse that he hadn't really eaten or had any water since his little relapse. He hadn't shaved, hadn't bathed. He felt dreadful. On the plus side, that probably meant he was going to be a lot harder to recognize by everyone in the Ivory District. On the minus side, he was probably a fair bit easier to clock down here with his compatriots. He rubbed the scratchy stubble growing over his scalp and pulled his cloak over his head. If there was one thing

Lucian had taught him, it was how to adapt his appearance to suit his environment. In this case, affecting poverty to the point that no one would even see him. Hells, as long as he kept his tattoos covered, he looked as generic an Iron derelict as one possibly could.

Colton crawled toward the nearest public fountain, maintaining a constant effort not to vomit. The Iron Belt wasn't known for the hygiene of its infrastructure, but this simple metal basin with its cooling crystal waterfall was heaven to Colton. He submerged his head in the stream, gulping down heavy mouthfuls gratefully as the life-giving liquid kissed his cheeks. He rubbed at the dirt and grime that felt like it was a part of his skin and was glad when the water began to run clean once more as it dripped off his hands and face.

He rubbed his face and sat perfectly still as a new wave of nausea rolled over him. Fuck. He needed a drink.

He found a bar that he'd never been to before and sat down at the back, the hood casting a shadow over his face. Eyes glanced in his direction, and Colton doubled over with a hacking, spitting cough that sang tales of consumptive contagions that seemed to dissuade further attention. The place was buzzing with energy and its clientele had better things to worry about than an exhausted, dehydrated, diseased stranger. Colton downed his first glass of beer in under thirty seconds and gingerly chased it with some hard bread and warm stew.

He picked up a newspaper that someone had left on the table beside him and flicked it open. Lucere's miserable face stared back at him, his toothy grin prominent, his left hand stroking a gold prosthetic arm that fit perfectly under his sleeve. Colton turned the page. *Fugitive Demon Colton Still at Large*, the headline helpfully informed him, and he bit his lip.

The nationwide bounty hunt had turned up nothing, although the article mentioned that several young men matching Colton's description had been burned to death in the effort to capture him throughout the Iron District: *"It's a shame,"* says Prime Minister front-runner Lucian Beaumont, "that so many wicked men are in our fair Iron District. When I am elected, I will put a stop to this. The fight for Silvermoor's soul will be a lengthy one, but I will never give up on you!"

Colton had to commend Lucere's skill at this whole public relations thing. He tried to order another beer, but no one was listening.

"Turn it up! They've gotta know by now!" someone called, and the bartender tutted as he clicked on the radio. Silence descended, and they had to sit through several minutes of advertisements before at last the familiar voice of Broadcaster Graves reverberated over the airwaves.

"Good afternoon, people of Silvermoor! The results are in! We have a new Prime Minister!" A pause for effect, and Colton wondered if anyone else could hear the way his heart was thundering away in his chest. "In a landslide victory, I am pleased to announce our very own Lucian Beaumont as our new leader! Congratulations, sir!"

That choking, barking laugh. "Well, thank you, Mr. Graves. Of course I am delighted and humbled by the results. It is my sincerest wish to be the harbinger of a new age for our people, an age of holiness, of purity, of freedom from wickedness and corruption. And I think that that must begin in our home and our hearts. I, like many of you, have been shocked by the horrific influence of demons within our fair nation. You know of course of my efforts to rid our best and brightest of the wickedness that plagues them, yes? I've seen a great deal during my tenure as the Ninth Archon, of course. I believe the source of this evil to be our nation's disconnect with the Holy Order, the people with their faith."

"Hear, hear!" called one of the patrons, beer sloshing around in his glass.

"And so I believe that we must begin my reign with a cleansing, shall we say. Silvermoor, like a phoenix, shall be reborn in fire. Vice and depravity must be excised and obliterated, and we shall rebuild once cleansed. The Iron District as it is now shall be cleansed."

Looks of confusion fell over every man's face in the pub.

"All properties within the Iron District shall be examined, evaluated, and demolished if they are not up to our national standards. In its place shall be built affordable, beautiful housing—hospitals, schools, temples. Wholesome, good places for the decent people of Silvermoor. Funded of course by liquidating the assets of anyone . . . *anyone* we determine to be morally unfit. We cannot stand upon a foundation of sin. The entire district will be swept through by my personal guard. Any person of legal age found to be partaking in criminal activity, illicit drug use, or unholy lifestyle shall, of course, be arrested and put to work for the state."

Wait. What?

"I promised you a clean and virtuous future. I promised you salvation. And I, Lucian Beaumont, will deliver. Bless you all."

The worst had happened. Lucere had the power to destroy every living thing in this nation if he wished to, and the rest of the Ivory monsters were eating it up.

I want you to read this letter.

The letter. The last thing that Lucian had tried to give him, locked away in a drawer at their old apartment in the Ivory District. Colton still had the key on a chain around his neck. He swallowed hard and pushed his beer glass to the far end of the table. He couldn't afford to fuck around anymore, couldn't afford to wallow in self-pity or self-destruction.

Surely—*surely* there would be something in that letter that could help him defeat Lucere. Lucian wasn't such a fool that he couldn't have seen some of this coming. The answer to all of this was there, locked away in his side table drawer.

It was just a matter of infiltrating the Ivory District during the Prime Minister's inauguration week. While there was a national manhunt for him with the primary aim to burn him alive.

Colton was going to get that letter, or he was gonna bloody die trying.

forty

It was all well and good for Colton to want to go back to their home in the Ivory District and find whatever message Lucian had left for him, but it was another matter entirely when Lucere had already begun to institute sweeping changes throughout the Iron Belt.

It had all happened so fast that Colton had to wonder how much of this had been planned ahead of the election. How much of a hand the Order had had in shifting the outcome, falling over themselves to enact Lucere's vision of the world.

White-coated officers stormed the district almost as soon as the decree left his lips, kicking down doors and finding the criminals that Lucere had warned them about. Young men with drug habits, women with fatherless children, truants, litterers—whatever particular evil Lucere had decreed was a top priority on any given day. He didn't arrest children, to his credit. Any minors left without caregivers were taken in by the state, and Colton could only pray that Lucere's sympathies extended to them.

For all of his faults, Colton had to admit that Lucere's bureaucratic efficiency was almost admirable. In the hands of a less corrupt politician, such organization could have saved the nation.

Colton had only watched a few of these sweeps before opting to avoid the white figures at any cost. They would arrest anyone involved with criminal activity, never to be seen again, and would smile piteously at whatever family was left behind. "You'll have two days. This structure has been found to be culturally insoluble." The police would take their iron brands and burn a crimson, smoldering *L* onto the facade of any doomed building.

Two days later, the home would be ash, whether the remaining occupants had left or not.

A problem one often encountered in the Iron District was the lack of mobility, lateral, vertical, or otherwise. There weren't so many free homes that these evictees could just pick up and land on their feet elsewhere. Nor could they leave the Iron District. Indigo had cracked down on Iron men without proper work passes, and leaving Silvermoor altogether meant at once facing the wilderness, the sea, or a bureaucrat at a border control desk.

As a result there was an onslaught of newly undomiciled, crowding the district and actually making Colton's national manhunt a lot easier to avoid.

Even so, getting arrested meant death. His face was plastered all over the district now, and a substantial cash reward had been advertised for his live capture. He'd had a number of close calls with Iron folk—gazes lingering on his face just a touch too long. Colton didn't dare move in the sunlight and didn't dare go somewhere familiar like Mai's house, lest he drag her down with him.

That being said, it was very unlikely he'd be able to source the disguise he'd need to infiltrate the Ivory District without her, and so he decided to trust in their relationship and her intelligence, and let her come to him. He spent much of his time in their old haunts from when they were children together, at the edge of the beach, the cave they'd discovered one summer that was full of tide pools and tiny sea creatures.

They'd been back plenty of times since then and had discovered little ledges they could perch on when the ocean came rushing in. Now, it was probably the safest place he could be. It was one of the only places in the Belt where he couldn't smell smoke, and he felt it was very unlikely that the police would come and bother him here.

If Mai was looking for him, this would almost certainly be the first place she'd start. Once he met up with Mai, he'd at least have an operative who could help him move—get him a disguise, check the path ahead for danger, allow him to get to the damned letter. More than anything, he wanted to know she was okay.

And so he waited. He came to this place each day as the sun rose, took off his cloak and just waited.

But Mai never came.

Had she succumbed to the infection? Recognized the hopelessness of their battle? Colton was about to give up on ever seeing her again when a long cloak obscured the light of the entryway.

"Mai!" he laughed, tears in his eyes as he stumbled over the pools to get to her, to pull her into his arms and kiss her face and tell her how much he'd—

He pushed the black hood back, and hoped the disappointment on his face wasn't too obvious.

"Odessa, your hair."

Her golden waterfalls had been lopped off, replaced with a boyish bob that made her look even younger. Her dainty sundress had been replaced with a plain blouse and set of trousers, a black cape obscuring much of her body. No one would recognize Lady Beaumont now. She seemed absolutely exhausted.

She reached out and touched the fuzz that was starting to grow on Colton's scalp. "Yours too."

"Where's Mai?" He was almost afraid to ask.

Her eyes avoided his. "She got arrested, Colton."

Colton staggered back. His skin blanched, and it was a blessing that he was able to keep himself from being sick. "He won't kill her." He was certain of that. "But he'll probably use her to get to me." Use her. What a lovely way of talking about torture.

"They came back and burned the house. Colton, honey, I'm so sorry." Odessa shook her head, tears running down her face. "Marbles ran off. Mai tried to escape, but her chest started bleeding, and I couldn't—I was too afraid to . . ."

Colton pulled her into his arms and sighed softly. It wasn't hard to figure out the rest. Mai had surely warned Dess that they might be separated, and in that event instructed her to come here and wait for Colton. Odessa probably hadn't been able to leave until now, terrified of being caught by the Iron men or the police and dragged back into Lucere's clutches.

They held each other for a moment, and eventually Odessa let go, taking in her surroundings. "It's beautiful here," she commented, crouching down and touching the tiny pools with her fingers. "Mai said you were so happy together." Her shoulders quivered.

Colton knelt beside her. "We were. The best sort of summer entertainment you could get as a poor kid, I guess."

Odessa's fingers followed an opal-scaled fish as it flitted around the stones. "Look at them all. Trapped because the world around them changed."

"Until the tide comes back in."

Odessa smiled. "Lucian loved your optimism, you know. He loved everything about you."

"Wish I could say the same, but he was just the worst."

Odessa reached over and pinched him on the arm with all her fury, and they both laughed for a time, until they remembered why they were here. Stony silence fell between them, and Colton muttered, "I'll end it, Dess. I'll kill that fucking *thing* once and for all."

She covered her face and nodded. They didn't have a choice anymore. Lucere was destroying a third of the country, he had the whole nation hunting them down like dogs, and he'd captured Mai.

The only question was, how could they manage it?

They hatched a plan together. With what little money they both had left, they would buy clothes beautiful enough to get them into the Ivory District. They'd go to Lucian's old flat and regain their strength. It was only a few days until the grand Inauguration Gala.

It wouldn't be that hard, surely. Colton just had to get close enough to stab one of the most powerful men in the world in the heart. With his entire security detail in place. In front of lots of people. While a national manhunt was on for him.

From the mouth of the cave, Colton could just about see the soaring marble spires of Beaumont Manor. The lights from the windows sparkled against the dark water of the sea, and Colton had to imagine that Lucere was standing beside one of them, cigarette in hand, sneering. The Inauguration Gala was only a few days away, and that would be Colton's best chance to strike.

Colton squeezed Odessa's fingers and gritted his teeth.

Watch out, you miserable fuck. We're coming for you.

forty-one

The solution to getting passable clothes presented itself to them one wet, stormy evening. When the winds got violent like this it wasn't safe to stay in the cave.

They had no choice, therefore, but to venture out into the Iron Belt to find some shelter that wasn't liable to flood. A squat, somewhere they could get their bearings and figure out how to get into the Ivory District once more. Odessa held Colton's hand tightly, not wanting them to be separated.

An officer spotted them in the distance.

"Oi!" he called, trotting closer.

Okay, their options were run (and risk having him call for his coworkers), allow themselves to be questioned (and risk being identified), or try and take him out quietly (and risk getting injured or captured). Colton supposed option two could easily slide into option three should the need arise, and he squeezed Odessa's fingers.

"I need some identification. It's past curfew."

Colton hacked a cough without covering his mouth and wiped at his nose. "Ain't got one. Lost in a fire."

The guard took a step back, his eyes trained on Colton's slender companion. He reached for his brand with a smirk. "Oh, ho. Take down your hoods."

Colton was confident he wouldn't be recognized, but Odessa's beauty had the tendency to draw the wrong sort of attention from men like this. Even dressed as a boy, even at night, that innate Beaumont elegance radiated from her whole body and captured the imagination. A white-gloved hand snatched at her chin and held her face in the dim lamplight above them.

"Pretty little thing, aren't you? Are you sure you're a boy, sweetheart? We've had some reports of cross-dressing in these parts. Maybe we'd best take you somewhere private and check."

Colton bristled and moved closer to her but stopped when he saw the sneer on her lips. "Why, Notloc, my dearest brother, I think I've just come up with a very good idea."

Notloc. Of all the ridiculous pseudonyms—

Odessa moved quickly, driving her knee up between his legs with as much force as a young woman could muster. He was fast though, able to avoid the blow, and stronger than she was by a factor of ten.

"Oh you little whore." He held her throat, clicking the brand on until it glowed crimson. Hah. It matched the mark on Colton's wrist perfectly.

"C-Colton!" she managed, clawing at his wrists.

"*Colton?*" That must have been very interesting to the guard indeed, and he wheeled around to apprehend Silvermoor's most wanted man.

"Hi." Colton offered a small wave. He stepped forward, his left foot planting firmly on the ground, and drove his right elbow upward into the guard's jaw. The effect was immediate and decisive. The guard's eyes rolled back, his body going limp as he crumpled to the earth. In the dark whispers of the storm, they were able to drag him into a secluded area, tie him up, and strip him of his enforcer uniform.

Coming to, he screamed against the rag stuffed into his mouth, and Odessa lightly kicked him to keep him quiet. "What do we do with him, brother? Do we kill him?"

"Mmm, I'm not sure. I suppose we can just maim him a little." He pulled on the white enforcement jacket and clasped the buttons around his throat. "Just as well we didn't spill any blood while he was wearing this. Maybe that's why they chose this stupid color."

"I was thinking the same." Odessa picked up the brand and fiddled with the handle, her eyes lighting up with pleasure as the iron went from black to simmering crimson.

"But then again," Colton considered lazily, "if he screams too much, we might have some trouble." He pulled her into his arms and squeezed, whispering in her ear. "I should take this chance, Dessie. Are you gonna be okay for a little while longer?"

She nodded.

"Stay safe. If I don't come back, I want you to leave this place."

Odessa looked into his eyes. Hells, she looked so much like Lucian.

"Stop it, you miserable beastie. It'll work. You have to believe it's going to work." She punched Colton half-assedly in the chest, right over the tattoo that spelled out the end of this story.

"I'll see you when you get home, okay? Take care, Notloc. I love you."

He fluffed her hair. "I love you too, squirt. Be safe. And find that stupid pig, all right?"

Colton turned away, not wanting to see the beautiful Beaumont smile on her face any longer. He adjusted his white cap so the brim obscured his eyes, catching a glimpse of himself in a broken window—his shoulders broad, his back straight, the brand in his hand. He looked every bit the White Flame enforcer. What a name for Lucere to have chosen for his not-so-secret police.

But it was just like any job in the Ivory District, wasn't it? A hollow smile on his lips, his heels clacking confidently alongside the dull thud of raindrops as he made his way up, up. Ironers cowered away from him, Indigos glanced at him with mild curiosity—and Ivory didn't even spare him a second glance.

The first time he'd witnessed Lucian's class bullshit in action, he could scarcely believe what he was seeing. It was like a magic power he possessed, that allowed him to do whatever he wished with impunity and without consequence. Colton was glad of the lesson. White Officer Colton marched right up to their old building, nodding politely at the guards stationed outside, and let himself in with his key.

"Official business. Secret mission," he said plainly to a lone enforcer perched beside the door. What else did he need to say? He was the law.

He had to take a moment to collect himself as he entered the home—the scent of vanilla, of raspberries, of the hideous spice cigarettes that Lucere enjoyed—so much of Colton's heart lay bare in this place. He clapped his hands on his cheeks to center himself and haltingly strode toward his old bedroom.

Lucere had trashed the place. He'd destroyed the bed, crushed the furniture, ransacked the drawers, torn up any documents that looked like they mattered to Colton. The dresser drawer lay toppled on the far end of the room, and the envelope containing Lucian's letter lay in several jagged pieces, its edges turned up slightly from the humidity in the air. Even so Colton could just about make out Lucian's elegant cursive dancing over the parchment. *To Colton, with all my love.*

It took him time to reassemble the document from the scraps Lucere had reduced them to. Fragment by fragment, Colton was able to parse envelope from message, putting the puzzle together like a mosaic containing the solution to everything.

Lucian's golden seal was cracked, and Colton pressed a soft kiss to the emblem before facing the envelope's contents. He thought he'd never have to open this letter. Felt on some level that reading it meant accepting defeat, that Lucian was gone, and he was never, ever coming back.

My dearest Colton,

    My hands are cold and unsteady, and I feel I can only apologize for the atrocious handwriting in this letter. You know how much I like things to be pretty, darling, and I know how much you like things to be in order. I fear this may be the first of many things this creature takes away from us.

    Colton, I feel myself losing control. My mind is not my own, my thoughts are not private. My body, too, is falling to this creature. This thing inside of me, it is strong, and wicked, and hungry, and it takes great pleasure in causing you pain.

    I want to say some things before my soul perishes, locked away in my chest. I want to tell you these things before this creature robs me of the ability to express how I feel for you.

    I love you. With every ounce of my being, I love you. You are the first thing I think about in the morning, the last thing I think of before I fall asleep at night. You are my sunshine, my joy, my pride, my everything. I watch you while you sleep, sometimes, and think how lucky I am that we met. You allowed me to accept myself for who I am; you helped me face my fears, find my voice, be myself. Even with all that has transpired—Colton, I wouldn't trade it.

    I never wanted to drag you down into this hell. If it comes to it, Colton, I would not resent you if you left and never looked back. I would not blame you if you wounded this body to protect yourself. And I would be grateful, if all was lost, if you would set me free.

    I have never known fear like this before. The dysphoria and terror of losing my body to a malevolent force I don't understand, it is worse than death, my lovely, darling. It is an agony I cannot describe.

    I fear this monster has more sinister designs than I can

conceive of—a wish for power that could unravel Silvermoor at its roots. In my study, you'll find a clockwork jellyfish. It's all terrible fun; it swims and makes noises and provides hours of entertainment. Turn it over, and there is a lock. Our mutual ally will help you.

I love you, Colton. You are beautiful, you are brilliant, and you mean everything to me. I am grateful, at least, that I got the chance to say it once more.

I love you, precious.

Goodbye.

Yours eternal,
Lucian Beaumont

This was it. Lucian's last request, and surely the key to everything. The weight of it was unbearable—Lucian's life, Silvermoor's future, his own safety, security, and freedom all hung in the balance. One chance. He'd only have one chance to get this right.

Can you even do it? Can you hurt someone with Lucian's face? His voice? You know Lucere is going to pull out all the stops, right? You know he's going to make it hurt.

It didn't matter.

There was no other way.

forty-two

The Royal Inauguration Gala was the grandest event that Silvermoor ever hosted, outside of royal weddings, military victory parties, and coronations. It took time to plan, and often occurred weeks or even months after the Prime Minister had begun his term.

"It makes the Winter Ball look like a pile of garbage!" Lucian had explained to him once, fussing with his hair. "Everyone who's anyone will be there, Colton." And Colton had grasped his wrists and held Lucian's hands against his cheeks, enjoying their smooth warmth.

But how would the most wanted man in the nation infiltrate the most highly guarded gala?

"With impunity!" Lucian probably would have said, and Colton just smiled.

With impunity, yes. Why not?

He let himself into Lucian's study and rooted around for the aforementioned jellyfish. He found it eventually, shoved to the back of Lucian's drawer with various bits of detritus. It was a sweet tiny thing, dotted with brilliant blue crystals, an iridescent metallic textile making up the bell that flapped adorably when a clockwork key was turned. It had a face too, with a dear little smile made up of black lacquer paint. Lucere had located it first, apparently, and had torn off a few of its wiggly legs in irritation. Colton held it close to his chest for a moment and closed his eyes. On the underside was a lock with a seven-letter code.

A mutual ally, he'd said. One Lucere wouldn't have known about when he'd watched Lucian write the letter through his eyes. *For fuck's sake.* Who else could it be? Colton smiled as he spun dials and input his very best guess: M A R B L E S. The lock clicked, and the belly of the beast opened up. Inside was a pure gold ring, studded with sapphires, the Beaumont signature *B* surrounded with glinting stars etched into the metal, and a small scrap of parchment.

This will get you anywhere, love. Use it with my blessing.
LB

Lucian's signet ring—the last thing he'd kept from his father before all this had started, the tiny loop of metal that carried as much power and influence in Silvermoor as any amount of money. And Lucian had had the foresight to hide it away in case they ever needed it for an emergency.

Colton allowed himself the luxury of a shower, a shave, and a nice long sleep in his old feather bed, and by the time he awoke it was just about time for the gala. He selected one of the beautiful bespoke suits that Lucian had commissioned for him and was tempted to put on the black cloak he'd worn at the Winter Ball, but ultimately he decided that the aesthetic of being a black shadow at the party would not be worth the risk of being recognized. Instead, he picked an outfit that Lucian had loved, with tones of chocolate and burgundy, crimson silk lining the vest, rubies holding his cuffs together, a sweeping charcoal cape clasped around his throat by a gold chain, and a garnet the size of an apricot.

Colton caught a glimpse of himself in the mirror and used it to center himself. He could barely recognize his own face anymore. Gone was the grime and soot, the swelling, the dry, bloodshot eyes that had come with his relapse. He imagined Lucian behind him, his hands on his shoulders, whispering in his ears.

Look at yourself, Colton. Look at how brilliant you are. This is who those nobles are going to see, all right? Not Colton, no—a noble who has been invited to the greatest party in the world. A man who orders action and it happens—he snaps his fingers and the world is his. A wanted criminal? Never. This is a guest befitting a private audience with the new Prime Minister!

The last thing he did was to grab his dagger, the one carved with the symbols his mother had left him, and drench it with lavender oil. He lined its sheath with the same, and at the very last moment he pricked the tip of his finger with it and let his exorcist blood slide down the edge of the blade. Whatever powers he had in him, he would use them to vanquish Lucere. And so he left the guard outfit behind, grabbed his bag of demon-hunting goodies, and selected Lucian's shiniest cane sword as he marched out the front door and past the sentinel beside it.

"Nicely done, chaps," he called, waving pleasantly. "See you at the gala!"

It wasn't hard to find the party. He just followed the flow of traffic, his heels clacking on the street as he moved toward the man he loved. Once he arrived at the front entryway, he was met by security.

"Name?"

"Excuse me?"

"What is your name, my Lord?"

Colton scoffed, holding his hand out for these peons to inspect the ring on his finger. Recognition failed them, and Colton shook it at them impatiently. "I'll have you know I am the Prime Minister's beloved cousin, Lloyd Beaumont," he huffed.

"Um—sir, your name isn't on the—"

"Pardon? You're telling me the *Beaumont* name isn't on the list? At *our* inauguration? Lucian will have your hands for this. Get him for me."

"My Lord, I don't think—"

"Get him for me!"

"Okay, Lord Beaumont, please—it must be a mistake on our end. Please, please accept our sincere apologies and enjoy the party. And pass along our congratulations to your cousin. What a wonderful man he is."

How was that, Lucian? he wondered, sneering at the guards.

It wasn't long before the Prime Minister himself made an appearance, a golden crown nestled amongst his golden hair, a mechanical hand at the end of his sleeve.

Imagine that around your throat, Colton. He was bad enough with hands of flesh.

Lucere waved at the crowd with it, to their coos and admiration of his strength and bravery in the face of adversity. "My friends! I thank you so much for sharing in my joy on this day! Please join me in welcoming a new era of purity and prosperity to our people—let the White Flame bathe over our fair Silvermoor, and let us be born anew!"

The ballroom erupted in applause, the noise of which, thankfully, drowned out Colton's sarcastic slow clapping. How would he get to him? How could he get through this crowd?

Their eyes met then, ice blue boring into Colton's molten molasses. Lucere smirked, leaned a chin on his mechanical hand, and flexed his metal fingers.

Colton tilted his head to one side and waved back with a sneer. *Your move, dickhead.*

The Prime Minister beckoned one of his guards close, pointed at Colton, and listened as the guard said something that caused Lucere to roar with laughter.

Colton counted to ten and felt the heavy thud of leather gloves on his shoulder. "Lloyd Beaumont? Your cousin wants a word with you."

"What an honor," Colton croaked, handing his glass to a woman standing beside him. "Let's not keep him waiting."

He was led to a private room just off the grand ballroom—a cozy, wood-paneled space with lush green carpets and opulent portraits hanging on the walls. The oak door creaked open once more, and the demon stepped in, flexing the individual joints at the end of his golden fingers. "Lloyd. What a lovely surprise to see you here. Please, gentlemen, give us some privacy."

Colton couldn't suppress the shiver of fear that went through him as Lucere looked him up and down like a piece of flesh. He hated himself for trembling before it, for not being able to contain his visceral terror. That pink tongue slid over the front of his teeth, and Colton nearly whimpered.

The door clicked shut, and Lucere smiled.

"Colton. I wasn't sure if you would come for my big day."

"How could I miss it?" he managed, taking a step back. "Congrats, by the way."

"Why, thank you." A pause. "Why are you here?"

"I—ah—I'm here to kill you, Lucere."

That croaking, miserable laugh. "Aha. I should have known. I'm glad, in a way. I think it would have been very ugly politically if I'd had to parade around that little bitch of yours and make her miserable until you crawled out of your hole."

Mai's alive. Thank all the heavens.

"Yeah, that's very nice of you that you didn't do that."

"Mmm. Well, I had a feeling you wouldn't stay away for long, Colton. Because this is the little dance we do, isn't it? You run, I chase, I wound you, and then you always, *always* come crawling back. Always determined at long last to rid precious Lucian Beaumont of his ailment, and yet never quite able to seal the deal."

"I could say the same to you, Lucere. You've not been able to kill me yet either. Lucian won't let you, right? All-powerful demon, my ass."

Lucere cocked his head to one side. "I suppose there's only one way to find out."

He moved in close, his metal hand icy and sharp against Colton's skin. It flexed against his throat, close enough to draw a line of blood that ran down to his collar. Colton lashed out with his foot, pushing away and forcing Lucere to pounce once more, striking him to the ground with a sneer.

Colton crawled backward, blood dripping from his mouth as he tried to find his feet. "Is there a reason you're dragging this out, Lucere?" He lunged forward, only to be struck down by Lucere's superior strength. "Any reason why you don't just kill me where I stand? I betrayed you, Herluin. I *hurt* you. On purpose."

The metal hand found Colton's throat once more, and once again the fingers quivered over his skin and released him. Lucere let out a frustrated bark.

"You can't," Colton breathed, looking into its horribly beautiful face. "He won't let you do it."

Lucere's nostrils flared and he threw Colton to the ground. "So? You can't kill me either." The demon took a moment and centered himself, breathing in and out through his nose. "Well, it hardly matters. I don't need you dead, strictly speaking. And, as we've established, it's much more fun to have you alive. I like punishing people, Colton. I like making people sorry that they hurt me." And surely no one had hurt Lucere more than Colton had.

Colton shakily put his hand on the hilt of his knife.

"Oh, yes. I'll lock you up in a room with no sunlight. I'll torture that woman to death in front of you, Colton; I'll make you *beg* me to kill you. I'll blind you, I'll cut out your tongue, I'll burn you until your fingers fall off." He snorted a laugh. "Why did you come here, Colton? Surely you knew you wouldn't be able to end it, no? You love him too much."

I'm doing this because I love him, he reminded himself, unsheathing the blade and filling the whole room with the scent of lavender.

Lucere shuddered at the smell, but he didn't move. "Oh, Colton. Come now. We both know you can't."

One step forward, just one, drive it into his chest, and he'll die, Colton. He'll torture you otherwise, he'll kill Mai, he'll find Dess, he—

His eyes landed on Lucere's, who manifested such a Lucian smile that Colton almost sobbed.

"Don't, Colton." His best Lucian voice, surely. "I love you."

How could he? How could he steal the sun from the sky? How could he kill the man he loved most in the world? Those smiles against his skin, that laugh like bells, his horrible cooking, his unbearable puns, the joy he gleaned from everything—he couldn't. He *couldn't*.

"Lucian—" The knife stopped midair. A spell held Colton still, a desperate hope that love would triumph, that they could be happy, that they could *fix* this.

Get ahold of yourself! You knew he'd try this, it's not Lucian! It's not!

Lucere smiled, all confidence.

I love you, precious.

I can't. I can't. I can't!

It is an agony I cannot describe.

Please, Lucian. Please no.

And . . . I would be grateful, if all was lost, if you would set me free.

Tears ran down Colton's cheeks, and he searched Lucere's face. "Please," he whispered.

For a fleeting moment, the warmth of Lucian's eyes bled through the icy blue gaze of the demon. It was Lucian. Colton knew with absolute certainty that it was. Beautiful pink lips moved silently, then fell to a sad smile. They didn't need words. Colton knew what Lucian had tried to tell him.

Do it.

Colton cried out as the blade found Lucian's heart with a wet thud. He stayed flush against Lucian's chest, still gripping the hilt of the knife even as Lucian's warm, desperate blood flooded out onto his hands. Colton was alone with his senses. The room smelled of lavender and iron, all he saw was red, the figure beneath him was warm and firm, and Lucian's gasping, gurgling body was thrashing underneath him. "I'm sorry," he whispered. "I'm sorry, Lucian."

Their eyes met for a moment, and Lucian smiled weakly.

"My Lord?" A guard opened the door cautiously, gasping as he took in the scene. "I need help! The Prime Minister's been stabbed! We need a doctor!"

He felt it then. Something deep in his bones as Lucian's body shivered—he could feel *evil* slipping through his fingers, weeping out from the hole in Lucian's chest.

Colton was torn from Lucian, his hands forced behind his back and tied. A bag went over his face, and someone cracked him on the skull. He was dragged away from the guard's frantic screaming, out into the cold air of the street. Panic was taking the crowd; cries of desperate fear rippled through the party guests.

It was over. Lucian Beaumont was dead. He'd won, he'd vanquished Lucere, he'd set Lucian free. A decisive victory that had ended both Lucian's life and probably his own.

It's worth it. Whatever happens from now, it was worth it. The people of Silvermoor deserved better than Lucere; Lucian deserved better too. And Colton had to wonder if his mother would have been proud of the exorcist he'd become.

You'll have plenty of time to wonder in prison. They'll hang you for this.

From within the burlap sack, Colton's shoulders shook as his laughter decayed into sobs.

forty-three

He'd signed his death warrant that night. There was no question about that—it was just a matter of *when*. Silvermoor didn't take kindly to assassins at the best of times, never mind those who stabbed popular Prime Ministers on the night of their formal inaugurations.

As much as Colton would have preferred not to be executed, it was a fact he could make peace with so long as Lucere was dead—so long as Lucian was free.

He tried to cling onto that thought, that at least he and Lucian would be together soon, rather than focus on everything he'd lost up until now. The beautiful life that he might have had with Lucian if only they'd ignored Lucius's invitation, if they'd just grabbed Odessa and Mai and fucked off to the country as soon as they had enough money to support themselves. They'd have bought a quaint little cottage (well, little to Odessa and Lucian, which meant a minimum of four bedrooms and a private gazebo), and surely it would have been beside a crystal lake in the mountains. They'd go swimming every day, maybe catch some fish or raise chickens in the garden, and at night he'd cuddle up with Lucian and look into those big stupid eyes and tell him how pretty he was and how nice he smelled. He could imagine Odessa sitting on the porch, braiding blossoms and ivy into Mai's beautiful black hair and leaning in now and again to kiss her shoulders. Hells, he could even imagine that stupid pig snuffling around behind the house, ruining the flower beds and generally being a pest.

His cell was dark most of the time, except when the guards remembered to light a torch for him. He'd get fed maybe twice a day if he was lucky, some sort of bland, lukewarm glue with bits of gristle dotted throughout, that dried out his throat and caught in his teeth.

What had happened to Mai? Had Lucere tortured her to death after all? Was she trapped as a slave somewhere in the bowels of Silvermoor? And Dess, how was she faring on her own? She'd have run out of money by now, surely.

Please, please be okay.

Colton had no idea how much time had passed by the time the guards eventually came for him. It was pathetic how he leaned into the rough touch of the strangers who gripped his shoulders and forced him to his feet.

"Get up, dog," one of them barked, pushing Colton forward. "You have a visitor."

A visitor? Odessa? Could she have—well, since Lucere was dead, then surely she would have felt safe enough to show herself and—

He couldn't help the excitement that made him rock on the balls of his feet, though his mind told him to be rational.

Colton's hands were tied behind his back, and he was forced into a splintered wooden chair, before his ankles were shackled to the ground. Uncomfortable, unpleasant, probably unnecessary. Colton shifted on the seat so he wasn't sitting on his fingers.

"Stop fidgeting," the guard ordered, punching Colton in the shoulder. "Just wait here."

What helpful advice to someone tied to a chair.

The door swung open, and the guards stepped aside with a bow. A tall figure darkened the threshold and stepped inside, the dim light from the window glinting off his golden hair.

Lucere.

He didn't look much different, really. His hair brushed neatly to the right, his eyes bright and alive, that mechanical limb dangling from the end of his virgin white sleeve. His hand of flesh moved awkwardly toward the metal one, fiddling with the cuff links with something akin to nervousness. He smiled at Colton, all warmth and uncertainty. He cocked his beautiful head to one side and took a step forward.

Colton toppled with his chair and scrambled backward as best as he could. His hands crushed under his body, his feet chained to the floor, he squirmed like a desperate insect trapped in the sticky tendrils of a spider's web.

"No! NO! You're supposed to be dead!" He looked to the guards, his eyes wide with terror. "Please! Please, you don't understand—don't leave me alone with him, please! He—he's dangerous, he'll—" Colton's voice cracked, and the Prime Minister kept a respectful distance.

"This isn't necessary. Please unchain him." Lucere's voice was calm, gentle, with none of its usual bite. *He sounds like Lucian,* Colton thought, but knew better than to trust this thing for one damn second.

"B-but my Lord, he stabbed you in the heart, and—"

"And at the moment, he is unarmed and terrified. Please release him and give us the room."

As soon as Colton was freed, he pressed himself flush against the stone wall of the room, his chest rising and falling as he panted in desperate fear. He side-eyed the window. Maybe if Lucere ran at the bars, they'd break—maybe fifty feet up, he could smell the ocean—were they on the water? It was possible he'd survive the fall if he—

Lucere took a step forward, and Colton let out a soft cry of terror.

Vanilla. He smells like—

"How? How did you survive, you fucking snake?"

He expected Lucere to laugh, to say something about how it was impossible for Colton to kill him, but he didn't. He looked like Lucian when his heart was breaking.

"It's quite interesting actually," he started, without confidence or bravado, avoiding Colton's eyes. "You never took the knife out, which somewhat stemmed the bleeding. There was a doctor on site as well, so they were able to keep me stable until we got to a medical facility."

Then there was the added bonus of Colton's blood thrown into the concoction. The whisper of the divine that apparently resided in his soul. *Could that have been enough to . . . ?*

Lucian chuckled softly. "I did die in the hospital, apparently. For maybe five minutes, they said. They got me back with drugs or cardiac massage or some sort of nonsense I wasn't really paying attention to, but then it turns out my heart was too badly damaged, so they replaced it with a mechanical one." He tapped on his chest twice, making that face Lucian did when he was about to say something stupid. "You know. A ticker."

Colton's jaw dropped. "Oh, my god."

Could it be? . . . Lucian?

"They only let me out of the hospital today. Apparently recovering from having your heart removed is quite an ordeal. It's such a clever little device, actually. Although it doesn't change the rate very easily, which is a bit odd when I'm excited. I'm not sure I like it, but it's definitely better than having a demon inside me."

A Lucian smile then, maybe a bit muted, uncertain, but it *felt* like Lucian. "You did it, love. You killed him. It's over."

It couldn't be. He'd believed it last time, and that had nearly gotten them all killed. He wasn't stupid; he wasn't going to fall for that same nasty trick all over again.

Colton shook his head. "I don't *believe* you, Lucian." His voice ached with desperation. "We thought we did it last time, and he—he was just waiting."

And we'll never know that it worked until you fucking die.

Lucian reached out his left hand, and Colton recoiled from it.

"Please don't," he whispered. "I'm so afraid of you."

Lucian wilted but stood steady. "Touch my hand, lovely. Please. My skin is warm again. Look into my eyes. Do you see any of that thing left in me?"

Take his hand? Sure. And then get pulled in and forced into a bite that would leave him with a chunk of his neck missing, have his face torn open again by those fucking claws. Starved for human contact as he was, he didn't dare touch something that could be Lucere. But then he looked at Lucian's face, at his tender smile, at the sweet little creases beside his eyes.

"What do you see, sweetheart?"

Warmth. Love. Trepidation. Hurt. *Lucian.*

But he'd seen that last time, when Lucere had taken his arm.

That was Lucere's favorite game, after all. Mimicking Lucian, luring Colton in, and laughing when he beat him down. Colton shook his head, pressing himself against the cold stone behind him. "I'm sorry, Lucian."

"I understand." Lucian took a few steps back, giving Colton all the space he needed. "I have a surprise for you."

He'll take an eye this time, right? One of yours, one of Lucian's.

Lucian moved to the door and unlocked it, gently ushering a young woman inside.

"Colton!" Mai rushed to him, her body whole and unwounded, her cheeks a bit thinner, her skin a bit paler, but she was—she was alive. Her arms went around his neck, his went around her waist, and for a moment it was just kisses and warmth.

"Are you okay?" he whispered, burying his face in her neck. "Did he hurt you?"

"I'm fine, Colton. No one touched me, no one did anything." She cupped his face. "You look horrible."

He just laughed. "I know."

Lucian kept his distance, and Colton's heart clenched. Even if Lucian could understand the rejection on an intellectual level, it still must have hurt. His father had rejected him in a similar way, he supposed. Turned him away for something that wasn't his fault, that he was trying to make better. Colton let go of Mai then and slowly approached Lucian, who held out a hand to stop him.

"It's all right. You needn't force yourself on my behalf." He manufactured a smile. "I've ordered your release at any rate. I'm sorry I didn't manage to do it sooner." Lucian bit his lip and ran his flesh fingers over his metal ones. "I'll always love you, Colton. And I appreciate how difficult this situation is, has been, and will continue to be. I can only imagine the terror that you've faced at my hands, and all I can do is apologize and try to make things right."

"Lucian, you don't have to apologize. You didn't do anything wrong."

He looked at the earth. "I destroyed a third of this nation with a smile on my face. I ruined countless lives, tore families apart, killed anyone who stood in my way." He swallowed. "I hurt you. I hurt Mai. I hurt Dess."

Colton took a step closer, but it was Lucian this time who stood back. "Don't worry, lovely. I'm not trying to make you pity me, nor accept me once more because of my remorse. I know you're not certain Lucere is dead, and I respect your apprehension."

Colton took his hand, though, which Lucian allowed.

His skin was warm. His fingers almost burned against Colton's, and he felt the steady mechanical beat of his heart under his skin.

"I'm going to make things right again. I'll release everyone I imprisoned, I'll rebuild the Iron Belt for the people, I'll make Silvermoor a place to be envied. I'll pay for it myself, and put the Beaumont resources to good use for once. And maybe one day, after everything is whole once more, you'll feel safe enough to be in my arms again."

Colton couldn't stop the way his whole body winced when Lucian pulled his hand toward his lips for a kiss, nor could he stop the apology from rushing to his lips when he saw him deflate from his rejection.

"Lucian..."

"It's all right. All I ever wanted was for you to be happy, even if it's not with me." He summoned the guards and gestured toward Colton. "He is to be released without charge. Get him whatever he wishes, and escort him safely out of the building or as far as he wants to go."

"But—but sire, he—"

"Has been released without charge, by decree of the Prime Minister." He managed a smile at Colton. "Take care, darling. I hope I'll see you again soon. Look after him, Mai. I'm so sorry for the trouble I've caused."

He exited with a flourish and left Colton and Mai on their own, surrounded by bewildered guards.

Lucian had said he could ask for whatever he wanted, right?

Within twenty minutes Colton and Mai were out on the pavement in front of the prison with new clothes on their backs, a sack of money in their hands, and a carriage waiting to take them wherever they wanted.

Mai tugged his sleeve. "I'm exhausted, Colton. We can both figure out our romantic bullshit once we've had a nice hot meal and a rest, right?"

He nodded and took her hand.

Even from the prison overlooking the ocean, he could smell the smoldering ash of the Iron District. It was going to take a tremendous effort to repair all that Lucere had destroyed, more still when faced with the inevitable opposition of the Ivory aristocracy.

But if anyone could do it, Colton supposed, it would be Lucian fucking Beaumont.

forty-four

Colton's initial idea was to head to the Indigo District and find a room there, so they could recover in relative privacy away from the Prime Minister and his staff, but Mai was opposed.

"Colton. We both just got out of prison and theoretically have infinite Prime Minister money—I want to stay at the Grand!" Which was, of course, the most expensive hotel in the Ivory District.

Well, he reasoned, if Lucere really did want to hunt him down then he probably would, and if they were going to get eaten, it might as well be in a hotel that had private bubbling pools in the rooms.

Mai could scarcely contain her squealing at the luxury of the place—not as nice as where she'd stayed in the Beaumont estate, perhaps, but still gorgeous. Everything was covered in silk and velvet and fresh flower petals, and she slipped off her shoes and wriggled her toes in the long threads of the plush carpet.

Colton moved to the window, which overlooked the sea and had a perfect view of Beaumont Manor off to the north, its ivory spires glinting in the afternoon sun. Mai took his hand and smiled.

"You smell horrible. Please take a shower and try not to drown."

Colton just laughed and fluffed up her hair, trudging into the porcelain chamber and turning the water on as hot as it would go.

He watched the filth of the last few weeks trickle off him and down the drain and scrubbed his skin raw until his tattoos were visible once more. The grime of the prison, the salt of the sea, the blood that had dried against his face from that last encounter with Lucere—how much of it was his, and how much of it was Lucian's? His heart was tired. Everything hurt.

He dried off his body, collapsed on the bed, and slept without dreams. He had no idea how many hours had passed by the time he woke up, but the sun was painting the Ivory District pink as it dipped below the ocean, and Mai was seated on the edge of the bed looking at him. She'd had a shower, too, and her hair was brushed and gleaming the way it was supposed to be. Hells, it was nice to see her.

"Hey," he croaked. "How're you feeling?"

"Better. I'm glad that you're not dead."

He sat up, his eyes still aching from exhaustion. "Will you tell me what happened to you?"

Mai just shrugged. "I got arrested in front of Odessa. It was terrifying. I didn't know what he was going to do to me." She held her arms around her waist and looked away. "But I didn't end up seeing Lucere. I had enough food, was warm enough, and no one touched me. I guess the worst part was just waiting for him to pluck me out and torture me to death.

"When he took me out of the prison I thought it was the end, but he was kind, Colton. He didn't even touch my shoulder unless I allowed him to. He told me he was freeing me, that he was taking me to see you. It wasn't like Lucere." She tucked some of her hair behind her ear. "I was surprised when you wouldn't even take his hand."

Sure. Because before, Colton would go in *knowing* Lucere was present, just for a glimpse of Lucian.

"I thought I'd killed him. I'd watched the life drain from his eyes. I don't know. Maybe I thought I was dreaming; maybe part of me died with him. It was the hardest thing I'd ever done, Mai. Killing someone I loved so much, and then he comes back like it's nothing, and I just—there's this *monster* inside him that *can't* be killed, and I guess I just couldn't."

Mai nodded. "I can't even imagine, Colton." She paused. "So, that's really it? You're not going back?"

He swallowed. "I didn't say that." How could he? How could he reject Lucian now, after everything they'd been through together? "I just . . . I've been locked in a dark room without enough food or water for days after being on the run on my own for weeks while my best friend was probably being tortured for fun and my lover was potentially mutilating himself while he killed everything I ever knew as a child, and it was all a bit much to take in all at once when he came back from the dead all of a sudden."

"Ah. Yeah, that's a bit of a pickle."

So what did that mean for them? Would he just run up to the Beaumont estate and demand an audience with Lucian? Throw his arms around him and kiss him and say all was forgiven? Would he ever be able to fully trust that Lucian was truly himself? Would he ever be able to forget how much they'd endured because of Lucere?

No, he'd never forget. And he might never fully trust again. But Colton knew, deep down in his chest, that he wanted to be with that sweet man once more.

Then there was Lucian. Would *he* be able to forgive Colton for rejecting him outright over something that wasn't his fault? Or, for that matter, losing his sister somewhere in the smoldering remains of the Iron Belt? Not to mention the fact that he was now saddled with the burden of being Prime Minister, having enacted an agenda that was antithetical to everything he believed in, and now committed to fixing it at great personal and political expense.

Tears came to Colton's eyes, and he covered his face. "I'm so glad. That he lived," he whispered. "But it's all so fucked up, Mai. It's not like it was before. You don't think it's possible that Lucere is still there? Just waiting for us to relax?"

"I think we did what your mother told us to do, Colton. We stabbed him in the heart, and he died. I don't see how Lucere could still be in him if he literally doesn't have a heart anymore." That was where the demon resided, after all.

Assuming that his mother was correct. Colton's hand went to his left breast, and his fingers skipped over the faded black letters that decorated his essence. "I don't know if I can ever trust that completely."

But that was part of love, surely. One could never truly know another person—but he knew Lucian Beaumont. They'd loved each other so desperately; they'd been *so* happy together.

And yet...

"Mai, I left Odessa behind in the Iron Belt. I don't know what happened to her. He'll never forgive me if—"

Mai smiled and whapped him on the top of the head with a newspaper. "Take a look."

Colton turned to the first page. There, waving from one of the great balconies of the Beaumont estate, was Prime Minister Beaumont, standing proudly beside his baby sister and a fat little pig nestled up to her chest.

A New Era for the Iron District! Sweeping Infrastructure Reform Promised by Prime Minister Beaumont! More on page 7.

She must have realized they'd done it and stormed the gates, puffed out her chest, and demanded to be treated like a Beaumont.

Mai's eyes lingered on Odessa's radiant face in the picture. "See? Dessie knows Lucere is gone. She's no fool, Colton."

No. She wasn't. Could it be possible? His smile was so broad that it almost hurt as it plowed across his face. "It's really him," he breathed. "Right?"

Mai smiled back. "You're adorable. So what's the plan, then? We storm the estate, and you demand a big wedding with elephants and crystal roses while I get reacquainted with Miss Dess?"

Hmm, that would be very on-brand for Lucian. Colton bit his lip. Maybe he needed to give them a little bit of space at first, to let everything get more settled. Lucian had enough on his plate without turning their house into a torrid love shack.

But of course, total silence would cause Lucian to fret and make a fuss. So Colton decided to write him a letter.

Dear Lucian,

I want to see the world you build when you put your mind to it. Wait for me, stupid.

I love you,
Colton

Yeah. This felt right.

forty-five

The world Lucian carved out was unlike any that had come before it in Silvermoor. Every person who had been arrested by the White Flame was released without charge, and with a generous apology in the form of gold coins to take back to their families. All the homes and businesses that had been destroyed were rebuilt at Beaumont Industries' expense, using Iron labor, Iron materials, and Iron ideas—which had the lower district flush with cash like they had only imagined before. His voting base was of course divided on these changes—the Iron District was obviously pleased, the Ivory elite not so much.

"He's been schmoozing a fair bit," Miss Radcliffe explained to Colton over coffee one morning, little Thomas nestled in her arms. "Soothing egos, working it from the exorcism side of things. I mean, demon hauntings have decreased considerably since you guys went out of business."

Colton snorted.

"It's a good thing, Colton. Silvermoor's soul is lighter."

Lucian increased taxes on large businesses and built hospitals, libraries, childcare facilities, schools, and anything else that might improve the lives of his citizens. He repaired the roads, incentivized workers' rights, enfranchised the downtrodden, and created substance addiction programs run by the state medical unit, free of charge.

Beyond all that, though, Lucian tried to change the way that the people of Silvermoor thought. To embrace their individuality, to not be restricted by their upbringing. He wanted every man, woman, and child to think they had the potential to make the world a brighter place for themselves, if they wished to.

Be who you want. Do what you want. Love who you want. And be kind to each other.

We are all human, and we all deserve to be happy.

Change, of course, was a gradual thing. There were factions in all three districts that resented and resisted Prime Minister Beaumont's ideas, not to mention the Order being a bit perturbed that their angel had done such an abrupt about-face. It would take time for all these dreams and ideals to manifest themselves into brick-and-mortar reality. And yet Lucian worked, every day, on making the world a better place.

So where did that leave Colton?

It was difficult for him to imagine Lucere just sitting back, watching Lucian turn all of Silvermoor into sparkles and rainbows without interfering in some way. He also couldn't imagine Lucere faking *goodness* for this long, *this* well, without vomiting.

Everything in his soul assured him that Lucian had returned and was doing all that he could to right the wrongs of the monster who had lived inside him. It had been weeks since they'd left the prison, long enough that Colton's hair had nearly returned to normal. And yet there was still a part of him that was hesitant. What if it really was Lucere? What if this was the best demon con anyone had ever pulled? But he owed it to Lucian to try. He *wanted* to try. And so Colton scribbled out a short note to his Lordship.

Dear Lucian,
Can we meet?
Love, Colton

The response came within an hour of his page being sent off, and read simply:

Anytime, anywhere, always, always.
LB

Lucian's handwriting was different now. His beautiful script had been lost to that mechanical hand, and although the perfect serif type carried none of Lucian's elegance, Colton could almost taste the excited frenzy with which he'd written it. No fluff, no peacocking, just—eagerness, adoration, yes, yes, yes.

I know just the place.
Colton

Summer in Silvermoor was too much to bear, sometimes. It was sunny for nearly a whole season, and the fields and farms around the nation bloomed with green life and brilliant produce. The people basked under the sun, and every street corner seemed to offer cool drinks or ice cream cones to escape the heat. The sea offered respite, of course, as did the crystal-clear fountains that covered the whole nation with a fine mist during the warmer months. There was one more place, of course, that Colton had frequented as a boy when he wanted to escape the oppressive oven that was the Iron Belt during the height of the season.

The cliffs to the south of everything, where the jellyfish danced under the full moon of winter. The winds blew a chilled air across the stones, and at this time of year the whole place was carpeted in grass and wildflowers. Colton was sweating and exhausted by the time he reached the top of the stone steps, and he took a moment to catch his breath before approaching at last. Butterflies and bees were kissing the petals, birds were singing in the distance, and there, standing beside the cliff's edge like a brilliant statue, was none other than Lucian Beaumont.

He'd taken off his suit jacket and was resting it casually over his shoulder as he looked out over the water. White shirt, crisp blue vest, no cape this time, surely because it was too hot for one, and his beautiful golden hair was billowing in the breeze. He caught sight of Colton, and his face broke into a smile, waving at him with such enthusiasm that Colton feared he might lose his balance and careen into the sea.

Colton's legs were moving before he knew it, kicking up pollen and blades of grass in his urgency. The distance closed between them, and Colton threw himself on Lucian, his arms around his neck, his lips pressed against any part of him he could reach. He felt Lucian's embrace circle his waist, his laugh against his cheek.

"Hi, precious," he managed, and Colton grasped his face with both hands and kissed him until neither of them could breathe.

"Hi," Colton replied eventually, releasing his grip just enough that his feet could touch the ground. "You—" What had he wanted to say? Surely something profound would be best, right? "You're so good-looking."

Oof.

Lucian kissed the tip of his nose. "Well, thank you, darling. I tried my best."

Colton wouldn't let go of Lucian, and he found his fingers gripping into that fine silk fabric. "You're doing so much wonderful work, love. I've been so proud of you, reading all about it." He met those big beautiful eyes. "How do you feel? Is there any part of *him* inside of you?"

"No. For the first time in a very long time . . . it's just me. I feel wonderful. It's some of the most fulfilling work I've ever done."

"More than pretending to exorcise demons?"

"Oh, no, precious, that was obviously my career highlight. But it's been great, making a difference in the world. Trying to, anyway. There's still the off chance that I might get assassinated, I suppose."

"Ah, that reminds me, I've actually been sent by your enemies to push you into the sea."

"Oh, have you!" Lucian laughed. "Terribly awkward business, that. Blast it all, I knew that kiss was too perfect to be real. Colton, darling, I know it worked last time, but assassins normally don't announce their intentions before carrying out murders, you know."

"Crap! Is that where I've been going wrong?"

Lucian kissed him again. "Seems that way. I have the distinct impression I might escape this encounter alive."

"Mm. I guess you are *possibly* too cute to murder in cold blood. Today, anyway." He touched Lucian's face. "You really think we . . . I mean, this time that we . . ."

"Got rid of Lucere? Yes, love. I wouldn't have dared meet up with you otherwise." Lucian cast his eyes at the water. "I wouldn't risk hurting you again. He's gone, precious. It's just you and me from now on. Forever, if you want."

Lucian's cheeks flushed.

"Lucian Beaumont. Was that a wedding proposal?"

That insufferable, dumbass smile. "Well. We can't elope, can we? We're not melons."

"Oh, my god," Colton murmured, shutting Lucian up with a deep and desperate kiss. "I hate you, Lucian. So, so much."

"Shall I take that as a yes?"

He crushed his lips against Lucian's. "Of course it's a yes! You stupid, miserable prick!"

Of course, even with Lucian's progressive agenda, it wasn't like two men could just get married out in the open. Hells, having the two of them presenting even the hint of a romantic relationship would have been disastrous for Lucian's burgeoning political career.

"We'll tell everyone someday, love," Lucian promised, pushing Colton's hair out of his eyes. "When my projects are more secure, when it won't be as much of a disaster if I have a scandal. I want to make Silvermoor a place where we can be together without consequence. Where you and I can live with pride."

This was everything that Colton had ever wanted. To stand

with the man he loved, with security, stability, a grand sense of purpose. A life where everyone who mattered to him was safe and warm, where one could wake up every morning and make some positive change in the world. It wasn't perfect. But it was a damn good start.

And so they had a private ceremony, right in Lucian's garden. They had the whole place decked out in ribbons and flowers, all their favorite foods piled high on polished wooden tables under the bright summer sun. Lucian, as ever, was clad in white, blue, and gold, and Colton looked elegant in his ebony-and-ruby regalia.

They'd gotten a pink ribbon for Marbles, and Odessa had taken Mai shopping for a gown befitting the occasion. Mai had chosen a brilliant rainbow garment that swirled around her feet, and she'd designed and tailored a beautiful pink dress for the lovely Miss Beaumont to wear.

Johan, as ever, butlered and said nothing.

Naturally, Odessa officiated, Lucian made stupid jokes that made Colton want to die, and they kissed and kissed until Mai threw peanuts at them.

The evening wore on, and the four of them had eaten more than it was safe or reasonable to eat in one sitting. Colton and Lucian sat on a wooden love seat surrounded by flowers, while off in the distance Odessa had taken Mai's hand, laughing at some shared secret Mai had pressed against her ear.

"What a beautiful day," Colton mused, his head nestled up against Lucian's chest. He shut his eyes and listened to his mechanical heart beating steadily under his ear, one two, one two. "Lucian? Do you remember, a long time ago, you were telling me a story about a prince?"

Lucian's smile was warm. "I seem to recall something like that."

"Tell me again?"

Lucian cleared his throat. "There once was a prince who had everything any man could ever want. He had more money than sense, he had access to all the education and drugs he could ask for, and he had a sister who loved him very much. But he wasn't happy, this prince, not really. One day, he met a brave knight who changed the way he saw the world. They came up against terrible odds, and the prince was taken captive by the evil country with which they were at war."

Colton smiled. "So what did the knight do?"

"Well, he fought harder than anyone had ever fought before. He overcame every obstacle that life threw at him, no matter how much it hurt him, and eventually he infiltrated the enemy palace. The prince was being held prisoner, and there was no way out. So the knight set everything on fire."

"Reckless sort, seems like."

"Mm. Not too concerned about collateral damage, our knight. But somehow they both survived, and they went back home and resigned to make the world a better place."

"This story doesn't have a good narrative flow, Lucian."

"Colton, shush. Well anyway, the prince gives the knight a very lucrative position on his cabinet and he has near total authority, nepotism be damned. They work together and try and make their nation the most lovely place it can possibly be. Education leads to innovation, everyone prospers, and eventually the prince and the knight get married."

Colton chuckled. "Yeah? How's that go over?"

Lucian kissed Colton's neck. "They spend the rest of their lives making each other happy, Colton. And it takes some time, but eventually, little by little, the world begins to change for the better."

Lucian had always been something of a dreamer. He'd always been prone to imagining the fantastic, the impossible, forging ahead into the future with a smile and little else.

Even so. Even bloody so.

I believe you, Lucian.

He always would.

Acknowledgments

To my parents, for their support—and for always reassuring me on demand that I am a good baby.

And to Greggles, for the encouragement, the patience, and the occasional head pats.

About the Author

Emma Deards grew up in New York City and earned her undergraduate degree at Barnard College at Columbia University, where she studied Japanese literature and biology. She was then accepted to The University of Edinburgh, where she completed her veterinary degree. She remained in the UK afterward, and since then has split her time between her day job as a vet and her truest passion: writing. Emma has authored a number of humor articles for *In Practice,* a veterinary magazine, and was the recipient in college of two writing awards: the Oscar Lee Award and the Harumatsuri Award. Her first book, *Wild with All Regrets,* came out in 2023.

Looking for your next great read?

We can help!

Visit www.shewritespress.com/next-read
or scan the QR code below for a list
of our recommended titles.

She Writes Press is an award-winning
independent publishing company founded to
serve women writers everywhere.